THE BET

WINSLOW BROTHERS BOOK ONE

max

New York Times & *USA Today* Bestselling Author

monroe

AUTHOR'S NOTE

The Bet is a full-length romantic comedy stand-alone novel in the ***Winslow Brothers Collection***. This book is chock-full of hilarious rom-com moments, but also, it's spicy as hell.

We're talking *alllllll the sexy*.

Now that you know, don't contact the authorities on us because ***The Bet*** heats up your device, makes your house feel like the A/C broke, and requires that you read while sitting in front of a fan. Monroe consumes a borderline illegal amount of coffee, and constantly checking in with a parole officer would really put a damper on our writing productivity—*aka make it really hard to write more hilarious rom coms for you. ;) ;)*

Also, due to the hilarious and addictive nature of this book's content, the following things are *not* recommended: *reading in public places, reading in bed next to a light-sleeping spouse and/or pet and/or child, reading on a date, reading on your wedding day, reading during the birth of your child, reading while eating and/or drinking, reading at work, reading this book to your boss, and/or reading while operating heavy machinery. Also, if suffering from bladder incontinence due to age/pregnancy/childbirth/etc., we recommend wearing sanitary products and/or reading while sitting directly on a toilet.*

Happy Reading!
All our love,
Max & Monroe

DEDICATION

To the Girl Scouts: We're sorry.

To orgasms: Holy moly, you showed up for this book. Not even Savannah Cummings (IYKYK) knows what to do with this many of you.

INTRO

Saturday, February 17th

Jude

I don't know what it is, but I feel like luck is in the air tonight—well, luck and an arctic fucking cold front. I smile at the thought, but also, with a bounce in my step, I pick up my pace to decrease the time I have to be outside in this blistery-as-hell winter wind.

Two blocks from my destination, my phone vibrates in my jacket pocket, and I pull it out to find a message front and center on the screen.

Bianca: You busy tonight? I'd sure love some company…

I grin and shake my head, typing out a quick text.

Me: Sorry, honey. Working.

Bianca: :(

I smile.

Bianca is a beautiful woman, but she's not my girlfriend or my ex-girlfriend. She's not even really a friend, if I'm being honest.

She's nice and sweet, and we hang out from time to time, and she's one *of* a million. A million who are just as good a fit for a temporary fun time or companionship or a distraction from life's complications.

Truthfully, when it comes to women, this is generally how I like to keep things.

No strings attached.

No relationships.

Just a whole lot of fucking fun. I learned thirteen years ago after watching my eldest brother Remy get left at the altar that it's better that way. No soul-crushing hope, no professions of love, no waiting for the one diamond that outshines the rest.

Because it doesn't break my heart to turn Bianca down, and it wouldn't break my heart if she were the one to walk away.

She's replaceable—and so am I. We all are. And I'm fortunate enough to live in New York, one of the biggest, busiest cities in the world, where the possibilities are endless.

I weave in and out of a small crowd that's gathered outside to freeze their balls off waiting to get into the new "hot spot" restaurant, WigWam, and pull my jacket a little tighter. Even though I'm moving, the frost in this bitch tonight could just about nip the nose off Jack himself.

Fuck, it's cold.

Realizing I'm still holding my phone in my bare hand in the freezing air like an idiot, I slide both back inside my pocket and shove them into the depths of warmth, just above the HotHands I slipped inside before I left my apartment. The phone vibrates again, but I'm completely prepared to ignore it—until it goes off again and again and *again*.

I sigh, pull my hand back out of my pocket, and look at the screen. Five message notifications from the group chat with my siblings sit front and center. Too curious not to check, I open up my inbox and start reading as I continue carefully making my way down the busy sidewalk.

Winnie: Uncle Brad's birthday is coming up, and I am not letting all of the party and gift responsibilities fall on my shoulders again. You bastards are helping this time.

Ty: But, Winnie, you're so good at all of it.

Winnie: Ty, I swear on everything, I will end you.

Ty: Can you at least make sure you end me AFTER you plan Uncle Brad's party and figure out what we should get him?

Remy: LOL.

I laugh out loud too. I could join in on the amusement—I mean, I am the funniest *and* funnest sibling of all—but the entrance doors of Club Craze are so close, and indoor warmth sounds like my current idea of a good time. Instead, I slip my phone back into my jacket pocket and focus on the priority task at hand—work.

I push open the large black glass door and step inside, and instantly, the pounding beats of a popular hip-hop song fill my ears. I can't not move my head to the bass as I walk through the cavernous space and toward the back hallway where the offices and dancer dressing rooms are located.

Ah, yes, I fucking love the New York nightlife.

"Jude!" Ki-Ki, the in-house DJ, shouts from her booth, removing one headphone to offer a wave as she continues to bop around to the catchy music. With a quick swipe of her hand, the song morphs into "Do I Wanna Know?" by Arctic Monkeys. Which she then brilliantly mixes with old-school Beastie Boys.

"Hell yeah!" I raise my hands in the air. "That's sick, Keeks!"

The pink-haired music pixie grins back at me, gives a thumbs-up, and then adjusts her headphones, getting back to prepping music for a busy Saturday night.

Since it's only a little after seven, she still has some time to get things prepared before we open the doors, but once nine hits, Ki-Ki's got to be ready to move and groove. Thankfully, she knows it and takes it seriously, or we would never be able to draw in the numbers we need to.

And bringing in the big crowds is my job.

Club Craze is brand-new, but J. Winslow Promotion is notorious for working with the hottest clubs for a reason. I need this place to bring wall-to-wall people and an even bigger personality. It has the potential to be one of my favorite hot spots in Manhattan, and if everything is done right for the launch, the owner says he'd be willing to sign a contract with my company for nightclub promotion for the next four years.

My job is to create the party, help people let loose, and make damn sure they want to come back and do it over and over again.

For a guy like me, I can't think of a better fit.

Once I'm past Ki-Ki's booth, I take a swift right and head down the "employees only" hallway. Another few feet and I spot Maverick, a relatively new friend of mine—one I made pretty easily upon finalizing the staff for this club. He walks in through the back door that leads in from the small parking lot off the alleyway on the side of the building. A gray duffel is over his shoulder, and a beanie covers his blondish-brown hair.

Maverick is hilarious, a real fucking good time, and a *dancer* for Club Craze. Picture Channing Tatum from *Magic Mike* doing "Pony" with a grinder, and you'll have a pretty good idea of what kind of dancing he does.

"What up, Winslow?" he shouts when we make eye contact. "What are you doing back here?"

"Actually, I was looking for you." I wasn't. "See, I remembered you still owe me money from that play-off game last month, and figured it was high-time I reminded you." I smirk, shrug, and stop to lean against the wall just outside the dancers' dressing rooms where I know he's headed.

"Of course, you cheap bastard." He throws his head back on a laugh.

"Cheap bastard?" I question and put a hand to my chest. "Are you talking about me? The guy who told you the Mavericks were going to win that play-off game, and you definitely *shouldn't* take that fucking bet?"

This isn't the first time the two of us have bet on something. Surely it won't be the last either. Maverick is addicted to trying to beat me, and I'm addicted to wagers and challenges.

He laughs and rolls his eyes, coming to a stop across from me. "Yeah, but the only reason you probably knew is because your sister is married to fucking Wes Lancaster. It's like goddamn insider trading."

"Don't be bitter, dude. I told you not to bet against them. Hell, the team has your damn name, for fuck's sake."

"Whatever." He rolls his eyes at that. "What do I owe you again?"

"One hundred big ones," I respond. "And don't try to sweet-talk your way out of it with cries of poverty. Even though you suck ass at dancing, I've seen the way women shove dollar bills down your pants. I know you're good for it."

Mav waggles his brows. "You jealous, bro?"

"Jealous? Of what, exactly? That you spend your nights letting women fawn over the idea of your dick so you don't have to cry when they see how tiny it *actually* is?"

"Fuck off," he retorts. "We both know there's a reason why you're the one who gets the people to the party and I'm the one who *entertains* the people at the party. Only one of us has real talent."

A laugh jumps from my throat. "Get real. I could dance. I could fucking dance circles around your ass. You think your tips are good? *Ha.* The number of tips I could pull in during one night would blow your mind."

"Man, I'd love to see you put your money where your big, obnoxious mouth is," he snaps back on a hearty chuckle. "There's a bachelorette party coming in tonight. It might disappoint the bride, but it'd be a fun opportunity to watch you fail."

"I'd rock that bride's world."

Mav cracks up. "Jude, with all due respect, you've never danced a day in your life. Much less danced like *I* dance. You'd fail spectacularly."

I waggle my brows. I can't help it. It's the thrill I'm always chasing, the high I can't seem to quit. And this bastard is going to pay for doubting my abilities.

I square my shoulders and lean forward, right in his face, and ask, "Wanna bet?"

ONE

Sophie

"Party of ten for Sophie Sage," I tell the big, burly bouncer behind the velvet rope.

The man is dressed in all black and has a perpetual scowl etched across his lips, but I'm assuming it comes with the job territory. Every Friday and Saturday night, he's tasked with the responsibility of filling this club with partygoers who will have a good time, but also, won't act like total assholes.

Sure, it sounds simple enough, but all it takes is standing in the never-ending line outside—*in the bitter February cold, mind you*—for a mere five minutes with people yelling and shouting toward the bouncers at the door to understand it's not simple at all. If anything, the man is being paid to deal with verbal harassment and demanding, drunk idiots. *All night long.* Add in a constant barrage of pimple-faced teens with fake IDs and the credit card they stole when their parents weren't looking, and I'd rather rub poison ivy on my eyeballs than switch places with him.

He glances down at his clipboard and then back up at me. "I take it you're Sophie?"

"That's right. I am her, and she is me," I respond somewhat awkwardly through a shivering jaw. My breath hangs in the air for a few seconds, and I tuck my arms deeper into my faux fur coat and try to keep the shivers from migrating to my knees.

He moves his gaze past me, to my twin sister Belle, our elder sister Katelynn, and then over the rest of our small group that includes seven of Belle's closest friends—Laura, Tasha, Kirsten, Jackie, Tonya, Bri, and Devon.

All of these women either went to college with Belle at NYU or work with her at MK Modeling Agency. I know some of them better than others since Belle and I spend so much time together, but these people definitely qualify as more "hers" than "mine."

"Who's the bride-to-be?"

"That would be this gorgeous girl right here with the sash," I comment and step back to wrap my arm around my twin.

Belle smiles, and the rest of our already-tipsy group hoots and hollers, which then makes my sister bury her face in my shoulder.

I giggle and give her a reassuring squeeze.

All thanks to the awesome bachelorette party I planned for my sister, our group is having the time of their lives, is well on their way to being three sheets to the wind, and is ready to bring the night on home at our fourth and final stop at one of New York's hottest new nightspots, Club Craze.

"Whoa. You two are—" the bouncer begins, and I immediately recognize his intro as the precursor to what everyone says when they see Belle and me together.

"Identical twins," I answer for him with a knowing smile. "You know, like a brunette version of the Olsens."

Belle snorts. "Though, we've never met Uncle Jesse. And we aren't recluses in our adult age."

I'm half tempted to roll my eyes at the two of us and the fact that it sounds like we give this rehearsed speech every hour on the hour, but the bouncer's reaction outshines my mental battle with self-deprecation. I don't know if this dude has never seen identical twins in person or what, but he just keeps glancing between Belle and me like we're two aliens that just stepped off our UFO. Our eyes may be green, but our skin isn't. *At least, not yet. Maybe after a few more hours of drinking, it will be, though.*

Thankfully, when Tonya obnoxiously offers to show the man her G-sized ta-tas if he'll get us inside before they turn into literal witch's tits, he focuses back on his clipboard, and that scowl of his almost turns into a smile.

"Clothes need to stay on for now," he says and shakes his head. "But once you're inside and escorted into your private VIP party room…" He winks at Tonya. "Then, you can live it up in whatever way you please." He licks his lips and mutters to himself, "I really need to think about asking for a job reassignment."

Tonya laughs and leans up onto her toes to place a drunk kiss on his cheek.

"Private VIP party room?" Belle whispers into my ear, obviously too panicked to focus on the episode of *The Bachelor: Nightclub Bouncer Edition* taking place in front of us. I turn away from the action to give her a reassuring flick of my eyes and squeeze around her shoulders, and by the time I turn back, our previously stoic bouncer is unclipping the velvet rope and letting us inside, hijinks with Tonya concluded.

I'm a little sad to have missed some of the action, but *Hallelujah!* for warmth.

"Have fun, ladies."

"Hell yes!" Kirsten cheers and wraps her arms around Laura's and Bri's shoulders. "Drinks first, then dancing!"

Katelynn discreetly slips a twenty-dollar bill into the bouncer's front shirt pocket and pats him on the chest. "Remember this and Tonya's boobs later when you're having to kick one of these bitches out of your club."

He actually lets a full smile consume his face then, and I grab Belle's hand.

"Let's go, sis! Time to bring this bachelorette party on home!"

As I step through the large doors, a burst of hot air hits my face, and I sigh in relief.

Thank goodness.

The pounding beats of house music grow impatiently as we walk down a dimly lit hallway that leads to the inside of the club. The closer we get, the more the music dominates my ears, and the more the ladies in front of me sway their boozed-up hips and shout their approval.

Club Craze is hopping, and it's not even *officially* officially open yet. This is just the soft run, for Pete's sake. The only reason I even got us in here is because, after hearing about the upcoming opening, I went on to their website to do some research for work and stumbled upon an all-call to apply to have your private event. I never thought we'd get selected, but we did.

I just hope it lives up to the hype.

Once we reach the end, it opens into a big, wide-open space that's packed to the brim with clubgoers, and a pretty blond woman dressed in formfitting, all-black attire greets us with a grin.

So I can hear her over the pandemonium, I shove my way to the front of our boisterous group and lean in toward her as she speaks. "If you ladies will follow me, I'll lead you to your private VIP room."

Evidently, she's already been updated by the bouncers of our arrival, and I wave a hand back at the group to follow her lead. Carefully counting off ladies and sending them ahead of me to make sure we all stay together, I make it through all but one when something grabs the back of my coat and drags me in the opposite direction.

"What the—?" I shriek in the pitch of a dying cat. It doesn't matter, though, because the atmosphere in this place is so dang loud, I don't think the women of my party would have realized if a bomb went off behind them.

My steps stutter and stammer as I fight to keep myself upright, the scent of my sister's perfume on my attacker the only thing that keeps me calm.

Before I know it, Belle's yanking me into the closest women's restroom. The instant the door shuts behind us, she up and locks the damn thing so no one else can get in.

"Soph, I can't do it," she whispers harshly into my ear before backing away toward the sinks and mirrors.

"What are you talking about?"

She's already shaking her head. "I can't do it."

"You can't do what?"

"I know I said I wanted the whole shebang for my bachelorette party, but I'm done."

I jerk my head back in surprise. "What do you mean, *you're done?*"

"I mean I'm done! I can't let some greased-up stripper dance up on me in front of everyone!"

I blink several times, open and close my mouth like a fish, raise a finger to speak, and then drop it again. *What in the ever-loving hell?*

"Sophie," she says and grabs both of my shoulders. "I'm not joking around. If I have to go sit in that private VIP room while all my friends watch some dude rub his dick on my legs, I'll freaking shit myself. Or have a heart attack. Or a brain aneurysm. Or—"

"Belle," I cut her off before she pushes herself into a panic attack. "Take a breath. Calm down."

"*Calm down?*" she repeats with stretched-out, crazy eyes. "I can't calm down! Soon, everyone in that stupid VIP room you rented will be watching me get dry humped by a stripper. I don't want to be a human pillow or sock or come rag or whatever. I can't do it. I can't."

"I'm pretty sure the politically correct term is *exotic dancer*, and it's not like he's going to jizz in your belly button. That's what backstage is for."

"Sophie, now is *not* the time to be a smartass."

I snort. "Listen, I don't want to be a bitch right now, but I feel it's important that I remind you that *you* said you *wanted* this. I remember it distinctly, actually." I change the pitch of my voice to mock her and continue, repeating her own words back to her. "*I just want to get crazy, Sophie. Live it up! This is my last hurrah!*"

"I know!" She tosses both of her hands up in the air. "I know. I thought I did. But I don't. I just want to go home and let John rub my feet."

"*Belle.*" A shocked laugh pops from my lungs. "Honey, we can't go home right now. Everyone came out tonight to celebrate with you, and our limo driver won't be here for another three hours. Plus, I'm pretty sure Tonya will throw a temper tantrum if she doesn't get to utilize all those dollar bills she brought with her tonight. You saw them in the limo. She has three hundred of them stuffed into the cavern between her boobs."

Belle huffs out a sigh and runs a hand through her dark hair. She's agitated. Nervous. But she's also starting to consider what I'm explaining. At least, I *think* she is.

"You have nothing to be freaked out about. For one, you look gorgeous," I say and turn her around by the shoulders, so she sees her reflection in the mirror. "And two, no one is judging you. Everyone here just wants you to have fun. That's it. And it's not like I paid the exotic dancer to give you a happy ending with his penis. Only dancing, I swear," I tease, trying to swing her emotions all the way back to where they started, but she doesn't even offer a smile.

Out of the two of us, my sister is the introvert, and I'm more of the extrovert. It's probably why I'm in the business of event planning and she's in the business of scouting out models to attend the events. She's never been fond of being the center of attention, always preferring to be a fly on the wall rather than the focus in the middle of the room. That's not to say she's not outspoken with people she's comfortable with—with Katelynn and her fiancé John and me, she's a brutal bringer of truth—but with friends and a complete stranger involved? Forget it.

Even growing up, I can't tell you how many times I ended up doing her oral presentations in class because the teachers could never tell us apart and Belle's social fears were too much for her to stomach.

It's the number one reason why I asked her over and over again if she was *sure* she wanted this kind of bachelorette party—you know, one that included her being the center of attention in front of a crowd of people, one that took us to several New York hot spots throughout the night, and one that ends with her getting jiggy with a sexy, exotic Club Craze dancer.

And while Belle *assured* me numerous times that she did want this, I probably should've anticipated the night would lead us here anyway. I've known her my whole damn life, obviously, and this fits her MO a whole lot more than her telling me *I just want to get crazy* did.

Honestly, at a time like this, I'm most thankful that she and John decided to keep their wedding small and intimate. A freak-out during your bachelorette party is one thing, but on your wedding day? Talk about *no bueno*.

I meet her emerald eyes in the reflection in the mirror, but when she tilts her head to the side and starts tapping her chin in a familiar way I've seen a thousand times, I furrow my brow.

"Why are you looking at me like that?"

She shrugs. But also, grins.

"What are you scheming?"

That grin grows so wide it forces her red-painted lips to spread out across her face. "Do you really want me to enjoy my bachelorette party?"

I roll my eyes. What kind of question is that? "Of course I do."

"Like you really, *really* want me to, and you'd do anything to make it happen?"

I narrow my eyes at her in the mirror. "Considering I gave you my very expensive event planning services for free and spent weeks planning this night, I'd say, yes, that's the general sentiment."

"Fantastic," Belle responds and takes off her black jacket, her white bride-to-be sash, and begins unzipping the back of her short, silver-sequined dress.

"Wait…what are you doing?" I query and turn my head away from the mirror to look directly at her.

"Making sure I live to see the morning after my bachelorette party."

I quirk a brow, but she ignores my confusion and shoves her jacket and sash into my chest.

"Switch me," she demands and slides her heels off her feet. "You play bride for the rest of the night, and I'll play maid of honor and party planner."

"*Belle*," I retort and shake my head. "No way."

"Sophie," she says and slides her dress off her body so she's standing in the middle of the bathroom in only her bra and underwear. "*Yes.*"

"This feels like high school all over again," I mutter and exhale a deep breath on a sigh. "We're twenty-eight, Belle, don't you think we're a little old to be Parent-Trapping your fucking bachelorette party?"

"We're identical twins, Soph," she retorts and takes it upon herself to remove my faux fur jacket from my shoulders. "No one is going to know the damn difference."

"Katelynn will."

"Katelynn is too drunk to care." She snorts and holds out a demanding hand that contains her dress. "Now, give me your clothes."

I glance down at my favorite high-waisted dress pants and silky blouse and then at the dress in her hands.

You'd think since I've made a career out of planning parties and events, I would've been able to make sure my own sister's bachelorette bash went off without a hitch, but here I am, right in the middle of a giant-fucking-snag.

When the sounds of pounding knocks filter in from the locked door of the restroom, I know I need to decide. And even though it's not the direction I wanted the night to go, there's really only one option here to keep things from spiraling out of control. *Goddamn my Type 9 Enneagram people-pleasing core.*

"You're lucky I love you." I snatch the dress out of her hands.

Belle beams just like a spoiled brat who got her way—because she is one.

I swear, the things I do for my sister.

"All right, it's time for the bride-to-be to take her seat!"

The lights in our private VIP room are dimmed, and I'm ushered over to a chair that sits in the center of the small but spacious room.

When my ass hits the velvet cushion, I try to adjust the tight material of

Belle's dress, but it's almost no use. The sequined-covered spandex is tight in all the wrong places, and I feel like I might inadvertently flash my goods at any second. To the untrained eye, our bodies are nearly identical, just like our faces—but my T and A have a little bit more meat than hers, and in a dress of this cut, a little bit goes a long way.

Good grief, for a girl who hates being the center of attention, my sister sure loves to dress in an attention-grabbing way…

I flash a discreet glare at Belle, but she just giggles and lifts her champagne glass in the air. "Cheers to the bride-to-be!"

My sister is a little biotch.

Katelynn and the rest of our group join in on her toast, and I'm tempted to flip Belle the middle finger. But I shake off my annoyance and try to remember the fact that my sister looks relaxed and happy—*playing me for the night*—and that's the whole intention of this party.

To make sure my twin has a good time.

Even if it means I have to spend the next sixty minutes playing grab-ass with one of Club Craze's male exotic dancers.

"Ladies, I'd like to introduce you to Jude," our female hostess announces and opens the door to reveal a man dressed in black slacks and a white button-down shirt with sleeves folded to his forearms.

He's tall, and the muscular lines of his body can't be missed beneath his clothes.

With light brownish-blond hair and a little scruff on his chin, this guy reminds me of a young Brad Pitt. I'm talking sexy Fight-Club Brad Pitt mixed with Ocean's-Eleven Brad Pitt to create some kind of insanely attractive superhuman.

"Good evening, ladies." He flashes a sexy smirk that slides through the room and ultimately lands on my wide eyes. "As Kelsie said, I'm Jude, and I'll be taking over to make sure you have a good time."

I swear, those eyes of his are as blue as the freaking ocean, and their depths are downright hypnotic. It's like I can't look away even if I wanted to.

Holy hell.

Self-preservation in the form of distraction speeds up in my head, and somewhere in the whirling thoughts, a bell of recognition rings. I pull myself out of the insane trance of his eyes to focus on an inconsistency. "I thought Maverick was supposed to…" I start, only to pause when I realize my faux pas. I definitely shouldn't be the one asking this question since, technically, I'm Belle for the night and every step of the itinerary has been a surprise for her, but luckily, no one picks up on the mistake. They're all too busy staring at *Jude*.

"Unfortunately, Maverick realized he wasn't man enough to handle this party of beautiful women, so I went ahead and stepped up to the plate." Jude winks, and I throw up in my mouth a little. *By God, the cheesiness of that line knows no bounds.*

Our hostess snorts and nudges him in the side with her elbow, but he just laughs it off and moves his gaze back to me.

"I take it you're the gorgeous bride-to-be?" he inquires with a little rasp in his voice.

I swallow thickly, trying to find the words in my dry mouth like an animal searches for water in the desert. It only takes a few moments to give up, however, because despite my debut as a mime, he's striding right toward me. Each step is calculated and with purpose, and a shiver threatens to slip up my spine.

"She sure is!" Tonya shouts at the top of her lungs. "That's our girl Belle!"

Kirsten and Laura pretend to fan themselves. Katelynn laughs. Belle stares at me over the top of a glass of champagne with wide, amused eyes.

With one long hand stretched out toward me and veins making themselves known on his forearms, Jude grips the fabric of the sash around my chest and smirks down at me.

"You ready to have some fun?"

Oh boy. Now that line or move isn't cheesy. At all.

I nod. Gulp. Nod again. "Uh-huh."

And then, he leans in closer to me, whispering directly into my ear, "Buckle up, gorgeous, because I'm going to make sure you have a good fucking time."

Oh, mamma mia. What in the Weird Al Yankovic has Belle gotten me into?

TWO

Jude

Right on cue, Kelsie hits play on the music I selected about thirty minutes ago for tonight's role as *Jude, the exotic dancer.* After listening in on Maverick's "instruction time" about how to become an exotic dancer in thirty seconds or less, she insisted on being the one to host, just so she could get a load of what I looked like on the other side of the coin—like a fucking episode of *Undercover Boss.* I'm not sure why I agreed, but if I'm honest, I'm not exactly ready to teach classes on the reasoning that led to accepting this little bet in the first place.

I do my best to ignore the employee voyeur, but when she doesn't exit immediately, I pull back from the bride, do a spin, and hit Kelsie with a roll of my eyes that suggests she'd better scoot if she wants to live to see another paycheck.

Finally, Kelsie steps out, a panicked yet elated smile painted on her lips making me purse my own. I take a full deep breath for the first time to settle into my role of uninhibited dancer Jude. Maverick told me I needed to come up with a "stage name," but there was no way in hell I was going to have these women calling me Fabio or some shit and getting confused every time they screamed. They can call me Jude, just like the women I take to my bed, thank you very fucking much.

The first song on my list is by the one and only Pretty Ricky, and when the opening beats of "Grind with Me" start to echo inside the private room, I smirk to myself. Frankly, if I weren't so focused on making sure I beat Maverick at his own game, I might even laugh out loud over this. I mean, when I headed into work tonight, playing stripper for the evening didn't even cross my mind.

Hell, if my three brothers knew what I was up to right now, they'd be begging these women to record it so they could razz my ass for the next fifty years. Also, I'm pretty sure Ty would keep it on hand for future blackmail purposes.

Normally, I spend my weekends schmoozing the VIPs at whatever club my company is currently promoting, not engaging in the customer experience. But I'm no stranger to a wager, and to be frank, resisting them is kind of my weak point. The thrill, the excitement, the bragging rights that come with besting a challenge—they're better than any drug.

I'm *always* up for a contest. And by tomorrow, Mav is going to have to cough up the dough when he realizes I can pull more tips than him in a night by a long shot.

The women inside the private room start to form a half circle around the bachelorette sitting in the center, and they don't hesitate to squeal and shout their excitement.

I work the room a little, gyrating my hips to the beat, and try to amp up the excitement of all the bachelorette's party friends by dancing and flirting with them a little. I don't give them much eye contact, though, reserving all of my looks for the bachelorette herself.

She's gorgeous, so it's not even remotely a shock that some sappy bastard has decided to lock her down for life, even if marriage is a fool's game.

I swerve and grind and mingle among the crowd, but when a tall blonde with a loud mouth gets a little too handsy, I smirk and gently excuse myself from her attention so I can put all my focus on the most important woman in this room—*Belle, the bride-to-be.*

Without delay, I stalk straight over to her, grip her thighs with my hands, and spread them wide so I can step in between them. She squeals, puts both of her hands between her legs to cover herself, and her beautiful emerald eyes expand when she looks up into my steady gaze.

I wink and whisper toward her, "Don't worry, gorgeous. I won't peek."

Slowly, I unbutton my white dress shirt, never once removing my gaze from hers. Which, oddly enough, isn't a difficult task at all.

No doubt, this woman is a fucking stunner. Big green eyes, full red lips, and the kind of long, dark lashes most women would sell their souls for.

She's the epitome of beauty, but it's not even by normal standards. She's just…*striking*. The kind of woman you can't just take one quick look at.

No. She makes it hard to pull your eyes away from her.

But beyond all the outer-layer beauty, something mysterious and intriguing lies below the surface. I like to think it means she has all sorts of dirty, sexy secrets that she's never told anyone about, but she's dying to find someone to spill them to.

Pretty Ricky sings about taking your time, and once the buttons of my shirt are undone, I slide the material off my body and toss it over her head, so it's wrapped around the back of her chair. Swiftly, I tie the sleeves into a loose knot at the front of her chest, pinning her arms down at the sides of her body. It's a pretty comical move considering she already seems to be sitting on her hands, but it gets the gaggle of ladies worked up, to say the least.

Dollar bills fly in the air as the women start cheering over the idea of their friend bound to a chair.

The pretty goddess in front of me blinks rapidly and laughs, digging her teeth into her bottom lip in the sexiest fucking way. It's a hearty mix of nerves and embarrassment and excitement, and I'd be willing to bet that I'm not the only one who's experiencing a firsthand exotic dance for the first time.

I smile back at her, running my tongue along my top lip in the hopes that she'll show me something new. It pays off as her eyes broaden, and the vein in her neck starts to pulse at a rapid pace.

Damn. Before I know it, I start to think about what she looks like when she's having sex.

Is she completely uninhibited? Or is she adorably shy? Are her moans loud and uncontrolled or soft as a whisper?

Fuck. I probably shouldn't go there. I mean, she *is* someone's fiancée, not a single woman who isn't spoken for, but in a way, that makes it even more fun to play. There's no pressure of dealing with overdeveloped feelings, no chance that she'll grow attached and become clingy—no danger of coming on too strong and scaring her away. Coming on strong, in fact, is kind of the fucking point.

I smile at the idea of toying with her, teasing her, taunting her.

I've never been one for long-term commitment, but don't get me wrong, I'm also not someone who doesn't respect other people's vows. But there's a drastic difference in actually taking a woman who's already betrothed to bed or simply making her fantasize about it.

I move my hips to the beat of the music, slowly, seductively, and I don't miss the way Belle's breath gets tangled up in her lungs for a second or two longer than it should.

It's a damn shame this woman is about to be someone's wife…

Obviously, not for the guy she's about to marry, but for me. The two of us could definitely make magic happen between the sheets; I'm sure of it.

When the song switches over to Lenny Kravitz singing about an "American Woman," the women in the room lose their ever-loving shit.

Yeah. I knew this song would be a hit.

I quirk an eyebrow at the bachelorette as I begin to unbutton and unzip my pants. She clenches her eyes shut, and I don't doubt, if it weren't for my shirt over her arms, she'd be covering her eyes with her hands.

Maverick gave me shit when I refused one of his stupid banana hammocks and baby oil to grease up my muscles, but I knew that sticking with the *au naturel* look, without all the weird stripper shit, was far sexier. Women like strong men. *Real* men. Not a greased-up monkey.

I shake my ass a little as I slide my pants down my legs, revealing my favorite pair of black Calvin Klein boxer briefs, and within seconds, I feel dollar bills being shoved into the back of my underwear, followed by hoots and hollers.

"Oh, yes please!"

"Hellll yessss! Take it off!"

"I'm so jealous of you right now, Belly!"

"Show us your cock!"

I chuckle at the last one, untie the knot at the front of Belle's chest, and lean forward to whisper into her ear, "Wrap your legs around my waist, gorgeous. It's time to really give your friends a show."

She gasps as I lift her from the chair to the small stage in the corner of the room, flip her upside down, roll her to the floor, spread her legs, and do a spinning handstand in between them. As I fall to a push-up position over her body, she squeals, and the other women shriek as I put my head between her legs, careful not to touch anything, and blow.

She shivers hard, *really fucking hard,* and my heart kicks up in my chest. *Did she just…?*

Holy shit.

THREE

Sophie

The water is cold and angry against my heated skin as I splash another handful on my face and lean into the Club Craze bathroom sink. Makeup be damned, I feel like my skin is on fire. Belle's in one of the stalls, happy as a clam, and for all intents and purposes, that should be a good thing. The only problem is, her happiness has come at my expense, and I am *officially* scandalized.

Tell me…is it ever possible to recover from the shame of having orgasmed in public—*discreetly, I think*—all because of the stupid exotic dancer I hired for my sister?

Because, if not, I won't bother sharing this with my therapist when we have our next session.

"Oh my God!" Belle yells from the stall, her feet teetering on *my* heels as she tries to squat and hover over the toilet. I swear, if she pees on my one and only pair of Jimmy Choos, I will hex her so hard. "Did you freaking see that guy? He bent you over backward and planted a baby in your womb through your dress, I swear to Jesus."

"Uh, yeah. I saw," I comment on the absurdly obvious. But truthfully, I didn't just *see* anything. I felt his heat and his heart thrumming in his chest and smelled the undeniably intoxicating subtlety of his cologne. I felt the stretch in my muscles as he manipulated my body left and right and sideways and upside down, all while somehow managing to make the ridiculousness of a male stripper seem sexy.

The only time I could truly say I saw, I suppose, was during the out-of-body experience I had while he straddled my body in the sixty-nine position and straight up sent me into purgatory. There I was, just hovering by the ceiling of the room like Mary fucking Poppins and the kids when they go to have tea with the loopy guy, wondering if that was really my face under his superior crotch or if it was all just a mirage.

And then I had to go and fucking orgasm, like a teenage boy in the middle of a wet dream.

I shake my head to clear it again, thanking my lucky stars that, in this situation, I was at least afforded the luxury of being a woman. No boner. No jizz-filled underwear. Just a hard twist of arousal and a pair of damp panties.

"I swear he tossed you around like a rag doll!"

"Yes, *Sophie*," I say, emphasizing my name instead of hers just in case any other drunken members of our group found their way in here and into another stall while I was busy with my emotional breakdown. "I'm well aware of everything Jude, the Magic Dancer, was, thank you very much."

She flushes the toilet and swings the stall door back toward herself, stumbling out into the open area and laughing hysterically at my revamp of Puff, the Magic Dragon, one of our favorite songs as kids before cynics ruined it.

I'm glad she's having a good time, but holy hell. I'm still shaking. And once I'm certain none of the gals from our group are in the bathroom with us, I give her the cold, hard reality.

"You owe me so freaking much, it's ridiculous." Pretending to be the bride at my sister's bachelorette party when I'm not even dating anyone would surely be something Dr. Winters would see as a "setback."

"I know I owe you, I really do, but I would have *died*, okay? You know I would have died. And that would really complicate your use of my Costco membership, wouldn't it?"

I snort. "Fine. But can we switch back now? Don't you want to enjoy the rest of the evening as the bride-to-be?"

Belle shakes her head almost violently and stands at the sink to wash her hands. She waves them obnoxiously in front of the automatic sensor several times but still never manages to turn the faucet on. I lean forward and wave my hand in front of hers, bringing it to life.

For some reason, she always struggles with that.

"No way. I've had a great time the whole night tonight, but I didn't realize how much better it is when no one is paying attention to me! Maid of honor is where it's at, and I can't go back now that I know how good it is here."

"Are you serious?" I snap.

"Please," she begs, pretending to pout. "I know it's not ideal for you, but pretty, pretty please with a cherry on top, do this for me? I'll bake you however many cookies and cupcakes and cakes you want for the next six months."

My sister is the baked goods goddess, and she *knows* I can't resist that kind of offer.

"Fine," I grind out. "But if I were you, I'd invest in stock for flour and butter and sugar and shit because I'm going to run your ass like a factory worker."

"Whatever you want. John's really good with investments, so I'll make him figure it out."

I laugh at her drunken seriousness—it's too hard not to—and finally pull her into a hug so I can whisper directly into her ear. "I love you, Bells. But I also fucking hate you."

She nods. "It's the Sage sister way."

"Well, two out of three," I correct, knowing that Katelynn is the least drama-associated sister of the three of us. At five years our senior, she was always more of a "Disciplinary Board" than a defendant when it came to Sage sister arguments.

"That's true," Belle agrees. "I'm seriously surprised at how drunk Kate's gotten tonight. It's a real mom's-night-out kind of vibe."

I roll my eyes. "Like you should talk. You're drunker than she is."

"Yeah, but it's my bachelorette," she asserts.

Immediately, I shake my head with a fake smile. "Uh-uh. Not anymore, it's not. Thanks to you, the glory of tonight seems to be mine."

FOUR

No matter what I do, I cannot get the sound and feel and look of the bride orgasming beneath me out of my head. For as talented as I am, I've never made a woman come without even touching her pussy before, and the rush of power I feel after having done it is exhilarating.

But she's not just any woman—she's the bride of a bachelorette party I danced for as a stupid fucking bet.

And, apparently, as I stand in front of the mirror in the back dressing room, pressing my hands into the tabletop in front of me with the force of a superhero, I don't know how to cope with that kind of dichotomy.

I can't pursue something like taking her home tonight, but for as much as I try, I can't seem to just forget about it either.

The door to the dressing room cracks against the wall as it slams open, temporarily undiluting the thump of bass from the DJ's music. I crane my neck to see who it is, but when Maverick's jovial eyes lock on to mine, I wish I hadn't looked.

"Oh, man, Jude, don't tell me it didn't go well," he remarks with entirely too much excitement. Clearly, he's misread the stress I'm carrying as being performance-related, and being the type of guy he is—and I normally am, frankly—he isn't hesitating to rub it in my face. "Did the ladies not like what you had to offer?"

I shake my head and close my eyes briefly before spinning around to face him, crossing my arms over my chest, and sinking my ass into the edge of the table.

"It went fine," I hear myself say, a huge understatement by any standards. Still, it doesn't seem right to disclose what I witnessed without the bride's permission, let alone to a bigmouth like Mav. He'd eat it up, that's for sure, if he could even find it within himself to believe it.

The truth is, it'll probably be much easier to pretend I flopped than contend with any of the other complications of the truth.

The only problem, of course, with that plan of action is my ego.

Fucking hell, I don't want to lose this bet when I really kicked its ass five ways to Sunday.

But I can't bring myself to prove it either. It looks like Maverick might get to keep that hundred bucks he owes me after all.

"You bombed, dude. I can see it written all over your face!" he practically yells, crossing the room to slap me on the back. One more hard slap and all the confessions about what really happened in that VIP room are libel to come up like vomit—word vomit.

"I didn't bomb," I hedge, gritting my teeth against the urge to wring my own neck. I don't know what is wrong with me all of a sudden or why I'm being such a pussy, but I don't like it one bit. "But I am inexperienced in the ways of your profession, and the lack of training was obvious."

Because I'm pretty sure making the women orgasm isn't part of the exotic dancer's handbook or official training video.

"I told you," he boasts cheerfully, slamming his palm into his locker and laughing. His muscles twitch obnoxiously as he holds his arms out to his sides and proclaims, "Everyone can't be as good as me, dude. It's just a scientific impossibility."

Somehow, I manage a nod, even though the tension in my neck feels like it could snap it in two.

"Well, I guess we're even on the money, then, huh?" he says through a growing smile. "Too bad you had to double down on that shit, but I guess that's to be expected. Jude Winslow can never resist a bet."

He's right. Up until now, I wouldn't say I've ever had the impulse control to resist much of anything that comes with a temporary high or instant gratification.

How is it, then, that I managed to stop myself from telling him all about how good I really am at his job?

Back in my normal clothes, I stand at the window behind the DJ booth in the top office and scan the crowd of partying New Yorkers and tourists. The mood is up, the vibe is right, and Club Craze is an undeniable hit among the young and fabulous.

Rainbow-colored lights strobe the dance floor, cascading over the writhing bodies of hundreds of coeds as they experiment with heavy bodily contact.

My gaze doesn't stay there for long, though. Instead, I'm drawn to the other side of the room, to the elevated booth where the bride-to-be and her group are congregated, sipping on drinks and falling drunkenly on top of one another while laughing. It's a diverse group of friends, ranging from crazy to quiet, but the bride at the center of it all is the one who commands my attention.

I watch as she takes a sip of her drink before setting it down in front of her and then laughs, her head thrown back and her throat exposed, when one of the other women launches her body on top of Belle.

They shuffle a bit, eventually coming to a stop while sitting next to each other on the couch, and when they look up, I lean a little closer to the window and squint.

"Are they identical twins?" I whisper to myself as I conduct my inspection. Obviously, having been in the VIP room with them before, I thought I would have noticed, but evidently, my focus on the bride pertained to more than just dancing.

The same proportions, the same features, the same bright-lipstick-lined mouths—they are. *Fucking identical twins.*

Suddenly struck by a twisted curiosity as to whether I react to them both the same way physically—and if the other twin is spoken for—I shove away from the window and make my way out of the office, down the stairs, through the back hallway, and out into the chaos of a lively club.

It's kind of messed up, I'll admit, to be thinking of twins as exchangeable objects, but I can't fucking help myself. I don't know these women from Adam. All I know is that I've reacted to one I can't have, and the selfish part of me is completely unwilling to let the rest of the night slip by without seeing if there's something to be done about it—a backup plan, so to speak.

The crowd jostles to the music as I push my way through as inconspicuously as possible. Maverick is back at it, dancing in one of the floating cages above the dance floor to some of the best mixes Ki-Ki's ever made. She's on fire tonight, and the crowd is responding in kind.

The business side of me knows I should stop by the bar on my way over to the group to see how they're handling the onslaught, but the foolishly fixated part knows it's not an option. Maybe on the way back, but not yet. Not before I talk to the bride and her friends *and* her identical twin again.

Finally through the dancing crowd, I readjust my suit jacket at my waist and hop up two steps at a time onto the elevated platform where their group resides. Several sets of eyes lock on to me—followed by even more catcalls and yells of a happy, drunken nature—and I feel the corners of my mouth lift into a smile.

"Well, well, if it isn't Jude, the Magic Dancer!" the bride's twin cheers, making the other women hoot and the bride herself blush and look toward the ground.

I chuckle at the moniker, feeling a little emboldened by the obvious pat on the back it gives me. "Is that what I'm supposed to go by from now on?" I ask the woman whose sash reads Maid of Honor in big, glittery letters.

I study her face closely, waiting for the deep burn in my gut that I get when I look at her sister to fire up, but it never does.

No flutter of butterflies, no intense arousal, no desire to find out all her dirtiest secrets—none of it. And yet, she looks exactly the fucking same. Given how little I know about these women other than their looks, the rest of it shouldn't matter.

But it does, goddammit. Why? Is it as simple as wanting what I can't have?

"Yes!" the loud-mouthed blonde shouts at me excitedly. "Jude, the Magic Dancer is a better high than any dragon I've ever puffed, and I wasn't even experiencing you firsthand." She turns to the bride and demands wildly, "Tell us, Belle. What's it like to be that close to exotic royalty?"

The rest of the girls dissolve into a cackle, and Belle's gaze jumps to meet mine with wide-eyed scandal just as I'm running the feel of her name over my lips.

"Belle," I mouth, rolling the Ls with a curl of my tongue. Her gaze flicks to my mouth and holds, her eyebrows pinching together slightly with a grimace. It's strange. I don't understand it. *Though, I'm sure there are a lot of things you don't understand about a literal stranger, Jude,* I chastise myself.

Belle's twin reaches over and squeezes her knee, visibly aware of her discomfort, so I change the subject. I don't want her to be embarrassed—not at all. As a matter of fact, I'm almost alarmingly attuned to her emotions.

I don't know. Maybe the unexpected act of intimacy we shared during my dance has bonded us in some strange way.

"Now, now, ladies, that's not actually the reason I'm here. I just came to check in and make sure you're all enjoying the rest of your night. Service is good? Drinks are plentiful?"

"You bet!" the girl with curly hair shouts, holding up her drink as evidence before taking a huge gulp.

"And what about you?" I say directly to Belle, demanding her eyes with my voice in a way that makes them jump to mine almost violently. "Having a good party? Everything you dreamed it would be?"

Her green eyes flash toward her sister before locking back on to mine, a small smirk curving up the perfect line of her red-stained mouth. "You have no idea how different this is from what I pictured, actually."

I laugh. "Oh yeah? And what did you picture?"

She pauses briefly. "You know, I'm not sure, but I thought I'd do a lot more dancing?"

Without thought, I take an extra step into the platform, breaking the barrier of the circle of gals, and reach across the table in front of her. Belle looks at my hand like it'll slink out and bite her if she reaches for it.

Still, I've come this far, so there's not much point in turning back now.

"Come on," I cajole. "If you want more dancing, let's do more dancing."

Her twin nods furiously, elbowing her in the side so many times that Belle finally jumps up just to escape the onslaught of pain. After a little more vibing from the group, she puts her hand in mine and makes her way around the low-set table to stand in front of me.

Her short dress hugs the long, lean lines of her body, and the neckline dips into a V between her breasts. They might not be as obvious if she weren't breathing like a chain-smoker at the end of a marathon, but to be honest, I'm not so sure. For some reason, I can't stop noticing everything about her.

"One dance," I say next to her ear. "Just to get you started. I promise it won't be like the last one."

Her heart kick-starts from a jog to a gallop, shooting a surging pulse through even the veins in her hand. It gives me a thrill on the inside, but externally, I ignore it.

"What do you say?" I add when she doesn't answer.

With a nod and a swallow, she moves around me, her hand still in mine, and heads for the dance floor while her friends yell and cheer behind her. They're locked into the good times of the party, so I'm not surprised that they haven't seemed to notice whatever is going on between their bride and me. But I'm not going to be the one to tell them.

As far as I'm concerned, once she leaves here tonight, I'll never come back to thinking about it again. Not only is she off-limits, but I'm not that kind of a guy. I don't need one woman to occupy my thoughts—I've got several.

Right?

FIVE

Saturday, February 24th

Sophie

Jude leads me to the dance floor, his arm cocked back to keep my clammy hand locked in the palm of his. Seeing him decked out in a suit is like a whole different attack on my nervous system, and it's all I can do to force myself to swallow my saliva every few seconds rather than choking on it.

A slow beat pounds from the oversized speakers next to the DJ's booth on the other side of the club, and every vibration hits me square between the legs. I'm swollen and sensitive—just as I'd be after actual sex, and nobody's even touched me.

I swear, tomorrow, I'm going to have to see if anyone else remembers anything from tonight or if this is all just a freaking weird dream.

Jude spins without unlocking our hands when he finds a small hole in the crowd on the dance floor and pulls my body toward him with a jerk. I hit him on a hard stop, all his muscles feeling like the smooth surface of a large boulder beneath my hands. For as much as we've already been through together tonight, this is the first time I've touched his body with my palms.

My mind races to figure out if it's wrong to be doing this—given that I'm not really the bride-to-be but am just pretending to be—but we're swaying to the beat with his thigh between my own before I even come close to landing on a conclusion.

There's no time to question, no time to wonder. It's all I can do to keep up with the normal bodily functions required for survival.

"What do you think, Belle? Is this more like what you had in mind?"

For my bachelorette party? No. I'd say not. Ha.

I watch as his pulse thrums peacefully at the side of his tanned neck, and—

"Sophiieee! Helloooo?"

With muddy recognition of my name, I snap my head up on a jolt, and the bouquet in my hands jostles accordingly. Strobing lights I once saw with the vividity of reality fade away, and my sister's sternly bridal face takes their place. I would have sworn on the dang Bible two seconds ago that I was still back in Club Craze, dancing with a freaking exotic dancer I had no business dancing with, given that he thought I was Belle and engaged to be married.

But no.

Strange as it seems, I'm apparently at my sister's wedding, having a possible psychotic episode.

I gulp down a huge batch of air, trying to catch my thoughts and shove them back into the deep recesses of my brain so that there's room for reality. Belle is getting married. Right now. Today. We're moments away from the actual wedding, and I haven't seen Jude, the Magic Dancer in a week. It's time to get a grip.

Sheesh. I can't wait to fill Dr. Winters in on this one.

"Geez, Soph. I've been calling your name for at least a minute. Are you having a stroke or something?"

I shake my head to clear it and then smile like the dutiful maid of honor I am. "I don't think so." Not that I know what one feels like. It's entirely possible I am, I suppose. I'm definitely acting crazy enough.

"Good," Belle huffs. "I mean, this is my day after all."

I roll my eyes at my twin's uncharacteristic dramatics. Lack of sympathy for a potential stroke victim is pretty callous, I'll admit, but in my line of work, I've seen many a bride go temporarily insane on the big day. Why should it be any different for my twin just because we share DNA?

"Of course. I'll delay my medical emergencies accordingly."

Belle glares, and I bite my lip to silence a chuckle. The truth is, after the amount of time and physical labor my event planning company put into this wedding, I'd sweep my own body to the side and declare that the show must go on from the afterlife if I needed to.

"Girls, please. Can we not even have a wedding without the two of you sniping at each other?" our mother Katerina asks from her spot at the ironing board in the corner of the room. Our dad Anthony's pants are in her hands, and she's working on them furiously. That, of course, begs the question of where exactly my father is without his pants, but I really don't want to know, so I don't ask.

"How long do we have? I'm starting to sweat through my deodorant," Belle remarks, making me laugh.

She's a pain in my ass, but I love her more than anyone else in the world. There's a special kind of bond that comes with being a twin sister—half devotion, half loathing, and another completely unexpected fifty percent dedicated to an understanding so deep no one else will ever comprehend. Our mother refers to it as "sniping," but in reality, it's all just a special part of our dynamic. Normally, she ignores it, but since our parents moved back to Miami, we don't see them as much as we used to. As a result, I think Katerina feels an extra need to mother us when she's around.

I glance down at the slim gold watch on my wrist that Belle gifted all her bridesmaids and calculate the time. It's her big day and she's anxious, so I'll do my best to be understanding. "Just about ten minutes to go. Last time I checked in with Julie, she said the groomsmen were getting themselves together to head into the atrium."

"Pretty sure you mean popping mints to cover the smell of all the alcohol they've been drinking," our elder sister Katelynn says from her spot on the couch. She's been married for five years already, and apparently, she gets it.

I laugh. She's pretty spot-on, to be honest. "That, among other things. You wouldn't believe how many grooms I've had to make switch pants with one of their groomsmen at the last minute because of a stain."

"Oh yes, I would," Belle interjects. "John is an actual attractant for sauces. I swear. Somehow, you can see stains on even his black stuff. I told him he's going to have to take all his shit to the dry cleaners if he wants our marriage to last."

She may be cracking jokes, but her hands are shaking, and I know my sister better than anyone. She's nervous as hell, and all this talk is just her way of trying to cover it up.

I step closer, handing off my bouquet to Tonya, who stops fluffing her boobs to take it, and pull Belle gently into my embrace. "You're getting married, sis," I whisper with a smile. "I'm so happy for you."

Her eyes are wide and innocent as she breathes, "I love him so much, but I'm terrified, Soph. What if…what if it doesn't work out or we start to hate each other or—"

"Belle," I interrupt calmly, cupping her cheek with my hand. "John loves you. You're going to fight and quibble and disagree sometimes, but I know you're going to work out."

"Really?" she asks hopefully.

I smile. "Really. And if not, I have a feeling I'm going to look damn good in an orange jumpsuit."

SIX

Hands full with beer, I bang on the front door with my foot and wait for one of my family members to answer my call. After Winnie assigned me the role of Beverage Bitch for Uncle Brad's birthday shindig, I went all out and got seven thirty-packs of beer, five cases of soda, a case of water, and a big jug of wine for the moms.

Evidently, something happens to women after giving birth that makes their bodies need wine to survive. At least, that's what I've been told. I'm not sure what brand I got, but with these lushes, I figured quantity was better than quality. As it is, I'll have to make several trips back to the trunk of my Audi A4 to get the remainder of the drinks. Living in the city, I don't drive a ton, but knowing I'd be hauling this much stuff, using my car was a necessity.

When the door finally swings open, a woman I don't recognize at all smiles and swings her arm gallantly into the house. She's got a frisky little blond haircut and dark-brown eyes, but I don't have one fucking clue who she is. I lean back to check the numbers on the house—*yep, this is my mom's place*—and then glance back to her with furrowed brows.

"Hi," she says then, smiling again, but this time, it's a bit self-consciously.

"Uh, hi." I want so badly to ask who the fuck she is, but when she reaches out to take the cases of beer from my arms, I think better of it. *At least she's helping, unlike the rest of my no-good family.* "Stay here," I tell her instead. "I've got more shit to carry."

She nods, and I have to laugh as I walk the distance back to my car. *You really never know what to expect at a Winslow gathering, I swear.*

I grab another load and repeat the process, until finally, the mysterious blonde and I have all the drinks inside the front hallway. Feeling a little like we share a bond now, I'm just about to ask her name when my brother Ty comes strutting toward us, and she clings to him like a fucking magnet.

Ahh. Okay, now this is making sense.

Ty has brought yet another completely random woman to a family gathering, thus garnering false hope in her heart. At the latest, she'll be gone by the weekend, wondering how things shifted so quickly from meeting the family to ending.

I shake my head. *Poor fucking sap.*

She has no clue that this isn't special—that my brother hasn't warmed to her with an unmatched connection. Unfortunately, bringing women around the family is just something he does for the fuck of it, I suppose. Truthfully, I don't know the real psychology behind it, but that doesn't change the facts. Ty Winslow is a serial dater with just as much contempt for commitment as the rest of us Winslow brothers, and that won't be changing anytime soon.

"Thanks for the help," I tell her, not bothering to ask her name.

Her voice is tentative and a little confused as she tells me I'm welcome, and I get it. I'm coming across as super rude, given the visual of what she thinks is going on. But to be honest, this is just par for the course with Ty, and the less I play into this girl's hope, the better off she'll be.

I shove Ty in the shoulder as a nonverbal gesture of how big of a fucking idiot he is, and he just smiles, the bastard. I roll my eyes and head down the hall toward the kitchen, the cluck of all the hens loud enough to invade my ears long before I get there.

My mom Wendy, my aunt Paula, my sister Winnie, and Aunt Paula's longtime friend Bev all stand at the kitchen island, working on various food trays and laughing hysterically.

"Ladies!" I greet enthusiastically, throwing my arms in the air and soaking in all of their responding smiles.

They giggle as I work my way around their campfire, kissing them each on the cheek and even going so far as to give Bev a small slap on the butt. She's a super-funny lady with a raspy, smoker's-style laugh, widowed three years ago, and I like to keep the spice alive in her life. Wendy Winslow, of course, hates it quite a bit.

"Jude!" my mom chastises as Bev blushes, and Aunt Paula and Winnie both giggle some more.

"Sorry, sorry," I apologize, lifting both of my hands in the air defensively. "I just can't help myself."

"I don't mind," Bev affirms, smiling like the cat who got the cream.

I wink, and the ladies dissolve in a titter again.

"God, please help my son," my mom pretends to pray, lifting her eyes heavenward. "One day, I pray that he be blessed with impulse control."

I chuckle and shake my head before placing another kiss on my mom's cheek. "Sorry, Ma, but I don't think it's going to happen if it hasn't already."

"Get out of here," Winnie says playfully, dropping her foodstuffs to shove me in the shoulder toward the back door. "You're better off out at the grill with the men where there's no code of conduct."

I agree with a salute and a bow, and then tuck out the spring-loaded back door as quickly as possible. Trust me, those women are the light of my life, but I'm much better suited to hanging out with the men of the family any day of the week, even if it is cold enough to freeze my nuts off out there.

"Heyyy!"

"*Yooo!*"

"Jude!"

The guys all yell as I step out onto the porch, and Uncle Brad smiles at me before thumping his palm on the back of my head.

"Hey! What was that for?" I cry, scooting away quickly while Flynn and Remy both laugh ruthlessly at my expense. My brother-in-law Wes smiles but at least has the decency to keep his hilarity on the inside.

"For the *gift* you got me," my uncle answers, shooting me with something red and lacy like it's a slingshot. After a quick juggle, I hold it up curiously, and then I drop it like a hot potato when I discover it's a women's thong of unknown origin.

"Wha... I didn't... That's not... Uncle Brad!" I stammer, making Remy nearly choke on his beer as Ty comes walking out the back door to join us. "I think there's been a misunderstanding."

"Yeah," Uncle Brad agrees. "I bet. You know, I think I might know what happened."

"Oh yeah?" I ask, swallowing nervously. No matter what, I don't think there's a good way for me to get out of this.

"Yeah. See, I think you deflected on the gift-picking altogether and expected your sister to get something for you. And, in a brilliant move of revenge, this is what she chose."

I chuckle uneasily and glance to my three brothers as they laugh behind their beer bottles. I'm immediately suspicious. "What the fu—dge? Why am I the only one getting crucified?"

"Remy, Flynn, and Ty all got me gifts of their own. Nice ones," Uncle Brad says, illuminating the depth of my siblings' betrayal.

"I thought we had an understanding!" I exclaim at the traitors.

"We did," Remy hedges while Ty snickers. "An understanding that we were all willing to let you bury yourself on this one."

Ty reaches out to high-five him, and I lift up my middle finger, swinging it wildly toward them all. "I hate every single one of you." I pause on Ty and give him another middle finger for good measure, emphasizing, "Especially you."

"Me? What did I do?"

"Give me a break, dude. Do you really not realize the torture you're putting all these women through?"

His eyebrows draw together, and he laughs. "You mean Stephanie?"

I shrug hugely. "I don't have a clue, dude. I don't know her name because we never know their names. Why do you always insist on bringing these randos to family shit?"

"What? I'm not supposed to bring women I'm dating to family get-togethers now?"

Even Flynn scoffs at that. "Come on, Ty. You're not *dating* her. Sleeping with her, maybe."

"All right, all right. Enough," Uncle Brad interrupts. "And Ty, bring whomever you want. I, for one, have actually started to get some enjoyment out of it."

Remy, Flynn, Wes, and I look at Uncle Brad curiously, and he just shrugs.

"What? Paula and I started a running pool for names. I get five dollars if I'm closest alphabetically."

"You and Aunt Paula gamble over me?" Ty bellows, and we're all mid-laugh as Winnie walks out the door with a tray of hamburger patties to throw on the grill.

For some reason, though, Ty locks on to me as the brother to strike back at. Which, honestly, probably isn't a bad idea. I *am* two years younger than him and a much better sport than our elder brothers, Remy and Flynn. The two of them would probably grind his nuts up and eat them for breakfast if he tried to throw down with them.

"What about you, Jude?" Ty asks snidely. "Dip your wick in anything of consequence lately?"

Winnie smacks the back of his head soundly, but years and years of demented sibling torture between the five of us have conditioned Ty's pain response into nothing more than a chuckle. It's impressive, really, that kind of compartmentalization while under physical attack.

"Can't say that I have, Ty. Just living the casual life the best I can."

Remy and Flynn nod, both taking swigs of their beers, and Winnie rolls her eyes. After this much time with the four of us as single bachelors, I can't imagine our baby sister expects anything else. Still, I know she's found her supposed happily ever after or whatever with Wes Lancaster, so there's a certain amount of desire to *spread the joy* that runs through every woman's veins.

I clear my throat as their laughter dies down, and the vision of the most interesting brunette woman I've ever encountered enters my mind.

It's probably not the best idea I've ever had to bring this kind of dirty laundry to a family party, but hell, I've never been the type to hold anything back, I guess.

"I, uh, did meet a pretty interesting woman last weekend at the new club."

"Really?" Winnie asks, her voice undeniably hopeful.

I lift the corner of my mouth into a pseudo-smile as I admit, "Well, yeah. I mean, she was the bride in a group there for a bachelorette, but she *was* interesting."

Ty's body folds in half as laughs overcome his muscles, and Remy's and Flynn's eyebrows shoot to their hairlines. Wes lets his head fall back toward his shoulder blades, his eyes closing in pain, and Uncle Brad just shakes his head and turns back to the grill.

"Nooo," Winnie cries, sinking her head into her hands. "Tell me you didn't, Jude. Please tell me you didn't."

"I didn't," I comfort, hedging, "At least, not really."

"What in the hell does that mean, bro?" Remy interjects.

"Either you did or you didn't. Right? What am I missing?" Ty says, looking around at everyone for an explanation that only I can give.

"I didn't sleep with her. We danced. Flirted a little, maybe. That's it."

Oh yeah, and she orgasmed while I was dancing for her, too.

"Promise me you won't mess with a married woman, Jude!" Winnie exclaims then, nearly coming out of her skin. "I do not want to have to disown you!"

"Relax," I assure her gently. "I don't expect I'll ever see her again, sis."

I picture her body and her lips and the sound of her breath leaving her as she orgasmed on the floor of the VIP room stage beneath me. And then I picture her in a wedding dress, marrying some other dude.

Nah. *Even fate wouldn't be that cruel. Green-eyed Belle is nothing but a flash in the past.*

SEVEN

Sophie

The door to the office opens, and Dr. Winters peeks her head out, her mouth curving up into a smile when she sees me. "You ready, Sophie?"

I toss the *Cosmopolitan* magazine back down on the coffee table in front of my chair, sling my purse on my shoulder, and push to standing with a nod to follow her into the office.

It's a routine I've done many, many times, and I still get butterflies in my stomach every time she pushes the door to a close behind me with a click. It's not that she's not an incredibly nice person—she is—and it's not like I'm here because my life is a disaster and everything is falling apart either.

I'm lucky. I'm fairly happy. I have friends and family, and I don't have cancer.

And that's a fuck of a lot more than many people can say.

But I hit a bit of a dark spot a little over six months ago after my grandmother passed away, and when I went to my regular doctor for a checkup, she recommended I start seeing Dr. Winters too.

It's not that big of a surprise that Mimi's death hit me the hardest—we were by far the closest out of all my siblings, and when I really look back on it, I can see that she was actually one of my best friends.

I had to find a way to cope, and rather than binge drinking and obsessing, I decided to give therapy a try.

Dr. Winters has been there for me for a long time, even if I haven't gotten the guts to tell most of the people in my life about my standing Wednesday appointments with her.

"Can we normalize putting a magazine other than *Cosmo* out there?" I say by way of greeting, smiling to take the sting out of my words. "That's seriously, like, the worst option I can think of if you're trying to build women's self-esteem."

Dr. Winters laughs as she takes her seat, picking up her pad and pen from her side table and pretending to scribble on it, dictating, "Patient shows signs of disproportionate anger for magazines."

I roll my eyes but laugh. "Okay, maybe I have a little bit of an attitude today." Dr. Winters smiles her annoyingly knowing smile, and I sigh, mocking, "*And why do you think that is, Sophie?*"

My therapist snaps the fingers on both of her hands like maracas. "Ah, yes! My plan to live inside your head is working! I love when you can self-actualize a question before I have to."

I shove my body back into the couch and consider my answer. There's obviously been a ton of stuff going on in my life over the last couple of weeks, and I figure that's as good of a place to start as any.

"Well…Belle got married this last weekend. And I'm, like, so, so happy for her, you know?"

Dr. Winters nods. "But?"

"Buuut…I don't know."

"You don't know, or you don't want to voice it? Because there's a difference."

"I just…you know I came here about my grandmother's passing, right? Not for relationship advice."

"Sophie, you spent three sessions talking about your sweet Mimi, and I enjoyed them immensely. But you've spent the last twenty or so talking about relationships. You drove the conversation there, not me. I'm just providing whatever guidance I can in the situation."

I gulp a little. "Have I really been talking about wanting a relationship for that long?"

Dr. Winters smiles. "It's not all you talk about. It's just a big part of your life. Which, quite frankly, is understandable. You plan weddings for a living. You live it, day in and day out, and I have to imagine that makes it a little harder to forget about. That's why I'm here. To help you."

"I guess I just really thought I'd be married by now. And seeing Belle…" I pause, trying to think of the word. "Achieve it?" I shake my head. "That sounds so stupid."

Dr. Winters raises her eyebrows but says nothing else, so I continue to babble. "I'm happy she's happy. I really am. And John is a great guy. I don't know that I would have been a good fit for him, but Belle is. They work, you know?"

"And watching Belle makes you want to have it for yourself?"

"I don't know that it's really Belle."

"So, just weddings in general? You feel like everyone in the world is finding it but you?"

I shake my head. "Other than my sisters, I've never really been to a lot of weddings, personally. Like, outside of work, I mean."

"Okay, so maybe you got too close before? Someone special in a past relationship that you really felt was the one, but it didn't work out?"

I shake my head again. Frankly, I've never really dated anyone I considered marriage material.

"Okay. So, what is it that brings out the need in you? Societal demands?"

"No, I don't think so. I mean, I'm proud of what I've built in my business, and I realize I might not have gotten to do it this way if I'd met someone sooner."

I can hear myself, and I imagine Dr. Winters must be getting frustrated with me at this point. Hell, even I am. But for as enraged as she may be on the inside, she doesn't show any impatience on the outside. Since I'm genuinely confused at my own complication, it's greatly appreciated.

"So, what's the missing link here? What drives you?"

I shrug, fiddling with my fingers as I try to deep-think, and admit, "I've always pictured myself as married. As a little girl, I dreamed of weddings. I thought I'd have my own by now. It was in my ten-year vision, but…that was fifteen years ago. Honestly, I know what I'm looking for in a man, and I eliminate the noncontenders right off the bat. It should be saving me time."

"Sophie, life doesn't manifest like an Erin Condren planner. It's messy. Unexpected. Usually drama-filled and ass-backward. You're going to have to open yourself up to going on some dates with men who might *not* be Prince Charming."

"I don't see the point in dating people I know aren't prospects for a long-term commitment. What's wrong with that?"

"It's judgmental. And shortsighted," she says, her tone of voice somehow gentle enough to keep me from feeling bad. "Would you buy a house based on what it said on the listing, or would you actually do a walk-through beforehand to see what it was really like?"

My eyebrows pinch together. "So, men are houses now?"

"Sort of." She grins. "You're looking to set up shop…stay there for a while with both, right? Maybe the vinyl siding is faded, but the inside's got a hundred-thousand-dollar reno, girlfriend."

"You should start an app." I grin cheekily. "HGTV meets that dating app TapNext."

"I'm just saying that you can't know the heart of a person until you spend at least five minutes in their presence."

"What do you suggest I do, then? Because I'm trying, Dr. Winters, really. I'm willing to meet men. I'm willing to get out there. I want it."

She considers me closely before leaning toward me again and tilting her head to the side. "Is that really true, Sophie? Are you really putting yourself out there? Because you just said before that you eliminate men who *aren't contenders* right off the bat?" I frown as she continues. "What if you're eliminating them too soon?"

The corners of my mouth turn down even farther, and she nods, decided.

"I'm giving you a homework assignment. Pick someone on the dating app of your choice, match with them, and go on the date. I don't care if you already feel like it's going to fail. I don't even care if you give it a real mental chance. Just *go*. Get dressed up, make the effort, meet the guy, try to engage in enjoyable conversation, wait for the date to be over, and then say goodnight. No strings. No expectations, no anything. Just a date. Period."

"You don't think that's a waste of time?"

"No. For you, I don't. Dating needs to become a habit. Something you're as comfortable doing as breathing. Once you relax and just take it all as a matter of course, one day, it really won't be a waste of time. Because one day, you'll meet the guy you've been looking for. And I can promise you this, he won't be the one because he checks all the boxes on your list. You're just going to *feel* it. And until you do, you need to go through the motions."

Just go through the motions. *Could I do that?*

"You can and you will," Dr. Winters replies as though she's read my mind. "And then I'll be here next week, ready to listen to everything that happened."

One date. One night. One random chance. I could do that for a shot at happiness.

I mean…*how hard could it be?*

EIGHT

Monday, March 5th

Jude

"Where are you headed now?" I ask my brother, sliding my hands into my nice leather gloves and zipping my jacket up to my chin. It's still frigid outside, even after the turn of the month to March, and the tunnel effect of New York's busy streets only amplifies it. Combine that with being fresh out of the gym shower with still-damp hair and my nuts are liable to freeze to my thighs on my ten-block walk.

Flynn smiles—just smiles. God, he is such a mysterious bastard. Seriously. I spend a lot of time with him, mostly working out in the early evenings—it's actually the reason I go to a gym in Midtown instead of by my place in SoHo—and yet, I don't know that I actually have any knowledge to show for it. I don't know what he does with his spare time, what kind of hobbies he enjoys—I barely even know where he lives, to be honest. I don't expect I'd do very well in a trivia speed round about his life. He's always been there whenever any of us has needed him, though, and that's a hell of a lot more important than knowing what kinds of books he's reading or if he's into white-water rafting.

"Oh, cool," I mock when he still doesn't say anything. "That sounds really interesting, Flynn."

He flicks his eyebrows up and down, a tiny hint of a smirk lifting the corner of his mouth, but otherwise, he ignores me, wrapping his scarf around his neck twice before sliding a beanie over his dark hair.

"I'm going to grab dinner at Grand Station," I tell him, silently letting him know he's more than welcome to join. "Maybe stop by Milwaukee's Bar for a beer after."

"Have fun," he says in dismissal, giving me a quick but loving punch to the shoulder and turning up the block to head the other direction. I watch his back for a moment as he retreats and eventually laugh to myself with a shake of my head.

I don't know that I'll ever understand the inner workings of my second eldest brother.

Pulling my jacket around myself more tightly, I power walk up the sidewalk on thighs that burn from Flynn's sadistic idea of a simple leg day work-out. The streets are bustling with cars, and tourists clamor on every corner, looking at their phones and maps and pointing in a million different directions as they try to navigate to their next landmark.

A fine cloud of steam hangs in front of me, spilling from nearly every building in the area and expanding in the chilly air. I love the sounds of New York even more than I did ten years ago, and back then, I was nearly obsessed. It's always moving, always changing, and as a man who forever likes to be on the go, I appreciate the complication.

That's not to say I can't appreciate the simple life every now and then—I can and do—but this is the place that makes my blood sing. This is the place that makes me feel alive.

I hurry my pace to cross the street before the light changes, earning a honk from a turning taxi and a middle finger out the window for good measure. I smile and wave. *God, I love this city.*

My phone buzzes in my pocket, but I ignore it, choosing instead to indulge in the random sounds of my brisk walk and the warmth of my gloved hands. It's not long before I've completed the ten-block trek toward Uptown, and the neon flashing lights of Grand Station Grill beckon invitingly.

This is easily one of my top two favorite restaurants in the city. It's got everything—good food, good service, and just the right ambiance for solo or group dinners alike. Monday nights are their prime rib special night, and as a result, I usually find myself here once every couple of weeks.

The glass door feels light in my hand as I step inside, but I have a feeling that's just some sort of sensory mis-signal created by the fact that my legs are absolutely shredded. I swear, I'm neck-deep in lactic acid.

Heidi, the hostess, smiles at me hugely as I arrive, likely encouraged by the pained chuckle spilling from my throat. "Hey, Jude!" she greets with a friendly, jaunty wave. "Good to see you."

"Good to see you, too. My regular table available?"

She nods excitedly, admitting, "I blocked it off for you in case you came in."

"Thanks, babe." I wink, pull the glove off one hand with my teeth, and then dig into my jacket pocket to pull out a VIP pass or two. "Here. These are good for VIP entry and a bottle of your choice at Club Craze on Thursday. We're closed to the public starting Friday for a private event this weekend, but if you like it, you should bring the rest of your friends some other time."

"Really?" she squeals excitedly, doing a little jump-kick donkey-looking thing with her legs and putting her lips to the apple of my cheek. "Thanks, Jude."

I wave it off. "You bet. Let me know anytime there's a club you and your friends want to go to, and I'll see if I can hook you up."

She smiles again, grabbing a menu and waving me toward a table. She's practically skipping she's so giddy, and I'm feeling pretty damn satisfied. The truth is, as personal as I made the exchange seem, young, pretty things like Heidi are the ones helping me do my job. A club can't be popular without customers, and she's the kind of customer that brings in the rest. One quick phone chain to her friends, and they'll have every college-aged guy in the city piling in after them to try to get a swing at their tail.

It's just a fact of the club promotion business. Get the women, and the men will come. Period.

She puts the menu on the table and thanks me again before skip-running back to the front podium. I take off my overcoat and lay it over the back of the opposite chair, take my seat, and drop the napkin from the table into my lap.

For the most part, I know what I want, but I still open the menu to get a look at what their side specials are today—since they like to focus on semi-local seasonal items—and take a deep breath. *Man, it feels good to relax.*

Between the club openings and family shit, I've had a tremendously busy few weeks. After a couple of minutes and a brief visit from the waiter to take my order, my body finally starts to unwind. My shoulders drop down from around my ears, and my breath steadies.

I love a party, but time to myself really is a godsend. Sometimes, it's just good to sit in the silence and contentment of your own company.

Once I've finished my first beer, I pull my forgotten phone out of my jacket and sit back down to read the text I received on the way here.

Vivian: Hey, sexy. Want to meet up on one of your nights off?

I smile. Sex doesn't sound like a terrible idea, honestly. It's been a few weeks at least, so the opportunity this message presents isn't a bad one.

I take a minute to think about how I want to answer her and scour the restaurant for my waiter, Blake, to order another beer. I search all the white shirts at the edges of the tables, but I don't see him anywhere. *Hmm. He must be in the kitchen.*

Resolved to go ahead and answer Vivian before looking for him again, I swing my gaze back down to my phone, only to have my eyes snag on something across the room.

In a bright-blue dress and dangerously high heels, the bride of my dreams sits at a two-top table across from a man who's gesticulating wildly with his arms. She smiles and listens, before glancing down toward the floor and tucking a loose strand of dark hair behind her ear. Her lips are painted red, and her skin glows in the soft light of the restaurant.

That's her, right? Belle, the bachelorette from Club Craze? It *has* to be. I can feel the sizzle and spark of our weirdly powerful connection all the way across the room in both the burn in my chest and the tingling in my pants.

Fuck. I cannot believe I'm actually seeing her again in a city of over eight million people.

Maybe fate is that cruel.

Phone forgotten again, I sit back in my chair and watch her for a minute. Her smile, her laugh, the way she bops her foot up and down on the floor.

Maybe I should go say hello, right? Just to be cordial. She hasn't noticed me yet, but if she does and I don't say hi, I'll feel bad.

I'm a nice guy, and she's a nice gal. I'll just go over and say hello.

I mean…*what's the harm in that?*

NINE

Sophie

I chew nervously on my lip as my date pours me a glass of wine from the bottle he ordered for us and try to smile as he meets my eyes.

His name is Nathan, and we matched on TapNext about an hour after I created my profile. To say I'm apprehensive to be implementing Dr. Winters's homework is an understatement.

Hell, I didn't even give myself time to make a pro-con list about the guy. Or to run a background check. *What if he's a murderer or something?*

Swallowing thickly, I force myself to focus on Nathan again as he speaks.

"Honestly, I was a little shocked to see a woman as beautiful as you are on TapNext. Normally, they're…" He laughs a little, and my eyebrows draw together. He's trying to give me a compliment, I know he is, but I can't help but wonder where he was going with that statement about the rest of the female population. Sure, I never thought I'd end up on a dating app myself, but it's not because there's anything wrong with them. The problem is with me and how awkward I am.

Funny you should mention it, Soph, because I'm pretty sure you're being awkward right now.

Subtly, I shake my head to clear it of all my rambling thoughts and focus on my date again.

With jet-black hair and a strong jaw, he's not exactly hard to look at. And he's been nice, too. He pulled out my chair when we got to the table and asked me about my wine preferences before selecting a bottle. And he hasn't been staring at my breasts or anything any more than expected. All in all, he's been a gentleman. I don't have a whole lot of tingles or the urge to jump him immediately, but that could come with time. Obviously, I just need to get out of my own way here and let the date happen.

I clear my throat and force a smile to curve the corners of my lips upward. "Thank you."

"Did you just get out of a serious relationship, or…"

I shake my head. "No. I mean, I've dated, but no…I haven't been in a serious relationship in a while."

"That's interesting. Huh."

God, why does this have to be so hard? Why can't coming up with things to say be as easy as coming up with excuses to leave? Honestly, I've got a ton of those.

Hamster care.

Needy mother.

Cat with cancer.

Grease fire in my apartment.

Really, the list of excuses seems endless.

"What about you? Why haven't you settled down?"

He shrugs then, glancing over his shoulder briefly before coughing and looking back at me. "I just…wasn't ready until now. I've been more focused on my career."

My eyes widen with excitement. *Finally, something we can talk about.* "That's great. I'm really career-centric too. What is it that you do?"

"I'm a gamer."

"A gamer?"

"Yeah. You know, like on Twitch? I livestream and people watch."

I nod, though I don't know that I could do much else if I wanted. I was expecting something, I don't know, a little less isolated.

His business is about keeping people in their houses watching their computers all day, and mine is about getting them out. To parties, to events, to all manner of social engagements. Fucking hell, I feel like I just consumed a bag of lemons.

Coincidentally, another viable excuse.

"What about you?"

I swallow hard to stave off a sigh. This is like hearing from a fish about how great the ocean is and then having to tell them you hate water. "I have an event planning business. Sophie Sage Events." I wave my hand in front of my face. "We do all sorts of stuff all over the city. Private parties, corporate events, weddings. That sort of thing."

He nods, and I have to wonder if he's just about as put off by my career as I am by his. I mean, I'm not knocking it for everyone—I know these are the times. But "Professional Gamer" is *definitely* not on the list of qualities I've been envisioning for my husband since I could write in my diary, that's for sure.

"That's interesting," he says again, trying his best to be polite.

I nod again before picking my menu up in front of my face. Man, this is going to be a long night if I can't get some kind of grip on making this conversation flow.

"Excuse me," a chillingly familiar voice says from the side of our table, making my eyes widen as I pull my menu down tentatively. I peek just enough above the top to get a glimpse, and I nearly faint as a smiling *Jude, the Magic Dancer* catches my eyes at that very moment and winks. My stomach immediately flips over on itself with memories and unbidden excitement, but it's not long before it changes its tune. Attractive or not, seeing this guy here, right now, is *not* a good thing. At all.

Holy shit. What in the ever-loving hell is he doing here? my mind screams as the true panic starts to set in. *This wasn't on my list of excuses at all, so I don't think I'm manifesting stuff.*

I cough, choking slightly on the building saliva in my throat, and Jude reaches over to pat me on the back. Nathan's eyes narrow at the gesture, and I'll be damned if I can't blame him.

If I could just get the awkward choking under control, maybe I'd be able to wade into the brink with…some sort of explanation.

Not that I know what that would be at all. I don't think any version of *this guy stripped so well I spontaneously orgasmed* is going to help me here.

"I'm sorry to interrupt," Jude continues, glancing between me and my date. "I don't know either of you very well, but I couldn't help but come over and offer my congratulations."

Oh God. Noooo. No, no. This is even worse than I realized.

"Congratulations?" Nathan asks. "On what?"

Jude laughs, slapping my date on the back with a big old healthy dose of consequences he can't even begin to comprehend. "On the wedding. I met your lovely bride here just the other night, and she told me she was getting ready to tie the knot. I feel honored to get the chance to meet the lucky guy."

Nathan turns to me immediately, his neck contorting with a whole hell of a lot of *what the fuck.* "You're *married?*"

"Nathan," I hedge, trying to figure out how to explain this whole thing without making a scene. I'm not my sister like Jude thinks I am. Though, I was pretending to be her, to be fair. So, I am the woman Jude thinks I am, even though I'm not the woman who was getting married. Simple, right?

Nervous laughter spills from my lips suddenly, and fuck if that's not, like, the exact opposite thing I needed to happen right now.

Nathan scowls.

"Oh my God. I knew it was too good to be true…seeing a woman who looks like you on a dating app." He shoves back from the table, and I scramble to stand. Jude's head whips back and forth between us, his eyebrows at his hairline.

"Nathan, I'm sorry. You don't understand. I'm not—"

"Forget it. I'm out of here."

He tosses his napkin on the plate in front of him and heads for the entrance, his legs churning at full speed. The rest of the patrons eye me with contempt—having overheard enough details to consider themselves judge and jury—and my whole body shakes with anger and embarrassment.

This is a freaking disaster.

"I'm sorry. I didn't—" Jude seems a little stunned and tries to apologize, but my crazy train has already left the station, and the horn of embarrassment has already been blown. There's no turning back now, so I don't even bother checking myself before I lay into him at a less than respectable restaurant volume.

"You ruined it! I cannot believe you ruined my freaking date! Have you lost your mind? Why on earth would you think it was appropriate to come over here?"

"I'm genuinely sorry, Belle. I just wanted to offer my congratulations."

"Well, I'm not Belle, and you've officially fucked me. So, thanks. Can't tell you how much I appreciate it."

Wrinkles form between his brows as they pinch toward each other. "You're not Belle?"

"No!" I nearly shout. "I'm Sophie. Her twin."

"Oh Jesus. Shit. Fuckinggg hell, I'm sorry."

"Yeah, well. Sorry's not going to turn back time, now is it? The only woman who can make me feel like it's possible is Cher. And I don't see her here."

TEN

Jude

She grabs her purse from the top of the table and skirts it to the other side, glaring at me as she goes. Her hips sway with the speed of her walk, and everything about the motion turns me on.

Combine that with how much her unexpected Cher reference makes me want to laugh, and I'm a steamy pile of *ready to fuck.*

But I'm confused. My hormones are raging, spiked up on the kind of adrenaline I was desperate to tap into with this sister the night of the bachelorette party. This is the way her twin, Belle, made me feel. That's why I could have sworn it was her. But it's not her; it's Sophie. The *available* sister.

Well now, Jude. That's a horse of a different color.

"I'm sorry," I call after her softly, hastening my step to catch up to her and grabbing gently at her elbow. "Really."

She spins around to glare at me. "Your assumption just ruined my date."

"Yes," I say, taking all of the guilt without avoidance. That's the good part about being the fall guy in a family of five kids, I suppose. I don't shy away from responsibility, even if it's uncomfortable. "And I really apologize. It was incredibly rude of me to interrupt, even if you had been your sister. And inappropriate, I suppose, given how you know me. I don't know why I thought it was a good idea in the first place, but please, now that the damage is done, let me make it up to you."

"How exactly do you plan to do that?" she challenges. "My date is already gone, and the night is effectively over. Unless you've got a time machine in your pocket, I'd say things are pretty much screwed."

I squeeze my lips tightly in an effort not to laugh at her—because though she's definitely being funny, I doubt any kind of amusement is the response she's looking for—and hold up my hands in a semi-shrug.

"I don't have a time machine. I wish I did because that would be really fucking cool, but even without it, the night doesn't have to be over. He's gone, but he's not the only guy on the planet." I slam my palm into my chest. "Hell, I'm one, and I'm standing right here. Spend the rest of the date with me."

"That's not how this works! That's not how any of this works." She shakes her head and turns to leave again, walking with determination toward the front door. The urge to reach out and stop her again is strong, but I know it's not even remotely my right to touch her without permission either. My best bet is to try to keep up with her quickly churning legs and reason with her while we move.

"Why not?" I ask, positioning myself just off her flank as we climb the stairs to the main reception area of the restaurant. Heidi notices us, and her head tilts in concerned curiosity, but ultimately, she settles back behind the hostess stand when I glance back and offer a calm smile.

"Because you're not part of the plan."

"So?" I question. "Plans change. Things happen. And when they do, you make a new plan."

"A new plan that includes going on a date with you?" She scoffs. "How convenient."

"Yeah," I agree. "It is convenient. That's why you should do it. Give me a good reason why you shouldn't."

"Because you're an exot—" She shakes her head briefly, sucking her lips into her mouth, but the cat's already out of the bag and I already know what she was going to say.

Maybe, if I were *actually* an exotic dancer, I'd be offended—though, knowing me, probably not. But the fact that that's not even really what I do for a living only makes me want to beam.

"Ahh," I breathe. "Too good to go on a date with a *dancer*."

"No," she rushes to disagree, embarrassed. I almost have to laugh. She's on the defensive now, and I kind of like the feel of stalking my prey.

She digs in her purse for her phone—at least I presume that's what she's after—and her body shivers in the bristling cold air of the sidewalk without any real barrier against the wind.

"I think that's it. I think you're embarrassed to go on a date with someone like me," I challenge. At the same time, I work on pulling my own sport coat from my shoulders to place around hers since it seems she didn't have standing on the sidewalk in the middle of winter waiting on a ride in her carefully crafted plans either.

"No, I'm *not*."

I smile and hold up the coat as a peace offering, and she eyes it closely. There's hesitation, sure, but the overwhelming expression on her face is abject longing. And I don't blame her. It's fucking cold out here, and I'm not in a skimpy dress and heels.

Finally, she accepts it, giving me her back so I can set the coat across her tanned shoulders while she slips her arms into the sleeves. It drowns her delicate frame, but at the same time, it somehow seems made for her.

"Well, good. Now that we got that out of the way, there's nothing else to debate. Let me run back in and grab the rest of my stuff from the table, and then we can go."

"Go?" she asks, spinning around to face me. "Go where?"

"On our date."

"But you didn't even know you were going to see me tonight. How could you possibly have something planned?"

"I don't," I say with a shrug. "We're going to make it up as we go along."

"Great," she grumbles, and I laugh.

"Not one for spontaneity, huh?"

"No," she admits. "I can't say it's my strong suit."

"Well, then, stick with me. Because I'm a pro."

While I made a quick trip back inside to leave money on my table—*and Sophie's*—and grab my belongings, I enlisted Heidi to keep an eye on my new date to make sure she didn't escape. Once everything was all set, the two of us stepped back outside into the blustery weather, this time with Sophie sporting not only my sport jacket, but my overcoat, too.

It was cold as shit without having anything to protect against the wind, but she needed it more than me, far and away.

Plus, I hailed a cab pretty quickly with a whistle and a wave, and now I'm perfectly toasty in the slightly stale air of a New York City taxi.

"Did you say Raines Law Room?" Sophie asks after I sit back into the seat and turn to face her. The fact that she's skeptical enough of me to eavesdrop on my conversation with the cabbie makes me smile. I might be the type to toy with my women every once in a while, but at the end of the day, there's nothing sexier than a woman with a brain.

And a woman who takes a personal interest in her own safety, no matter how trustworthy the guy may actually be, is a smart woman.

"I did," I confirm easily, not wanting to keep her on edge. "Have you been there before?"

She shakes her head once, glances out her window and away from me momentarily, and then turns back. "I haven't. I've heard of it from a couple clients, but even in all the years I've lived here, I've never been."

"How long have you lived here?"

She laughs a little, licking her lips and blushing. "Twenty-nine years."

"And how old are you?"

"Twenty-eight and a half," she says comically, and a chuckle spills from my throat.

"Okay, you're going to have to explain that one."

Her face is beautifully confident, lifting and crinkling in all the right places as she elucidates. "My parents made the trek from Miami to New York when my mom was a few months pregnant with Belle and me so my dad could take a job in the ironworkers union."

I laugh. "So, your first six months in New York were as a fetus."

She nods.

"I have to admit, I've met a hell of a lot of people in this city over the years and listened to all manner of stories about how they came to be here, but yours might be the best I've ever heard. At least in the category of delivery."

She beams, and my chest tightens noticeably. She's so goddamn sexy, I can hardly stand myself around her. I just wish I could understand what flipped the switch in my body so hard from her sister to her.

She *seems* like she's Belle, but I'm no expert in telling twins apart.

Still, feelings of self-doubt niggle, and I can't help but make one final apology.

"I really am sorry that I mistook you for your sister. I…I don't know what it was that made me feel so certain you were her." I shrug. "You both have this freckle," I explain, reaching out and touching her neck gently, right above her collarbone. "I noticed it on Belle the other night, but I didn't realize you had the same one."

Newly attuned to her neck, I find it impossible not to notice that her pulse is thrumming at double a normal speed.

She's nervous or anxious or excited, and her eyes hold a secret I can't even begin to discern.

I only wish I had the power to read a woman's mind.

We pull to a stop in front of the completely nondescript entrance to one of the most famous speakeasies in New York, and I pass the cabbie some money and then turn for the handle of the door.

But just as I'm about to pull it, her hand comes down on my forearm.

"What is it?" I ask softly. I have no idea what she's got to say, but for some reason, I can't wait to find out.

ELEVEN

Sophie

My heart pounds, and the heat of his arm bleeds into the palm of my hand.

I cannot fucking believe he noticed such a subtle difference between Belle and me, and beyond that, remembers it weeks later.

None of the men I've ever dated has been able to tell us apart, and this practical stranger knows me for me, down to the fucking freckle on my neck.

I have to tell him.

"What is it?" he asks again when my terror robs me of the ability of speech.

I shake my head to clear it, squeeze his arm, and then pull my hand back like it's been burned when I feel a jolt of *something* between us.

I mean, what the hell is it with this guy that turns my body into a live wire?

"I…well, I guess I have a bit of a confession to make. I *am* Sophie, obviously, and Belle *did* get married, but at the bachelorette party at Club Craze…I *was* Belle. I mean, I was pretending to be." I shrug as his eyes widen. "Yeah, I'm sorry. But she freaked out when we got in there about being the center of attention all night and, well, you dancing for her, so she forced me to pretend to be her." I wince. "So, yeah. That's probably why you thought I was Belle…because that night…" I shrug again. "I was."

"Well, *shit.*"

I nod and wince again. "I'm sorry. But the whole freckle thing?" I wave a hand in the general vicinity of my throat. "That was pretty impressive. Sometimes my own dad has trouble telling us apart, so really, props to you there."

He smiles then, shaking his head quickly before turning back to his door and climbing out of the cab. My shoulders fall with defeat as I picture him walking up the block and disappearing around the corner.

I wouldn't blame the guy. I made him think he was crazy, and then shamed him for being an exotic dancer, and then practically obligated him to take me on a date—

"Oh!" I squeal as my door unexpectedly opens beside me, a wave of cold air rushing in from the busy sidewalk.

Jude leans down into the open door and smiles at me. "Are you coming?"

"I…" I pause, looking him in the eyes. "You're not mad?"

He chuckles. "Are you kidding? I'm fucking thrilled. I'm not crazy, for one. And for two, now I can scrub the idea that I got a little too flirtatious with a soon-to-be-married woman from my conscience. I'm ecstatic. My family will be relieved. My sister, especially, will be overjoyed with the news."

I stumble to make sense of everything he's saying, and my heart kicks up in my chest. "You told your family about me?"

He shrugs. "It's a little weird, but I assure you it wasn't in any kind of detail. Very informal conversation, really."

"You have a sister?" I ask, to which he laughs uproariously. "What?"

"I really love that you're curious, babe. And I'll be happy to answer your questions. But, uh, do you think maybe you want to let this nice guy pick up another fare while we go inside the bar?"

Whoops. Way to go, Soph.

My cheeks heat with embarrassment, but Jude doesn't say anything else. Rather, he reaches down with his hand to take my own, helps me from the taxi, and walks me inside.

The lighting is low, but the ambiance is high. The furniture is all carefully selected to look appropriately from the twenties, and all the barstools but two are taken. I'm impressed that they manage to pull this many people into a location that's not obvious, but apparently, I'm one of the only people in New York who hasn't gotten with the secret.

"This place is amazing," I say, already envisioning half a dozen different events I could utilize the space for. "Do you know if they do private events?"

Jude laughs, turning to me and stopping so abruptly that I actually run into his side. It's awkward, but his smile is enough to disarm me from completely crumbling. "I'm sorry, but are you working or dating right now?"

I shrug as the corner of my mouth curls up. "I'm self-employed, baby. No matter what else is happening, I'm always working."

He chuckles, nodding with understanding and turning back to walk toward the bar again, taking my hand in his. It's such a simple and fanfareless gesture, and yet, my whole nervous system is acting like it did not get the memo.

Geez, chill. He's just holding your hand.

"I admire your work ethic, Sophie. Now, I have an assumption, but I still feel like it's always best to ask… What is it that you do for a living?"

I smile proudly. "I have an event planning business. Sophie Sage Events. My company actually planned my sister's bachelorette party and wedding."

He smiles as he carves out a spot at the bar for us, pretty effortlessly getting another couple to scoot down a bit so that we can sit together and seeing that I get seated on my stool before taking his own spot on his.

I pull his jackets off my shoulders, and he takes them both before I can even question what to do with them, snaps his fingers at someone at the front, and then, *voilà!* The jackets are gone.

"Does that guy work here, or is that your idea of charity work?" I can't help but tease as Jude turns back to face the bar.

As expected, he takes it good-naturedly. "Robbie's been here a few years, and he knows me. He'll label those as mine and put them in the coat check."

I hum. "So, you know a lot of people in this city, don't you?"

His smile is bright and damn near hypnotizing, it's so sexy. "I do."

"Interesting."

"That's me," he agrees. "Interesting."

I roll my eyes with a snort.

"What? You don't believe me?" He narrows his eyes playfully. "A *dancer* can't know people?"

I shake my head and open my mouth to apologize for being rude when the bartender stops in front of us. "Hey, Jude," he says first, reaching across the bar to give my unplanned date a fist bump. Jude turns to me and waggles his eyebrows, and I have to laugh.

"Hey, Gavin. I'll have my usual, and Sophie will have…"

My teeth are the most prominent feature of my mouth as I try to look amicable while not having a freaking clue what to order. Gavin and Jude both have the good manners to ignore just how odd it is.

"Not sure what to get?" Jude asks sweetly, and I shake my head. "Mind if I choose something for you?"

"Please," I agree with relief.

"Bring her the same as me," he says to Gavin, to which the friendly bartender replies, "You got it," with a nod and a smile.

Once he's retreated from in front of us, I venture, "So…what drink am I getting? You never said what your usual is."

"An old-fashioned," Jude answers. "You can't do a speakeasy without having an old-fashioned."

I nod. "Makes sense."

Once Gavin returns with our drinks, we spend the next half hour chatting about mostly nothing but laughing quite a bit along the way. Jude's attitude is seriously pleasant, and as far as I can tell, it's not an act at all.

He genuinely seems to be the kind of guy who grins all day long.

"So, what other secret tricks do you know in this city?" I ask, finishing the last of my old-fashioned, which has turned out to be surprisingly tasty for someone like me who doesn't drink a whole lot. "Are you in a gang? Do you have a secret lair?" I narrow my eyes. "Are you Batman?"

Jude shakes his head, his throat rolling deliciously with humor at the same time. "No lair of my own. But…" he hedges, leaning closer to me. "I do know of another, even more clandestine part of New York that branches off of this place. Do you want to see it?"

"Are you kidding? Is that a real question?"

Climbing up and off his stool, he holds out his hand for mine. "Come with me."

I follow, obviously, because he hasn't let me down tonight so far, and because… Well, frankly, I can't even imagine ending the night right now.

Maybe Dr. Winters was right about not prejudging people—because Jude, the Magic Dancer is a hell of a lot of fun.

Back through the front of the bar, we turn down a dark hallway where only a bright exit sign illuminates the space at the end.

My heart picks up its pace, a lifetime of survival instincts screaming at me that going down a dark hallway with a stranger isn't a great idea, but for all the doubts I have, my legs keep moving.

I'm too invested. Plus, people here obviously know Jude, and they seem to like him. I know nothing is absolute, but I feel like the risk factor is at least a modicum lower than it could be.

I squeeze tight on to his hand as we approach the door, and he bangs on it one time with a loud, unmistakable blow.

It takes a few seconds, but when it swings open, a big, muscled guy and a velvet curtain block the view of what lies beyond.

"Jude," the bouncer-type guy says, his smile blindingly white and authentic.

"Do you know *everyone* in New York?" I ask sarcastically into Jude's ear.

He turns back toward me, whispering cheekily, "Not everyone. I didn't know you."

"Hey, Jimmy," Jude says then, greeting the bouncer with yet another fist bump. "Okay if we go inside?"

"Sure thing," the man replies, pulling the curtain back for us.

And I have to admit, for as secretive as I knew this place was going to be, I'm still surprised when I get a look at what it actually is.

It's dark and pulsing and immediately ripe with sexiness. It's the kind of place that makes your stomach heavy and your knees weak, just by walking inside.

Couples litter the deep-cushioned sofas along the walls, their bodies intertwined with each other like ivy vines. They don't know of anyone else's existence but themselves and their partners, and it's the same for each and every set of them.

Okay. This is the super-sexy secret part of this club, and by God, I don't know if I'm fully prepared for it.

My heart knocks in my chest, thumping like a speeding train on an old set of tracks. Jude takes my hand in his, his grip sound and steadying, and pulls me toward the other side of the room where neon-trimmed windows feature scantily clad women dancing to the beat of the pulsing music.

I watch them closely, trying to tap into the tiny, minute part of myself that enjoys the unexpected. It's not huge, but it *does* exist. I mean, I'm not a total prude.

I tighten my fingers around Jude's hand reflexively when the woman in the center window looks directly at me and licks her lips, and he responds by pulling me closer to him with a gentle tug, and places a comforting arm around my hip as we continue to walk.

I don't know what it is about him that makes me feel like he's my ground wire, but for all I know, in this situation, it could just be that he's familiar.

He walks us to the bar, squeezing my hip before releasing it, and orders us a couple of drinks. And the bartender smiles at him knowingly, as though this is far from his first time in this place, too.

I spin around to take in the room again, completely unable to quench my curiosity.

Jude's lips skim the side of my neck as he leans in to whisper in my ear. "You okay?"

I swallow hard as I nod. I am. Really. I'm nervous as hell, but I have to admit, I'm also kind of enjoying it. This is so far out of my normal, I almost feel like I'm having an out-of-body experience.

"Good."

Unexpectedly, he kisses the skin directly under my ear, grazing the flesh with the very tip of his tongue. I shiver, and my abdomen pulsates with the heaviness of arousal.

I swear, I'm close enough to coming without any actual stimulation again that I almost throw myself on the ground.

What is it about him that sends me right over the cliff so quickly?

"Come on," he prompts, lifting two drinks that he's procured for us in the air. "Let's go sit down."

I follow him dutifully, unwilling to stay here alone with all that's going on around us, and slide into a deep, plush, velvet-covered sofa in the corner. Jude follows, setting our drinks on the table in front of us, and leans back to hook his arm over the back of the couch, somewhat around my shoulders.

I shiver again, and this time, he notices.

"Are you cold?"

I shake my head. The truth is, I'm anything but. I'm on fucking *fire*.

TWELVE

Jude

Four hours we spent together tonight in the bowels of one of New York's sexiest underground clubs, and I'm so ready for sexual contact I could snap. Touching, teasing, taunting, we've essentially been challenging each other to a duel—who can drive the other to distraction the most without making contact.

Aside from the small flick of my tongue against her neck, I've done nothing but *suggest* the power of our arousal, and she's done the same.

We haven't kissed. We haven't fucked. Hell, I haven't even rubbed my hand up the skin of her thigh.

As a result, my nuts feel as if they're going to explode.

She turns the key in the lock on her door, and I hear the click of the bolt as it disengages with the jamb. I watch the line of her throat closely, observing as her perfect little freckle vibrates up and down with the zing of her excitement.

She swings open the door, gesturing for me to step inside first, and I don't bother with objecting to the offer. Seeing as this is her place, I don't imagine she's going to lock me inside and take off, destination unknown.

I nearly laugh at myself, but frankly, I'm too far gone in my need to fuck her until she can't breathe to give it any real energy.

She steps inside behind me, closing the door, and I take the opportunity to survey the space.

Her apartment is roomy for New York, with a separate kitchen, living room, and an actual hall that leads to a couple other doors that I assume are for bedrooms. It's comfortable and girlie, and when I turn back and see her standing awkwardly at the kitchen counter while I appraise her place, that only makes it better.

"Do you, um, want something to drink?" she asks, shifting herself from one foot to the other and then turning to the cabinet behind her to pull out a glass.

I cross the room toward her, grabbing her by the hips and pulling her back against me. She gasps at the unexpected contact—and likely, the feel of my hard cock as it presses into the crack of her ass—and drops the glass to the counter with a clang.

Thankfully, it doesn't break.

I shake my head behind her, sneaking my lips around to the shell of her ear. "The only thing I'm thirsty for…*is you.*"

"Oh God," she breathes in reply, her entire body starting to tremble.

"I plan to fuck you so good you won't walk straight in the morning," I tell her, nipping at the line of her throat beneath her ear. "Are you all right with that, Sophie?"

She nods, the air from her lungs coming out in sharp, distinct pants.

"I need you to say it aloud, baby."

"Y-yes," she manages shakily.

Spinning her quickly, I grab her by the hips and lift her onto the counter, sliding my hands to grip the backs of her bare thighs.

She gasps, and I pounce on the opportunity to put my mouth to hers.

She tastes sweetly of alcohol and those fucking cherries she taunted me with toward the end of the evening.

"Mm," I hum directly into her mouth, moving one of my hands to the back of her head and sinking it into the long brown tresses.

She moans, and I grip the strands and pull, exposing the long line of her perfect throat.

"I might be rough the first time, Sophie. Can you handle that?"

She nods and then quickly voices her answer too, clearly a fast learner. "Yes."

Shoving my hands under her ass, I lift her off the counter, and our next destination is simple—*her bed.*

We'll save the adventure of the kitchen counter and the shower and all the places that require some acrobatics for the second and third rounds. For this one, I just need room to work.

I walk quickly down the hallway while she takes control of the kissing, pausing briefly at the first door I come to until she groans and shakes her head, throwing an arm back behind herself to point to the end of the hall.

"That one," she mumbles against my mouth, making me grin.

Resuming course, I travel the rest of the hallway and turn the knob to open her door, pulling my head away for just a moment to get a lay of the land in the room.

The last thing I want to do is trip and take us both down in a heap.

Her bed is just as I'd expect from the rest of the apartment, girlie and dainty with a deep-purple comforter and white-tufted throw pillows. There's a plush white blanket tossed across the bottom of the bed as well, but as soon as I get close enough, I drop her down on her back and shove the loose blanket out of the way.

She scurries up the mattress some in a modified crab walk, and I don't hesitate to follow her right in.

She lies back, her hair fanning out on her pillow, and her knees come up as she places her feet on the bed.

As I shove her thighs apart, her dress slides farther up her hips, and I close my mouth over the thin scrap of lace she's using to cover the promised land and suck. Her back arches, and the most amazing taste hits my tongue.

"Mmm," I moan against her, making her head thrash back and forth.

Her skin is tanned and silky-smooth, but I know immediately I can't yet see enough of it.

I need her bare.

Roughly, I grab the straps of lace at the sides of her hips and pull, scooting the thin thong material down her legs and out of sight with a toss over my shoulder.

She moans, and I put my mouth back to her, this time without anything in between.

Fucking hell, she tastes good.

Up and out, her knees spread to give me better access, and I groan my approval. Too many women do *the clench* when I go down on them, scared to fully let themselves go in the moment. But there's nothing sexier than a woman who knows how much a man loves to lick her pussy and owns it.

Scooting my hands under her ass, I bring her closer to my mouth and eat like a man starved.

She gasps, breathing harder and harder and harder until a gush of deliciousness hits my tongue.

I drink all her goodness down until she stops shaking, and only then do I roll onto my back, shove my pants down, grab a condom out of my pocket, sheath myself, and reach for her.

Swiveling her hips, I position her on top, those glorious thighs of her straddling my hips, and feed myself inside her, inch by inch.

Her pussy clenches and her body shakes with adrenaline, and I have to close my eyes briefly because it all feels so fucking good.

"Come on, baby," I tell her. "Show me what you can do. Your turn to have fun."

She bites the flesh of her bottom lip with her straight white teeth and closes her eyes as she lifts up gently and sets herself back down.

I reach for her face, grazing her cheek with the pad of my thumb. "Keep your eyes open. I want to look at you."

The green of her irises sparkles with indecision and insecurity as she follows my command, and I immediately soften my voice.

"Go fast, go slow. Whatever you want, Sophie. And I promise, whatever you do, it won't be wrong."

She nods slowly and then lets her head fall back until the tips of her long brown hair skim the tops of my thighs. It's the most intoxicating sensation.

Slowly, she moves up, letting me fall from her center slowly, and then sinks down, in one smooth stroke that nearly robs me of the ability to think at all. She's sexy as hell, that much I knew, but this unexpected level of shyness is a turn-on I never knew existed.

"That's it," I encourage. "Take me how you want me."

Bolstered by my words, she moves up and down again, this time taking me a little faster and harder. Her ass puts just the right amount of pressure on my balls during her downstroke and makes me groan.

"Goddamn, you're sexy. Again, baby. Do it again."

Up and down, up and down, slowly, ever so slowly, she builds both confidence and a rhythm that drives me crazy. I don't know if it's the fact that it's been a few weeks since I've fucked or what, but goddamn, does she feel good.

Grasping her hips, I hold on tight as she rides me, swirling her hips and licking her lips while her tits bounce beneath her slinky dress.

Damn. Sophie Sage is hot as fuck.

My pulse pounds and my ears start to ring as my climax climbs to escape from my dick.

"Faster, Soph," I coach her, knowing she's on the brink of coming again and wanting so badly to make sure she does it before I do.

"Oh God," she whimpers, her head dropping back as the wave of pleasure starts to roll over her. "Oh God, oh God, oh *God!*" she yells then, her tits bouncing so deliciously during her frenzy that I know, without a doubt, they have to be the next thing I taste.

"Yeah, Sophie, come," I beg, feeling my toes curl involuntarily with impending orgasm.

Finally, she lets go, dropping her chest forward and onto me, and my own climax hits me so hard, I swear to everything holy, I think I see stars.

Our breathing is ragged and our skin is flushed, and still, all I can think about is having her again.

"Next round," I say softly, "you're going to be naked and riding my cock in the shower."

THIRTEEN

Tuesday, March 6th

Sophie

My legs feel like lead and my arms are sore, and opening my eyes feels as though I'm doing it under a heavy blanket. It takes me a minute to come into any kind of awareness, but once I do, memories hit me with a vengeance.

I'm tired, I'm sated, and *holy hot sex*, I cannot believe all the things that happened last night.

Scouring the sheets next to me with tentative fingers, I hope with all my might that this doesn't have to be super awkward. I mean, we're adults, right? So what if we got a little wild and spent the night together without me even knowing his last name?

It's not a big deal.

It's *not* a big deal.

Holy aching vageen, this is kind of a big deal.

Let's be real here. This isn't something I typically do. I'm not a casual dater, and I'm sure as hell not the woman who brings an exotic dancer to her house and *sleeps* with him.

Cripes. And now I have to get this guy out of here. Plus, he knows where I live!

When the sweep of my arm is unsuccessful in making contact, I squeeze my eyes shut tight one last time before releasing them. The light of my room is stagnant, the sun clearly having made its ascent into the sky a while ago. Tentatively, I turn my gaze from the window to the bed, but instead of hard, muscled flesh and the smell of man, all I find are the slightly rumpled remnants of his sleep spot.

My eyebrows draw together, and I shove up to sitting. My heart starts to pound involuntarily in my chest.

Did he leave? Or is he just, like, in the bathroom or something?

The door to my en suite bath is partially shut, so I lean almost comically in that direction and redirect all my focus to my ears. They ring with the effort to catch any sort of minuscule noises, effectively blocking out the possibility of *actually* hearing them.

Frustrated, I sigh and climb from the bed, stumbling a little when I realize just how raw I feel. My legs are fucking bowed, I think.

I rub at the top of my full feeling vagina, and my stomach flips over on itself with misspent excitement. I don't know how she can even be considering taking another ride on the freaking baton-sized schlong from last night, but evidently, she's got her own set of priorities.

Carefully, I waddle-walk over to the bathroom door, leaning into the jamb with my hand and listening intently. When twenty seconds go by without any noise, I push the door open.

Nothing. Only an empty bathroom and a sex-shower that now mocks me.

I turn immediately, stalking down the hallway as much as my aching kitty will let me, slamming the bedroom door behind me as I go.

Even the hall mocks me with her memories of the dirty things that occurred there, and I wrinkle my face into an expression of disgust.

"Shut up," I tell the slutty hallway as I set foot into the living room.

I wish I could say I don't jump out of my skin when the hallway answers, "I didn't say anything." But I do.

"Cripes!" I yell on a shriek, noticing my sister Belle sitting at my kitchen table like she belongs here. "What are you doing here?"

Belle glances up from the newspaper, shrugs, and then scoops up a bite of cereal—my cereal—and shoves it into her mouth. "Eating," she says then, the word garbled slightly around Frosted Flakes.

"Yes, I can see that. But why are you doing it in *my* apartment?"

She shrugs again. "What's that supposed to mean? I've lived here for years."

"No. You *used* to live here, and then you married a guy named John—not sure if you remember him—and you moved out."

"Trust me, I know. But living with a boy is weird sometimes. Like, he's got a penis, you know?"

I snort. "Seeing as you're a straight woman, I kind of thought that was a selling point."

It sure as hell sold my soul to the one-night-stand devil last night.

"Yeah. I don't know how to explain it."

She goes back to reading and eating cereal like our conversation is done, and I'm so flabbergasted—and likely volatile thanks to having been snuck out on by Sir Sex-a-Lot—I smack her spoon right out of her hand, and it goes clanking to the floor.

"Hey!" she shrieks. "What did you do that for?"

"Where does John even think you are? Does he know you're delusional?"

Belle rolls her eyes. "He thinks I'm running."

"Has he even met you?"

My sister Belle may be skinny, but in her case, it's entirely genetic. I swear she's allergic to exercise.

"I told him I was on a new kick. It's no big deal, geez."

I let out an annoyed groan and head straight for the coffeepot. I don't have the energy to get into all the things wrong with this. I mean, I know she and John have their own relationship and shit, but does she really think lying to him right out of the gate is a good idea?

Dr. Winters would have a field day with this.

Actually, she'd probably tell you to stay in your own lane and ask yourself why you're so bothered this morning, of all mornings.

Almost as if she can read my mind, Belle fires back with twin-style mirror attitude. "What's your deal this morning anyway? You seem super crabby."

I stick out my tongue as I sit down at the table across from her with my coffee cup and sigh.

I *really* don't want to get into all the details of this whole thing just yet. Not only is the sting of rejection a little too fresh, but there's also a whole backstory with my therapist and her dating assignment that will undoubtedly cause some sort of a shit fit from my sister when she finds out I've been hiding my therapy appointments from her.

Thankfully, my house phone rings in a timely distraction, sending Belle into a whole other tirade. This one, however, is one I'm prepared to handle.

"What…what is that?"

I shake my head and shrug innocently as the phone continues to ring.

"Did you hook that thing back up?" Belle interrogates, jumping up from her seat.

"I don't know what you're talking about," I deny, just as my old-school answering machine picks up and starts to play my outgoing message.

"Hi, you've reached Sophie. I'm not here right now, or I am and I'm busy, but feel free to leave me a message and I'll get back to you." BEEEP.

"Oh my God, you dirty skank! I'm barely out of here, and you've already got that fucking thing hooked back up!" Belle yells.

I widen my eyes innocently as our sister Katelynn comes over the speaker. *"Hey, hooker. Call me back. I'd call your cell, but my little shits are already tearing my house apart as we speak, so I don't have the time. Byeeee."*

"Sophie!" Belle snips again. "I want an explanation."

I shake my head with a laugh. "You don't live here anymore, Belly. That means I can have whatever outdated technology I want, and you can't stop me."

"You're helpless."

I shrug. "I like it. So, sue me."

"You know, maybe I will," Belle says with narrowed eyes as she pours herself another cup of coffee. "John's got this lawyer friend I could talk to."

I snort.

Belle stalks back over to the table and sits down again, picking up her newspaper and opening it so dramatically it sends a crack through the air.

I shake my head behind the thin paper wall she's formed and take another sip of the sacred bean juice.

"Oh my gosh," Belle says suddenly, the change in her tone of voice catching my attention. Whatever it is, it seems unrelated to our tiff.

"What?"

"Isn't this the guy who danced at my bachelorette party?"

Immediately, all the hair on my body stands on end and my vagina spasms. *Isn't what the guy? Is his underwear somewhere or something?*

Frantic, I look around the room nonsensically, trying to find some sort of article that's given away the fact that I slept with Jude last night. The notion is preposterous—this isn't the kind of thing that's easily deduced with hints like an episode of goddamn *Blue's Clues*, but I'm nervous as all get-out.

"Look," Belle finally says, seemingly ignoring my mental breakdown and shaking the paper. "Here. In the paper."

"What?" I shriek, ripping the thin sheets from her hands and flipping them around to look.

Recognition hits me like a sock in the damn gut.

There, dead center and larger-than-life, Jude's smiling face looks back at me, his full body shot showing him at ease and confident in a blue-gray suit with his hands tucked across his chest.

He looks drop-dead gorgeous and then some, and a sick twist in my stomach makes me feel a little like I'm going to throw up. Seeing him like this, the morning of his sneak-out after the hottest sex of my life?

This is a cruel one, even for a bitch like fate.

Agitated, I scour the article for pertinent information as quickly as I can.

Club Promoter Jude Winslow Brings Fresh Fun Back to Manhattan, the title reads.

After nearly a year of renovations on the old SoHo building, Jude Winslow says Club Craze is the next big thing in New York. "This is a place where people are going to line up to come," Winslow said. "We've done some soft openings already, and the response has been amazing."

This weekend, Winslow will close the club to the public again, welcoming the most elite private events specialists in the world for a marketing event. "The idea is to get some exclusive clientele interested in having their next big party here. It's the perfect location, and I'm going to make sure they know about it," Winslow explained.

I drop the paper and sink back down into my chair, a starkly stunned expression on my face.

Well, at least you know his last name now.

"That's him, right?" Belle asks, before narrowing her eyes on me to survey me closely. "Why do you look as if you've seen a ghost?"

I shake my head a couple times, silently of course, since words completely escape me, and she eventually moves on.

The weird thing about being as closely bonded as we are, is that, sometimes, that means not reacting to the strange behavior that sets off red flags. We are each other's safe havens of space and understanding.

"Wild," she says then with a snort. "I guess Jude, the Magic Dancer isn't just a dancer after all, huh?"

I shake my head.

I guess not.

FOURTEEN

Jude

Tossing the remote down on the coffee table after shutting off the Knicks game, I walk into the kitchen and over to the counter where I'd put my phone on charge a couple hours ago. It's been going crazy with messages ever since the fourth quarter started, but fuck if I was going to miss the Nets getting their asses handed to them.

The sun glows through my floor-to-ceiling living room windows on its descent into the Lower Manhattan skyline. With a colorful abundance of nightlife and bars, SoHo is a natural fit for me and my lifestyle and has been since I moved to this apartment five years ago. It took a little while to afford a place this nice—and certain milestones in my career like stepping out from under Cruz Nightlife and into a leadership role at my own promotional firm—but I now live more than comfortably.

I pull the phone off the plug and scroll into the messages, and the running chat with my siblings is at the top of the list. I tap the screen to open it and read through what they've said.

Winnie: Hey, guys. Just wanted to let you know that we're going to do family night at seven this Friday instead of at six. Lex has Mathletes practice, and I want to make sure I have time to get home and get dinner started.

Remy: Does it help if I pick her up for you, Win?

Ty: Oh, look out. Remy the suck-up has entered the chat.

Remy: Fuck you, dude. Don't take your insecurities about being an inferior uncle out on me.

Ty: Excuse me? I'm the fucking greatest. And I'm a professor. Lexi relates to my intellect.

Flynn: You're not even in the neighborhood, dude. In all honesty, you're probably in fourth place.

Winnie: LOL

Instantly annoyed, I type out a message with hostile fingers. I don't mind spending my time alone, but fuck if I haven't been in a funk for the last day or so. It's weird, and I don't know how to explain it. But time with my family always pulls me out of shit like this.

Me: Why do you fuckers always make family nights happen on the weekends? You know I work every Thursday, Friday, Saturday, and Sunday night.

Ty: Sounds like you just answered your own question, bro.

Me: Wow. I didn't know I had a turncoat for a brother. And after all the time we've spent together over the years.

Winnie: I'm sorry, Jude. It's just much easier for me to cook on Friday or Saturday nights during the off-season. I'll go back to including you when I'm working weekends too.

Fuck that. I'm just as much a part of this family as anyone else. It's not like I need to see them all weekly, but it might be nice. Immediately, I click to open a new message and start entering contacts—all the same, minus my beautiful sister. I feel a little bad cutting her out like that, but it's a necessary evil in this case.

Me: Okay, fuckers. I'm going to Winnie's house tonight for family dinner. Who's going?

Remy: Did you not read that last message where Winnie expressly told you it wasn't happening tonight?

Flynn: I'm not sure Jude reads.

Me: I don't. At least, not well. No WoNdEr I GoT cOnFuSeD aBoUt WhIcH nIgHt tO cOmE.

Ty: Winnie's going to fucking murder you, Gen Z sarcasm typing or not.

Me: I'm not a complete assmunch. Winnie said it's easier for her to cook on the weekends. She didn't say anything about it being easier if she didn't cook. I'll go by the store, grab some shit, and you fuckers can help me cook while she relaxes.

Remy: You don't know how to cook.

Me: True. But you and Flynn will be there to supervise.

Ty: I'm pretty sure when Jude says "supervise," he means you'll be there to do all the work.

Me: Shut up, Ty. I'm going to help. Plus, I'm going to get all the groceries. What are YOU doing?

Ty: Oh, me? I'll be helping Winnie hide your body.

Me: Bring extra tape and garbage bags. You know I'm SWOLE as a motherfucker.

Flynn: Eh, what the hell. What time are you getting there?

Ty: Are you serious, Flynn? Aren't you supposed to be the voice of reason?

Flynn: Says the man who's talking about hiding bodies.

Ty: Whatever, dude. I'll help Win bury you both.

Remy: I'll be there at seven.

Ty: You too??

Me: Fuck yes. That's what I like to hear, boys. See you then.

Plan successfully achieved, I click out of my messages, shove my phone into my pocket, grab my keys off the hook, and head out the door. One quick stop at the grocery store and then Uptown to my sister's house.

It's fifteen minutes before seven, and I'm not at all expected, but I ring the doorbell anyway and stand back and wait to be greeted.

I figured the least I could do for my two eldest brothers in appreciation of their loyalty was to show up first, help Winnie get over her initial anger, and welcome them with open arms and smooth sailing upon their arrival.

The light on the porch flicks on above me, and I plaster on my most charming of smiles.

There's a slight squeak as the door swings open, and Wes's face stutters to a scowl as soon as he sees me. I don't let it discourage me, though. People glower at me all the time, to be honest, and I don't give a shit. I'm not about to start now.

"Wes!" I greet cheerfully, holding my sack of groceries up and out to the side. "How are you, bro?"

"What the hell are you doing here, Jude?"

"What do you mean?"

"I know my wife told you that family night is on Friday."

"She did," I agree, stepping forward and crowding him out of the doorway so I can step inside. It's a bit of a dick move, and on any normal day, Wes Lancaster could do some damage to me if he wanted to, but I'm counting on the element of surprise to throw him off his game. "And then I responded that I'm unavailable and that I'd like to reschedule."

I shrug, turning back to look at him from my place inside the front hallway, having successfully infiltrated behind his line of defense.

"Jude—"

"Thanks so much, Wes," I say in avoidance. "But I think I can handle carrying everything."

There's not a snowball's chance in hell that offering to help me with the groceries is even remotely close to what was about to come out of Wes's mouth, but that doesn't matter. What matters is that I beat him to the punch.

Lexi appears at the bottom of the staircase, spotting me easily as I pass her by and immediately questioning my presence. "Uncle Jude? What are you doing here?"

"Making dinner," I say, smiling and waggling my eyebrows. "I got all the stuff for your favorite."

"Spaghetti?" she asks hopefully, and I nod.

"You bastard," Wes mutters under his breath, and I can't stop myself from looking back at him and winking. I may be the goofball of the Winslow clan, but that doesn't mean I'm a fool. The way to the heart is always with food, and the best heart to infiltrate is the one the others can't stand to deny. *That of their beautiful baby girl.*

Continuing into the kitchen, I find Winnie at the counter, looking through takeout menus intently. She glances up at the sound of my entrance, spots the bag of groceries, and damn near growls.

"You've *got* to be kidding me."

"Now, now," I soothe, setting the bags on the counter and raising my hands in the air defensively. "I know this looks bad, but I promise I heard you about the cooking. I don't expect you to cook at all, I swear."

"And who's going to? You?" She does a half scoff, half laugh that doesn't really offend me in the slightest. I'm definitely not the chef in the family, but I'm a single dude and I survive. So, whatever.

I shake my head. "I called in reinforcements."

"What are—" she starts to ask, just as the front doorbell rings again.

Winnie narrows her eyes. "You think you're so clever, don't you?"

I shrug and stretch my neck forward like an ostrich. "I mean…I don't think I'm *not* clever."

"Uncle Jude brought the stuff for spaghetti," Lexi says factually, having finally found an opening to add her opinion.

Winnie glowers, and I practically rub my hands together with glee.

"Just look at it this way," I say. "Now, you don't have to order takeout and you don't have to cook and Lex gets to have her favorite food. All around, I'd say this is a win, *Win*."

She tosses annoyed eyes at my pun, but personally, I think it was pretty damn cute.

When Wes returns from the door, Remy, Flynn, and Ty are all behind him, looking nearly as satisfied as I am. There's also a random woman, whom I can only assume is Ty's flavor of the day.

I only have eyes for the youngest brother of the three, though. The traitor. "I thought you weren't coming," I accuse pointedly, taking a seat on one of the stools at the Lancaster kitchen island.

Ty gives me the finger. "It wasn't my idea, but I wasn't going to be the only asshole out." He pulls a twine-tied package out from behind his back and smiles. "Plus, Flynn drove me by the bakery."

"Cannoli?" I ask hopefully.

"And chocolate chip and almond cookies."

Well, hot damn. Food, family, and cannoli.

Today started in one hell of a funk—*that I haven't been able to explain*—but my mood should be back to normal in no time.

FIFTEEN

Sophie

My cab swerves to a stop in front of the Mandarin Oriental in Columbus Circle, and I accidentally tap my forehead on the plexiglass divider between the driver and me, I'm so eager to hand over his money and get out.

He looks at me sideways a little, but I don't linger. Not only would that worsen the embarrassment, but I'm already running horrendously late to set up for an important corporate event. So late, that my assistant, Julie, is probably on the brink of setting the room on fire and hopping a jet to Bora Bora.

Normally, between the two of us, we manage to get more done than a whole staff from one of the larger event firms in the same amount of time. But it's the setup that makes the magic, and neither Julie nor I alone is equipped to outfit a six-thousand-square-foot space by ourselves.

"Come on, come on," I mutter under my breath as the almost-spring influx of tourists makes it hard to get into the whitewashed building. Cameras in hand, they snap shots of Columbus Circle and the entrance to Central Park with little to no awareness of just how much of the sidewalk they're blocking.

Add that in with the *reason* I'm running so behind—spending my normal hour and then some lying to Dr. Winters about my experimental date and the way things turned out—and I'm more than a little frazzled.

Out of time and patience, I karate chop my way through a group of teenage girls clamoring to find the right angle for their social media shots and skid toward the door like I'm on skates.

The light shifts slightly when I step into the lobby, causing my eyes to do a funny sun halo thing that makes it hard to see where I'm going, but I don't bother slowing down.

If I run into a thing or two, the bruises I earn will just have to be a casualty of war.

"Hold the elevator," I yell toward the closing doors, but when no hand reaches out to stop them, all I can do is whine in my head.

Why? Why did I have to spend so much time avoiding Dr. Winters's questions about my date? And why do the people in New York have to be so damn rude?

Power walking, I hit the elevator call button, expecting to have to wait, but the same cart opens immediately, revealing itself as empty.

Oh. Well. I guess that's why no one held it. Ha.

God, I'm a mess.

Obviously, getting snuck out on immediately following the type of sex that transcends all metrics of reality isn't the kind of event I'm built for.

And to be honest, I'm not even sure why.

When it comes to relationships, I like defining events and lines in the sand because they're paths to clarity. And those lines say, in no uncertain terms, that the person who commits the acts are not worth my time. Not worth my thoughts, not worth my worry, not worth the very distinct fantasy for life and marriage and babies I have.

But something about this strikes me as different. It doesn't feel final like it should, and frankly, that terrifies me.

For as perpetually single as I am, I haven't often dealt with feelings of rejection or loss. I haven't been the one left standing there holding the proverbial bag. I've been the roadrunner, nothing left to deal with but a puff of smoke.

The elevator dings its arrival at the ballroom-floor level of the Mandarin, and I scamper out like a newborn colt, all arms and legs and incoordination.

"Shoot," I mumble as I almost trip over my own damn feet in the hall, stutter-stepping on the carpet and throwing out a hand into the wall to stop my face from eating floor.

Forcing myself to pause and reset, I take a deep breath in through my nose, hold it, and then blow all the toxic energy out through my mouth.

Get over it, I coach myself. *So what if you told Dr. Winters that your date with your TapNext match Nathan ended badly and didn't go any further into the story? It's not like you don't see her every week…you can easily clear your conscience next Wednesday by hashing out all the details then.*

I nod. I'm right. This isn't a big deal. I'm freaking out for nothing.

It's over and done. He snuck out—the end. I'll have plenty of time to let Dr. Winters take a deep dive into the psychological consequences, and for now, I just need to concentrate on setting up for this event. The event that's probably about to start any minute.

Shit!

I glance down at my watch and break into a jog immediately. Julie really is going to kill me.

I round the hallway to the far side of the ballroom and bust in like a bull in a china shop. The door bangs against the wall and echoes throughout the large space, but I don't pause to do anything about it. As far as I know, doors and walls don't respond to apologies anyway.

Julie is on the far side of the room, bent down over a cart of supplies, when news of my boisterous arrival cracks throughout the space, bringing her gaze to me straightaway.

"I know," I say with a raise of my hands as Julie gives me the stank eye of an employee. It's half respectful, half hateful and reeks of both hating me and wanting to keep her job. "I'm sorry I'm late!"

"It's okay," she says, even though we both know it's not okay at all.

"Where are we? What's left to get done before the guests start flooding in here?"

Julie points to the other side of the room. "Centerpieces still need to go on all the tables, and I'm finishing up the tablescape for the buffets. Audiovisual is all done, and the sponsor gift bags are all arranged."

"What about the step and repeat outside? I know that was one of the most important things on the sponsor's list."

"It's all set up. I started with that as soon as I got here…two hours ago."

I gulp and laugh, though I know to Julie nothing seems even remotely funny. "Point acknowledged, babe. Really. Thank you for taking up the slack."

"Of course, boss."

I roll my eyes. "You know I hate when you call me that."

"I do, boss."

I laugh. I deserve it, honestly.

I hustle to grab a couple centerpieces, and she follows me, grabbing two of her own. "Tell me you were at least doing something interesting in your absence. Having a tryst with Johnny Depp. Licking Channing's Tatum. Starring in an adult film? Something."

I snort. "Oh, Julie, you know I'm not that noteworthy."

"You could be," she insists. "If you just let down your guard a little bit.

You're freaking supermodel-level gorgeous without even trying, and you're one of the nicest women I know. If you're any good in bed, you're like the lotto jackpot of women."

"Maybe. But I'm also a head case. Trust me."

"Oh yeah. I know that, too."

Having set the centerpieces down, I shove her in the shoulder as we head back to grab more. "Thanks."

"Hey, we've all got our issues, you know? I'm not judging. But you are definitely crazy. And occasionally late."

I laugh.

"Okay, you lush. Stop chugging the truth serum, and let's bang this out. Before long, some of the richest, most successful, powerhouse men and women in the world are going to be in this room, and I don't think they're going to want to hear about how crazy I am."

All manner of suit-wearing men start to flood through the doors, many of them heading directly for the bar. A couple go straight for the table of hors d'oeuvres, but the rest are too busy mingling to focus on anything but one another.

One man, in particular, seems to have drawn a bit of crowd around himself as he talks and laughs and gesticulates wildly. All the men around him break out into a mixture of laughter and guffaws as he finishes whatever tale he's weaving.

"My God, I need one of those," Julie mutters under her breath, staring at him longingly.

There's something familiar about his big, muscled frame, but I'm not entirely sure what it is.

What I do notice, however, is the sparkling metal on one of his very important fingers.

I turn away and warn her, discreetly looking out at one of the giant, eighteen-foot-high glass walls over the twinkling lights of Manhattan. "He's married, Jules. Sorry."

She doesn't turn, instead choosing to keep ogling the guy shamelessly. "I didn't say it had to be *him*. Just one like him…or twenty like him. Whatever."

I grin. "I don't know." I glance back, away from the glitz of city streets and at the man in question with a craned neck over my shoulder. He's got dark hair and bright eyes and a smile that could fill this entire ballroom, but he also has the air of a wild man—the kind that I'm not sure ever really settles down—and enough charisma that suggests women will always be hitting on him. I don't know if I could handle being with someone like that, ginormous frame and huge, honed muscles or not. "He's not really my type."

"What?" she nearly shrieks, making me reach out to clutch her elbow, afraid she's going to make a scene. "You're joking me right now, aren't you? Because if that man," she says, pausing only long enough to point directly at him and make me reach out to grab the offending finger and turn it away, "is not your type, you really do have impossible standards, and I'll think about just getting you a couple of cats now."

I roll my eyes. "Just because I say one guy in the world isn't my type doesn't mean I'm ready for spinsterdom. Come on."

"You come on!" she insists. "Do you see him? Or do I need to get your eyes checked?"

"Thatch!" someone else yells across the room, catching the subject of our conversation's attention.

Julie's still focused on me, waiting for an answer, but as my brain starts spinning over the shouted name, I finally make sense of the familiarity.

And boy is it comical.

He looks familiar because I've seen him in *Cosmopolitan*, on the dreaded coffee table in Dr. Winters's office.

For the love of everything.

"Julie, slow your roll, sister, because I know who that man is," I say quietly, and she quirks a brow. "It's Thatcher Kelly, for fuck's sake."

"Who?"

"The billionaire!" I whisper-yell.

Julie swings her head around sharply, and she compresses her chest with a hard hand. "Okay, he's perfect."

I scoff. "He's also married to Cassie Kelly, one of the most beautiful women on the planet, and they have a, like, one-year-old kid or something."

"How do you know all of this?"

I wave her off. "It doesn't matter. What matters is that Thatcher Kelly is so far out of both our leagues, we're practically on different planets."

"Out of my league?" Julie shakes her head. "I'm not afraid of a challenge."

"Jules! He's married."

She rolls her eyes. "Yes, *boss*, I know. Don't worry, I'm not going after him. I'm just saying that I don't set boundaries for myself without even trying. Nothing is unattainable, and it'd do you some good to get the same attitude."

"What do you mean?"

"I meeean…don't take no for an answer. Never give up on the first try. If you don't ask, they can't say yes. The only person capable of holding you back is you. And I, for one, don't consider myself a cockblock."

I consider her words closely as I watch Thatcher Kelly schmooze a dozen and a half businessmen at once. They all look at him like he's a god, and for all I know, maybe he is. The point is, he doesn't cower under the pressure—he revels in it.

Maybe Julie's right.

Maybe I do give up too quickly.

Memories of Jude's head between my legs make me feel light-headed, and I stumble to the side, my heart racing so fast it's liable to be in my throat soon.

I envision the picture of him in the paper, smiling for the camera like he's larger-than-life, and I recount the headline of the article and the reason for its placement there.

Club Promoter Jude Winslow Brings Fresh Fun Back to Manhattan.

The private marketing event for elite private event specialists.

Elite Private Event Specialists. _That's me. I am one of those._

"Julie, does your cousin still work on the advisory board for the Event Planners Association?"

She cocks her head to the side. "Yeah. Why?"

"There's an event at Club Craze this weekend. And I want into it. But I'm pretty sure you have to know someone to get in there."

"Oh, yes! I heard about this. By invitation only or some shit." She rolls her eyes. "Like they really know who to invite."

"Do you think your cousin could get me one?"

She shrugs. "I'm not sure. But I could definitely find out if you want—"

"Find out," I say quickly, unable to stop myself from interrupting. "Just one day out of the two will be fine. Just get me in there."

"You got it, boss."

God help me, but I'm going out on a limb. I just hope it's strong enough to hold the weight of my expectations.

SIXTEEN

Jude

"You got a minute?" I ask Ki-Ki, stepping up onto her platform as she's cueing up her laptop and taking out all her extra equipment. Her cute pixie nose practically twitches with excitement, and I automatically grin while she nods.

I've never actually met anyone as happy as she is, and I'm pretty sure it's because her parents did some sort of crossbreeding experiment with a unicorn or that Disney fairy with the tight green dress.

"I just want to go over a couple things before I do the meeting with the rest of the staff, if that's cool."

"You bet," she agrees. "I've got a pretty standard playlist, but I can easily mix something up if you've got a different request."

"No, no," I say with a shake of my head. Ki-Ki is definitely the expert in the music department. It's not that I don't listen to music per se, because I do, but I'm not the guy who knows the name of every song and artist. I just vibe to whatever I vibe with at the time, be it country or rap or hip-hop or alternative or whatever. I am a musical chameleon. "I trust your style. I just wanted to talk about volume levels, really. Tonight is a little different from our normal heavy hit, you know? Early on, we need to meter the volume down so that conversation is discernible."

She nods and gives me a thumbs-up, flicking her wrist on her soundboard and then clicking a couple of keys on her laptop. Immediately, a smooth beat picks up at probably half our normal volume.

It's mood-influencing—in a good way, of course—but not overpowering. "That's perfect, Keeks."

She smiles huge and clicks off the beat. "So, I'll just run this for the first hour or two, and then as the atmosphere picks up, so will the volume. Cool?"

I lean forward and place a quick peck on her cheek, making her giggle. Our relationship is platonic in every way, but we just get along. I like seeing her happy, and she feels the same.

"They say you're the best for a reason," I continue with a wink, climbing down from the platform and taking off for the kitchen staff. We've got two extra waitresses tonight, all because we've taken on the task of adding food. On normal nights, we don't bother trying to accommodate anything other than fluids, but on the private side, we're all about catering to a client's every whim.

That, of course, means we have to show the people who are most likely to bring the clients here that we have the capability.

I round the corner into the kitchen, which is wild with activity, and scoot past the waitstaff meeting currently underway with our head floor manager, Dave. While I'm in charge of getting the people here, Dave is more in charge of making sure we have the means to get them all served.

I do a quick scan of the extravagant setup provided by my brother-in-law Wes Lancaster's restaurant, BAD, but I'm completely surprised to see the devil himself walk in through the back door, carrying a tray of food.

His eyes flick up and catch mine, and I can't help but make the quick trek across the kitchen to give him a hard time.

"Hey, bro, what are you doing here? I thought you billionaire types had, like, servants for this shit?"

Wes shakes his head and chuckles, and I slap him on the shoulder lovingly. I have to admit that when he and my sister first got together, I was a little worried he was always going to be a bit too uptight for my taste. But after a couple of years with him in the family, I've come to know better.

Sure, he can still be a little moody and a touch serious, but he's also pretty fucking funny, and beyond all that, he's the kind of man my sister needs and deserves. Plus, even though Lexi isn't his biological daughter, he loves my niece like she's his own—with his whole, wealthy heart. Anything she wants, she gets. Anything she needs, he does.

I'll probably never stop giving him shit, but down deep, I'm Wes Lancaster's number one fan.

"We aren't all just content to coast through life without actually working like you, you know?"

I scoff through a chuckle. "Bro, I'm at work right now. You need to work on your comebacks. Lexi can teach you."

He flips me off, and I laugh. "Seriously, though. Thanks for catering. I'm really hoping this is beneficial for both of us."

Wes claps my shoulder and squeezes. "No problem, man. Glad to do it. Though, after the stunt you pulled on Wednesday, my wife almost made me write you off altogether. Told me to let you hang."

I chuckle. "No way. My baby sister loves me."

"Normally, yes. When you invite yourself over and show up without permission? Not so much."

"Come on," I challenge. "We had a great time, didn't we?"

"I've endured worse."

"Exactly!"

Wes laughs. "All right, man. I'm gonna take off. If you have any problems, though, you can call or text."

"Thanks, bud."

Wes nods. "I hope it goes well for you."

"Me too," I admit. "You really never can tell."

Without much further ado, Wes leaves out the same door he came, and I snap back into work mode. All the guests will be arriving momentarily, and it's my job to make sure we're ready.

⤫

Music thick and bodies thicker, Club Craze is officially jamming tonight, and after a couple hours of formalities, the world's most elite private event planners are letting their hair down in a major way.

Men and women intertwine on the dance floor, bodies grinding like they don't have any lives outside of these walls, much less a wife in Minneapolis.

The energy makes me smile, and Ki-Ki gives me a thumbs-up through the window of the office over her back shoulder while she jams. I'm not entirely sure how she knows I'm in here watching without turning around, but I'd wager that she knows if I'm not out there, this is where I am.

Dancers gyrate in the cages above the floor, and neon lights strobe like ribbons in the wind. All in all, I couldn't be happier with the way things are going so far. I've had two immediate bookings and forty-seven commitments of interest. At the rate it's going, Club Craze could end up doing more private events than public.

Scanning the crowd at large, I plot out my next schmooze strategically, looking for someone who looks particularly open to persuasion, and lock on to a woman in her forties, who's bent over backward on the dance floor doing a shot of hard liquor. I smile to myself and shift my weight toward the door of the office, ready to pounce, when another woman in a blood-red dress catches my eye through the masses.

Long, sleek limbs, silky dark hair, and the kind of features that could stand out on a pitch-dark night, Sophie Sage is unmistakable.

My eyes know her, and my body certainly *remembers* her.

Can't seem to forget about her, actually.

I wasn't in charge of the invitations—one of the assistants in my promotional firm was—but damn if I don't get one hell of a thrill out of the coincidence that Sophie was part of the list.

She did mention that she's an event planner on our date, but I didn't connect the dots to this event.

I smile. *Tonight's shaping up to be even better than I thought it'd be.*

After one last, *long* look at Sophie, I tear my eyes away from her wildly sexy body and stunning face and make myself re-home in on my original target. Because the fact remains that I have a job to do tonight, first and foremost, and then I can move on to pleasure.

For now, I'll keep an eye on the lady in red and repeat to myself that *good things come to those who wait.*

SEVENTEEN

Sophie

Event planners are in hog heaven all around me, chowing down on food, guzzling endless drinks, dancing like they're set to star in the remake of *Dirty Dancing*, and losing their ever-loving minds. These are literally the who's who of private event planning, some of them having been involved in celebrity weddings, state dinners at the White House, and even one guy who's best known for running all the setup for New York Fashion Week! Honestly, if I weren't freaking out so much about the seriously delusional fantasy of *Jude seeing me and having some sort of ultra-swoony explanation for his disappearance* that got me here, I might actually be in awe.

But the fact is I am wigging out while some of my biggest idols are getting their freak on like this is happy hour at spring break, and Jude, for the love of everything, hasn't even fucking noticed I exist.

Coming here was definitely not a good idea.

I scour the room again, passing right over Cara Ming, one of the top wedding planners in the world, while she drops it like it's hot to Snoop, and zero in on the man in the suit.

Just as I remembered, Jude looks every bit as handsome and self-assured as I'd expect a man of his credentials to be. He smiles easily, he's charismatic, and for lack of a better description, he works the room like a whore on a popular street corner.

They're all eating out of his hand, and by all appearances, the event is a great success.

"Excuse me," a man calls from beside me, startling my attention away from Jude and up to him. "Is this seat taken?" he asks, pointing to the spot directly next to me.

His dark hair, dark eyes, tanned skin, and trimmed beard are undoubtedly noteworthy, and I try my best to close off my stupid running mind so I can give him all my attention. I mean, there's a reason they say *tall, dark, and handsome*, right?

I don't need Jude's light hair and bright eyes. I need mystery. *Yeah, that's it.*

"No," I finally answer. "Please, sit."

He smiles, the look transforming his face from *Mafia Boss Kingpin* to *Man Next Door*, and I shift in my seat.

Once situated at my side, he sticks out a hand for me to take and introduces himself. "Hi. I'm Bennett Nickelson. What's your name?"

I smile, trying my best to leave the awkward pressure of meeting someone for the first time behind and just converse like a normal human being. "Sophie," I say. "Sophie Sage."

Well, so much for not being weird. I sound like 007, for shit's sake.

Nevertheless, Bennett smiles. "Nice to meet you, Sophie. I don't know about you, but I'm feeling a little out of my league tonight. Some big names here."

I nod. "I know."

"I'm not even sure why I got the invitation."

Oh. I know how I got mine. Ha.

Secret embarrassment flushes my cheeks pink, so I turn away briefly to save myself from exposing that to him. Almost without my permission, my gaze immediately snags on Jude.

He's smiling broadly, in the middle of an exchange with several different women at once, all of them hanging off him like he's a damn pull-up bar.

My stomach twists—the traitor—and the urge to get the hell out of here overwhelms me. *What was I thinking coming here? He fuck and snuck, right out of my apartment like a bandit in the night. And he didn't even give me the decency of a goodbye. There's no coming back from that.*

Pushing quickly to standing, I manage only a hasty glance over my shoulder at a startled Bennett. "I'm sorry," I say, already in a near-run off the platform and toward the front door. "I have to go. Nice meeting you!"

I push and shove my way through the throngs of people blocking me from some much-needed fresh air, my consideration for their personal space practically nonexistent. I take a deep gulp to keep myself from descending into a full-blown panic and barrel past the interior security guard and coat check area like a woman possessed. The dark glass entrance taunts freedom across the room, and my heart races inside my chest with the first vestiges of an actual anxiety attack.

I don't know what's got me this worked up, but *Lord almighty, I have to get out of here.*

Jogging as fast as my five-inch heels will let me, I cross the space and grab on to the handle of the door to pull it wide open, but before I can, a heavy body hits me, forming completely to my back.

"Leaving already?" a deep, rich voice rasps in my ear, his hand coming up to press into the door in front of me. I recognize him immediately, and my body melts backward like butter without my permission.

"What are you doing here?" I ask on a lie of sorts, already very much knowing the answer. Him being here is the very reason *I'm* here. Which, given the fact that this could have been one of the biggest career opportunities of my lifetime if I'd stopped being so fixated on a stupid guy, is pretty pathetic.

God, Sophie.

"Don't kid yourself, sweetheart. You know why I'm here. You've been watching me all night."

I whip my head to the side.

"And how would you know that?"

I can *feel* his provocative smile against my throat.

"Because I've been watching you."

I hate myself so much for how easily I give in—for the way my body pulses toward him and my breath escapes my lungs. This is a man who left my bed without so much as a goodbye, and yet, here I am, panting over him.

This is not on Sophie Sage's list for acceptable behavior when it comes to suitors. Not at all.

But Dr. Winters says to have fun. To not think so hard. To just enjoy dating for a while, right?

Just *enjoy.*

Sucking in another gulp of air, I steel myself against my racing blood and spin in his arms, reaching out immediately and grabbing him by the tie. He smirks, the asshole, and I just about want to crawl out of my skin and wrap it around him, anything to get him inside me faster.

Oh my gosh. This is demented. If I didn't really need therapy before, I definitely need it now.

"Who gave you permission to touch me again?" I challenge boldly, completely contradicting how I feel just to prove to myself that the rational version of me is still in there somewhere.

The corner of his mouth kicks up, and my heart flips over in my chest.

"Don't worry, babe. If you want me to earn it, I'll earn it. All you have to do is say please."

Bless my own heart, I'm in trouble.

EIGHTEEN

Jude

At my words, Sophie's body shivers in my arms, and I smirk mischievously, knowing I've hooked her. Combine her newfound determination to challenge me with the fact that I can barely feel the rest of my body for all the blood that's now in my cock, and I know one thing without a shadow of a doubt.

She's not going anywhere but a bed tonight, and she won't be alone.

"Come on," I urge when she doesn't verbally refuse my efforts. "Let's go back inside and act like we know each other."

As I pull back from her grip, my tie slides through her hand until we're a full two feet apart. I reach out an offered hand, and after a few long moments of careful, slightly angry consideration, she takes it, sliding her petite hand inside my palm.

I don't wait—in the game of women, there's no room for hesitation—and lead her back through the lobby entrance, down the hallway, and into the main room of the club. The din of partygoers and Ki-Ki's full volume crushes us immediately, sucking us further into its vortex with every step we take toward the dance floor. I've almost broken through the crowd at the edge when an irate tug at my hand pulls me to a stop.

I spin to face her and place my lips at her ear to ensure I'm heard and ask, "What's wrong?"

"I'm not this easy, you know?" she spits, flaming leaves whipping wildly in her unique eyes.

"I never said you were," I correct mildly, the ignition of my arousal by her sexy attitude becoming harder and harder to ignore. As a man who's never had a type other than hot, eager, and willing, I'm surprised to find that, evidently, argumentative is a turn-on.

"Well, even if you didn't say it, I just felt like you needed to know it. I don't spread my legs for anything that sniffs in my direction, and I don't need you to take some weird form of sexual pity on me either."

Shaking my head with a smile, I can't help but bend down enough to take her mouth with mine. Her emotions are all over the place right now, but I spent enough time with her on our last date to know that the end is most definitely worth the means. And in this case, having her argue with me even seems a little fun.

There's resistance to my mouth's effort at first—though, it's clearly half-hearted at best—but the deeper I delve into the flesh of her lips, the more malleable her body becomes. I take advantage by pulling her hips into my own and showing her just how turned on she makes me feel.

When I pull away, her eyes are wild and pale, warning of a storm like the underside of a leaf. I lean back to her ear, the air from my words vibrating off her neck and bouncing back to my lips to make them tingle.

"All I'm thinking about right now, Sophie, is feeling you on my cock. If I thought you were easy, I'd take you to the bathroom right now and fuck you."

Her breathing escalates, reverberating in the pounding bass from Ki-Ki's mix, and for a fraction of a second, I think about doing just that.

But instant gratification, as it turns out, isn't always the best, and I know for a fact from my last encounter with this very woman, that the longer I prime Sophie tonight, the hotter the sex is going to be.

She's begging to be toyed with, and I aim to please.

Done with conversation, I grab her hand again and pull her the rest of the way onto the dance floor, spinning her around in a full circle and slamming her front to my own. Her tits press deliciously into my chest and her hips are restless against me.

Slowly, ever so slowly, I bring a hand to her hip and start to move in tune with the thick, throbbing music.

The beat drops, and the lights fall, and I make my next move. Her slinky dress bunches up atop her thighs as I scoot my leg between hers and pull her hips toward me to grind deeper. It's dirty dancing at its finest, and the last time I came this close to coming because of it was in high school.

Sophie's eyes are locked on my face when I lift mine to look at her, and the emerald color of them looks like a sparkly onyx in the low light of the dance floor. I don't know how one set of eyes can have the power to shine like so many different shades in the span of minutes, but they change like the mood rings my sister used to have as a kid.

I never expected to be back in this club with her after the first night, let alone dancing and breathing her in again—except, this time, with the intimate knowledge of what sinking myself between her legs really feels like.

I pull her hips firmly against mine, tighter, harder, and a moan leaves her lips on a silent gesture covered by the music. She looks like pure sex, and I can't help but put my lips on her exposed throat and suck gently. Edging closer, she digs her fingernails into my shoulders and moans again, but this time, it's loud enough for me to hear it, even over the crush of the crowd and bass.

With one eager hand, I dig into the back of her hair and pull her face up toward mine, sealing our lips together. She tastes like pure candy, compliments of the fruity drinks she's been diving into all night while pretending not to notice me.

I lick the tiny space between her lips to get her to open them more and slide my tongue fully inside her perfect mouth on invitation. I swear she's got the kind of lips I could explore for a night all on their own. Plump and responsive and as if they were meant to mesh with mine.

Everything else about the night starts to fade away. The clients, the job, all the details I should still be paying attention to.

Regardless of the importance of all of it, the only thing I can focus on is her.

Her sweet body. Her small but heavy tits. Her delicate collarbone and moody eyes, and the most perfect space between her legs that awaits me.

This night may have started out about winning over as many event planners as possible to ensure the long-standing success of Club Craze Manhattan. Winning over *one* planner, though, has become an event of its own.

Get ready, Sophie. I never back away from a challenge.

NINETEEN

Saturday, March 10th, Early Morning

Sophie

My front door slams into the wall first, and then my back hits the door, Jude's entire body weight pressed against me as he licks a line of unimaginable foreplay through the crease of my lips.

It promises a plethora of things, many of which I've spent entirely too many hours fantasizing about. It's still dark outside, but the precursors of dawn are all around us. A hazy softness whirls in with the stark blue of night, painting the sky above the buildings out my window a shade of cerulean Miranda Priestly would be proud of.

My whole body burns and aches from the strain this many hours of arousal without culmination have put on it, and I don't know that I'll be able to continue much longer without shattering.

Jude doesn't wait for direction, instead grabbing my hand, pulling me away from the door, and slamming it behind me. The sound echoes into the otherwise quiet space like a snap of a rubber band.

Pulling me behind him, Jude moves at a fast clip down the hallway toward my bedroom. The fact that he knows where to go already gives me a small thrill I'm not entirely expecting—*almost as if we're a couple or something*—and I triple the speed of my feet to keep up with him and then some.

Brushing past him, I turn to move backward, pulling him along with me, and watch as his face transforms completely from the teasing man who spent the night trying to balance work and taunting me, to a man who means fucking business.

No more messing around, no more foreplay—Jude is going to fuck me like I've never been fucked before. I can feel it.

When the backs of my legs hit the bed, I fall to my ass and shove into it, crooking a finger toward him that amplifies the look of his lust with a smile.

"Eager, huh, baby?" he asks, making me bite my lip and nod.

The truth is, I *hurt* I want him so bad.

He climbs in the bed after me, unbuttoning his shirt so slowly I could cry. He knows what he's doing, though, the smirk lifting the corner of his mouth and the dancing light in his eyes all the evidence I need.

Finally undone, his shirt lands on the floor somewhere behind him after a quick toss, and he travels the rest of the distance up the bed to me. My back pulses against the mattress, practically begging me to arch up in climax.

"Jude," I prompt, and he leans forward into the bed, drops down on his stomach, and shoves my thighs apart. My breathing picks up in cadence, and my knees shake with anticipation and need.

Up my thighs, Jude skates the palms of his hands lightly across my feverish skin until he reaches the hem of my panties.

Gently, crooking his fingers beneath the red lace material, he curls the pads of his pointers around the fabric and slowly, ever so slowly, runs them up my bikini line to the curve of my hips.

Suddenly, he grips the waistband violently and pulls, ripping the fabric right off my body altogether.

Glory be.

Not done, he takes the hem of my dress and tosses it up my body, ordering, "Take it off. I want to see your tits while I eat you."

I nod quickly, writhing anxiously on the bedding until I can get the red satin number up and over my head, and toss it to the side.

The only element of my outfit still in place are the calf-laced red stilettos I got last year for my birthday, and as far as I can tell, he doesn't intend to get rid of them.

"Hook your legs over my shoulders," he orders instead, lifting the weight of my legs to help me without waiting for me to comply.

Cool air hums against my bare clit, reminding me just how exposed I am. For some reason, though, I'm not nervous. All I can focus on are the lean, powerful muscles in Jude's shoulders as he reaches down, grabs the cheeks of my ass, and pulls me toward him, sealing his lips over the whole of my sex at once.

My head shoots back like a rock out of a slingshot at first contact, and my cry rends the air.

"Oh my *God.*"

"No, baby," Jude teases as he pulls back to lick his lips. "Just Jude."

Something inside the ego-driven comment strikes a chord in my own pride, and before I know it, I'm using the strength of my thighs to roll him over, spin around, and sit on his face. Our last romp left me with memories I can't forget, but this time…this time, I'm going to make sure I leave the same with him.

He doesn't complain. In fact, he groans in excitement when I hastily undo the buckle of his belt, unfasten the button of his pants, and release the zipper, shoving the fancy wool material down toward his thighs, right along with his boxer briefs.

His dick bounces as it's freed, and everything inside me turns animalistic. I have to taste it, suck it, make it *mine*.

Without delay, I grip him hard at the base and lick a line around the crown at the top. Using the moisture from my tongue, I rub circles into the head, and he moans against my clit.

Oh yes.

Starting at the tip, I curl my tongue around his shaft and widen my jaw, accepting his large girth inch by inch until he touches the back of my throat. There are still a couple inches left of his exposed cock, so I work them with my hand, letting the moisture from my mouth drip down to lubricate it.

His hips dance wildly, startling me briefly with a thrust upward that gets him another inch deeper.

Surprisingly, I'm not uncomfortable, and with the way his mouth is sucking me and the feel of his heavy cock in my mouth, I'm on the very brink of coming.

By all accounts, I should have already. Sometimes, though, when I prolong a climax this long—and holy moly, I've been staving it off for *hours*—it takes a little extra work to break it free.

Up and down, I skate the very edge of my teeth along his delicate skin, sheathe them again, and then pop my mouth off at the top to allow myself a deep breath.

My hair skims the tops of his thighs, and the beauty of my hands and hair and his cock together is something completely unexpected. A jolt of immense enjoyment at the sight makes the center of my chest burn.

So much so, I zone out a little until he flips me handily to my stomach, kneels behind me, rustles briefly with what I imagine is a condom, and drives his dick so deep I cry out loudly enough to wake the neighborhood stray cats.

"Oh my God," I rasp, making Jude grab the hair at the back of my head and pull gently.

"It's Jude, baby. And I'm going to fuck your little pussy so many times tonight, even it will know my name."

Fuck. Me.

The bed dips beside me, and it's apparently just enough to break me from my almost-slumber, and my eyes flutter open. Jude stands beside the bed, hunting and pecking through our tangled mess of clothes on the floor and pulling out his apparel one item at a time.

His boxer briefs are already back in place, and his deliciously ruffled hair hangs down in front of his eyes.

The searing pain of rejection hits me square in the chest, and I have to clench my eyes tight to stop the sting of tears in my nose from developing further.

I can't believe he's sneaking out again. Everything inside me vibrates with betrayal and a heady feeling of triviality, and the only two options left are to tuck my tail between my legs and suffer silently, or to give him the shit he deserves.

"You're leaving again?" I ask harshly, my brain having clearly chosen the latter.

He jerks his gaze up, startled that I'm awake, I think, but it's only a moment before his trademark easy smile slides into place. "Yeah, babe. I have to get home."

I shake my head at myself, backtracking my sliding scale in the direction of flight rather than fight, but as he continues to get dressed, a fire burns inside me that I just can't seem to extinguish. If I don't speak up now, I never will. The chances of running into him again in a city this large are statistically nil, and while last night I would have characterized that as a bad thing, now, I should let it work in my favor. The worst that could happen is that he leaves—which is obviously already happening. Fuck being meek. This is my life and my bed and my intimacy, and I shouldn't be afraid to ask.

"What is this?" I implore, shoving up in the bed with a hand until I'm sitting. I take the sheet with me, covering my exposed breasts.

Jude brushes his hair out of his eyes and smiles. "What's what?"

I don't appreciate the seemingly intentional inanity. I want answers, dammit. Not only that, I deserve them. It's one thing to have a one-night stand that leads nowhere, but there's got to be some kind of rule after the second night that at least entitles you to a succinct conversation. Hell, I don't know. Maybe he's comfortable with no boundaries at all, but I need the border of what zone we're in to be at least faintly defined.

"What's happening here? With *us*. This," I finally emphasize, dropping the sheet to wave both hands wildly between us.

Jude shrugs, a shameless smile lighting his undeniably gorgeous face, and flicks his gaze from my eyes to my bare breasts and back. "It's fun."

Fun, he says. It's *fun*. That's great and all, but what in the hell is that supposed to *mean*?

My mind races neurotically, and he slides his feet into his shoes.

I watch silently as he grabs the pen and notepad I keep on my night table and scribbles down a series of numbers across the top. It's the chicken scratch of a typical man, but it's definitely legible—whether or not I want it to be is another question entirely.

"Use this to call me when you want to have some more." Everything inside me stops as he leans forward and places a gentle kiss to the apple of my cheek and tucks the paper into my palm.

He shuffles out of the room then, still settling his pants into place on his hips and then buttoning the open shirt on his shoulders. It takes all the effort I can manage to keep myself from jumping from the bed and chasing him down the hall just to read him the riot act again.

I feel volatile and completely unstable and, quite frankly, insane. *How in the fucking world can someone spend the night doing the things we just did, in the positions we did, and not feel some small ounce of…connection?*

How on earth can he walk away so easily?

Manic, I push out of the bed and start to stalk in the direction of the hallway, but I stop myself when it hits me. Months of forced self-reflection courtesy of Dr. Winters have apparently honed my skills.

I'm angry and emotional and undeniably confused, yes, but…well, he hasn't *actually* done anything wrong. He's been upfront and honest, and I'm completely responsible for the consequences of doing this again after watching him walk out the first time. I knew. I knew that this was a man who'd walked out before and was just as likely to do it again, and still, I chose to subject myself to it again.

And what do you even expect him to do instead of leaving your apartment after two hot sex marathons? Wake you up with flowers and breakfast in bed?

Besides the intense orgasms only he seems to be able to give me, I don't necessarily know what I'm even wanting from him at this point. Bottom line, I signed on for this, willingly, whether I want to admit it or not. I practically stalked the man to make it happen, for goodness' sake.

I glance down at the paper in my hand as the front door to my apartment clicks shut, and I study the numbers with stark precision.

The ball is in my court, and the future is in my hands. Jude Winslow is the good-time guy, and he's ready and willing to keep having them with me. But it's never going to check all the boxes on my list, and it's not going to end with the two of us tucked away behind a symbolic white picket fence.

I have to decide if *just fun* is something I can handle or not.

And right now…the truth is, I don't know.

TWENTY

Jude

Two kids race past me on scooters, yelling riotously, and I lean deeper into the brick column at my back to avoid getting skimmed by their lanky limbs.

"Don't be a little shit, Hunter!" one of them yells to the other, earning the ire of the school administrator at the top of the stairs.

"Excuse me, Byron Hawthorn! Don't make me call your mother."

I laugh quietly and look back down at my phone to check the time. It's two minutes past six, and Lexi should be out here any minute. I briefly click through my call log, just to make sure I didn't miss one from anyone, and then do the same in my messages. Both come up empty, and I brush aside the bothersome notion that there's anything wrong with that.

I don't actually spend that much time on my phone when I'm off the clock, and often with my brothers, I'm not the first one to start a message thread. I have a couple buddies I occasionally get beers with, but for the most part, I spend a lot of my time alone. Traveling the country to different club openings, relaxing in my downtime, and spending time with my family have always been my priorities. Well, all that, along with the occasional hookup, of course.

So, it really doesn't make any sense at all why I feel this way—expectant.

I shake my head to clear all the weird thoughts and tuck my phone back into my pocket where it belongs.

My niece will be out soon, and her smart-as-a-whip mind will give me more than enough to concentrate on. She's normally out by now, but I'm not in a rush. Even at thirty-six years old, being outside of an elementary school like this brings waves of nostalgia crashing over me.

It's the same dynamics, the same principal at the door with her keys and walkie-talkie, and the same unadulterated joy of childhood. I like getting a little taste of it occasionally. It reminds me not to take life so seriously and to just enjoy the ride. Time truly flies, whether you're having fun or not. So, I prefer to have it.

"Hi, Uncle Jude," Lexi greets without preamble, and I spin around to greet her in her position directly behind me.

"Hey-o, Lexinator. How's it hanging?" I take her backpack and sling it over my shoulder.

Lexi's eyebrows draw together as she smirks. "This is another one of those weird things you say that I don't understand, isn't it, Uncle Jude?"

I laugh. My niece is the smartest person I know, but she's pretty damn funny too. No one straight-talks me quite as fiercely as she does, and I have to admit, it makes me enjoy the time we spend together even more.

"Yes, I guess it is. How was Mathletes practice? Did you ace everything?"

"Of course. I'm an expert in math."

I laugh again. Damn, I love how her brain works. She never even considers belittling herself for the sake of others, and in today's world, I feel like that's a godsend for a little girl. So many societal constraints and voices would tell her to be humble or not to brag, but I'm fucking here for it.

I hope she keeps it up until the day I die and beyond.

"Damn straight, girlfriend. Most of us wish we could do only half the stuff you can."

"I could teach you."

I smile. "I bet you could, baby girl. Probably not without a lot of frustration, though. Your dear uncle Jude excels much more at other things."

"Like chasing tail?"

I cough on my saliva, choking around it while I try to find some air. "Where did you hear that?"

She shrugs nonchalantly. "I don't know what it means, but Uncle Remy and Uncle Flynn talk about it all the time."

"They do, do they?"

She nods. "Yes."

"What else do those bast—brothers of mine have to say?"

"Not much else about you. They say Uncle Ty is a serial polygamist. Which I learned about on TV, but I'm not really sure how it relates to Uncle Ty unless he's got wives I don't know about."

I nearly snort. "Does your mom know you've heard Uncle Rem and Uncle Flynn talking about this stuff?"

Lexi shrugs. "It hasn't come up."

I smirk. *Oh man. Sounds like Jude is about to be the favorite brother pretty soon.*

"Well, no matter what Rem and Flynn say, everyone has the right to be whatever kind of person they want to be. Especially since those two don't have a whole lot of room to talk."

Lexi sighs. "Uncle Flynn doesn't talk that much anyway."

I laugh. "No, you're right. He doesn't. And that's fine too."

"Okay."

I nod, first to her and then to myself. I'm not an expert in childcare, but I think I do all right with my niece. And as a bonus, living the life I do, I get to take her to dinner, have a good time without worrying too much about teaching her life lessons and shit, and then drop her off with her parents so I can go home to peace and quiet. It's pretty much the perfect arrangement, being an uncle.

Now I just have to plan a strategy to secure the *favorite* uncle position, effectively robbing it from Remy.

"Where do you want to eat, kiddo? Somewhere casual or fancy?"

Lexi ponders for a moment, answering, "Fancy. We deserve to treat ourselves every once in a while."

"Hell yes, we do," I agree, succinctly considering our options while looking up and down the block from Lexi's school. We're Uptown already, but that's no big deal. We can easily take a cab or ride the subway if we need to.

"Do you feel like Italian or a nice juicy steak?" I ask in an effort to narrow it down.

"Spaghetti," she says excitedly. "Definitely spaghetti."

This kid could eat spaghetti every day for the rest of her life and still not have enough spaghetti.

"Mm-hmm," I hum. "I had a feeling." Reaching out and wrapping my forearm around her shoulders, I guide her to the left and head straight for the subway station on the next block. "Little Italy, it is, then."

Lexi smiles, counting off the buildings as we walk and giving me a tally at the end of the block while we wait to cross the street. "There are fifteen buildings between this side of the street and the other. Typically, a city block consists of somewhere around twenty or twenty-five buildings, but since my school is a part of this one, it's fewer."

I nod. "That makes sense."

"How many buildings are on your block?"

I have to laugh. "You know, kiddo, I've never checked."

"You should."

"You're right," I agree, ushering her in front of me and holding on to both shoulders as we pass through a large crowd of people cluttering the entire sidewalk. "Or maybe next time you're over, you can count them for me."

She nods. "When's the next time I'll be over?"

"I'm not sure, but I'll check with your parents."

"Will it be soon?"

"I'll make sure it is," I say confidently. The thing is, I know, for Lexi, that this question in her mind won't just disappear. It'll be the first thing she asks me about the next time she sees me, and at least part of the thoughts she has daily. With the way her extraordinary brain works, it's not acceptable for a question to go unanswered forever.

Several years ago, Winnie revealed to the family that Lex had been diagnosed as high-functioning on the autism spectrum. I know it was hard for my sister at first, but none of us were all that surprised. Lexi has *always* been special. She isn't your average kid—she's mountains above it. And her magnificent mind is something to be marveled and cherished. Revered by everyone around her.

My phone buzzes in my pocket, and I remove one hand from my niece's shoulders to dig it out. But almost immediately, a knot of anticipation dissolves when I see that it's Ty.

Maybe I'm not so cool with questions going unanswered forever either.

As quickly as the thought comes, I shake it off and tuck my phone back into my pocket. As we descend the stairs into the subway, focusing on Lexi takes priority, and my shithead smarty-pants professor brother can wait.

Pasta and fresh bread abound on our table at Prima, one of my most frequented restaurants in Little Italy. It's upscale without being pretentious, and as a bonus, my brother-in-law and sister know the chef.

Lexi's eating can sometimes be picky, so having someone who understands at the helm in the kitchen really is invaluable.

She digs into her perfectly plated spaghetti with enthusiasm, twirling the strands around her fork and practically unhinging her jaw to get the large bites inside. One of the many reasons that I love hanging out with my niece so much is that she always makes me smile.

I peek briefly again at my phone, just to check and see if there have been any missed texts or calls, and then slide it back into my pocket and pick up my fork again. I've got a slice of chicken Parmesan halfway into my mouth when Lexi takes a break from scarfing to speak.

"You're looking at your phone a lot today," she muses, just as my chicken hits a spot in my throat that makes me choke.

I hack my way through the discomfort until I get a handle on it, dabbing my mouth with my napkin and setting my fork on my plate to ask, "Excuse me?"

"You've looked at your phone a lot today," she repeats slowly, as if I'm not fluent in English or something.

My eyebrows draw together, a little defensive. I mean, I haven't looked at it that much. Have I? "Why would you say that?"

"Because, on average, you look at your phone five times a night when we're together, and so far tonight, you've looked at it fifteen times."

"Fifteen?" I question with a shake of my head. "That can't be right."

She eyes me earnestly, and I immediately shake my head. *C'mon, Jude, who do you think you're talking to? You can't snow Lexi on the facts.*

My chest burns with unease at having completely lost my normal indifference, and as it's not something I'm used to, I don't like the feeling.

I suppose I could ask myself why I'm waiting so eagerly to hear from Sophie Sage, but being that I'm here with my niece and the thoughts associated with Sophie are anything but appropriate in mixed company, that doesn't seem like a good idea at all. My only other option, of course, is to deflect. Thankfully, executing an old swerve and strike on one of my brothers is much easier. It's like second nature, to be honest.

"Yeah, but I bet your uncle Remy looks at his phone way more when he's with you."

He's a day trader, for fuck's sake. He has to keep up with stocks and shit.

Lexi shakes her head, and I swear, if I didn't know her better, I'd think she was smirking and mocking me. As it is, I know better. Still, the look stings. "Uncle Remy doesn't get on his phone at all when I'm with him."

"Not at all?" I ask disbelievingly.

She nods. "Only to call my mom or dad when he's bringing me home or they're picking me up."

Well, hell. No wonder the suck-up is the goddamn favorite uncle.

Determined, I resolve to dispense with the phone shit for the rest of the night.

If only getting rid of the nagging need to hear from Sophie were that easy.

TWENTY-ONE

Sophie

The now infamous paper feels damp between my fingers as I flip it over again and read through the numbers one more time.

917-555-8858

With the number of times I've read through them in the last few days, I most definitely have them memorized. And still, I haven't been able to bring myself to throw it out or burn it or even stow it away.

Instead, it lingers. In my purse, in my pocket, and when I get a free moment like right now, in my hand.

Despite all of that, I haven't decided. To call him, not to call him, to let fate take its course or to pointedly avoid him. All of them have some level of appeal, and the more I think about it, the more I talk myself in circles.

My phone vibrates in my pocket, and after a quick glance at the still-closed door to the office, I take it out and tap on the screen to wake it up.

A message from Belle sits front and center on the screen, but before I can open it, another one layers itself on top.

Clicking on the stack of them both, I open her message thread and scan quickly.

Belle: Why the hell are you so busy all the time? Isn't working for yourself supposed to provide flexibility?

Belle: I want to get a drink. Come with me.

I wish I could ignore her, but I know my sister better than that. The more I don't answer, the more she'll text, and my phone will be doing a perpetual dance of vibration until it's time to go to sleep.

Me: I can't tonight. I'm busy. Sorry. Ask Kate to escape New Jersey. She probably needs the night out.

Belle: You know she can't just do shit spur-of-the-moment! She's got the hellions and Todd. I need you!

Me: I'm sorry. No can do tonight. But we'll do something soon, I promise.

Belle: What are you too busy doing to hang out with me? Rerecording a new outgoing message on your answering machine? LAME.

Me: Working. When it's your business, there's no one to fill in for you.

Sure, that's a lie at the moment, but that doesn't make it not the truth. And the last thing I have time for right now is a game of twenty million questions about why I'm at therapy at all.

Yeah, no thanks. I'm enough of a head case already without bringing my sister into it.

The office door creaks open, and a man walks out, smiling civilly at me as he passes and heads out the main door. Several seconds later, Dr. Winters appears in the open space and cranes her head toward me.

"Hey, Sophie. You ready?"

I nod avidly, tucking the paper deeper into my palm and my phone back into my bag, slinging my purse onto my shoulder and jumping up to walk inside.

Dr. Winters closes the door to her office behind me, and I sit down in my spot on the supple, tan leather couch across from her chair and place my purse on the seat next to me.

Jude's number, however, stays in my hand like a ticking time bomb. The truth is, I'm hoping that by holding on to it, I don't lose the nerve to tell the truth when it comes time for Dr. Winters to question it. Because, knowing her like I do, she'll definitely notice.

Dr. Winters strolls over to her seat and sits down again, taking a sip of water from one of those giant jugs on the table beside her. You know the ones…they tell you how well you're doing throughout the day, so you don't lose motivation to drink.

Barely alive.

Skin doesn't look like the undead.

A little more and you'll have to pee.

YEP, GOTTA PEE.

Hey, look at you, hydrating and shit.

Or whatever it is they really say.

The sight of it makes me smile a little. Every once in a while, it's nice to see that therapists are humans too. And needing a reminder to drink water—a resource vital to our survival—is the most Homo sapiens freaking thing I can think of.

"All right," she breathes, finally settling in her chair again and fixing the lay of her shirt. "How are we this week? What's going on? Anything really pressing that you want to talk about?"

I shake my head immediately, like a little scaredy-cat. She narrows her eyes slightly but doesn't press me on it either. Unequivocally, harshness isn't her style. Honesty and culpability, yes. But she's never tried to rush me.

"Okay. What about dating? Have you tried putting yourself out there again yet? Gone through the motions again?"

Immediately, I glance down at the paper in my hands and swallow thickly, and Dr. Winters, the smart woman that she is, lets the silence load itself.

It takes several more seconds to get up the nerve, but I finally start into the truth—or at least, *half* of it.

I don't know what it is, but I'm still unwilling to admit aloud that I let a man sneak out on me once and then went *searching* to find him again. It sounds painfully pathetic in my own head. I can't even imagine how it would sound to my actual ears.

"Yes. I-I went on another date, sort of, I guess. I had a work event, very recreational in nature."

She raises her eyebrows, and I laugh. *Yeah, that doesn't even sound remotely real.*

"Okay, I was at a nightclub. Technically, though, it was a work event of sorts."

She nods, jerking her chin out as though to say, *Go on.*

I take several deep breaths and chew on my lip, staring down at the number in my hands. Jude's face comes to mind—flirty and carefree and so dang happy as he left me lying in my bed Saturday morning. He was so assured that just having fun together is the best idea in the world, but I'm…completely and utterly lost. Spiraling, really, in a vortex of feelings I can't even begin to sort out on my own.

Essentially, Dr. Winters is my only hope of getting clarity. *I can't leave here today without getting some advice.*

"I…well, I kind of hooked up with someone. It was completely casual, he's made that clear, but he left me his number and said to use it if I want to have more fun."

When I don't say anything else, Dr. Winters smiles understandingly and prompts me, "And…how does that make you feel?"

I scoff a little, slamming my back into the couch in physical defiance of what, deep down, I know is necessary prying. "Is that question somewhere in the therapy handbook?"

Dr. Winters is unfazed. "First day of class, actually."

I roll my eyes, but I also laugh. At least my therapist is funny and doesn't take herself too seriously. It's probably why I was able to open up to her at all in the first place.

She's the only one who knows the depths of my obsession with saying *I do*, and she's one of only two people who know I'm in therapy at all. The only other person I've told is my elder sister Katelynn, and the reason I chose her to share with is obvious by the number of times she's asked me about it—zero.

Don't get me wrong; it's not that she doesn't care. She does. I know she does. But she's got kids and a husband and a job and a yard to mow, and frankly, I don't even think she gets all that much time to sleep, let alone ask me about my therapy sessions. Plus, last time she called me, I never called her back, and I don't have the excuse of toddler terrorists running around. So, I guess it's not all her fault.

Dr. Winters raises her eyebrows at me, clearly having noticed that I'd veered mentally into my own little version of a telenovela inside my head and waiting patiently for me to finish.

I guess patience comes pretty easily when you get paid by the hour, though.

I sigh heavily, knowing she's not going to prompt me again but that she's still waiting for my answer.

How in the world does Jude leaving his number for me on the bedside table and telling me to call him for a good time make me feel?

"Honestly?"

"You know how much I love honesty," Dr. Winters jokes, but also adds, "Yes, Sophie, honesty would be good."

"It makes me feel a little bit like a hooker."

She smiles at that, taking her cute oval-shaped glasses off her nose and setting them on the table beside her chair. She leans forward, her elbows to her knees, and I prepare myself to listen.

After six months of coming here, I know that's the position she takes when I'm about to get slapped with the truth.

"Okay, let's break that down. Hookers get paid for a service, correct?"

I nod. I suppose.

"So, if you're the hooker in this scenario, how is it that you see yourself getting paid? He's not *literally* leaving money on your bedside, I'm assuming. Right?"

I shake my head. "No, no money."

"So…what is it that he's leaving you with, then? If you were going to call him, there'd have to be a reason. What's the reason?"

I shrug. "I'm…attracted to him. Kind of a magnetic type of feeling, actually.

And I do have fun when I'm around him. He's not exactly wrong about that."

"Good."

"But it seems like such a waste of time. If he's not going to be willing to commit to anything serious, why should I even bother?"

"From a therapist's perspective, I could give you all manner of answers to that, Sophie. And I think you know that. But what's your answer to it? If you think it's such a waste, why are you even pondering it? Why are you holding what I presume is his number in your hand like it's a thousand-dollar bill? Why are we talking about it? Those are the questions you have to explore first. Then, I think you'll know the answer."

I sigh. Truthfully, I'm pretty sure I already know—have *known*. Since the moment he put the number in my hand four days ago.

I can't get him out of my head.

TWENTY-TWO

Jude

"Yo, Jude! I got a bachelorette party coming in at midnight!" Maverick calls toward me from the opposite end of the staff hallway, and I turn on my heel to find him grinning like a confident bastard. "You feeling lucky tonight? Wanna make another bet and see if you can actually win this time?"

His words strike the match of memories, and unbidden visions flicker into my mind.

Sophie's parted lips and her mouth cresting into unexpected pleasure as I danced against her in one of the private VIP rooms.

Hot-as-fuck visuals of her naked body beneath mine. The way she tastes. The way her skin flushes red when she's getting close to climax.

The mesmerizing way Sophie looks when she comes.

And the fact that you left her your number six days ago and she still hasn't used it.

Quickly, I shake the thoughts from my mind and push a cocky smirk to my lips. The expression comes more naturally than anything else in my repertoire, and the enjoyment I get out of sparring with Maverick even makes it genuine.

"Don't you think you should be focusing on picking out which G-string you're wearing tonight, Mav?" I toss back. "Or what shade of sparkly body glitter will look best under the strobe lights? Instead of, you know, trying to get me to do your job for you?"

Truthfully, Maverick never sports G-strings or body glitter when he's dancing, but shit-talking doesn't always have to be rooted in truth. As long as you sound confident that it *could be* accurate, it strikes the nerves just as deep.

He guffaws. "Nice deflection, Jude."

"Oh, I'm not deflecting. But are *you* deflecting?" I clap back with a smug quirk of my brow. "Because if all the stress is getting to you or you're having an insecure moment, that's all you need to say, bud. I have no qualms about being your Kris Jenner and telling you that you're doing great. Because you are, sweetie. You're doing great."

"Sometimes, it's scary how naturally bullshit comes to you." He snorts and lifts his duffel bag higher onto his shoulder.

"What can I say? Combine raw talent with four siblings and you've got a recipe for smack-talking greatness." I hold out both hands and grin. "Now, if you don't mind, I'm going to head back inside the club and make sure shit is running smooth. See you out there?"

"Yeah, you bastard," he comments and heads toward the staff dressing room. "I'll be the one with the women fawning all over me!"

"I believe in you, sweetie!" I yell with my hands cupped around my mouth. "And I'm sure whatever G-string you pick, the ladies are going to love it!"

Knowing he can't out-banter the master, he just shakes his head on a chuckle and steps through the dressing room door. And I head back in the direction of the club.

A quick glance at my watch confirms that it's already half past ten. In another thirty minutes or so, Club Craze will be at maximum capacity and hopping.

I know this because I planned it that way. Before this Friday night even kicked off, I gave the bouncers explicit instructions on how to fill the club tonight, and after the initial burst of people at opening, the name of the game is slow and steady and a two-to-one female-to-male ratio.

I've said it before, and I'll say it again. *Women are always more fun at a club.* They'll laugh. They'll dance. They'll have cocktails. And they'll undoubtedly bring all the boys to the yard.

The pounding beats of house music start to echo off the walls as I get closer to the side entrance that leads into the bar area, but before I can step inside, I feel my cell vibrate a few times in my jacket pocket. Promptly, my chest expands with an inflated level of curiosity, but when I pull it out and check the screen, I find notifications from the group chat with my brothers and one message from Bianca.

Still no word from Sophie Sage.

I let out an annoyed breath and open up the text inbox to see if there's anything urgent.

Bianca: What are you doing tonight, handsome?

I'm pretty sure it's been a month since I last spoke with her, and normally, I'd try to meet up with her after I finish at the club, but...I don't know... I'm just not feeling it tonight. Not really feeling it at all, if I'm being honest.

Me: Sorry, B. Working all weekend.

She responds with another message, but I'm already inside the group chat with my brothers and reading through the various texts I've missed.

Ty: Any one of you fucks getting into anything fun tonight?

Flynn: Not in town.

Ty: What? Where are you?

Flynn: Montana.

Ty: What the fuck are you doing there?

More messages pop onto the screen, and I keep reading.

Flynn: I was here for a client, but I ended up joining a motorcycle club. Probably gonna move out here permanently.

I laugh. Flynn is the quietest Winslow brother out of the four of us, but man, whenever he does say shit, it's always laced with the best fucking sarcasm and dry humor.

Remy: LOL.

Ty: Just because you're Mr. Cool on your Harley, doesn't mean a motorcycle club would actually accept your pansy ass.

Remy: Don't act like you haven't been on the losing end of a brawl with Flynn before, Ty. We all have. He'd be a fucking asset to any group of roughnecks. I'm two years older than him, and he can still kick my ass—barely.

Flynn: You wanna join the MC too, Rem?

Remy: Sure, why not. I'm down. But only if Ty can't.

Flynn: Ty surviving in an MC? That's hilarious.

Ty: Fuck you guys. And what is up with Jude tonight? Someone must have taped all his fingers together to keep him this quiet during a session of shitting on me.

Knowing that's my cue, I quickly type out a response.

Jude: Working. Club Craze. Don't worry, though. I'm saving up some insults for the next time I see you.

Ty: Yeah, whatever. What about next weekend? Are you working then too?

For good measure, I add one more message into the mix before shifting back to work.

Jude: Probably heading to Montana to join Flynn's MC.

Ty: FUCK YOU GUYS.

I laugh to myself as I slip my phone back into my pocket and step through the side entrance. The bar area is active with bartenders making drinks and clubgoers on the other side clamoring to get their orders taken.

And when I look out toward the center of the dance area, I'm met with way more writhing bodies than I can count.

All in all, everything is going as planned. Club Craze is packed, the music is popping, and the drinks are flowing. It won't be much longer until I feel confident enough in the staff and the way things are running that I won't have to dedicate so much of my weekend time here and can start focusing on my next big promotional project.

In the early days, after I first left Cruz Nightlife, I really had to pace myself. J. Winslow Promotion didn't turn a profit as quick as I wanted, and regret for stepping out on my own was a constant threat. But I knew if I stuck with the mind-set that quality outweighs quantity and stayed focused, I'd eventually be able to ask for bigger numbers with each gig, thus rendering the necessity for overcommitting myself unnecessary. And the six-figure paychecks the owners of this joint are currently paying me to make sure their nightclub is all the rage prove that my methods were spot-on.

It's been thirteen years in the making, but finally, at thirty-six years old, I'm not only considered one of the best in New York, but I also have Vegas, Miami, and LA investors looking to hire my firm for consulting and pro-motional advice.

Instantly, thoughts of Sophie Sage and her event planning business come to mind. I haven't talked to her about it all that much, but with what we have talked about, I've gotten the sense that her work ethic is reminiscent of my own in my late twenties. Hustle hard, and don't take no for an answer. But that doesn't answer the most prying question of the moment—why am I even thinking of her right now?

Because you want to have more *fun with her.*

I'm not going to deny that. Sophie Sage is one of the hottest women I've ever been with, hands down. So, it makes sense that I wouldn't be spent after two quick rounds of play. But the ball is officially in her court, just like I prefer it to be, and all I can do is wait and see if she decides to take the shot. Pursuit turns women into romantics, and Jude Winslow has no fucking interest in chasing anyone's dreams but his own. Life's a hell of a lot happier without the complication.

In the meantime, though, I have a club to run.

After a quick check-in with the bartenders and the cocktail waitresses, I stride out of the bar area and in the direction of my VIPs.

Through the center of the dance area and toward the red velvet ropes of the upper floor, I smile and shake hands with familiar faces, check in with more staff members, and give a thumbs-up to my favorite pixie-haired DJ.

But once I make it through the crowd and my vision adjusts to the change in lighting—from bouncing strobe lights to softly lit ambiance—I'm pulled in the direction of one of the velvet couches lining the walls around the dance floor.

One couch where a brunette beauty with an all-too-familiar and downright unforgettable face sits.

Sophie Sage.

Hot damn. She's fucking *here*. At my club. It's almost like I willed her here, for shit's sake.

A pair of sexy stilettos are clasped to her feet, and her crossed legs look a mile long beneath the sexy green dress that hugs the curves of her body. Her hair hangs across her shoulders, and her blood-red painted lips curve up and into a smile.

But it's not at me. It's at some dude in a pair of jeans and a collared shirt sitting beside her on the couch.

What the fuck? Is she here with that guy?

I shake my head. It wouldn't be the first time one of my hookups tried to play petty bullshit games of jealousy in the interest of gaining more of my attention, but Sophie really hasn't seemed like the type.

Picking my way through the fringe of people standing in front of her platformed section, I move in her direction carefully, hoping to get a better idea of what's really going on before I jump to conclusions. As I get closer and the music threads lower between songs, I overhear him ask, "C'mon, honey, let me at least buy you a drink."

Sophie offers a conciliatory smile but also shakes her head at the dude who looks like he just left a fucking frat party. I'm honestly surprised the bouncers even let him in here. I mean, he just oozes douchebag.

On what planet does this guy even think he stands a chance with a woman like Sophie? The situation is the epitome of him trying to play out of his league.

"What about a dance, honey?" he pesters as I climb up the steps in front of them, ready to intervene on her behalf, but Sophie responds before I can open my mouth.

"I would love to, but my parole officer gave me explicit instructions that the judge said I can't do that."

The dude's face scrunches up like he just ate a piece of bad fish. "Parole officer?"

"Yeah. Truthfully, my court order even says that I'm not supposed to be *here* since it's within four miles of the guy's apartment." Sophie's smile turns conspiratorial as she leans in a little closer to add, "But you won't tell on me, right? I just finished up a three-year stint at Bedford Hills, and there is no way I want to go back there. I'm sure you can understand why."

Bedford Hills is a women's-only correctional facility that most New Yorkers know about because it's where Amy Fisher did her time after she shot Joey Buttafuoco's wife.

Basically, there is *no fucking way* Sophie Sage spent three years there. But the fact that she's pretending to be a secret, undercover felon in the name of making this guy leave her alone amuses the hell out of me. I'm going to have to thank Ki-Ki for the smooth, understated vibe of this song she's playing now, because normally, there's no way I would've been able to make out what they were saying at all.

"Uh…Y-yeah. Of course…" The dude pauses and swallows hard around a mouthful of shock as his eyes dart around the nightclub. In mere seconds, his face has morphed from douchey and flirtatious to a man who fears the woman beside him is going to pull a shiv out of her purse and stab him in the dick.

"Oh shit!" he shouts far too loudly and holds his hand up to his ear like he's actually hearing something from the other side of the club. "I-I think my buddy is yelling for me. Yep. That's him. Definitely him. I…uh…better go see if…he's okay…yeah…I should do that…uh…bye."

Like a sprinter out of the gate after the gunshot, he's off the couch, gliding past me with a whoosh, and heading straight for the dance floor. I track his momentum over my shoulder to steal a final glance of his warp-speed departure, and man, it's worth it. Like a pinball in an active machine, he bumps into several people as he tries to put as much distance between himself and Sophie and her prison stories as quickly as humanly possible.

It's comedy in its purest form and a situation I could spend a good ten minutes laughing about—if it weren't for the woman on the couch. When I turn back toward her, she's staring at me with wide, tumultuous emerald eyes.

I grin down at her and scoot past the low-set table between us to settle a small kiss on the apple of her cheek. Her whole body shivers as I put my warm palm to the opposite side of her throat and whisper softly into her ear. "Hello, Sophie. Fancy seeing you here tonight."

"Uh…hey, Jude," she greets quietly, her voice shaking slightly with something I can't fully discern.

Satisfaction? Surprise? Nervousness?

I don't know. But I'm undeniably glad to see her and get the chance to find out. Taking a seat next to her, I skim my hand over the top of her bare knee and cross my ankle over my own, stretching an arm across the back of the sofa behind her. Her body turns toward mine subtly, and my grin kicks up a notch or two.

"Parole officer? Court order? And a three-year stint in the slammer?" I repeat her earlier words, and a little laugh jumps from her throat.

"I take it I've been caught red-handed in the middle of my web of lies, huh?"

I nod. "Where in the hell did you come up with that shit?"

"Truthfully? I'm not quite sure." She shrugs one bare shoulder. "Lifetime movie. *Dateline.* Too many Netflix crime documentaries. Any of those could be to blame for my depravity."

"Why do I get the feeling that's not the first time you've done something like that to scare off a man's unwanted advances?"

"Probably because it's not the first time." She cringes, but also, the hint of a guilty smile kisses her perfect mouth.

It's so fucking cute I wish I could snap a picture to remember the adorable expression on her pretty face. Not to mention, the realization that she's not giving me even remotely the hard time she did Brad Phi Kappa spurs a thrill of satisfaction in my veins.

Something tells me Sophie Sage enjoys my kind of fun. And more than that, I think that's why she's here right now…

"Are you by yourself tonight?"

She nods, and her eyes flash like a traffic camera after she's just run a red light. They tell a story, one made up of highs and lows and a conclusion that ends at this club with me, serving her willingness on a platter much larger than a simple text to my number. I've never been more certain of one thing—*she* is *here for me.*

And now the fun can begin. *Game on.*

I smirk, stand up, and reach down to take her hands into mine. Once I gently pull her off the velvet couch and to her feet, I wrap my arm around her waist and bring her closer to my chest so I can whisper, "You're here," into her ear.

"I am." She nods again, and the shell of her ear brushes across my lips.

"You look beautiful," I tell her truthfully and reach up to tuck a piece of her silky brown hair behind her ear. "That dress of yours is reason enough for you to actually have a parole officer, or hell, maybe for me to have one."

"What do you mean?" she asks.

"I'm liable to get into fifteen brawls on the dance floor tonight, Soph, and that's just with the men who are brave enough to touch you. I can't even consider the ones who are bound to be looking at you in this thing."

Even to myself, I sound oddly territorial. I reason internally, though, that no boy likes to share the newest of his toys, and boys never really grow up. I want to kiss and dance and fuck. I don't need any other men coming over with their bullshit one-liners and distracting her. Right now, I want all of her attention.

Her cheeks redden a little at my words, and my nose doesn't miss the fact that she smells insanely good. The soft hints of vanilla and sweet sugar and something else I can't determine fill my head and damn near make me high.

I have to get confirmation of her intentions quickly, before I get completely lost in her. "Are you here for me?" I ask bluntly, and Sophie leans back to search my eyes.

"Well…it's either that or I'm having a temporary moment of insanity." She scoff-laughs. "Hell, maybe it's both."

"Temporary insanity isn't always a bad thing." I smile and let my gaze flit from her gorgeous eyes to her full, red-painted lips before locking my eyes with hers again. "In this case, I think it means you've given yourself per-mission to have fun."

"Yeah. I think that's what it means, too."

Instantly, a buzz of excitement blasts into my veins and sets my blood to singing. If Sophie Sage is here for fun, I'm going to make sure I give it to her. And with the club running as smoothly as it is, I have the freedom and time to make it happen.

Oh yeah. Tonight is going to be a good fucking night.

TWENTY-THREE

Sophie

Jude winks, takes one step back, and holds out his hand toward me.

Holy shit. Am I really doing this? Going out on a complete limb, ditching everything I've always known, and taking a chance on straight up not giving a shit about all the fine print?

Dr. Winters would be proud of me for stepping outside of my comfort zone, and both Julie and Belle would lose their shit. Katelynn would sort of freak out, but she'd at least make an effort to cover it up until she knew how close to the edge of my own cliff I was, but the real mess would be my mom. She'd be stealing holy water from the Catholic Church for me and smuggling it out in her purse, I'm pretty sure.

But this is the decision I made, *this is what I want,* and I'm going to see it through. No second thoughts. No doubts. No stressing about the future or making sure a guy checks off all the potential-husband boxes on my list. I'm just going to let Jude and the night lead me wherever they may.

On a deep inhale of fresh oxygen into my lungs, I dive headfirst into spontaneity by placing my hand in his. And Jude doesn't waste any time taking us in an unknown direction.

As he guides us through the crowded dance floor, he places a gentle but steady hand at my lower back, and my body hums. I can feel the warmth of his skin through the insanely short dress I decided to wear, and my heart starts pounding at the mere sensation of having him touch me.

God, what is it about him?

Just the simplest of touches from this man and my nerves light up like a Christmas tree. My body feels greedy for more of whatever he has to give that it's practically searching for the devil himself, ready to make a deal. It's thrilling and disconcerting at the same time, but holy moly, I'm digging the adrenaline rush it provides.

Up to the VIP area of the club, Jude flashes a little grin in my direction as he pointedly directs us to a familiar spot—*the private rooms.* And it's not just any room. It's *the* private room, the one I first met him in during Belle's bachelorette party.

The room is empty, save for the two of us, and when he closes the door with a resounding click, my hands shake, and a throbbing, anticipation-filled ache starts to build between my legs.

Set up a press conference and alert the media because my body is officially at war with itself. Nerves and excitement both creep forward with stealth and precision, hoping to overtake the crucial heart-shaped overlook in my chest. I'm already two halves instead of a whole, and for all intents and purposes, nothing has even happened yet. Sweet baby Jesus. I've only had a handful of encounters with Jude, and yet, I already feel like Pavlov's dog, where Jude is the bell and hearing it ring means I'm moments away from mind-blowing pleasure.

I stand in the center of the room, my body facing the plush couches that line the wall.

I don't know how long I'm just standing there, waiting, *anticipating,* but it feels like an eternity until Jude comes up behind me. His chest presses against my back, and he places two warm hands onto my bare shoulders.

"Do you want to know what I'm thinking about right now?" he whispers into my ear, and his warm breath brushes against my neck.

I shiver. Nod my head.

"I'm thinking about the first night I met you," he answers, his voice the kind of deep and husky that turns my mind into a one-track loop of hot sex and dirty, wicked things. "The night I made you come without removing a single item of your clothing. Without sliding my cock inside you. Without even putting my mouth on your sweet-as-fuck pussy."

I should probably be mortified that he knows about that, *that my body's reaction to him on the night of Belle's bachelorette party was that freaking obvious*, but I can't seem to find the strength or concentration for mortification right now. All I can do is wait with bated breath over what he's going to do and say next.

Jude Winslow is a wild card. I can't anticipate his next move any more than I can anticipate the first drop of rain on a stormy day, and right now, I have to admit that it's addictive.

It goes against everything I normally do or say or think about—it defies every previous reaction and response I've ever had toward the men who came before him. But I don't have control over it. All I seem to be able to do with him is experience the present.

The past. The future. For some reason, they don't exist when he's around.

With him, it's only the here and now. And man oh man is that a really wonderful thing for an overthinker like me.

He releases his hands from my shoulders, stepping away from me, and immediately, my body feels discomfort from the loss of contact. My lips quirk down at the corners, but my gaze never stops studying him as he steps in between me and the couch.

In rapt fascination, I watch as he removes his black suit jacket, tosses it onto a velvet sofa, and sits down. He rolls up the sleeves of his shirt, and I find a sick amount of enjoyment from seeing his strong, sculpted forearms come into view. They're tanned and muscular, and thick, corded veins can be seen beneath his skin.

Instantly, my nipples turn downright traitorous and harden beneath my dress.

Seriously? How can a man's forearms turn you on like this?

Honestly? I don't have a clue, but I'm certain of one thing—this man looks like a god just sitting there on the couch. The first two buttons of his crisp white shirt are undone. His arms are stretched out wide across the back of the sofa. And his crystal-blue eyes glisten with filthy secrets that I'm desperate for him to tell my body.

The ache between my thighs grows more demanding, but I'm helpless to do anything but keep standing there, in the center of the room, looking at him, while the vibrations from the house music from the inside of the club provide a rhythmic, heady soundtrack.

He crooks one finger in my direction. "Come here, sweet Sophie."

I swallow hard against the pulsating eagerness that's building inside my chest.

Good grief, he's sexy.

My steps falter a little as I move toward him, but all thoughts of hesitation and unwarranted doubt are pushed right out of my head when Jude takes both of my hands into his and guides me onto his lap.

As I straddle his hips, my dress slides higher up my thighs. With a knowing smirk, he takes one long index finger and gently runs it up and down the newly exposed skin of my legs.

"*Fuck*, this dress should be illegal. It's driving me crazy," he whispers, his gaze lingering wantonly on my thighs before traveling up to meet my eyes.

You are driving me crazy, I think to myself.

We are face-to-face, my legs straddling his hips, and his *ahem* pressed right against me. The evidence is *hard* and proves that I'm not the only one who is turned on, and when I inhale through my nose, the delicious aroma of his cologne makes my eyes shut momentarily.

With hints of cedar, mint, and lavender filling my head, I feel like I'm in the strangest of fantasy purgatories, bound between the sweetness of heaven and the naughty nature of hell.

He slides his hands into my hair and gently pulls my head back, and a soft moan escapes my lungs when the warmth of his lips hovers right above my throat. "I want to make you come again," he whispers. "Just like I did all those nights ago. Without removing a single inch of your clothes."

I can feel his mouth move down my neck, but it never actually touches my skin. Only the fluttering wisp of his warm breath makes real contact. It's the most intense form of teasing foreplay I've ever experienced, and when he places his hands at my lower back and leans my body farther away, those lips of his drift over my chest, then each of my breasts.

My body reacts of its own accord, my nipples hardening even more and my breaths becoming needy pants of air in and out of my lungs.

But Jude never falters. He just keeps on teasing me, *playing with me*, making me hopeful that soon, that mouth of his will make contact with my skin.

Not to mention that he's so hard now, I can feel the tip of him against the one spot that aches and throbs the most.

"Touch me," I beg, and his blue eyes flame with satisfaction and heated desire.

"Not yet, Sophie. Soon." He thrusts up against me, and a sexy-as-hell groan escapes his lungs. "Fuck, the things I want to do to you."

Yes, please. Do them. Do me!

My silent wish isn't his command, though. Instead, he eases my body off his lap until I'm on my feet again.

"Take off your panties," he orders quietly, rendering me functionless. I can't move; I can't speak. All I can do is stand there, my chest heaving with my frantic breaths. "Take off your panties, Sophie. Now," he repeats. I toy with the hem of my dress with shaky fingers, and he shakes his head. "Don't lift up your dress. Just slide them down your legs and hand them to me."

A whimper-filled moan jolts from my throat.

God, he's killing me.

Jude sits there, looking up at me through hooded, confident eyes until, eventually, I find myself doing as he asked. With two hands, I carefully slide my panties down my legs, and when they reach my ankles, I bend over, pick them up, and hold them out toward him.

Jude grins mischievously and takes the silky black material in one big hand. He gazes down at them for a few seconds, before lifting them toward his face and inhaling deeply.

Everything inside me seizes. A guy sniffing my panties? That shouldn't be hot...*right?*

That should probably be weird. Maybe even concerning?

Should be. But it's not.

In this moment, it is the exact right thing to lead my body into a frenzy. A shiver rolls up my spine, and I have to clench my thighs together just to ease the now intensely pounding ache that's starting to build from within me. They feel slick against each other, the presence of my excitement unmistakable.

"Your panties are wet," he says and looks up at me from beneath his lashes. "Downright soaked."

I nod. Or at least, I think I nod. All conscious function of my body has taken a temporary hiatus.

"You want to come, don't you?"

This time, I know I nod. And it's not just once or twice; it's at least five fucking times.

Jude smirks, slides my panties into his pocket, and crooks one finger toward me. "Come back over here, babe."

He doesn't have to tell me twice. Back over to the couch, I let him guide me onto his lap again until my thighs straddle his hips.

Without the barrier of my panties, I can feel how big and thick and hard he is beneath his pants. Sensation and memories alike urge a thrill of pleasure to surge in my bloodstream, and I grip his shoulders tightly as the impulse to rub myself against him becomes too intense to deny.

Jude's hands are in my hair again, and he tugs gently on my locks so that my body is stretched out far enough for his mouth to reach my breasts.

But he never removes my dress. Instead, he sucks at my nipple through the material, and for some insane reason, it feels like the hottest, most illicit thing I've ever done with someone.

I mean, we're in a private VIP room, inside a busy, packed nightclub, doing things that we definitely shouldn't be doing. I never thought I'd be the type of girl to get off on doing dirty, bad things in public places, but hell's bells, I'm apparently that girl with Jude.

He moves his hand down to my lower back as he switches his mouth to my other nipple, and in perfect sync, he sucks at the pliant flesh in rhythm with the way he grinds his still-covered cock against my bare pussy.

Every thrust forward, the tip of his cock strokes against that one perfect, swollen, needy spot that causes little shock waves of pleasure to build in my belly.

It feels incredible, and I'd do just about anything to be able to unzip his pants and slide him inside me, but his hold is steady and solid, and the only chance of orgasmic relief stems from the way his warm mouth sucks at the material of my dress around my nipples and each grinding thrust of his hips.

The me of a year ago never would have thought it'd be possible to actually get off, *all the way off the climax train,* with this kind of foreplay, but when the throb between my thighs begins to spread down my legs and up my spine and multiplies tenfold, the me of now remembers that it's different with this man—intense, unexplainable, mind-bending.

I'm so close that it only takes a few more strokes of his covered cock against me before the first waves of pleasure hit my nerves.

Holy shiiiiiit. I'm coming. I'm literally coming.

Shock and awe consume me at the same time that Jude pushes me over the edge, and just as the biggest wave takes over, he presses his lips to mine and swallows all the moans and whimpers that escape my throat.

I have zero control, and all I can do is just shut my eyes and let my orgasm devour me, all the while kissing Jude as if my life depends on it.

And I don't know how long it lasts or how long I stay like that, moaning and panting in his arms, but when I finally come down from my orgasmic high and open my eyes, I find Jude staring at me, his blue eyes still blazing.

"Fuck, you're beautiful when you come," he whispers, and his mouth is just a few inches from my parted lips. "I need to see you do that again, but this time, I need my cock inside you."

Oh boy.

"Ready to get out of here, Sophie?"

I only have one response to that.

"Yes."

TWENTY-FOUR

Jude

We could've walked the ten blocks to her place in Nolita, but the name of the game right now is *speed*.

The city lights flash past the taxi windows as our driver heads in the direction of Sophie's apartment. It's a little after one in the morning and I left the club about two hours earlier than I normally do on Friday nights, but it's all because of the little temptress sitting beside me.

That green dress of hers skates dangerously high up her thighs, and every time I glance in her direction to take in the beauty that is her gorgeous body or her mesmerizing eyes or soft, perfect, red-painted lips, I feel like my cock grows longer by an inch.

Frankly, I'm so turned on right now I can hardly stand it. Give me some wood and a couple nails, and my sidekick could hammer the damn things clean through.

Her gem-colored eyes meet mine in the back seat of the dimly lit cab, and I don't miss the way she bites down on her bottom lip.

Pointedly and without breaking eye contact, I reach up and rest my hand atop the right pocket of my suit pants, where Sophie's silky black panties sit inside. And she sees me do it because I *want* her to see me do it.

Her body's reaction doesn't disappoint. Her teeth dig farther into her bottom lip, and she shifts her hips and thighs ever-so-slightly in her seat.

Her pussy is bare, my mind taunts me. *Completely fucking bare. And wet. And just begging for your mouth.*

The more I think about that mind-blowing fact, the more I itch to cover her up with my suit jacket. There's no fucking way I want the cabbie to catch a glimpse of the gloriousness that sits between Sophie's perfect thighs.

And without hesitation, that's exactly what I do. Once my suit jacket covers her lap and legs to my liking, she looks up and meets my steady gaze with a curious crinkle lifting up her nose.

I lean closer to her and whisper directly into her ear, "There is no way I'm letting our cab driver see your gorgeous pussy. That view is mine and mine alone." In addition to any and all of my somewhat proprietary feelings, I also know that by taking her panties and keeping them for myself, I've put her in the position to be exposed without her consent in a situation like this. As such, it's my responsibility to ensure that doesn't happen.

A small, surprised, and sexy laugh escapes from her lungs, and somehow, my eyes home in on the way it makes her perky tits bounce beneath her dress.

Is there anything about this woman that doesn't turn me on?

The answer to that question is a resounding *no*. So resounding, in fact, that I can't stop myself from discreetly sliding my hand beneath my jacket and up the smooth skin of her bare thigh.

I should stop. I know I should stop, but my fingers have a mind of their own, and before I know it, they're skating across the spot where she's wet and warm and ready for me.

Fuck, she feels good.

Her lips part into the hottest little "O," and it only makes me more impatient to get this cab ride over with so I can do all of the dirty, delicious, wicked things that consume my mind.

Kissing her until she's moaning against my lips.

My mouth on her bare pussy.

My tongue inside her.

My cock inside her.

I want it all, and I want it right now.

Sophie's eyes flame with need, and she drives me wild by pushing her bare pussy against my hand, silently begging me to slide my fingers inside her.

I want to. I'm fucking desperate to. But I'll be damned if I'm going to share the orgasm *I've* earned with the cab driver. This is New York City. His fare is high enough.

"Please," she whispers toward me, her hips shifting in her seat again and her voice a compelling mix of needy and demanding, but I use all my will-power to toss a subtle shake of my head in her direction.

"Not yet," I tell her quietly. "Soon. But not yet."

A little pout turns down the corners of her mouth, and it's this crazy mix of adorable and sexy. And when those mesmerizing eyes of her turn big and pleading, I'm so close to giving in to her demands, so close to sliding my fingers inside her and showing her what my cock will be doing the in-stant we get inside her apartment.

Luckily, though, not even ten seconds later, the cab driver comes to a stop in front of her building.

There's a small part of me that feels like shouting *Hallelujah!*, but the larger part of me, the one that's entirely focused on getting Sophie inside her apartment as quickly as physically possible, takes full control of the situa-tion and has me tossing a fifty-dollar bill over the seat.

It's about double the actual fare, but I've never cared about anything less.

"Keep it," I call toward the cabbie as I hop out of the back seat when he shakes the extra money at me. And with a little jog around the back of the taxi, I make it to Sophie's door in record time.

I help her out with a gentlemanly hand, toss my suit jacket over my shoulder, and all but drag her toward the entrance of her building.

"Slow down, please!" She giggles. "I'm in heels!"

Impatient with her shoes, I come to a dead stop just outside her building, lean down, and toss her over my shoulder, all the while making sure her ass and bare-and-glorious pussy remain covered by the suit jacket that was formerly over my shoulder.

Sophie squeals but, thankfully, understands where my head is at. And it takes hardly any time for her to get her keys out of her small purse and start shouting important instructions over her shoulder.

"Use the small silver key for the main door and the larger gold key for my apartment door!"

I smirk. "Got it." The truth is, I watched her closely enough the last time we came barreling in here, hot for each other, that I already know what to do.

Once we're in the lobby area, I head toward the elevator, and just before I hit the call button, she updates me, "It's broken."

"What? The elevator is broken?"

"Yeah."

I spin on my heel, looking for an alternate option. "Where are the stairs?"

"At the end of the hallway over there," she says and starts to make a move to get off my shoulder, but I keep her body firmly in place with two strong hands. "Jude! Let me down! There's no way you can carry me five flights!"

"The fuck I can't."

And I do. Up five flights, I jog the whole way, silently thankful for the daily, hard-as-fuck gym workouts I've been doing with Flynn for the past few years.

Sophie giggles in disbelief the entire way up, but when I manage to unlock her apartment door and set her to her feet, those giggles of hers change to moans.

All thanks to the fact that my lips are on hers, kissing the hell out of her.

My suit jacket and her purse hit the hardwood floor of her still-dark apartment just as I kick the door shut with my foot. And in no time at all, I have her back pressed against the wall, and her hands are in my hair.

Fuck, she tastes good, and the sheer idea that her red lipstick is now smeared all over my face turns me the hell on. It also makes me desperate to kiss her somewhere else.

So, I do exactly what Jude Winslow does when he wants something—*I fucking go for it.*

To my knees, I kneel down in front of her, and she stares at me with wide, shocked eyes.

"W-what are you doing?"

"Kissing you." I grin as I lift one of her thighs over my shoulder. The change in position is downright delectable, giving me a delicious view of her bare pussy.

I lick my lips and slide her dress all the way up and over her ass until she's completely nude from the waist down. "Now that's a fucking view if I ever saw one."

Between one breath and the next, my mouth is on her. And the instant my tongue sneaks out to flick against her clit, Sophie's fingers are in my hair, tugging tightly at the strands as her hips jolt forward to push her pussy harder against my face.

Yes please, baby.

She is a delicacy against my lips, and when I slide my tongue inside her, she clenches around me in the sexiest way that makes my cock stir beneath my zipper.

Fuck. I need to be inside her.

Soon. Not yet. But soon.

I suck and eat at her needy flesh, and every time another moan spills from her lips, I look up and am blessed with the sight of her exquisite tits bouncing with each panting breath that glides from her lungs.

And when her skin starts to flush red, showing me she's close, I stop and rise to my feet.

Sophie looks at me with dazed, disappointed eyes, but I know that in about two seconds, she'll understand why I had to press pause on her pleasure.

Pants unzipped and condom out of my back pocket, I pull my hard cock from my boxer briefs and slide the rubber down my length.

But I don't take off my pants or shoes. *Fuck no.* I don't have the patience or time to waste.

I need to be inside her. *Now.*

Sophie back in my arms and her legs spread around my hips, I push myself inside her entrance, and once I'm seated to the hilt, I have to clench my jaw because of how intense it feels to have her wrapped around me.

Tight. Wet. Warm. *Fucking heaven.* Just like the first two nights.

In that moment, I'm certain I could fuck Sophie Sage a million times and never have enough.

It's also the reason this won't be the only time I'm inside her tonight or anytime soon. She's greedy and needy, and fucking her fills me with a satisfaction no amount of sleep ever could.

"First, I'm going to fuck you right here," I whisper against her lips as I thrust deeper inside her. "And then, once you come on my cock, I'm going to take you right over there to the couch and make you come again."

Sophie moans.

"Tonight, I'm going to make you come on as many goddamn surfaces of your apartment as I can."

"Yes, please," she whispers just before her mouth sucks at the skin of my neck.

Man oh man, I was definitely right when I said tonight was going to be a good night…

One for the damn record books.

TWENTY-FIVE

Saturday, March 17th

Sophie

A rush of cold air jolts me out of unconsciousness, and I open my eyes to find what I think is a blurry vision of my sister standing above me.

What the heck is happening?

"Holy boobs and beaver, you're naked!" Belle shouts so loud that I jerk to a sitting position, all haziness of sleep gone, and grab at the comforter to pull it up to my chest. "Sophie, you sleep in the freaking buff?!"

"What?" I question, blinking several times to clear the jumbled hysteria from my mind. Eventually, the situation becomes evident. I'm in my own bed and, yes, I *am* naked. I'm also, other than my obnoxiously loud sister, very much *alone*.

Which is not how I entered this bed last night.

Club Craze. Jude. Private VIP room. Taxi ride. My place.

Jude naked.

Me naked.

Hot sex. All over my apartment.

"I didn't know you slept in the damn nude!" Belle keeps shouting, but this time, her words are followed by the kind of cackles that feel like a cheese grater to my nerves.

"Belle, for the love of God, stop yelling." I groan and grip the comforter tighter around my chest. I didn't drink that much last night, but I *feel* hungover. My limbs are heavy, my energy spent, and the sound of Belle's yelling feels like an ice pick to my brain. Add in the fact that I need two to four hours with a cold compress between my legs, and it's no wonder I'm not feeling particularly ready for my sister's company.

My twin laughs like a hyena, and I rub at my eyes with my free hand to try to make sense of the world around me.

I widen my eyes and scout the room for signs of my late-night guest. The spot on the floor where I know we shed our clothing is empty and cleared, Jude's attire gone like it never existed. My dress, however, is folded nicely on my chaise lounger on the opposite end of the room.

Did he seriously fold my laundry before he left?

That's kind of sweet. And a bit odd, considering it seems like he left my apartment again like a bandit in the night.

But did he really leave? Or is he still here somewhere? Even if I'm ninety-nine percent sure he's long gone, a one percent chance of him popping out from my bathroom with a top hat on his dick while my sister watches is still a little disconcerting.

It's not like I can ask her if she's seen him, though, so the only thing I can do is assume he's MIA.

"What time is it?"

"Eleven," she answers and plops down on the bed beside me.

I shut my eyes briefly and put a hand to my forehead.

Shit. I slept in that late? That's so unlike me.

And it's all thanks to the good-dicking from Mr. Sexy Good Time.

"Where were you last night?" Belle asks, and I look over to meet her probing eyes. "I texted you five million times for shit's sake, and when I woke up this morning, I got worried that you, like, died or something and I was going to have to call the cops." She lies back on my mattress, crosses her boot-covered feet, and stares up at the ceiling. "So, I made John stop here on the way to brunch so your dead body wouldn't start stinking up your apartment."

"How kind of you," I respond and reach out toward my nightstand to grab my phone. "As you can see, there's no need to contact the authorities to remove my rotting carcass. I'm still alive and kicking."

She nods, and her eyes light up with amusement. "Great news."

I glance at the screen of my phone and find so many notifications that I have to scroll down to see them all.

Most are text messages from Belle that revolve around asking where I am, mingled in with social media notifications. There's one text from Julie about getting confirmation on the last-minute menu change for the Babkus wedding tonight.

But there's one notification that stands out the most. A text message from Jude. Evidently, he did *something* before sneaking out this time, by getting my phone number out of my phone so he'd be able to send me this message since I never actually texted him.

That's one tick in the win column for my inability to remember a damn passcode. Sure, I'm at severe risk of getting all of my personal information stolen by a stranger or hacker, but at least Jude was able to procure my digits.

Immediately, I tap on the screen to open it up.

Jude: Monday, 8 pm. The Champagne Bar, Plaza Hotel. Wear another sexy little dress.

That's all it says.

Nothing about last night. Nothing about when he actually left my apartment. Just the promise of more fun to come if I choose to follow his instructions. It's all a bit overwhelming, and I have no idea what I want to do, but my sister doesn't give time to ponder on it.

"What the hell were you up to last night, Soph?" Belle asks again, and I try my best to redirect the conversation toward something that doesn't make my head want to spin.

"Nothing really," I answer. "But do you mind getting out of my bedroom so I can get dressed?"

"Only if you're getting dressed to go to brunch with John and me."

I quirk a brow.

"Oh, c'mon, Soph," she whines and stands up from my bed. "It's the least you can do for making me think you'd gone missing."

"Stop being so dramatic." I roll my eyes and shake my head, but my sister is determined.

"Put on some clothes, you little nudist, so John can buy us some fucking French toast."

I laugh at *The 40-Year-Old Virgin* movie reference. But also, I agree because…French toast. I'm a sucker for all things delicious breakfast foods.

Plus, after the erotic events of last night and Jude not leaving any trace of his presence in my apartment besides a text message with instructions for a future clandestine rendezvous, I'm pretty sure I could use the mental distraction that my sister and brother-in-law can provide this morning.

Amelia's Diner is always moving and shaking during Saturday brunch hours, but since Belle and I have been regulars for the past five years, Danielle, the hostess with the mostest and a good friend, managed to sneak us in past the waiting crowd and seat us in a booth near the kitchen.

It's also how we managed to get our food within fifteen minutes of arriving. Otherwise, we'd still be sitting outside with the rest of the crowd, waiting to be seated at a table.

In New York, it always pays to know someone.

I cut into my last piece of French toast, but when I shove another bite into my mouth, I realize it's going to be a no-go on finishing my plate.

"I'm stuffed," I mutter, set my fork down on the table, and lean back against the cushioned booth on a sigh. "I want to eat more, but I can't."

"I feel like a bloated whale," Belle announces just as she shoves the last two bites of her French toast into her mouth.

John smiles lovingly at her from across the table. "Am I going to have to carry you out of this place, sweetheart?"

Belle grins around a mouthful of sugary carbs and shrugs. "It's either that or ask Danielle if they have a wheelchair we can borrow."

"I'm just glad you didn't go nuts and order the waffle sundae like you did that one time," I tease, and an amused laugh departs from John's lungs.

"On that, we can agree, Soph."

"It wasn't that bad," my sister retorts, and both John and I give her a look.

"Wasn't that bad?" I question. "Belle, you ate an entire Belgian waffle covered in ice cream, chocolate syrup, and whipped cream in five minutes flat."

"I was hungry."

"You were nauseous for the rest of the damn day and spent a good two hours on the toilet," John comments, and Belle snorts.

"It's because I ate it all too fast. I just need to go slower next time."

"Or you need to realize that you're not a teenage boy who can eat anything in sight. You're an almost thirty-year-old woman with a history of IBS."

"I'm twenty-eight," she corrects what I already know. I mean, we are fucking identical twins. "And that waffle sundae definitely gave my intestinal tract a run for its money."

"Pretty sure that waffle sundae is a GI death sentence for anyone who orders it," my brother-in-law adds, and I laugh.

"You're spitting facts, John."

"Whatever," Belle retorts and takes a sip of her coffee. "One day soon, I'm going to woman-the-hell-up and order it again. Because that shit is delicious."

"Remind me not to join you guys for brunch that day."

John grins across the table at his wife. "Yeah, and give me some advanced notice so I can make sure I load you up with Gas-X and Pepcid."

Belle crinkles her nose at us. "You guys are so lame."

"If we're lame, then you're downright cuckoo. Especially when it comes to breakfast foods."

My sister has a serious addiction to baking and eating anything carb- and sugar-loaded. Her eyes are bigger than her stomach, but she never actually listens to her stomach. Instead, she scarfs that shit down until she practically has to put herself on bed rest to recover. To be honest, she's damn lucky her genetics have blessed her with a freak-of-nature metabolism.

Belle just grins and tosses her napkin onto the table. "Now, if you'll excuse me, I'm going to head to the ladies' room. But don't worry, you guys. It's just to pee. Not to shit myself silly."

John shakes his head on a laugh. "Sometimes, Belly, you are so sexy I can hardly stand it."

"You love me," she retorts and blows a little kiss in his direction.

The responding smile that consumes his face pulls at my heartstrings.

"That I do. *Madly.*" He slides out of the booth, places a sweet kiss to Belle's lips, and snags the check off the table. "I'll go cash us out."

My heart aches a little at the whole scene. The loving relationship that John and Belle have is exactly what I hope to have one day. It's what I've become obsessed about having for what feels like an eternity. But it's also what I need to *stop* fixating on.

Belle didn't find John because she was a neurotic lunatic with a mile-long checklist of expectations. She found him because she was open to dating and giving men an actual chance. She found John because she was letting herself live in the moment and have fun. Not because she was writing off every man from the start without even getting to know them.

And Katelynn was the same way with her husband Todd.

Both of my sisters found love when they weren't even really looking for love. They were just open to the idea of it, not on some CIA-style search that always led them to a dead end and a lonely Friday night.

You could probably learn something from them…

I sigh, and while Belle and John are away from the table, I busy myself by pulling my cell out of my purse and looking at my missed messages again.

The first thing I do is send Julie a quick text back.

Me: Great news about the caterer. Glad that pulled through so we didn't have to ruin the bride's wedding by serving the guests McDonald's chicken nuggets. LOL. Meet me at the venue at 5pm tonight.

Once I hit send, my finger hovers over the one text exchange in my inbox that's been on my mind since the moment I saw it this morning.

Yes or no?

Do I go to The Champagne Bar, or am I asking for trouble by messing around with a guy like Jude?

He's not a commitment kind of guy, so I know what I'm getting myself into. Last night, I knew. And yet, I'm still here, questioning it all over again.

I reread his message.

Monday, 8 pm. The Champagne Bar, Plaza Hotel. Wear another sexy little dress.

So… which is it? More Jude-flavored fun on Monday night or the stability of the predictable?

I don't even have to think about it.

Me: Okay.

And then I lock the screen of my phone and shove it back into my purse before I can give myself time to second-guess.

But my phone vibrates in my purse, and I can't resist the urge to check it.

Jude: I still have your panties. And I'm keeping them, by the way.

A thrill of excitement creates a path of goose bumps up my arms. And his hot and dirty words are all the confirmation I need to stay resolute in my decision.

Sophie 2.0 isn't going to obsess over the future. She's only going to enjoy the present, and she's definitely going to be at The Champagne Bar on Monday night.

If there's one man who makes the present the most fun this girl has ever had, it's Jude.

TWENTY-SIX

Jude

A little before eight in the evening, I walk down the marble staircase that leads into The Champagne Bar. The room is calm and quiet, and besides the chatter from the Monday night regulars and occasional wealthy guests blowing through town for the evening, only the soft cadence of classical music can be heard in the background.

I make a mental note that the massive space is only half filled and grin to myself. *Oh yeah, the atmosphere is ripe with the slow and anticipatory vibe I wanted when I told Sophie to meet me here.*

This bar isn't my usual place, but more of an occasional, every-great-once-in-a-while place that is a well-known and iconic New York spot inside the Plaza Hotel. Anyone who is anyone in this city has been inside these walls and experienced the sophisticated ambiance that is floor-to-ceiling windows highlighted by thick, luxurious curtains and large crystal chandeliers providing the right amount of lighting to keep guests feeling cozy without understanding why.

It's also the perfect place to show Sophie how good being bad can feel.

I sit down at the mostly empty bar and pull my phone out of my suit pocket, setting it on the marble surface in front of me.

"Can I get you anything to drink?" the bartender asks, and I offer a small smile.

"A scotch on the rocks. Thanks."

He makes quick work of my drink, and once he sets it down in front of me, the bartender moves on to a new customer who just found a seat at the far end.

After a quick sip of chilled scotch, I grab my cell to check emails and to make sure I didn't miss any text messages. Inside my inbox sits confirmation from my assistant Macy regarding a consulting gig in Las Vegas for a nightclub called Electric. It hasn't opened yet, but it will be nestled inside a popular casino on the Strip, and the investors are hoping to have their first soft opening eight months from now.

A lofty fucking goal, but not unachievable.

And this kind of project, where I'm simply consulting, isn't as hands-on as what I've been doing at Club Craze. Instead of being there in person and juggling all the things, I'm the go-to guy when it comes to creating the plan of how to properly kick off and promote their nightclub. If I agree to work with them, they'll tell me their strategy and I'll tell them what they're doing right, wrong, and give them fresh ideas to add an edge to their launch.

Basically, they'd be paying me to optimize their blueprints and give them my expert advice on everything from staff, setup, music, drinks, food menus, security, marketing, advertising, and the like.

To be honest, it's a fairly cushy gig that always pays really well.

I quickly scan the email for all the pertinent details.

Yo Boss,

Everything is set for this week. There'll be a private plane for you at Teterboro, and it's scheduled to leave at midnight on Wednesday. A penthouse suite will accommodate your stay in Vegas, and because Billy and the rest of the investors are thankful for your last-minute

trip (aka doing everything in their power to kiss your ass so you agree to help them), they've added a few extra goodies to show their thanks.

One goodie I'm certain you're going to love includes $20,000 in casino credit to satisfy your ongoing gambling addiction.

I pause and laugh to myself when I read her last comment.

Pretty sure it's not considered gambling when I only take bets I'm sure of, Mace.

Macy has been my assistant for the past five years, the woman behind the scenes who keeps my schedule in order and ensures everyone who is supposed to get paid or is supposed to pay does exactly that, and her use of sarcasm knows no bounds. Honestly, it's one of the things that made me hire her in the first place, and at this point, I'd be disappointed if she sent an email without some kind of sarcastic jab.

She keeps shit entertaining, and it's a well-known fact that I like to be entertained.

The email goes on to mention several other comps the investors are sending my way, including the fact that if I want to bring a few guests out for my stay, they'd be happy to accommodate.

And Macy doesn't hesitate to add her teasing two cents to that update.

I'd like to take this time to remind you that it's not a good idea for you to bring a plane full of women to Vegas. Pretty sure we both know how that ends. And it's not good. It's actually a huge pain in my ass trying to fly rando women back to New York on commercial flights.

In my defense, I've only done that once. Over four years ago. And it was enough of a clusterfuck that I vowed to never do shit like that again.

I might be a noncommitment kind of guy, but these days, I prefer one woman at a time, thank you very much. Threesomes and crazy shit like that are only fun when you're dumb and in your twenties. Once you hit your thirties, you realize they're more of a hassle—*and a fucking mess*—than anything else.

Also, I can't deny *this email* shows the glory in doing what I do. Most jobs don't include free casino credit to play blackjack and craps and generous offers of accommodating extra guests.

I quickly shoot Macy a short response—*letting her know she's a smartass and I saw her email*—and then I move on to my text messages, where I find a bunch of random chatter from my brothers in our ongoing group chat.

Before I read whatever bullshit they're spinning this evening, I steal a quick glance toward the staircase. I have no idea if Sophie Sage is going to follow through with her **Okay** to meet me here, but I guess I'll find out soon enough.

Truthfully, she's a bit of a conundrum.

I can tell she's the type of woman who prefers a plan, a well-thought-out scenario. She wants to know what she's getting herself into before she agrees. And she wants to feel secure in knowing what to expect.

But she's also someone who can thrive in spontaneous situations. Hell, more than that, she fucking blossoms. She can be impulsive and spur-of-the-moment and even find immense pleasure from those things, but it's a matter of if she'll let herself give in to it.

If I'm being honest, I normally wouldn't bother trying with a woman like her. In the past, I'd consider her hesitancy far too much work for a guy like me, but there's just something about Sophie that makes me want to spend more time with her.

Have a lot of fucking fun with her.

Do all sorts of dirty, sexy shit with her.

She's the ultimate challenge—the one woman who wants to experience all the fun I can give but struggles with giving in to that desire.

Man, it'd be a trip to bring her out to Vegas and show her the kind of fun the City of Sin can provide…

The fact that I even have the silly thought to invite her on a work trip makes me shake my head. I'm fucking drugged on her pussy, obviously.

I resign myself to kicking back at the bar and relaxing until she arrives, and with my eyes back to my cell, I check out what my brothers have to say.

Ty: Anyone want to hit a party in the Village with me?

Flynn: Nope.

Ty: You still in Montana?

Flynn: Nope. Just don't want to go hang out at some hipster party in Greenwich with you.

Ty: It's not a hipster party, you jackass.

Flynn: Who told you about the party?

Ty: Kip Morlein.

I laugh to myself, already knowing what Flynn's reaction will be. Ty somehow manages to have the most eclectic groups of friends, and Kip Morlein is a perfect example of that. The man runs an art gallery in Bushwick and is weird as fuck. Super nice, but a total fucking weirdo.

Flynn: LOL. Now, I'm definitely not going. The last time I went to a party that Kip Morlein told you about, they were serving organic wine, and everyone was wearing white dresses like it was some kind of cult.

Ty: You're fucking dramatic, dude. It wasn't that bad. And they weren't dresses, they were togas because it was a theme party.

Flynn: You know, that distinction doesn't make it sound better.

Ty: The chick he was dating at the time was into all the vegan shit, and the togas made it easier to ensure no one was wearing, like, fur or something.

Remy: How's that shovel feeling in your hands, bud? Is it heavy? Do you want to stop digging for a while?

Flynn: Haha

Remy: You need to take a page from Flynn's book and start hanging out with his MC buddies.

Ty: Stop acting like Flynn is hanging out with badass biker dudes on the regular. He spends his time with us, not the Sons of Anarchy.

I can't stop myself from jumping on the Ty-razzing bandwagon. When you're the youngest brother out of four, you learn quickly to take every opportunity to join in when you're not the butt of the joke.

Jude: $100 bucks says Flynn's MC could take on Ty's artsy, vegan friends.

Ty: Kip isn't an artsy vegan, you dick.

Remy: What's Kip do for a living again, Ty?

I grin, knowing full well where this is headed.

Ty: Shut the fuck up.

A quiet chuckle slides from my lungs, and I fire off another message.

Me: Pretty sure what Ty means by "Shut the fuck up" is that Kip runs an art gallery in Bushwick. Thereby, making ole Kip very much artsy. And, well, the vegan thing we've already established.

Ty: Sometimes, I really hate you guys.

Remy: Aw, you don't hate us, Ty. You love us. And you know what? We accept you for your artsy, vegan lifestyle.

Flynn: 100% acceptance, my man. Tomorrow you could tell me you're a fruitarian who prefers wearing togas and Crocs, and you know what? You'll have my full support, bud.

My phone buzzes in my hand with another message, most likely from Ty calling us assholes, but my attention is completely pulled away when I glance toward the staircase again and spot a fucking vision of beauty. She's in another dress, but it's not green like last time. It's this mesmerizing shade of gold that shimmers and shines beneath the soft lights as she gracefully moves down the stairs.

She followed my instructions.

A rush of exhilaration dumps into my veins.

Fuck yes. This is going to be a fantastic night.

I put my cell in my pocket, slide off my barstool, and stand to my feet.

Sophie is still looking around the room, trying to scout out a familiar face, and I'm looking at her. Her dark hair falls in waves down her shoulders, and her tight little body looks like a fucking dream in her shimmery dress and rose-gold stilettos.

Damn. This woman never disappoints.

Honestly, I couldn't pull my eyes away from her if I tried.

In three long strides, I cut the distance between us, and that's when she spots me. Her stunning green eyes flash with recognition, and one corner of my mouth quirks up into a grin.

"You made it," I say, coming to a stop right in front of her at the bottom of the staircase.

"I did."

"Color me pleasantly surprised."

She tilts her head to the side, and her long dark hair falls across one shoulder. "You thought I was going to stand you up?"

"I wasn't sure." I hold out a hand toward her, and when Sophie places her hand in mine, the warmth of her small fingers resonates against my skin. With a gentle tug, I pull her toward me, wrap one arm around her waist, and press a kiss to the spot just below her ear. "But I'm real fucking glad you came."

She leans back and meets my eyes, and I don't miss the way her long dark lashes fan across her cheeks with each blink.

"How about a drink?"

"Okay." She licks her lips, and it takes everything inside me not to drag her out of this bar and back to her place.

But instead, I remind myself of *the plan*. A genius fucking plan that revolves around teasing and anticipation that leads to hot, illicit sex where I get to enjoy watching the enthralling view that is Sophie coming on my cock again.

With a gentle hand to her lower back, I lead her toward the bar and help her onto one of the stools before sitting down beside her.

"What do you want to drink tonight?"

She opens her mouth to answer but wavers for a moment before finally saying, "Surprise me."

I grin. *Oh yes, sweet Sophie, I can promise you that tonight will be full of surprises.*

A few minutes later, the bartender slides two drinks across the bar. A fresh scotch on the rocks for me and a drink that serves an exact purpose for Sophie.

"An old-fashioned?" she questions as she stares down at the glass of amber liquid.

"For memories," I tell her and take a sip from my rocks glass. "A reminder of the Raines Law Room."

"Hmm. Memories, huh?" she asks through a little giggle. "Kind of like how I'm still missing my favorite pair of black silk panties?"

"Exactly like your missing panties. Only, this time, *you* get to keep the drink."

She quirks one curious brow in my direction. "But you're still keeping my panties?"

"Uh-huh."

"Is that something you do often, Jude? Collect women's underwear?"

"Actually, no." An amused laugh jumps from my lungs. "You're the first."

"The first of your collection?"

"Babe, it's not a collection if there's only one pair in it." I flash a wink in her direction. "Though, I may add another pair tonight."

She takes a long sip of her old-fashioned before turning in her seat and crossing her legs to face me. Her mouth quirks up in a mischievous smile as she leans closer to whisper, "What if I told you I'm not wearing anything under my dress right now?"

My gaze can't stop itself from glancing down at the apex of her thighs, and my mind flirts with the reality that beneath the gold material lies her perfect pussy. *But…is it magnificently bare?*

I lick my lips. "Then I'd tell you to lean back and close your eyes because I'm about to lick your sweet cunt in front of a whole lot of people."

When I finally lift my eyes back up and onto her face, she's grinning like a little minx, her cheeks crimson with embarrassment. Whether it's at the threatened gesture or my use of the c-word, I don't know, but either way, it looks really sexy on her.

"Wow, okay. Well, don't get too amped because I'm not going commando tonight."

"So, there's another pair of sexy panties beneath that dress?"

She nods.

A soft chuckle slips from my lungs, but also, outright satisfaction makes my mouth lift at the corners. "Good."

"Good?" she asks. "Why is that good?"

"Because I want to add to my collection."

She snorts. "You're kind of a pervert, Jude. You know that?"

"What can I say?" I shrug one shoulder and lift my glass in the air. "You bring out the best in me, Sophie."

"God, you're incorrigible." Her amused laughter is music to my ears, but when she lifts her glass to take another sip from her drink, my gaze homes in on her mouth. Her throat vibrates in the subtlest way as she swallows it down, and once she's done, she licks a few drops from her lips and carefully sets the glass back down on the bar.

Fuck, the things I'd love to see that mouth of hers do.

But not right now. *Not yet.* Tonight's game is focused on *prolonging* the anticipation.

So, instead, I purposefully place my hand on the bare skin of her thigh and squeeze tenderly.

Her eyes flash back to me, the depths of green curious and hopeful that my touch will lead to something, but I school my face into neutrality and pull my hand away to grab my drink off the bar and take a hearty pull of scotch.

Though, once my glass is back down on the marble, I reach out and lightly brush my fingers across her bare shoulder and slide a few rogue pieces of her hair behind her ear.

"You look stunning," I tell her and move that pesky hand of mine back to her thigh. Though, this time, I just let my fingertips linger over the skin in a soft, delicate motion. Just enough to make her think about my touch, but not enough to give her any sort of satisfaction.

"T-thank you," she whispers back, and I don't miss the way her hips shift and fidget a little in her seat. By sexualizing things right out of the gate, I've got her right where I want her. Desperate and anticipatory, she doesn't know when I'm going to touch her or how, and for the sake of her future orgasm, I'm going to do my best to keep it that way.

"So, tell me, how was your day?"

Her eyes search mine. "My...*day?*"

"Yeah, how was it?" I move my hand higher and higher up her thigh. "Good, I hope?" I add when my fingers skirt along the hem of her dress.

"Uh-huh…" She pauses, swallows, and her gaze dips down to where my hand meets her skin.

"That's great to hear. I take it the event planning business is still booming?" I question, using small talk as a means to keep her wondering what in the fuck is happening.

"Um…*what?*" she blinks and looks up to meet my eyes, and I have to fight back the urge to smile.

"The event planning business? It's still booming?"

"Oh…uh…yeah…I guess you could say that." She shrugs, and her ability to concentrate almost comes back at full force.

That is, *until* I slip my fingertips beneath the hem of her dress. But my hand is still only on her upper thigh. And still too far from where she's most likely awaiting my next move with a wet and wanting little pussy.

Her gaze is back to where my hand meets her thigh, and I have to bite down on my bottom lip to stop a satisfied smile from consuming my mouth.

Oh yes, sweet Sophie. We are about to have some fun.

No doubt, when I do give in to the nearly irresistible urge to make her feel good, Sophie Sage will be dripping wet for me.

"How about some dinner, babe?"

"*Dinner?*" She furrows her brow "As in eating actual food?"

"Of course. Aren't you hungry?"

"Uh…yeah…right. Food. Let's eat some food," she answers, and she has to clear what sounds like disappointment out of her voice.

I fucking love it.

Sure, disappointing her, of all people, isn't my priority. But in order to give her the most intense pleasure possible, this state of confusion she's currently experiencing needs to occur.

It's a means to one hell of an orgasmic end.

I stand up from my barstool, pull my wallet out of my back pocket, and slide a hundred-dollar bill onto the bar to cover our tab. "Come on. I made a special reservation for us at The Palm Court."

Last-minute reservations at The Palm Court are hard to come by, especially when you're requesting for the chef to make the full Plaza Hotel in-room dining menu available to you, instead of the restaurant's standard appetizers and small bites with afternoon tea or evening cocktails.

But my career has blessed me with lots of friends in high places.

"That sounds…great," she answers like she's not sure if she actually believes her words.

But *I* know it's great.

In fact, it's about to be *mind-blowingly great.*

TWENTY-SEVEN

Sophie

Jude has pulled out all the swanky stops tonight. From the posh drinks at The Champagne Bar to the very special, VIP-esque reservation at The Palm Court, he's spared no expense in providing me with the kind of evening a lot of women would fantasize about.

You'd almost believe that this is, like, a date or something.

But…I know better than to misplace that kind of expectation on it for the sake of my comfort. The truth is, Jude's a nice guy with nice tendencies. Just because we're strictly messing around doesn't mean he has to treat me like dirt. No, he's making it pretty clear tonight—it's entirely possible to fuck around and eat at the same time. And *holy hell on a hot fudge sex sundae,* I'm pretty sure I've *never* been this horny and turned on while eating filet mignon.

Honestly, the state of my arousal feels like it should be a sin, given the situation. I mean, this restaurant is about as fancy and upscale as you can get, and I'm just sitting here with wet panties and a persistent, throbbing ache between my thighs that makes me feel like I'm inadvertently scandalizing the waiter every time he stops by our table to make sure we're enjoying our meal.

It's insane. I *feel* insane.

But Jude appears completely unfazed.

I watch as he takes a bite of his steak, and I hate how my eyes fixate on his strong jaw and full lips with every chew. Or the way my gaze moves to the Adam's apple at his neck when he swallows.

Why am I so turned on, yet he's just sitting here, enjoying his meal like one of us isn't about to have a spontaneous orgasm in the middle of dinner?

And why in the hell does he have to look so damn good, too?

If there's one thing that's a certainty, it's that Jude Winslow can *wear* a suit. Black jacket, crisp white shirt, and black slacks, the man looks better than the filet mignon sitting before me. He isn't just a tasty snack; he's the whole damn meal. Six full courses, with the biggest, most delectable chocolate cake dessert at the end.

And I haven't even started on his eyes or the way the dimmish lighting of this sophisticated restaurant only adds to the allure of them.

They are these crystal-clear, blue-as-the-sky eyes that hold secret promises of sex and sin and the kind of delicious acts that you fantasize about but never say out loud because they're far too dirty.

But damn it all to hell, I'm starting to feel like I'm the only one who's sitting here thinking about hot sex and going crazy with anticipation.

He told me to meet him tonight. *In a dress.* Surely that was for a reason… *right?* Normally, wearing a sexy dress around Jude Winslow ends with happy endings of a climax variety.

And what about the drinks at the bar? *Good grief.* The way his hands kept lingering on my thighs and my shoulders and brushing my hair behind my ear… Why in the hell did he keep doing that? Was he trying to push me off the horny ledge?

Gah. I have to get it together.

I yank my eyes away from their current fascination with his mouth and stare down at my plate, but my attention is immediately pulled straight back to him when he asks, "How's the filet?"

"Um…" I look up and clear my throat to force the rasp of neediness out of my voice. "It's good. Very good, actually."

Jude's smile is relaxed and friendly. "Glad to hear it."

"Yep. Good. Very, very, *very* good."

Ugh. You're being weird. Stop being so weird.

I clear my throat again. "How's yours?"

"Delicious," he answers, and the way his voice is all deep and throaty makes me shift a little in my seat.

"Good. That's good."

Holy hell, can you say anything besides good?

Apparently, I can't because I am a ticking time bomb of horniness, and every second feels like I'm one persistent throb closer to bursting into flames. Or, worse, climbing over the table and straddling his lap and begging him to just fuck me right here in the middle of this fancy-schmancy restaurant.

Oh, for goodness' sake, you're losing it.

On a deep inhale, I shut my eyes briefly in an attempt to gain some control, but when Jude shifts his seat closer to mine and his warm hand reaches out to rest on my upper thigh, any chance of reining myself in goes *poof.*

His fingers skate along the edge of my dress again, just like when we were sitting at the bar, and my nipples take it upon themselves to harden and let me know they'd like some attention from him, too.

And when those fingers of his slide beneath the material of my dress and carefully make their way farther up my thigh, my breath gets tangled in my lungs.

Higher and higher and *higher* he goes.

It all feels painfully good, and in the spirit of keeping this moving in the right direction, I open my mouth to tell him just that, but our waiter chooses that exact time to step up to our table.

"How is everything?"

"Fantastic," Jude says, and the instant the last syllable of that word slips past his tongue, one finger slides beneath my panties and directly inside me.

Holy hell.

A rush of arousal consumes my nerves, and I clench around him.

The waiter nods and smiles at Jude before looking directly at my face, and I have to bite down on my bottom lip when that pesky finger slowly starts to move inside me.

In and out. *In and out.* Each time, he adds a little curl in the middle that has bull's-eye–like precision on a particular spot that pushes a pant of air out of my lungs.

"Did you enjoy the filet?"

When I realize our waiter is talking to me, waiting for me to respond, I nearly choke on the urge to moan and have to pretend to cough my way through it with my napkin held to my mouth.

Once I gain some semblance of control, I answer, "Mm-hmm." However, Jude chooses that exact moment to add the use of his skilled thumb into the mix and starts making smooth circles over my clit. *"Oh boy."*

"Excuse me?" the waiter questions with a quirk of his brow.

All the while, Jude's hand keeps treating me like its own personal jungle gym. Playing with me. *Toying* with me. Sliding me straight toward the climax cliff. It's wild. And forbidden. And the craziest thing I've ever done in my life.

Damn does it feel incredible.

But the waiter. The fucking waiter is still standing at our table, waiting for me to say something.

*"Holy moly…*it was…uh…so good. The best feeling…I mean, *meal*, yeah, the best meal I've ever had. Thank you, Jesus, Mary, and Joseph and all the saints!"

"Uh…okay… I'm glad you enjoyed it." The waiter's smile is uncomfortable, and I start to worry he's a little too keen on my current state of perpetual orgasm doom. Thankfully, he moves his eyes back to Jude. You know, the one person at the table who isn't acting like a lunatic. "Have the two of you saved some room for dessert?"

If the dessert is anything but an orgasm, I don't want it.

"I'm sorry, what was that?"

When I realize I'm not keeping my thoughts to myself, my eyes go wide in embarrassment, and Jude smirks at me like the fucking devil from across the table.

But. He. Never. Stops. Sliding. His. Finger. In. And. Out. Of. Me.

The waiter regards me with confused eyes, most likely waiting for an explanation for the odd things coming out of my mouth, but I'm all tapped out on words. I can't focus on anything but what Jude's fingers are doing to me.

"We're actually planning on getting dessert somewhere else tonight," Jude comments, and the waiter simply nods.

"Oh, okay. Can I get you two anything else, then? An after-dinner coffee? Or a cocktail, maybe?"

Jude shakes his head. "Just the check would be nice. Thank you."

The waiter clears a few of our plates from the table before heading in the opposite direction, and once he is completely out of earshot, Jude meets my unsteady, most likely glazed-over gaze. "You need to come, don't you?"

"Badly."

"Can you wait until we make it back to your place, or do you need relief right now?"

Make it back to my place? That's like…whatever exploding-vagina plus apocalyptic-dread plus spontaneous-combustion equals, and it's that far away. Which, in normal, not-about-to-burst-from-sexual-frustration terms means *very fucking far.*

Clearly, my answer is simple. *"Now."*

Immediately, he pulls his hand away from me and smirks. "Hold that thought for five minutes."

"F-five minutes?" I question, and the outright disappointment is embarrassingly evident in my voice.

I mean, *five minutes?* That might as well be an eternity.

But Jude just leans forward and whispers into my ear, "Just five minutes, Soph. And then I'm going to make you come so hard you'll feel it in your toes."

I swallow down the urge to blurt out something crazy like, *"Just bang me right here!"* and try my best to keep control of my body for the next four minutes and forty-five seconds.

I know this because I'm now counting in my head. And each second that ticks by makes me certain that once these five minutes are up, I can't be held liable for what I do or say.

⌒

Thirty-three.

Thirty-two.

Thirty-one.

"How much time do I have left?" Jude asks, his hand gripped tightly around mine as he leads us out of the restaurant and into one of the mostly empty hallways of the lavish hotel.

"*Huh?*"

"How many seconds, Sophie?" He smirks down at me, and I try to play it cool like I haven't been counting since the moment he set the deadline at five minutes.

Twenty-nine.

Twenty-eight.

Twenty-seven.

"Uh…I don't know. How would I possibly know that?"

"Because I've been watching your mouth move with each second that passes by."

Well, *shoot.*

"How many?" he repeats, and his blue eyes call my bluff so hard that I answer with the cold, hard facts.

"Nineteen."

"Looks like we're going to have to take a detour, huh?" He winks in my direction, and before I know it, he's pulling us into one of the bathrooms of the freaking Plaza Hotel.

"W-what are you doing?"

"Keeping my word," he says and shuts the door behind us.

"What if someone comes in here?"

"I guess we're just going to have to take our chances."

My jaw practically hits the tops of my stilettos. "Jude! You can't be serious!"

"And there's also a lock on the door that I might've just utilized." He grins and stalks toward me like a big, sexy lion ready to consume his prey. The instant he reaches me, he kneels down, yanks up my dress, and grips my ass with his strong hands just as he buries his face against my panties.

On a deep inhale, he looks up at me with hooded eyes. "You always smell so fucking sweet when you're wet like this."

I whimper.

"Can I make you come?"

"Should that even be a question right now?"

His eyes are amused at my sassiness. "You've been waiting for this for a while, huh?" he questions, and his wicked fingers slide my panties down my thighs. "Ever since I told you to wear a dress, I bet you've been thinking about my tongue right here." He pats two fingers on my clit, making my back bow dramatically.

I swallow. Nod. And suck both of my lips into my mouth.

With purpose, he shoves my nude silk panties into his pocket and shoots a little waggle of his brow in my direction. "For the collection," he comments, and I'm not sure if it makes me a total pervert to be aroused that Jude Winslow keeps stealing my underwear, but *man oh man*, it's one heck of a turn-on.

"You know, Sophie," he says, staring directly at my pussy. "I've been thinking about the same thing." He floats his lips across my bare skin, dangerously close to the one spot that's become so needy for his touch, I feel as if I could burst into flames. "Thinking about putting my mouth on you. Right *here*. On this very spot. I've been dying to taste you again," he whispers just before he gently licks his tongue across my swollen clit.

My hips jolt forward at the unexpected but intense sensation.

Slowly, he slides his index finger up my inner thigh and doesn't stop until that finger is inside me. He moves it in and out in the most delicious rhythm, and I moan.

"And right here," he whispers, and he licks his tongue across my entrance. "I've been dreaming of burying my cock here ever since I left your apartment the other morning. Hell, I almost woke you up just so I could feel this perfect cunt of yours wrapped around me again."

"You should have," I say, and my voice is so breathy that it hardly makes any sound at all.

"Next time, I probably will."

"And what about right now?"

He grins up at me. "Right now, I'm going to make you come. Once on my tongue and then again on my cock. And babe, let me tell you—that second orgasm, it's going to wring you fucking dry."

Yes, please.

His finger keeps sliding in and out of me, and with each stroke, I can feel how insanely wet I am. But just when I think he's finally going to put his mouth on me, he pauses and looks up again through heated eyes.

"One question."

"Huh?"

"You think you can get out of work obligations for a few days this week?"

"Work?" I blink three times. "*What?*"

"I want to take you somewhere."

"Take me somewhere?" I ask, and my face scrunches up in outright confusion. "Are you seriously asking me this? *Right now?*"

"It's important."

"More important than making sure I don't explode from pent-up sexual frustration? I mean, seriously, Jude, I always thought guys were full of shit about the whole blue balls thing, but I'm starting to believe it's real."

He laughs. "Well, considering it would lead to a hell of a lot more orgasms, nearly two days straight of orgasms, then I'd say yes, in this case, it is of the *utmost* importance."

I shake my head to try to understand what in the hell he's even asking. "W-when is this?"

"We'd leave late Wednesday night. Come back Saturday afternoon."

"W-where?"

"Somewhere that isn't New York."

"Uh…" I shift my hips, and my head falls back at the building sensation that his fingers are currently providing. "I…uh… Maybe… I don't know…"

"How about you get back to me on that one?" A warm, husky laugh leaves his throat and brushes against my skin. "And I get back to making you come."

"Yes." A relieved sigh escapes my lungs. "Brilliant plan."

Another soft chuckle leaves his lips, but it's quickly quieted down when he quite literally buries his face against me and eats at my pussy with the kind of fervor that has me screaming out the craziest, most incomprehensible shit that I swear everyone inside this hotel can probably hear.

But it's hard to care when a man like Jude is giving you one of the best orgasms of your life.

And it's *really* hard to care when he ups the ante, procures a condom from his pocket, slides his cock inside you, and makes you come so hard you forget you're in a public bathroom in the middle of an upscale hotel.

Have mercy. Now, I'm really starting to understand why Dr. Winters said it was a good thing for me to just let go and enjoy myself.

Because if *this* is living in the moment and having fun? Before now, I haven't been living at all.

TWENTY-EIGHT

Wednesday, March 21st

Jude

The Winslow gang is all here.

My brothers Remy, Flynn, and Ty. Winnie, her husband Wes, and my niece Lexi. And, of course, since we're currently sitting inside her kitchen, my awesome mom is in attendance, too.

There's also a random woman named Shirley or something that Ty brought with him, but that's to be expected.

For the last five or so years, Wendy Winslow has made a point to bring all her kids together for Wednesday dinner. With everyone's schedules *and* my siblings' tendencies to schedule shit on the weekends when I'm working, it's not something we manage every Wednesday, but we generally achieve it once a month.

And considering what happened two weeks ago when I had everyone show up at Winnie's place unannounced, I have a feeling my sister made damn sure this family dinner worked out.

Tonight, an Italian-style feast of spaghetti and meatballs, lasagna, garlic bread, antipasti, and various other side dishes are on the menu. And with the way my niece Lexi is grinning from ear to ear, I have a feeling she had a say in this tasty setup.

My mom and Winnie finish setting big platters of food in the center of us, and I look across the table to meet my niece's eyes. "Did you tell Grandma what to make tonight?"

She nods and flashes a full-toothed smile in my direction.

"Fantastic choice, Lexi Lou."

Lex giggles as my sister begins to dish out a healthy helping of spaghetti onto her plate, and I start to reach forward to do the same for myself, but my phone buzzing in my pocket pulls my attention.

My chest expands as I tap on the screen to check my notifications, but when I see **Bianca,** the expansion turns to deflation. *No offense, Bianca, but you're not the person I'm wanting a message from.*

I haven't given in to any of Bianca's hookup requests—or anyone else's, for that matter—for nearly two months now, and I don't have an explanation for it. But something tells me it's because I've been having so much fun with sweet Sophie Sage that I haven't needed to find it anywhere else.

It's been nearly two days since I asked her if she could get out of work obligations so I can surprise her with a trip to the *real* city that doesn't sleep, but she still hasn't given me her official response.

The last message she sent was as vague as a jilted mom on social media trying to air out her dirty laundry without losing little Timmy's spot on the T-ball team. Sophie's, apparently, trying to "figure it out."

Frankly, I don't know if it's a logistical delay or if she's not getting enough satisfaction from me anymore…

Psh. *It can't be that.*

I saw how she looked when she came on my cock in the Plaza bathroom, and it wasn't the look of a woman who was thinking about how long it was going to take to finish her laundry when she got to it later.

Ha. Yeah. She definitely wants more of the fun I can offer.

I unlock the screen of my phone to double-check my ongoing chat with her just to make sure I didn't miss a text, but all that's there are the mocking words of her alter ego, *Sophie, Team Mom.*

Just the thought of that night, the one where I made the snap decision—*right before I buried my face in her delicious pussy*—to ask her to open up her schedule for a trip makes me smile.

Damn. That was a good fucking night.

If only she'd say yes to leaving town tonight, I could show her *more* good nights.

"You think Mr. Important over there is going to put his phone down for five fucking seconds to enjoy dinner with us?"

"Ty! Language!" my mom chastises with a click of her tongue. I look up to see my brother staring at me with a smug-as-fuck grin on his face, unfazed by the halfhearted snap from our mom. The truth is, we've been cursing up and down the streets of Manhattan for too damn long to be stopped. My mom knows. Everyone knows. But it's part of a mother's obligation to keep trying to turn us into decent humans, no matter how far down the path of being scumbags we may be.

"Sorry, Mom, but I think we can all agree that Jude is being a real rude prick right now."

"I make a point never to agree with Ty on anything," Remy chimes in, "but I'm pretty sure Jude knows that cell phones are not allowed at Wendy's table. By doing it anyway, he is, in fact, acting like a prick."

"Do you mean he's a prick because he's a penis or because he's a man regarded as stupid, unpleasant, or contemptible?" Lexi asks around a mouthful of spaghetti. "Because I've seen both in Webster's."

The whole table nearly combusts, the laughter is so raucous, and Ty nods so hard, I think his head might fly off.

"I definitely mean he's a penis. Definitely."

"Ty!" Winnie chastises through her teeth, her cheeks heating to a rosy pink of embarrassment at having to deal with this shit.

"Though, by these terms, this would make Uncle Ty a penis as well, since he used his phone during family dinner too, two months and three weeks ago. We were eating tacos, and he kept checking his phone to get an update on a boxing match."

Her commentary makes Flynn chuckle. "I think our little genius has your number, bro."

Ty just rolls his eyes and forks a bite full of lasagna into his mouth. Winnie's head is in her hands, and she's given up on trying to get this whole thing reined in. But my mother has now moved her focus to me.

"Jude, you know the family dinner rules," she says and showcases her infamous *mom look* at me. You know, the same look every mother uses to instill the fear of God in their children so that they can keep them in line, even when they're rowdy, nearly uncontrollable teenagers.

"You know what, Mom? This is the best lasagna and spaghetti I've ever had. You've truly outdone yourself," I announce, and she shakes her head on a snort.

"Don't try to butter my biscuit to get yourself out of trouble," she retorts. "And considering your plate is still empty, that tells me you're full of shit right now."

I glance down at my plate to find it is, in fact, still empty. *Whoops.*

"Mom just said shit at the dinner table!" Ty teases, and our mother scratches the side of her face with her middle finger.

"Mind your business, Ty."

Wes, Winnie, Flynn, and Remy all laugh at the rare sight of Wendy flipping someone off, and I use the distraction to check the screen of my phone again. The dinner is now in pandemonium thanks to me, but I feel no shame. A man will use any means necessary for sex; it's a scientific fact.

Still, *nothing*.

"All right, Jude," Remy comments. "Why are you checking your phone like Ty when he's waiting to hear back from one of his hippie vegan friends about a clown party?"

Ty glares.

I chuckle at Ty's glare, and then, knowing I'm not going to be able to slither out from under Rem's radar, I shrug. "It's just work stuff, bro."

There is no way in hell I'm going to tell him what it really is. Especially since my sister would read into shit and try to make it sound like it's something more. Lord knows, she'd be chomping at the bit over the idea of me bringing a woman on a work trip. Probably start rambling on about relationships and love shit again like she did last summer at our Fourth of July getaway at Uncle Brad and Aunt Paula's lake house.

Just the amount I'm checking my phone proves that this isn't anything except having fun, because if it weren't, I'd be running so fast in the opposite direction, the people from Guinness would hire a jet car to drive them along and catch up with me, just so they could record the new champion. Sophie has more than proven she's *a lot* of fucking fun, and I'm eager for the opportunity for more.

Yeah, so much so that you haven't thought about any other woman since she made her big debut at Club Craze…

I don't have time to address that stupid thought because Rem is still staring at me with one quirked brow. His face downright calls me out, and I know I need to give him a little more or else he'll just ride my ass for the rest of dinner.

"All right, fine," I admit. "It's half work stuff and half…" I grin and waggle my brows. "Other kind of stuff that I can't say right now or else Mom and Winnie will get pissed at me."

Winnie scoffs. "What's the flavor of the moment's name?"

Flavor of the moment? I almost laugh. Maybe people need to focus a little more on the woman sitting beside Ty at my mom's dinner table. The redhead —*Carrie?*—has barely eaten anything and has said even less, and we all pretend like it's just normal.

Yet they want to worry about Sophie Sage? Internally, I scoff.

"Mind your business, Win," I respond to my sister, keeping it simple rather than hurting her feelings by repeating our mom's earlier words, and she snorts.

"*What?*" That snort turns into an outright cackle. "If you're starting to get all hush-hush with your weekly conquests, I'm going to think you've suffered a head injury somewhere along the line."

"You say that like I'm always blabbing about my business." I shake my head. "I don't need to flap my gums. My mouth gets plenty of exercise in *other* ways."

"Oh my God," my sister counters and fakes a gagging motion with her finger. "Gross, Jude."

"Do you do some form of oral calisthenics I haven't heard of? Is it recommended by the National Board of Health?" Lexi asks, and that makes all the adults at the table, myself included, have to fight to keep a straight face.

"Definitely recommended," Ty interjects, playing for my team for the first time during this meal. The woman at his side turns beet red, my mom looks to the ceiling—likely praying to God for salvation—and Winnie looks ready to inject some shit under my toenails and leave me to rot while she goes on with her life, having committed the perfect murder undetected.

"It's basically just a…uh…well, it's like writing cursive with your tongue," Wes tries to smooth it over, but in reality, makes it a hundred times worse.

Remy, Flynn, Ty, and I all dissolve into full-bodied guffaws, and my mom turns to violence, smacking each of us who are within reach, one by one.

"Oh. Could I do it with numbers? I like writing numbers better."

Winnie glares at me, and I shrug. It's not my fault, really. *I mean, fuck, how was I supposed to see this coming?*

Desperate to move on, Winnie changes the subject bluntly. "Oh, before I forget! Lexi's Mathletes competition is next Thursday night at her school. And we want everyone to be there, right, Lex?"

My niece nods. "Right."

"Oh, that is so exciting, honey!" my mom comments and claps her hands together. "I can't wait to see it!"

"I wouldn't miss it, Lexi Lou," I answer, smiling over at her as I finally dish some food onto my plate, and Rem, Flynn, and Ty respond with similar sentiments.

Finally feeling a little hungry thanks to the unexpected laugh session, I toss my first bite of spaghetti into my mouth. Simultaneously, my phone buzzes on the table, and despite the nosy-ass family members surrounding me, I check the screen to find a message that makes me smile so big, my fucking face starts to hurt.

Sophie: Okay. This is a crazy request, you realize that, right? Asking me to leave town and go to an unknown destination for two days with a guy I barely know?

Immediately, I type out a response and hit send.

Me: So is having sex in a public restroom, but hey, look how well that turned out. Also, I have too many pairs of your panties at this point to be called "a guy you barely know."

Sophie: HA. God. Okay, hypothetically, if I say yes, when would we leave?

Me: I'd pick you up around 10 tonight.

Sophie: That's in, like, three hours!

Me: In my defense, those three hours are like the last 3 of 48. I gave you the same amount of time as detectives have to find a missing person before they turn up dead! I'm not sure if you realize or not, but they have to do a lot of stuff in that amount of time, and with the number of episodes I've seen of that show, they're successful like eighty percent of the time. Surely you can make a simple decision.

Sophie: Jude, you asked me right before you made me come inside a public bathroom at the Plaza. That's grounds for a mistrial, at least.

Damn, I love when she gets all sassy like this. Even if we're mixing jargon, they're still some of the wittiest messages I've ever shared with a woman.

Me: I plead guilty, your honor. But I don't really think you can convict me of anything other than satisfaction. I made you come TWICE, by the way.

Sophie: I'm so rolling my eyes at you right now.

Me: Well, I'd like to remind you that time is ticking, babe. Come have the time of your life with me for a few days and more orgasms than your body can handle OR…you know…stay in New York and do boring shit. It's up to you. Take it or leave it.

I watch as the text bubbles on the screen float up and down. And I swear a good minute goes by without an actual response.

But then, one chimes in.

Sophie: Okay. Fine. This is NUTS. Pretty much insane. But count me in.

Hell motherfucking yes.

Me: You won't regret it.

Sophie: Can you give me a hint on where we're going so I know what I need to pack?

I smirk and type out one final response.

Me: Anything you want. Plus, lots of sexy panties. See you at 10.

I lock the screen of my phone and go back to eating dinner. Thankfully, everyone's moved on to ribbing someone else, and they don't have the energy to pay attention to me.

I smile.

Vegas, baby. With Sophie, her sexy panties, and her magically delicious pussy.

TWENTY-NINE

Sophie

Two months ago, if you would've told me I'd agree to go on a last-minute trip to an unknown destination with a man I've been having secret-rendezvous sex with, I would've told you that you were psychotic.

But here I am. On a freaking private jet with Jude Winslow, heading for god only knows where.

My standing appointment with Dr. Winters earlier today was one of the catalysts for me saying yes. I told her the gist of what's been happening with Jude and me—*minus all the panty-stealing and illegal sex in public places*—and when I mentioned that he asked me to go on a trip with him, she tossed her normal therapist's open-ended questions my way until I admitted the truth—*that I really wanted to go.*

Now, though, I'm wondering if maybe my therapist has lost her ever-loving mind.

I mean, rearranging my work calendar and rescheduling two meetings so that Jude can take me to the unknown to get my rocks off for a few days?

Like, this whole thing is pretty out there.

Goodness, if Julie only knew that my supposed last-minute trip to Miami to see my parents was actually a trip with Mr. Sexy Good Time, she'd have a stroke. Especially since she doesn't even know about Jude. In fact, my sisters don't even know about him.

I'm just spinning this giant web of lies, and somewhere along the line, it's probably going to catch up with me. Hopefully, Belle won't have a shit fit over the next few days when I vaguely have to tell her I'm busy when she asks to grab lunch or something. Or, you know, talk to Julie and blow the lid right off my can of deceit.

Sheesh. Am I making a big mistake right now?

I stare out the window as the plane drifts higher into the dark night sky and try to wrap my head around all the crazy things I've been doing since I met Jude. All the secrets I've been keeping from my family and friends.

All the damn lies I've been telling them to keep said secrets.

Yeah, but don't forget about all the excitement. Or the wild sex. Or the orgasms.

I can honestly say I can't remember the last time in my life where I've felt free enough to just give in to my wants and desires. Where I've felt this uninhibited to feel what I want to feel. To do what I want to do. And to say what I want to say.

Jude might just be a guy I'm having fun with, but he makes me feel more like me when I'm with him. He quiets my tendencies to obsess over the future and overthink minute details that probably shouldn't matter.

I pull my eyes away from the window and look right at the good-time devil himself. He sits in a cushy leather captain's chair directly across from mine, and his body just vibrates this playful confidence.

Dressed in jeans and a collared white shirt, his style is more relaxed for the flight, but there's no denying he looks good. Then again, Jude always looks good.

"So…" he says, grabbing my attention. "What kind of panties did you bring for my collection?"

"Oh my God." A very unladylike snort jolts from my nose. "Did something happen to you as a kid? Were you in the Boy Scouts or something and had to collect stuff for badges? Is that where this obsession stems from?"

"I steal your panties because I know it turns you on," Jude answers through an amused chuckle. "*Actually*, it turns us both on."

I don't know why those words threaten to do exactly what he said they do, but yeah, I have to shift a little in my seat.

"And I was never in the Boy Scouts," he adds. "But now, that's got me wondering. Were you in the Girl Scouts? Because I'd love to see you at my front door in one of those outfits, trying to sell me your cookies."

"Why do I get the sense that *cookies* is code for something else?"

He waggles his brows. "Because it is."

"Sorry to disappoint, but no, I was never in the Girl Scouts," I answer honestly. "Although, I wanted to be."

He quirks a questioning brow. "Parents didn't let you?"

"My twin sister Belle didn't let me."

"Now, that, you're going to have to explain."

"Well," I say through a soft exhale of air. "Belle was always a bit shy growing up, and in elementary school, we tended to stick together. Her by my side because I was good at doing all the talking for both of us. And me by her side because I felt like I had to protect her, I guess."

"I take it she wasn't a fan of being a member of the Brownies?"

"Nope." I shake my head. "She wanted to play soccer instead, but she didn't want to play by herself."

"So, you never got to sell any cookies?"

"*Or* wear the sash and get all those badges."

"Ah. I see." A big smile consumes his lips. "That was the draw for you. The badges."

I widen my eyes and nod. "The Girl Scouts were like an awesome secret club. Man, I swear, if only I could go back in time and tell Belle to grow some balls and play on the soccer team by herself, then I could fulfill my Girl Scout dream of having a sash full of those *hella cool* badges."

He grins. "Sophie Sage's one regret in life. Never being a Girl Scout."

"Ha! Yeah. Well, one of many regrets, I guess."

"You have that many regrets?"

I search his eyes. "Don't we all?"

"I don't," he answers with the kind of confidence that makes me a little jealous it's even possible to be that self-assured. "I try not to spend my time regretting shit. And I definitely try not to spend my time doing shit I don't really want to do. The combination makes it pretty easy to have zero regrets."

"You mean to tell me you don't have any regrets? *At all?*"

He shrugs. "Nothing comes to mind at the moment."

Good grief. All I can do is stare at him like he has two heads. *No regrets? Must be nice. There're about a million things I'd like to change from my past.*

"Jude and Sophie," the pilot's voice rasps over the intercom and grabs both of our attention. "I'm happy to update that we are now at cruising altitude. Feel free to take off your seat belts and enjoy the rest of the ride. We'll be in Vegas before the sun comes up."

I whip my head back to Jude. "Did he just say *Vegas?*"

"Shit," Jude mutters, shutting his eyes for a beat before opening them up again and looking into mine with a guilty smile encompassing his mouth. "I guess the cat's out of the bag, huh?"

"Wait… You're really taking me to Vegas?"

"I am."

His answer makes my head want to spin right off my damn neck. "What are we going to do there?"

Not once in my life have I ever been the type of woman who just jets off last minute to a city like Las Vegas. I mean, this is…*flipping Vegas* we're talking about here. The city of sex and sin and a place where even hookers are legal!

I've never been there, but you'd have to live like a caveman to have never heard someone tell a wild Vegas story. Hell, their whole motto is *What happens in Vegas, stays in Vegas.*

I'm not sure if I should be thrilled or terrified. I mean, *Vegas* with a man like *Jude?* It feels like big-time trouble. However, I don't know if it's the good kind or the bad kind.

Or maybe it's a little bit of both…

"We're going to have a good time, that's what we're going to do," he replies simply like we're not heading across the country to Las Vegas, but instead, going to feed some damn pigeons in Central Park. "Well, in between the meetings I have scheduled."

"Wait…this is a work trip?"

"Yeah, but don't worry. You're not going to be left to your own devices the whole time," he tells me. "I only have two meetings and, well, the investors that are flying us out there want us to enjoy ourselves. Hell, they've been trying to get me to move to Vegas for years so I can do more than just consult for them. Trust me, I'll be with you ninety-nine percent of the time, experiencing everything this city has to offer."

My chest feels like a vise around my heart, and one particular question stands out in my mind. Now that I know this is a work trip, I've got an entirely different perspective on his job. I don't know why, but I'd assumed he only worked in New York.

"Would you ever…uh…move to Vegas?"

"Fuck no," he responds on a scoff. "I'm a New Yorker through and through, babe."

The breath I didn't realize I was holding escapes my lungs on a deep but silent exhale.

Almost as if his answer gave me relief. Which is…*strange.*

"Are you trying to get rid of me or something?" he teases, and I shake my head on a giggle.

"No. Well, not yet, at least."

"Not yet?" he repeats and places a hand to his chest like he's in pain. "As in, one day soon, you'll want to? Damn, Sophie, you wound me."

"Oh, get over yourself." I reach out and slap a playful hand onto his thigh. "You and I both know that you're not about the long-term commitment kind of thing. This, all the fun we're having together, it will end one day."

Gah. I know it's true—that's why I said it. I just didn't expect voicing it to feel so uncomfortable.

Jude doesn't say anything but, instead, searches my eyes for a long moment. I can't quite figure out what's rolling through his head, and when he still doesn't say anything, I have the urge to find some kind of distraction. So, I take it upon myself to get up from my seat and walk around the cabin.

I look at the food and champagne that have been set up for us by the flight attendant named Peggy, who is currently busy in the galley.

I run my fingers across the cream leather seats toward the back of the plane. And when I stop at the end of the small hallway, I peek into a room and find that it's the bathroom.

But it's not a typical plane bathroom. It's a *fancy private plane* bathroom.

More spacious and modern than I've ever witnessed inside a cabin. But that doesn't mean anything because I've only ever experienced the sardine-can–sized bathrooms on commercial flights. You know, the ones where trying to pee feels like you're auditioning for Cirque du Soleil.

The longer I gawk at the massive shower and spacious sink, the more my mind is blown.

This is the Taj Mahal of plane bathrooms!

"What are you looking at, babe?" Jude asks from somewhere behind me.

"Uh…have you seen this bathroom? It's freaking huge!" I call over my shoulder. "I feel like Julia Roberts in *Pretty Woman*. Give me a phone, Jude, because I need to call Kit and tell her this bathroom is bigger than the Blue Banana!"

"Fan of the bathroom, I take it?" he asks, and I look over my shoulder to find him grinning.

"Who wouldn't be a fan of this bathroom? Pretty sure there's a plane full of people on a Delta flight right now who would give up their right kidney to have this bathroom inside their cabin."

He laughs at that, and I look back inside the spacious room, my mind still reeling that this kind of bathroom is even possible on a freaking plane.

"You know, the Mile High Club never made sense to me," I comment. "Logistically, I mean. But now, after seeing this bathroom, I get it. Sex in an airplane really is possible if you're flying on a swanky private jet like this. But those tiny-ass excuses inside commercial ones? I still say you're just asking for a concussion and a pulled groin muscle."

Within seconds, Jude is on his feet and all up in my personal space. He grabs me by the hips, pulls us both into the bathroom, and shuts the door with a kick of his heel just as he gently pushes my back against the wall. "Lift up your sexy little skirt and take off your panties, babe."

"Excuse me?" I question, but also, a panting little breath slips past my lips.

Jude doesn't falter. Doesn't hesitate. His blue eyes blaze as he stares down at me and repeats his demand. "Take…off…your…panties. I'm going to give you a banana you can call Kit about."

It's almost sad how quickly I obey, a grin drifting over my face at the cuteness of his joke.

But…this is Jude. And while I might never see these panties again, I know I'll at least be getting an earth-shattering orgasm as a trade-off.

THIRTY

Thursday, March 22nd

Jude

After a five-hour plane ride and an Escalade escort to our hotel, Sophie and I have officially made it to Las Vegas in the wee hours of Thursday morning.

The town is bright and lively, proving it truly is the city that never sleeps.

"Oh my gosh! This living room is bigger than my whole apartment, Jude!"

And the penthouse Billy Jones and the rest of Electric's investors put us up in at the Venetian apparently doesn't disappoint either.

I set our luggage down in the large master bedroom, and when I walk back out into the living space, I watch Sophie meander around the room, still taking in everything with big, gorgeous eyes.

"Damn, these investors must really want your help with their nightclub," she says as she runs her fingers along a black leather sectional that sits in the corner of the living area. It faces both the large flat-screen TV hanging on the wall above the fireplace and the massive windows that give one hell of a view of the Strip.

"This is Vegas, babe."

"I wouldn't know because I've never been."

"Wait...this is your first time?"

She nods and walks toward the kitchen area that's decorated with all-black marble countertops and sleek chrome appliances. "That's a fact, Jack."

"First of all, I love that I'm popping your Vegas cherry," I comment, and she giggles.

"Of course you do." One glance over her shoulder, she eyes me with a knowing smile. "And secondly?"

"Well, you'll find this is the norm here. I know they say everything is bigger in Texas, but Las Vegas sure as shit gives the Longhorn State a run for its money."

"So..." She pauses and turns to rest her hip against the countertop, her gaze latched on to mine. "What kind of trouble are you going to get me in?"

"The entertaining kind." I smirk, but before I can elaborate, three soft knocks sound against the front door.

Sophie furrows her brow. "Are you expecting someone?"

"Actually," I answer, "I *am* expecting someone to drop something important off."

Her nose crinkles up, but I just offer a mischievous smile her way before moving to the front door to answer it.

Just as I expect, a bellhop stands outside with a white gift box in his hands. "Hello, sir, I apologize for the late hour, but I've been instructed by the concierge to deliver this to your room as soon as possible."

"No apologies necessary, my man." I offer a thankful grin and take the proffered delivery from his hands. "I'm actually really fucking happy to see you."

The young guy smiles, and I reach into my back pocket to pull out my wallet and give him a generous tip. Once the cash is in his hands, his smile grows tenfold.

"Wow. Thank you, sir. Have a great rest of your stay here in Vegas."

"No problem, man. Thanks again."

Once I shut the door and head back into our suite, I find Sophie standing at the edge of the entry hallway, looking at the white box in my hands with curious eyes.

"What is that?"

"Extra panties for you."

"What?" she barks out, and a suspicious smile kisses her pretty mouth.

Her shocked reaction makes me grin, but I keep my mouth shut until I'm in the living room, sitting down on the sectional.

Too intrigued at this point, Sophie follows my lead and sits down beside me. And when I hand her the white box, her eyes move back and forth between my face and the gift in her hands at least ten times before she asks, "Is this really a box filled with underwear?"

"No." I laugh. "It's better."

"Better?"

I laugh again. "Just open it, babe."

Sophie's smile is hesitant as she unties the white bow and lifts open the top of the box.

But in a matter of seconds, her eyes flash with what feels like a million emotions when she sees what's inside. Surprise. Excitement. A little bit of confusion. And a few other things I can't quite put my finger on.

"*The Secret Club?*" she reads the words from the Sophie-sized gray T-shirt that she pulls out of the box. "Hold up...are these freaking badges?"

"It's time for Sophie Sage to be the Girl Scout she's always dreamed of and earn herself some *hella cool* badges," I repeat her words from our plane ride.

To be honest, I had no idea what Mona from the Venetian's concierge team was going to be able to come up with in the department of badges, but I can't deny she did an amazing job with my odd, last-minute request. I'm sure it helped that she knew my connection to Billy Jones *and* that I'm staying in one of the penthouse suits, but still, this request was pretty out there.

Truthfully, I didn't know if she could pull off getting a T-shirt printed for me. But damn, clearly I owe Ms. Mona one hell of a thank-you tip because the woman came through.

Sophie's jaw drops open farther as she picks up each of the badges, inspecting them one by one.

All different colors and sizes, and at least thirty of them sit inside the box. There's a blue one with a tent surrounded by trees and mountains. One with a kitten holding a ball of yarn. One with a cute puppy with a stick in its mouth.

There's even a pink one with a goddamn unicorn jumping over a rainbow.

They're all girlie as hell, and I can't be sure, but I get the feeling they'd be one-hundred-percent Girl-Scout approved.

"W-when did you have time to do this?"

"When you were taking a nap on the plane. You know, after you made me have Mile-High-Club sex with you."

She snorts and eyes me with a knowing look. "Pretty sure that was your idea, not mine."

"Actually, babe, if I recall, *you* brought it up."

She just shakes her head, half amused at my words but also still pretty damn flabbergasted by the contents of the box in her hands.

"So…you like it?"

"I love it." Her voice is a near whisper. And the way her eyes look into mine makes my chest feel all fucking gooey or something. "Thank you. This was…really sweet."

For a moment, my throat goes dry, and I feel like I can't push words out, but ultimately, I manage a, "You're welcome, babe."

Sophie stares down at the T-shirt and badges for another long moment, but eventually, she looks back up and tilts her head to the side. "So… uh…Girl Scouts have to earn their badges…?"

Now, *that* is the best part about this gift. "They sure do."

"And how do I…*earn* these badges?"

This, right here, was my favorite aspect of the whole fucking idea when I thought of it on the plane.

"With orgasms."

Her mouth gapes open like a fish. "Wait…I get a badge for every orgasm…"

"Exactly. You get a badge for every orgasm *you* have."

"That *I* have?" She gulps. "*Oh holy moly.*"

"You okay with that, babe?"

"Um…*yes.*"

"Good. Because, my sexy little Girl Scout, it's time for you to try to earn your first badge." I wink and stand to my feet. "And it starts with you getting naked and me fucking you up against those big-ass windows over there."

She glances over her shoulder to the windows in question. "*Jude*…but…people might be able to see us…"

"They might," I acknowledge and start to unbutton my shirt and shrug it off my shoulders. "But do you really think you'll be thinking about that when my cock is inside you?"

Her cheeks flush red. "No. I can't say that I will."

"Precisely." I unzip my jeans, letting them fall to the floor. "So, like I said before, it's time to earn that first badge, baby."

Sophie giggles, but also, she stands up and does exactly what I'm hoping she'll do—gets naked with me.

And the second her perfect body is bare of any clothes, I stride right over to her and run my hands all over her silky-smooth skin.

Damn. She's a fucking goddess.

I lift her up into my arms, wrapping her legs around my bare hips, and take her sweet mouth in a deep kiss.

It doesn't take long before my cock is hard and she's grinding against me, and I have no choice but to lead us over to the windows, set Sophie back to her feet, and press her tits up against the glass.

The view from behind her is…*incredible*. Her arms rest above her head, her thighs are spread, her back is arched, and her firm, perfect ass is lifted high in the air.

It's so good that I have to give myself at least thirty seconds to just stand there and admire her while taking about a hundred mental pictures to store away for a later date.

But once the urge to slide inside her becomes too great to deny, I stalk toward her, put my hands on her hips, and guide my now condom-covered cock deep into her warmth.

She moans, wiggles her hips, and clenches her pussy around me.

And it all feels so intense that I have to let my head fall back and inhale a deep breath of oxygen into my lungs just to prevent myself from coming right on the spot.

Because the goal for this little Girl Scout isn't about my orgasm. It's about *hers*.

Once I gain control, I start up a rhythm, and I relish the way Sophie just gives in to her pleasure. She's not hesitant or holding back, and she sure as shit isn't thinking about the fact that her naked body is pressed up against the windows that look out on to the Strip where hundreds of thousands of tourists could be milling about.

No. She just lives in this moment. And focuses on her pleasure.

It's hot as hell, and for some insane reason, it makes a sense of pride widen my chest.

"Oh, sweet Sophie," I whisper into her ear. "I gotta say, you're the best damn Girl Scout I've ever met."

A half whimper and giggle escape her pretty lips.

I push myself deeper and pick up my pace. "Get ready, baby, because you're about to earn that first fucking badge."

And damn, does she do just that.

Her orgasm doesn't disappoint. It hits her hard and makes her pussy clench me so tight, I feel as if my balls might fucking explode.

This might be the best idea I've ever had.

Fuck yeah. Vegas just got a lot more fun now that Sophie the Girl Scout needs to earn herself some *hella cool* badges.

THIRTY-ONE

Friday, March 23rd

Sophie

"If I go all in, does that mean I'm putting all my chips on the line?" I ask, my voice filled with the kind of innocence and naïveté to make the five men at this Texas Hold'em table inside the Venetian's poker room practically lick their chops.

"Yeah, honey," a guy with a black moustache, a bald head, and a thick Boston accent answers. "All in means you're wagering all your money on the hand."

"Oh, okay." I nod and stare down at the stack of chips—*worth twenty freaking thousand dollars*—that Jude handed me before he went to his meeting.

Honestly, I about passed out when he put the clear plexiglass holder in my hands and said, "*Have some fun, babe.*"

Apparently, when Vegas nightclub investors are trying to schmooze you, they pull out all the stops. Which includes an insanely large amount of free casino money to gamble with.

I tried to tell Jude *no way*, but he was persistent in convincing me it was okay to use the chips for whatever gambling desires I had.

"*Babe, if we don't use it, they're going to give it to the next person they're trying to get something out of it,*" he'd said. "*Trust me, the purpose of it is to spend it. Go play the tables or the slots. Just have fun and remember, it's not your money or my money that you're putting on the line. It's the casino's.*"

Somehow, those words of his had given me permission enough to bring all these chips to the poker room without feeling the least bit guilty.

I'm not a huge fan of gambling, but I *love* playing poker. The game of Texas Hold'em was instilled at a young age because my dad taught my sisters and me how to play. And although Belle and Katelynn pretty much hated it, it became my dad's and my thing.

I can remember a lot of nights watching World Poker Tour events on television with him and listening to him analyze each player's moves. There's no doubt that Anthony Sage knows himself some poker, and frankly, if he were sitting here at this table, he'd run all five of these men right out of money.

Me, on the other hand, I still consider myself novice enough that I have to use other techniques to get an advantage. Acting *completely clueless* being one of them.

The dealer deals the next round of cards, and I make a show of acting a little confused before folding my fifth hand since I sat down.

While the game continues, I pull my phone out of my purse and check my messages.

Belle appears busy enough with work that she's not nagging me about not agreeing to meet her for lunch today. And things appear to be running smoothly for Julie.

So far, so good.

Of course, I can't stop myself from sending a text message to the one person who has been on my mind since I sat down at this table. *My dad.*

Me: You'll never believe what I'm doing right now. But when I tell you, you have to promise not to tell Mom or Katelynn or Belle where I am.

Besides being a fantastic father, he's also the best damn secret vault of anyone I know. If you tell Anthony Sage something that you don't want anyone to know about, he'll take that secret to the grave.

Truthfully, it's probably one of the reasons why I've always been closer with our dad and Belle has always been closer with our mom.

My mom is sweet as pie, but she handles things a lot like Belle—by getting all up in your personal space until you break. My dad, on the other hand, takes a subtler approach and just lets you know you can come to him about anything but doesn't pry.

Katelynn always manages to land somewhere in the middle. Half like our mom and half like our dad.

Pops: You know I've got tight lips, Soph. Not even the Feds could break me.

I laugh. Truth is, I was probably going to tell him anyway—I feel the urge too strongly. But I really love his earnest effort to convince me.

Me: I'm in the Venetian's Poker Room playing Texas Hold'em.

Pops: Tell me my daughter is running the table, and I'll be a happy guy.

I grin.

Me: I just sat down, but that's the plan.

Pops: You using the sweet and innocent act?

Me: Oh yeah.

Pops: That's my girl.

Me: Love you, Dad.

*Pops: Love you too, Soph. Call me sometime soon, yeah? Maybe even come *out to Miami and see your mom and me. I'll make sure she makes the good fajitas. The ones with the steak from San Pedro's.*

Me: I'm hoping to get out to Miami in April or May, but the promise of fajitas smells like April.

Pops: Good. Can't wait to see you.

Me: Me too, Dad. I'll call you soon.

"The Secret Club?" a guy with a white beard and a worn-in cowboy hat asks from across the poker table, and I pull my focus away from my text messages. "Darlin', what's that mean?"

I set my phone facedown on the felt and flash him a little grin. "Well, it means exactly what it says. *A secret club.*"

The man chuckles at my sarcasm, but another older gentleman in a navy-blue suit adds to the conversation.

"Are those badges on your shirt?"

I glance down and smile. "Yes."

"Like the Girl Scouts?" White Beard asks, and it instantly makes my cheeks pinken over the dirty truth.

"Well…I guess you could say it's something like that," I answer vaguely, and White Beard lifts his thick, caterpillar eyebrows.

"How do you earn 'em?"

"Sorry to disappoint, but what happens in The Secret Club, stays in The Secret Club."

Both men just chuckle at my beat-around-the-bush answer.

Frankly, if these old-timers knew how I earned these badges or *where* I earned these badges, I feel like at least one of them would have a heart attack right at this damn table.

Ten badges, in fact. Each one ironed-on to my Secret Club T-shirt after Jude gifted me with an orgasm. Ten orgasms in less than twenty-four hours, mind you, and every single one of them was earned in a different spot, a different location, all over this wild town.

Four of them occurred in our suite—against the windows, in the shower, in the big-ass jacuzzi tub, and one on the plush king-sized bed while I rode Jude's awesome penis reverse-cowgirl–style. That badge, ironically, actually has a cute little cartoon cowgirl on it and now sits at the spot just above my right breast.

The other six, though? Well, they are a whole other story, and if the Las Vegas police knew about the public spots where my badge-earning occurred, they'd probably have me arrested and confiscate this T-shirt.

Pretty sure Jude fingering me beneath my dress to a full-on climax while we were on the X-Scream roller coaster at the Stratosphere hotel would definitely qualify as indecent exposure.

Or the quiet booth at Tao when I sat on his lap during the whole meal with his cock all the way inside me.

Or at the Paris Hotel on the observation deck of the Eiffel Tower Experience.

Needless to say, I've never been this wild or spontaneous in my whole life, but somehow, it just comes naturally when Jude is at the helm of my desires.

The dealer begins to deal another round, and I decide this one will be my next move toward steamrolling these men out of some chips.

I peek at the two cards that are facedown before me—**Jack of Hearts.**

Queen of Spades. Not that great of a hand, but that's okay because I'm going to act like it is.

A big-ass smile pushed to my lips, I giggle. "Oh boy."

Moustache and White Beard peer up at me from over their cards, but the other three men at the table don't give me much notice.

"Uh…All in!" I shout before the dealer shows the flop and fumble with my chips as I shove them toward the center of the table.

Now, I have the attention of the other three men.

Navy-Blue Suit furrows his brow. Hawaiian Shirt runs his fingers along his chin. And the man I've nicknamed Mr. Buckteeth looks up and scrutinizes my face.

I lift up the edge of my cards to peep at them again and make sure my eyes go wide with delight.

"Fold," White Beard and Moustache announce to the dealer, shoving their cards toward him.

Navy-Blue Suit and Hawaiian Shirt don't hang in much longer either.

But Mr. Buckteeth mulls over his options for a good two minutes.

"All in, huh?" he questions, and his eyes observe my body language like any good poker player would do. Although, it's more of a show than anything else. I can already tell he's about a minute away from folding his cards.

And with a swift shake of his head and his beefy fingers swiping his cards toward the middle, he does, in fact, *fold*.

"Oh boy!" I let out a giddy giggle as the dealer shoves the chips back in my direction. "That was kind of exciting. But I was also so nervous at the same time. Is that normal?"

White Beard grins. "Yeah, darlin'. I guess you could say every hand can provide a bit of an adrenaline rush."

I make a mental note to fold my next few hands to keep these men guessing, while occasionally asking questions like, *"Is a straight better than a flush, or is it the other way around?"*

The second hand I fold turns into quite the standoff between White Beard and Navy Suit, and while they decide their move at the turn, my phone lights up with a text notification.

Jude: I just got back to the room, and you're not here. Is Mike Tyson's tiger in the bathroom? Should I start checking the roof now?

I laugh, typing out an answer that's slightly more grounded in reality than Hollywood.

Me: I'm losing all your free casino money.

Technically speaking, I'm up about five hundred.

Jude: HA. Did you leave a trail of cookies to help me find you, or should I just ask you where you are?

Me: At our lovely casino's poker room.

Jude: Hold up. You're playing poker in the Venetian?

Me: Texas Hold'em, to be exact.

Jude: Babe, no offense, but do you know how to play poker?

Pfft. Of course, I know how to fucking play. I'm almost offended that he asked me that question, but then I realize it's that kind of thought process that's going to allow me to steal all of these old dude's chips.

So, I keep that mind-set and shoot a rambling text back.

Me: I mean, I know that a straight means that all the cards have to go in order. And a flush means that all your cards have to have the same cute symbol at the top. Like, all the hearts need to match. Or all the spades. Personally, I like diamonds the best.

Jude: LOL. Sounds like you're all set, then.

Me: Does being back at the room mean you're done with your meeting?

Jude: Yep. And I'm on the prowl for my sexy little Girl Scout.

Me: Well, I'm pretty sure you can find her in the Poker Room. She'll be the one wearing a pair of jean shorts and a T-shirt that says "The Secret Club."

Jude: Wait…those cutoff jean shorts where I get to see the bottom curve of your ass?

I furrow my brow. This is the only pair of jean shorts I brought with me, and, to be honest, I don't recall my butt cheeks actually hanging out of them.

Me: Uh…pretty sure you can't see my ass in these.

Jude: I did.

Me: When?

Jude: When you were bending over this morning to get something out of your suitcase.

I shake my head on a silent laugh. I swear, sometimes, he's like the pervy, underwear-stealing stalker I didn't even know I wanted.

Jude: I'll be there before you can say the Girl Scout Promise.

THIRTY-TWO

Jude

Right in the middle of a table full of big, burly, poker-playing men, I find Sophie.

She looks so damn tiny compared to the rest of the table, but she also looks crazy hot. Her legs are crossed beneath a pair of cutoff jean shorts, and her badge-covered T-shirt stretches across her breasts in the most tantalizing way.

Ten fucking badges she's earned thus far. And if all goes well, I'll get her to earn another ten before we leave this town.

When she meets my eyes, her lips crest up into the kind of smile that creates one of my own, and I pick up the pace to close the distance between us. Once I'm standing directly beside her, I press a kiss to the side of her cheek.

"How's it going, babe?" I ask as I pointedly make eye contact with all the men at this table, even the tall, gangly dude in the casino uniform and name tag that reads **Dealer.**

It's not so much that I'm marking my territory, but more that I'm making sure they understand that if they fuck with Sophie, they're going to have to fuck with me.

Most men at the tables in the high-roller poker rooms at any of the big Vegas casinos are chill, but every once in a while, you get a real asshat who thinks he can push people around. Even if those people are women.

Luckily, no one gives off a dickhead vibe, and I move my focus down to Sophie's chips.

"Babe," I whisper into her ear, "I thought you said you were losing. That doesn't look like losing."

If my count is correct, she's up a few hundred from what I handed her this morning before I left to meet with Electric's investors over breakfast at The Palm.

She just shrugs, and her mischievous body language makes my bullshit detector go *ding-ding*.

I narrow my eyes at her, and when she shoots an awkward but adorable wink in my direction, I know, without a doubt, something is afoot. I'm not sure what it is, but I'm pretty sure Sophie is up to no good.

More curious than ever now, I press another kiss to her cheek and step back and let her play the cards the dealer just dealt to the table.

Three of the men immediately up the ante, and two of them fold.

When it's on Sophie to decide, she peeks at her cards once more, and it almost looks like she might throw in the towel, but when she playfully shrugs one shoulder and lets out a little giggle, she ends up matching the bet and hanging in the game for the dealer to show the flop.

Ten of Spades. Two of Hearts. And the **Ace of Clubs** hit the table.

A guy in a Hawaiian shirt makes the bet a thousand to play.

A man with a big ole white beard and crinkles around his eyes shakes his head, but then, he ends up matching the grand and staying in.

The play is on Sophie again, and she looks around the table, glances at the flop, takes one more peek at her cards, and once she does some kind of visible mental count in her mind, she shoves a thousand bucks worth of chips to the center.

Well, shit. I guess she's going for it.

A **Jack of Clubs** hits the turn.

Hawaiian shirt guy makes the wager two grand to stay in this time, apparently a real fan of whatever cards are in his possession.

The old dude with the beard folds straightaway, but I'll be damned if Sophie doesn't shove another bunch of chips toward the center to stay in the hand.

Once the dealer is satisfied that everyone is all set, he flips one last card to make the river.

Another **Ace**. But this time, it's a **Spade**.

Hawaiian guy wagers five grand this time, but Sophie? Well, my girl just silently shoves all her damn chips toward the center of the table.

"Wait… Are you all in?" her opponent asks, and Sophie nods.

"I'm all in."

"Looks like the little lady came to play!" the old guy with the white beard exclaims through a chuckle.

The other men at the table are a combination of amused and outright shocked, and I can't deny I'm feeling both of those things myself.

But when I step to the side a little to look at Sophie's face, I can see there's a change. A certainty lying behind her eyes. A confidence that is undeniable. It reminds me of that night she told that douchebag she was an ex-convict from Bedford Hills.

Wait…she hasn't been doing what I think she's been doing, has she?

I furrow my brow and try to make sense of it, but when her opponent eventually calls, everything moves at rapid-fire pace.

He shows his cards—a pair of **Queens**.

"Queens and Aces. Two pair for the gentleman," the dealer announces.

"Good hand," Sophie says, but when she flips over her hand, she adds, "But it looks like mine is better."

I look down at the spot in front of her, and there sits a pair of **Aces**.

Did she really just slow-roll these old dudes with a pair of fucking Aces in her hand?

When I check her cards again, a stunned laugh barrels out of my chest.

Holy fucking shit. She just played these men like a fiddle.

My eyes laser in on Sophie again. She just sits there, all fucking smug, and it might be the sexiest thing I've ever witnessed.

"Four of a kind for the lady," the dealer states, and it takes a lot of effort for him to keep his amusement to just a tiny quirk of his mouth. "The lady wins this round."

The dude in the Hawaiian shirt just sits there, his mouth gawked open wide.

But the old guy with the beard busts a fucking gut, slapping his leg with each hearty laugh. "Well, hell. Looks like we have a hustler in our midst!"

The three other guys join in on the laughter, but considering he just lost twenty grand in one hand, all the man in the flowery shirt can do is shake his head and mutter, "Fuck me. I just got snowed."

"Dude, your girlfriend is nothing but trouble," a guy with a moustache says directly to me, but his voice is purely amused. "She's been cheating us for the past two hours. Making us think she didn't know jack shit about cards, but it looks like she knows *a hell of a lot more* than she was letting on."

I don't even bother correcting him on the girlfriend comment because, fuck,

I'm too turned on to make sense of anything right now but the fact that I need to get Sophie up to our room to earn another goddamn badge.

Sophie just rakes in all her winnings and flashes a little wink at everyone at the table. "It's possible that I might know a thing or two."

The confidence vibrating off her body might as well be a fucking siren's call for my dick, and the instant she has all her chips stacked up and in order and tells the men goodbye, I practically drag her toward the elevators.

"W-what are you doing?" she asks as I hurriedly shove us inside one of the empty carts. "Jude? Are you okay?"

"Are you kidding me?" I retort just as the doors close shut. "I'm more than okay. That was the hottest fucking thing I've ever seen. Hell, I'm surprised I didn't try to fuck you right there on the table."

Her eyes go wide, but then, something changes inside her. Like a flip of a switch, that confidence of hers is back and flaming, and she's moving toward me. One shove of her free hand into my chest, she pushes me up against the wall and kisses me with the kind of fierceness that makes my dick twitch beneath my zipper.

Damn, girl.

"I'm ready to earn my next badge," she says, steps back, sets her chip-holder on the ground, and hits the emergency stop button on the elevator so that we're hovering about ten floors from our suite. "But I want to earn it for *your* orgasm. When I make you come. *With my mouth.*"

All I can do is blink.

"Do we have a deal?"

Is she for real? Fuck yeah, we have a deal.

"Babe, I'll take that deal any-fucking-day of the week."

"Good." She grins at me like a little sexy devil.

And then, she doesn't waste another second of time.

To her knees, Sophie yanks down my pants and briefs, and while her big green eyes look up at me, she sucks my hard cock into her mouth.

Hands down, it is the most erotic thing I've ever experienced in my entire thirty-six years of life.

Her devious little tongue circles my tip while her mouth creates the most delectable sucking sensation around my cock, and I just stand there, watching her work me over like the self-assured goddess I always knew she was deep inside.

With each stroking suck of her mouth, the pleasure starts to build, and it doesn't quit until my breaths come out in harsh pants and my thighs start to burn.

And she keeps going until I come hard. *In her pretty mouth.*

But I hardly have time to catch my breath before she's tucking me back into my pants and standing to her feet.

"Looks like you owe this Girl Scout a badge," she says, pointedly *licks her fucking lips*, and then hits the button on the elevator to make the cart move again.

Well, fuck. *Someone stick a fork in me, because I might be done for when it comes to this woman.*

It's nearing ten in the evening, and Sophie and I decided to stay in the room for the rest of the night. Surely that has everything to do with how damn busy we've kept ourselves running around Vegas, fucking like a pair of horny rabbits.

Not to mention, I was up pretty early this morning for my meeting with Billy and the investors. Thankfully, that went as well as I'd hoped, and I'm now officially a consultant for Electric's team.

The aromas of food waft into my nose as I wheel in a cart full of dinner that a bellhop just dropped off at our door. Everything on it is courtesy of the hotel's in-room dining menu, and I guide it into the master bedroom, where I find Sophie sitting on the bed in one of the Venetian's plush cream robes.

I toss the two badges I grabbed from the box on the dining room table onto the bed beside her. One of the badges is a picture of a sunset, and the other is that goddamn unicorn because I'm certain the round of oral she gave me in the elevator is about as close to feeling like a mythical creature who can jump over fucking rainbows as I'll ever get.

"For your collection," I tease with a little waggle of my brow. "And dinner is served, madam." I lift the silver metal covers off the plates. "I hope you're hungry because I pretty much ordered anything that sounded good."

"Which is apparently a lot," she says when she gets a load of all the food on the cart. Burgers, tacos, chicken fried rice, even pancakes and eggs and bacon—I spared no menu item that looked like a good possibility.

I wink at her. "I guess you could say all your badge-earning has worked up an appetite."

"Tell me we're going to eat all of that in this bed, and I will let you steal another pair of my panties."

"I'll take that deal, babe. And I choose those sexy pink ones you were wearing last night."

A shocked giggle vibrates her throat. "You mean, the ones you tore in half?"

"Exactly those ones."

"Jude, do you think that maybe you should seek therapy for this panty addiction you're developing?"

I smirk. "Why the fuck would I do that?"

"Because a lot of people would possibly think you're deranged."

"But do *you* think I'm deranged?"

"I think I should think you're deranged, but…" She pauses and then snorts. "I'm probably far too biased because every time you steal my panties, I end up with orgasms. So…" She shrugs. "I don't think I'm the right person to ask."

I chuckle at that.

"But don't worry, your pervy secrets are safe with me."

Before Sophie, I've never had the urge to steal someone's underwear. It never even occurred to me, if I'm being honest. But fuck, I've never been one to be embarrassed by what turns me or someone else on. And I have to say, knowing I have a secret stash of Sophie's panties in my bedroom drawer is a fucking turn-on.

It's also hot as hell when I get to witness her reaction when I shove them in my pocket. A combination of blushing and panting and hooded eyes that are just begging me to do dirty, pleasurable things to her. And, well, a man can only be so strong while looking into Sophie Sage's heated emerald gaze.

Eventually, I start the process of setting up our dinner display. Once I cover the bed with one of the large bathroom towels, I set out two forks and a few of the plates.

Sophie makes it very apparent that pancakes covered with whipped cream and strawberries are her top choice. I know this, because she grabs the plate with two greedy hands and moves it to her lap.

"Not sharing that one, eh?" I question as I sit on the bed beside her, my body only clothed in a pair of black boxer briefs.

"Nope." She shakes her head and laughs around her first bite.

I waver between the burger and tacos for a good ten seconds, but eventually, the tacos win out. One crunchy bite in and I nod. "Oh yeah, these are good."

"The decision to eat room service in bed is one of the best decisions I've ever forced you to make," she states around another bite of pancakes.

"Not nearly as good as what went down in the elevator earlier, but it's up there."

She blushes and grins, and just when I'm about to start waxing poetic about her mouth's superior oral skills, my phone chimes loudly with a text message from the bedside table. I snag it off and see a message from the last person I'd ever expect.

Someone I haven't heard from in forever.

Kyle: *Do you know any good lawyers in Cuba? Currently in a bit of a pickle.*

I laugh. Outright.

"What is it?" Sophie asks, and I turn the screen of my phone to let her read the text. Instantly, her eyes go wide. "Uh…that doesn't sound good…"

"Yeah, it doesn't," I agree. "But that's how shit always is with Kyle."

"Is he a friend of yours?"

"Well, it's been years since I've talked to him, but yeah, growing up, we were pretty close as teenagers. Although, all three of my brothers hated him."

She quirks a curious brow. "It sounds like there's a story behind that."

"Kyle was known for trouble," I elaborate. "When I was seventeen, the FBI came to my door looking for him. Not even kidding. All because he stabbed himself with a K bar knife while playing 'Commando Games' in Central Park."

Her face pinches into disbelief. "That doesn't sound real."

"Oh, but it is. And that incident was pretty much the last straw for his dad. Right after that, he shipped Kyle off to military school. We kept in touch here and there, but I swear, it's been, like, thirteen years since I last talked to him."

"So…are you going to respond?"

I nod and quickly type out a message. Once I hit send, I turn the phone so she can read it.

Me: Dude, the only things I know about Cuba I learned from the movie Dirty Dancing: Havana Nights. I don't think that's the kind of expertise you need.

Sophie covers her mouth to laugh at my cinematic tastes, and I roll my eyes, saying simply, "My sister." And Kyle responds while both Sophie and I are looking at the screen.

Kyle: Ah, hell. Thanks anyway. Hope you're good, man!

"That's it?" she questions with an incredulous gawk to her mouth. "No explanation. No nothing?"

"Yep. That's Kyle. The most random motherfucker you'll ever meet."

"This might be irrational, but I feel kind of angry that I have no idea what's happening with him in Cuba," she comments. "I guess I'm starting to understand why your brothers hated him."

"Uh-huh." I nod. "Remy, my oldest brother, hated him the most."

"What are your other brothers' names?"

"Well, actually, I have three brothers and one sister," I expand. "Winnie is the youngest out of all of us Winslows. Then there's me. Then there's Ty. Then Flynn. And Remy."

"That's quite the brood," she comments. "I have fewer siblings than you. Only two sisters for me."

"Clearly, I remember Belle," I tell her with a grin. "Kind of hard to forget all that confusion."

She snorts. "Yep. Belle, my twin, and then Katelynn. She's the oldest."

For some strange reason, I find myself asking her more questions about her family. "So, are both your parents in the picture?"

She nods. "My mom and dad have been married since before Katelynn was born, and they're now happily living the retiree life in Miami. What about you?"

"Dad left when we were young. My mom is very much present. Strongest woman I know. I also have my uncle Brad and aunt Paula, who have always been like second parents to us."

"Damn, your dad left your mom with all those kids?"

I couldn't agree more. "Talk about a real bastard, huh?"

"I'm sorry that happened to you." She reaches out and places a gentle hand on my thigh, but even though it feels nice to have someone be that kind, my inclination to brush it off is strong.

"Thanks, babe. But there's no need for sadness or sympathy on my behalf. If anyone deserves that, it's my dad. I think we can both agree it was truly his loss leaving us all."

"I don't know your siblings, but if they're anything like you, I can't even imagine being able to walk away." Her smile is soft and caring, and all of a sudden, my heart gets all twitchy inside my chest.

Fuck, that's weird. Maybe I should get that checked out when I get back to New York?

Or maybe you should realize that it's not your heart, but what this woman is doing to your heart…

I shake off that ridiculous idea, but I don't hesitate to answer Sophie's next question about if any of my siblings are married or have kids.

"Only Winnie. And my niece Lexi is the coolest kid you'll ever meet."

"Both of my sisters are married. And Katelynn has two little boys, Ben and Alex. They're two and three and keep her on her toes," she says with a warm smile, but then she furrows her brow a little. "So…wait…*none* of your brothers are married?"

"Nope." I shake my head. "To my baby sister's dismay. Ty is always bringing random women to family events, but that's about as close as any of us get to settling down," I answer honestly, but then I remember one very poignant moment in our past. "Although, Remy was engaged once, but that ended pretty terribly."

"Terribly?"

"He got left at the altar."

Her head jerks back. "No shit?"

"It was a rough time."

"Damn," she mutters to herself more than me. "That's horrible."

"That, it was," I say, and suddenly, I have the urge to direct us toward a less heavy subject. "But don't fret over it, babe. It's in the past. And right now, we're in the present, and I'm sitting here realizing that you're eating pancakes with a bare pussy beneath that robe. Which, I have to say, is quite an interesting situation we have on our hands."

She quirks a brow. "What are you getting at?"

"How you're going to earn that next badge."

"Okayyyy…"

"And I'm pretty sure it starts with seeing how long you can sit there and eat those pancakes while I'm licking your pussy."

She just stares at me. "You wouldn't."

"Oh, but baby, I would, and I will."

Giggles jump from her throat as she tries to juggle her plate of pancakes in one hand and scoot her body away from me with the other.

But I'm quicker.

And the instant my head is beneath her robe and my tongue gets a taste of her sweet pussy, I actually hear Sophie's plate hit the floor. Surely that's a fucking mess. But right now, who the hell cares?

Sophie's got a badge to earn, and I've got a delicious pussy to feast on.

Sounds like Vegas luck is on my side.

THIRTY-THREE

Sunday, March 25th

Sophie

In between focusing on the Crenshaw wedding currently surrounding me, I can't seem to stop my brain from floating back to memories of Vegas with Jude.

Mile High Club. Girl Scout badges. Room service in bed.

Having more sex than my vagina should be able to tolerate in three days.

No doubt, a lot of awesome shit happened in Vegas, but tonight, I feel a bit out of sorts. I'm hardly able to concentrate on the songs the DJ is currently playing, and it takes a Herculean effort to keep checking in on the bride to make sure she appears happy and at ease.

Is this jet lag? I mean, our flight back home to Teterboro got in yesterday afternoon, but it's like my body is still on West Coast time or something.

More like, your body is on Jude Winslow time.

"Hello? Earth to Sophie?"

I look up from the cake table to find Julie standing beside me with a hand on her hip.

"You okay, boss?"

"Yeah." I nod, clearing my throat. "Of course. I'm good."

"Are you sure?" she questions with narrowed eyes and steps closer to me. "Because you're, like, really out of it tonight. Come to think of it, you've been out of it a lot lately."

"What?" I blow out an exasperated breath. "No, I haven't."

I mean, sure, tonight, I am. But prior to this? I don't think so.

"Oh, yes. You have," she whispers and begins to help me set up the area for the bride and groom to cut the cake. "I mean, you just took a few days off to go see your parents in Miami, which was kind of strange because you *never* do *anything* last minute. Trust me, Soph, you've been in la-la land for the past two months."

Have I really been that out of it?

I meet her eyes, and the look on her face says, "*Yes, girl, you definitely have.*"

Shit. I guess all of this secret-rendezvous fun with Jude is starting to show its effects.

Well, you did sneak off to Vegas with him…

I grimace.

"All right, spill it," Julie comments. "What is going on with you?"

Oh boy. There's the big, million-dollar question, and the answer revolves around an irresistible, larger-than-life man with witchcraft-like abilities to bestow mind-blowing orgasms.

Otherwise known as Jude Winslow.

I haven't told anyone but Dr. Winters—vaguely—about how I've been filling my time lately, but there's a huge part of me that feels like I need to tell *someone*. Maybe if I could confide in Julie, then I wouldn't appear so fucking out of it when we're working.

If anything, I probably should tell her…*right?*

When I realize Julie is still standing there, waiting for me to answer, I bite the bullet and dish some of the dirty details of my ongoing, top-secret… whatever it is Jude and I are doing.

"Okay…so…I've kind of…sort of…been seeing someone," I confess, and Julie's eyes expand in surprise, and her mouth quirks up in a giant, happy smile.

"*What?*" she nearly shouts, and thankfully the music coming from the DJ at the front of the venue prevents her outburst from drawing attention. "You're seeing someone?"

I nod, but also cringe. "It's actually who I was on a trip with. When I told you I went to Miami to see my parents, I lied. Which I'm really sorry about. I know it was a shitty thing to do. Please don't hate me."

"Okayyy…definitely shitty and I wish I could hate you because I was stuck dealing with the bride from hell's meltdown for nearly three days, but I can't. At least, not until I find out if the reason for your absence is something I want to hear about. I mean, I've been waiting for the Ding-Dong Dish from you for *years*." She offers a small, forgiving smile. "So, tell me, what in the hell were you doing? Where did you go if not to Miami?"

"We went to Vegas."

"Vegas?!" Her jaw damn near hits the tops of her nude pumps, and this time, her voice rises over the DJ's music enough to grab a few wedding guests' attention. "Holy balls, Soph! Did you, like, run off and get married?!"

"*Shh,*" I say and lift my index finger to my lips. "And oh my God, *no,*" I quickly answer and shake my head maniacally. "*No.* I did not get married. It was just for fun. That's it."

"Phew. Okay." She puts a hand to her chest and lets out a relieved breath.

"Because I was going to say if you went off and got hitched and I didn't get to be a part of planning your big day, I'd straight up murder you."

"It wasn't like that. I promise," I add. "He's just a guy I've been spending a lot of time with. A guy I've been having a lot of fun with. A guy I haven't told anyone but you about."

"You haven't even told Belle? Or Katelynn?"

I shake my head.

"Man ohhh man…" She lets out a low whistle as another stupid smile covers her face. "This is seriously the best news I've heard all week."

"What?" A barking laugh pops from my throat. "Why?"

"Because you never let yourself do anything like this, and I'm just happy you're finally having some damn fun."

She's not wrong. I mean, it's a point my therapist has been trying to get through my head.

"So…" She scrutinizes my face like she's trying to solve a crime. "I know you're having fun with him…but do you think it's going to go anywhere?"

"Uh…" I pause, completely unsure of what to say. Frankly, the whole prospect of that question makes me feel like I've come down with a sudden bout of vertigo.

Jude Winslow isn't the kind of guy who settles down, but when I think about the time we've spent together, how close we've been getting lately, it definitely doesn't feel like we're just a random hookup.

I mean, he took me on a work trip with him. Told me about his family. Heck, he even remembers when I tell him things like I always wanted to be a Girl Scout, and then, takes it a step further by trying to make that dream come true in a sexy, dirty, but super-sweet way.

"I don't know."

It's all I can answer. Because I really, truly don't know what it is that we're doing. Still, though, I kind of wish I'd have just said no. Because it feels like hope is already creeping in.

"Gotcha." Julie just nods. "Well, I'm hoping it turns into something and I can meet this guy, whoever he is. Because a man who can get Sophie Sage to take a last-minute trip to Vegas must be pretty damn spectacular."

I open my mouth to respond, but when no words come out, I quickly shut it and busy myself with a double-check of the cake table.

And by the time the DJ announces for everyone to gather around the rear of the room to watch the happy couple cut the cake, I head back toward the kitchen area to make sure waitstaff is ready to start serving the extra dessert add-ons the bride wanted for her guests.

But just as I step through the doors, my phone buzzes in the pocket of my jacket. When I check the screen, I find a text from the man who's been taking up a lot of flipping real estate in my head.

Jude: What are you doing right now?

Me: Working a wedding at NoMo.

Jude: Shit. You're in SoHo? That's like three blocks from this kick-ass apartment where a guy with an awesome cock is currently sitting with about an hour to waste before he has to head to Club Craze. Think you can sneak out of there and meet him?

I laugh to myself, but then, my face expands—eyebrows, mouth, cheeks— when I think, *is he asking me to come to his apartment?*

I've never been to Jude's place. *Which is definitely creating the urge to actually leave this wedding to meet him.*

Me: My assistant might kill me if I skip out on this wedding reception. The bride is a bit of a lunatic.

After I send that message, a question that's been floating around inside my head for a while makes its way to the forefront of my mind.

Me: Speaking of Club Craze, I have a question for you.

Jude: And what's that, babe?

Me: Why were you the exotic dancer on the night of my sister's bachelorette? As I know now, your job is a whole lot more managerial in nature than that.

Jude: Because I can't resist a bet.

Me: A bet?

Jude: Yep. With Maverick. The guy who was supposed to dance for your sister's party. He's a cocky little shit, and I was in the mood to prove myself as the better dancer.

Me: Did you win?

Jude: Technically, yes.

Me: What the hell is that supposed to mean?

Jude: It means, yes, I did win the bet, which revolved around bringing in more tips than Maverick—most of it was thanks to a tall, handsy chick at your sister's party who shoved like three hundred bucks in my underwear.

I laugh. *That was definitely Tonya*

Jude: But a gentleman like me never kisses and tells—or, in your case, never makes a fake bride-to-be orgasm during an exotic dance and tells—so I didn't actually claim the money I was rightfully entitled to.

I don't know why that revelation makes me feel good, but it does.

Although, there's also a part of me that isn't too thrilled over the idea of Jude stripping for other women. Especially when I think about what that dance of his did to *me*.

Me: And how often do you take bets like that?

Jude: HA. Once and only once, babe. Now, go tell your assistant that you have a very important Secret Club meeting, but you'll be back before she even misses you.

Me: You're nuts, sir.

Jude: Nah, babe. I just miss your sweet-as-fuck pussy, and I'm very determined in my support of you earning all those badges.

Damn, he makes it so hard to say no. With my phone pressed to my chest, I glance around the kitchen and see that everything is still in order. And when I step back through the door and into the main venue area, I note that Julie looks relaxed and hasn't developed that weird vein in her forehead that only comes when she's about to lose her fucking mind.

But can I really sneak out of here for an hour?

Oh yes, you can, and you're already figuring out how you will.

Next thing I know, I'm sending a text confirmation that showcases my possible lunacy.

Me: What's your address?

THIRTY-FOUR

Sophie

"Damn, baby, you look good all dressed up for work," Jude says the instant I step foot into his apartment. "Like a fuckhot librarian or something."

I glance down at my cream silk blouse and formfitting blush pencil skirt and jacket and laugh.

But also, I'm too inquisitive to see what Jude's apartment looks like not to shift my focus and walk around his place a little.

It's big. Bigger than mine. Clean, sophisticated, and minimalist in style, the smartly decorated space matches him to a T. It's a bachelor pad, so to speak, but it's also very cozy.

In the living room, there's a plush velvet sectional with big cushy pillows that sits in front of a large flat-screen TV. A couple pieces of art hang on the walls. And the coffee table has a few sports magazines and newspapers scattered across it.

"Your place is really nice," I comment just as he comes up behind me and places both of his big hands on my ass. He gently squeezes the flesh through my skirt, and the rush of arousal it provides between my thighs is undeniable.

"Not as nice as this ass of yours."

I glimpse over my shoulder to find him smirking down at me.

"Did your assistant get pissed when you told her you had to leave to go ride a stallion?"

I scrunch up my nose. "Oh…was I supposed to say stallion? I told her it was a pony."

"Don't fuck around, babe. Your legs aren't even straight anymore."

I laugh. "Okay, Mr. Stallion, sir. No, she wasn't mad. But she said she'd *be mad* if I didn't get my ass back to NoMo in an hour."

"Sounds like we're on a deadline then, huh?"

I nod. "Precisely."

"Well, I guess it's a good thing I'm prepared," he says and moves his hands to my shoulders and presses his now-hard cock against my ass.

My eyes fall shut of their own accord, and a shiver runs up my spine. "That's a very good thing."

And next thing I know, Jude is spinning me around and tossing me over his shoulder.

I squeal at the change in position, but he just chuckles and strides out of his living room, down a medium-sized hallway, until he's carrying me into what appears to be his bedroom.

It seems nice from my upside-down view, but I don't have time to get a good look at it because once my back is on the mattress, Jude's body is hovering over mine and his lips are persistent against my mouth.

"Fuck, I'm glad you got out of work for an hour," he whispers in between deep kisses.

Me too.

My skirt and panties hit the floor just before Jude's jeans and boxers do the same. And it's not long before he's lying on his back, lifting my body over his hips, and filling me up. His blue eyes glaze over with pleasure as his big hands reach up to grip my breasts.

"Oh God. That feels so good." I moan, my head falls back, and I match my hips' rhythm with each of his deep thrusts.

"Yeah, baby. That's it. *Ride me.* Take your pleasure."

And just like all the times before, I follow his command, riding him until I can't hold myself up any longer. It's a shockingly short time before the waves of my climax take hold of every single nerve inside my body and I'm falling down onto his chest.

"Oh, sweet Sophie," he murmurs into my ear as his hands reach out to slide a few pieces of hair away from my eyes. "It's always so fucking good with you."

Truthfully, it's borderline scary how right those words are.

As I hurriedly walk the three blocks back to NoMo, I run my hands down my skirt several times, hoping like hell I don't look like a woman who just begged off work for an hour to go have sex.

Even though, yeah, I *am* that woman.

When I step in through the main doors and make my way into the Crenshaw wedding's reserved room, I'm happy to find that nothing looks out of order. The bride and groom are happily dancing with their guests to the DJ's approved playlist. My assistant's forehead vein still hasn't made a debut. And nothing is on fire.

Once Julie makes eye contact with me from across the room, she walks toward me, waggling her eyebrows like a weirdo.

"Everything go…*orgasmically,* boss?"

Maybe I shouldn't have told her as much as I did about why I needed to be MIA for an hour. I mean, I could've just said I had diarrhea or something.

"Everything okay here?" I ask, redirecting the conversation to less-risky territories.

"Oh yeah, our bride has consumed enough champagne that she didn't notice when the extra desserts came out about fifteen minutes later than she wanted. So, my little sex fiend friend, I can confidently report that all is good in the wedding hood."

"Oh my God," I groan. "Shut up."

She laughs and nudges me playfully with her elbow. "So…I'm not trying to be nosy or anything, but it feels like a good sign that your mystery guy is inviting you over to his place for hot hooky sex right after he took you to Vegas on a whim. I mean, are you sure this isn't turning into something more? Because, to me, it's kind of seeming like it…"

"Not trying to be nosy?" I retort. "You're definitely being nosy."

Julie just shrugs, and I choose that time to head over to the gift table at the exit doors to make sure all of the little Tiffany-blue boxes are in order for the guests' departure in about an hour.

But halfway through my count, my phone steals my attention from my jacket pocket with three texts.

Jude: *Loved seeing you come on my cock tonight, babe.*

The second text is an address, and the last one includes instructions.

Jude: Clear your schedule for Thursday. 6:30pm. Dress casual.

Another surprise meetup. With Jude.

The smile that consumes my face should be downright embarrassing. And that's followed by Julie's questions floating around inside my head.

Is this starting to turn into something more?

THIRTY-FIVE

Jude

I stand out in front of Lexi's school as parents and small kids file inside the building, following the sign that reads, **Mathletes Competition**. My mom, brothers, and Winnie and Wes are probably already inside the auditorium with Lexi, but I'm waiting on the arrival of one final guest.

Glancing down at my Rolex, I see it's already half past six, but when I look up again, I spot her, *Sophie*, walking toward me.

She looks beautiful in a pair of jeans, boots, and a beige sweater, but her eyes are wide and imploring. The instant she closes the distance between us, those eyes of hers only get bigger.

"Glad you could make it, babe. Even if you're late."

"Jude!" she whisper-yells. "A school? I'm not having sex in a school! That's how you end up on the sex offenders' registry!"

She looks downright scandalized, and I just wrap an arm around her back and tug her closer to me. After one soft press of my lips to hers, I grin. "We're not having sex here."

Sophie leans back to meet my eyes. "Okayyy…but that still doesn't answer the blaring question of the night."

"Which is?"

She huffs out an annoyed breath. "Why are we at a school?"

"It's for a good reason. Nothing nefarious, I swear," I answer loosely and glance down at my watch again. "Now, come on. We better get inside because we're already late."

Sophie just stands there, staring at me with narrowed eyes. Her whole demeanor is sassy as hell, and of course, I find it fucking sexy.

"The longer you just stand there, the higher your chances of me actually coming up with dirty, fucking scandalous things to do at said school," I whisper to her. "I mean, I do have a badge and a condom in my back pocket, so…"

The smallest hint of a smile crests the corners of her full lips, and I can't stop myself from pulling her closer to me again and kissing her.

She tastes like her favorite fruity mints, and the aroma of her delicious perfume goes straight to my damn head. *Fuck. This woman.* She never fails to be all the addictive things that keep me coming back for more. I can't resist her. Never grow bored of her.

I just want to spend time with her. *Do dirty, bad things with her.*

When a little moan escapes her throat and my cock starts to like that train of thought a little too much, I pull away from the kiss and gently press a hand to Sophie's lower back.

"Have you ever been to a Mathletes competition?"

"A what?" She blinks three times, and I chuckle.

"Yeah. Me neither." I press one final kiss to her forehead. "Let's go see what all the hype is about."

"You do realize that I still have no idea what's going on, right?" she asks, and I smile down at her as I open the entrance doors to let us in.

But I don't say anything else. Instead, I lead us down the main hallway of the school and toward the sign that reads **Auditorium.**

Once we're inside, I search the crowd of seats for my family. My brothers' big-ass heads are easily spotted near the front, and I guide Sophie down the red velvet walkway and toward the two empty seats that reside to the left of my three brothers and whatever random woman Ty has brought to this event.

Thankfully, Sophie just follows along, her eyes taking in the current change in scenery with both bewilderment and interest.

I come to a stop beside Wes's aisle seat, and he looks up with a friendly smile, but when he spots the woman standing behind me, the one whose hand is currently locked with mine, his expression changes from relaxed to a calculating head tilt.

"Mind if we slide in here?"

"Oh yeah. Of course," he says and taps Winnie's shoulder to get her attention.

She pulls her eyes away from the stage where all the students, including Lexi, are beginning to file out and into their assigned seats. First, her gaze meets mine with a slightly irritated smile. "You're late, but glad you could make it," she whispers toward me, but when she notices Sophie easing into the aisle with me, my sister's head jolts back and her lips form a little circle of surprise. "And you brought a guest…?"

"Winnie, this is Sophie," I quickly introduce as we slide in past my sister and brother-in-law. "Sophie, this is my sister, Winnie."

"Hi," Sophie says, her voice timid and more reserved than I'm used to. "It's… uh…really nice to meet you. I've heard a lot of great things about you."

Her honesty is unnerving. Mostly because Sophie actually *does* know a lot about my family.

She knows even more about you. More than any other woman ever has.

I guess if I weren't standing in the middle of my niece's school's auditorium, that realization might feel like a real kick in the gut, but for some reason, it doesn't.

I mostly just feel happy that Sophie is here.

Remy, Flynn, and Ty, and whatever random woman Ty's brought to this event, notice the interruption our late arrival has caused, and just as Sophie and I slip in past them, I don't miss the snooping stares that follow us.

We sit down in the two empty seats, and I ignore the questioning looks from my mom, sister, and brothers to whisper into Sophie's ear, "We're here to cheer on my niece."

"Oh, okay. Awesome." Her eyes search the stage. "Which one is Lexi?"

I point toward the spot where the little cutie sits. "The adorable blonde in the center right there."

She smiles. "Got it."

Not even a minute later, a teacher steps up to the podium and begins to introduce the contestants of the Mathletes competition. Each kid walks up to the front of the stage and waves, giving the families a chance to clap for them.

When Lexi's name is called, that's when I realize it's not just my family that has come to cheer her on, but Thatch and Cassie and Georgia and Kline, Wes and Winnie's closest friends, along with four New York Mavericks players.

The mere thought makes me grin. *Of course Winnie's kid would have the fucking Mavericks come to her school competition.*

We all stand up to cheer for her, and by far, Lexi's squad of supporters is the biggest and the loudest.

"Get 'em, Lex!" Thatcher Kelly shouts with a fist pump.

"Go, Lexi!" Quinn Bailey, the famous quarterback for the Mavericks, yells through cupped hands.

Three other well-known Mavericks, Sean Phillips, Cam Mitchell, and Teeny Martinez, also join in with wolf whistles and cheering at the tops of their lungs.

And everyone else is being just as obnoxious.

Including Sophie.

She claps and waves both hands in the air and yells, "Go, Lexi!"

It's fucking adorable and makes me chuckle, but it also makes my heart feel like it forgets how to beat inside my chest, and I have to swallow hard to quell the odd sensation.

THIRTY-SIX

Sophie

I clap and cheer along with the rest of Jude's family while his niece Lexi stands in the middle of the stage and waves toward us. With blond hair and big blue eyes, she is downright delightful.

And when I glance around the crowd that's on their feet, I realize just how many people have come out to support this little lady. It's heartwarming, to say the least. Part of my crazy "I do" dreams always involved having this kind of crowd at my back. A loud, boisterous, unencumbered family of wildly loving people—the kind of people who drop their other plans to come watch your kid in a math competition at school.

The woman standing at the podium smiles down at the large crowd that is here to cheer on Lexi, her eyes crinkling with amusement, and gestures for everyone to take their seats so she can announce the next student.

Both Jude and I sit back down, and he reaches out to wrap his arm around my shoulders, his fingers gently running along the bare skin of my arm.

Several people glance in our direction, his sister, a lady who I'm pretty sure is his mom, and three incredibly attractive men who share enough of the same traits as Jude to lead me to believe they're his brothers—Ty, Flynn, and Remy.

Frankly, they appear just as curious, just as confused, about me showing up with Jude as I feel about Jude bringing me. I mean, he brought me to his niece's school function knowing full well that all of his family would be here.

This isn't Jude's style. At all.

He's Mr. Sexy Good Time. The man who sends me text messages with secret meetups that always lead to insanely hot sex. He's the man who gets me to let loose and be spontaneous and not fixate on things like long-term commitment and marriage and having babies someday.

He's not a meet-the-family kind of guy. Or at least, he *wasn't* that kind of guy.

Was Julie right? Are we starting to become something more than just wild hookups and hot sex?

A war of emotions spurs within me. One part of me is excited and hopeful. But another part of me feels panicky over having any kind of hope. The point of spending time with Jude Winslow wasn't to catch feelings. It was to have fun without fixating on the future or where the future would take me.

And I can't decide if it's a good or bad thing that hopefulness is beginning to grow inside my heart.

"Just so you know, my niece is a fucking genius," Jude whispers into my ear, and I blink out of my thoughts to meet his handsome face. "She's going to crush every kid on that stage."

I can't not grin at his enthusiasm or his pride. And when I watch the way he looks up at the stage, his focus purely on Lexi, it does nothing to suppress the rose of hope that's started to bloom inside me. If anything, it's only making it flourish more.

A lot more.

Two servers from Marco's steakhouse—the restaurant Jude's mom was adamant about having Lexi's after-competition celebration at—step up to our table and start handing everyone a dinner menu, along with their drink order.

Once they give us the spiel on the specials and leave the table to give us some time to decide, Jude stands up from his chair and lifts his fresh drink in the air. "I'd like to propose a toast to our little Lexi for kicking some serious as…*butt* at her Mathletes competition."

A peal of giggles leaves Lexi's lips as she grins up at her uncle. "You were going to say a bad word, weren't you, Uncle Jude?"

"I was," Jude answers and eyes her knowingly. "But how about we ignore that and focus on the fact that you're awesome and we're all so proud of you?"

"I second that!" Wendy, Jude's mom, chimes in and lifts her glass in the air.

Everyone else at the table—all three of Jude's brothers, his sister Winnie and her husband Wes, and a woman whose name I still don't know who has jet-black hair and appears to be with Ty—along with me, join in on the toast, holding our glasses in the air and congratulating Lexi on winning her competition.

The girl did great; there's no doubt about that. She squashed her competitors like a shoe smashing a couple of tiny ants on the sidewalk. Hell, ninety percent of the questions she answered, I didn't even understand.

When Jude said *she's a fucking genius*, he wasn't wrong. His niece's brain is an incredible thing. It's almost scary that she's *this* smart and only in elementary school. *Watch out, world* once she's a full-blown adult.

"So, Sophie, tell me a little about yourself," Jude's sister prompts and props her elbows on the table, fully invested in whatever I have to say. "With the way you were cheering for my daughter, I'm certain you're a blast. Plus, you can somehow tolerate Jude, which is a miracle in and of itself."

Jude chokes on a laugh beside me. "You say that like I'm some kind of lu-natic, sis."

"Because you are," Winnie retorts with pursed lips. But then, her attention is back on my face, ready for me to spill the tea about myself.

"Well…I'm twenty-eight. I run an event planning business. I have two sisters, one of whom is my identical twin, Belle. And, yeah, I don't know. That's about it, I guess." I shrug and take a sip of my iced tea. "I'm kind of devastatingly boring when I think about it."

"Now, that's not true," Jude chimes in, and when I look over at him, his eyes spark with the kind of mischievousness that I've come to know as trouble. "You *love* things like playing Texas Hold'em and *the Girl Scouts,* and you always tell the best damn prison stories."

My eyes might as well be flying saucers when those words leave his lips, but Jude's mouth just keeps chugging along, his lips far too amused with what he's currently telling his sister about me.

"You're fun to grab a drink with at The Champagne Bar. Have a great sense of fashion. So much so that a lot of people would probably want to *steal* your clothes," he says and wraps his arm around the back of my chair, squeezing my shoulders playfully. "Honestly, sis, she's outright lying. Soph is the opposite of boring."

I take a long blink and move my gaze back to Winnie. The furrow in her brow says it all and spurs the need for me to explain.

"I hope you realize that half of the things he just said are total crap."

"Oh, I know." Her laugh makes her neck elongate in the most elegant way. "Trust me, I have over three decades' worth of experience with this jack-wagon. But I'm thrilled that he now has you to call him out on his bull-shit. It's a relief, to be honest."

Jude just grins, and when Winnie's focus gets pulled to the other end of the table, I reach out and discreetly pinch my fingers into the meat of his muscular thigh.

Ouch, he mouths, and his fingers find their way into the sensitive spot just below my armpit that he *knows* makes me giggle.

Which I do, and then, I shove him away from me before we cause a scene. Or I piss my pants. Or both.

"Stop being crazy," I whisper toward him. "Or else you're going to make me look crazy in front of your family."

His arm is back around my shoulders again, and he leans over to whisper into my ear, "Oh, baby, you have nothing to worry about because everyone at this table is fucking nuts. Especially," he adds and nods purposefully toward his three brothers, who sit a few seats down. "Those bastards right there."

"You got something to say, bro?" Ty retorts with narrowed but teasing eyes. "Because if you've got beef, I have no problems settling it promptly."

"Hey now, boys," Jude's mom announces on a sigh. "If you make a scene at my favorite steakhouse in this city, I won't hesitate to make you pay."

"Make us pay?" Ty questions through a jokester's smile. "What's that mean, Ma?"

"It means you don't want to know."

"Uh oh, Wendy is getting pisssssed, Ty," Jude comments on a chuckle. "You better shut your trap."

"When I said boys, I meant *both of you*," Wendy snaps back, and when she meets my eyes, an exasperated but happy smile lifts her mouth. "Sophie, I'm sorry my sons are idiots. We'll all understand if you decide to leave Jude before they even bring the food."

Ty bursts into laughter.

Remy and Flynn just grin from over their menus.

And Jude coughs out a laugh. "Damn, Ma. That was harsh."

But she just blows him a kiss in response. "Love you, honey."

It's all pretty damn hilarious, and the more time I spend with Jude's family, the more I find myself happy to be with them.

They're fun, that's for sure. And they never seem to stop cutting up on one another. Never stop teasing and joking and just…laughing. When the Winslow family is together, laughter is never in short supply.

In a way, it kind of reminds me of my own family and how close-knit we are. My parents might be in Miami and my sister Katelynn might not always be around because of her busy life, but when we're together, we're thicker than thieves.

And I'm surprised with how well I get along with all of them. His sister Winnie and his brother-in-law Wes are so laid-back and easy to talk to.

His mom and Ty are a hoot. Remy is chill, but welcoming.

And Flynn is nice, even though I don't miss the way his eyes observe me closely. His perceptiveness is a little disconcerting, to be honest. It's like he knows more than what's on the surface.

Like how you've caught feelings?

I wish I could deny it, but I can't. I *have* caught feelings. *And your eyes are already starting to get filled with ideas of weddings and marriage and babies.*

THIRTY-SEVEN

Jude

"We're going to head out, guys. Lexi still has some homework, and I have to be at the stadium early because my boss is a real hard-ass," Winnie declares and sends teasing eyes my brother-in-law's way.

Wes just laughs and snags their check from the table.

Everyone follows their lead, my mom, Remy, Flynn, Ty and his random chick, all get ready to leave the restaurant.

"Thanks for coming out tonight to support Lexi," Winnie says and wraps an arm around my niece's shoulders.

"Way to kick some serious mathlete ass, Lex," I tell her, and her face scrunches up in the cutest way.

"That's a bad word, Uncle Jude."

"Yeah, but remember what you told me last summer about people who curse a lot?"

"They statistically have a higher intelligence level."

"Exactly." I tap her nose with my index finger and am rewarded with her toothy smile.

Winnie, Wes, and my niece make their rounds around the table, saying goodbye to everyone, and when they reach Sophie and me, Lexi goes to Sophie first and gives her a big hug.

"Hey, now," I tease. "Why does she get hugged first?"

Sophie smiles, and Lexi just giggles.

And when my niece finally decides to give me a hug, I stand up and squeeze her tight enough to lift her little feet off the ground. "Proud of you, Lex. You did awesome today."

"Thanks, Uncle Jude."

"Thanks for coming and supporting Lexi today, Sophie," my sister tells her and gives her a friendly hug. "I hope we'll be seeing more of you."

At those words, she glances pointedly in my direction, and I do my best to ignore whatever crazy shit Winnie is trying to communicate to me with her eyes.

"I hope so too," Sophie agrees. "This was really fun."

I don't know what I expected when I brought Sophie to Lexi's Mathletes competition tonight, but I'm not surprised that my family appears to get along with her. Sophie is incredibly likable. She's outgoing and beautiful and smart and kind. Her laugh is contagious, and she's always fun to be around.

So fun to be around that you invited her here, knowing that the threat of prison as a registered sex offender made the possibility of sex less than nothing.

"I'm just going to run to the ladies' room real quick," Sophie whispers into my ear, pulling me from my weird-as-fuck thoughts.

"Meet me out front?"

She nods, and for some strange reason, I can't hold back from leaning forward to press a kiss to her lips before she heads in the direction of the bathrooms at the back of the restaurant.

And I definitely don't miss the way my brother Flynn eyes me from the other side of the table, but I ignore him and throw a hundred-dollar bill down on Sophie's and my check—more than enough to pay for our dinner and tip the friendly server named Raymond over thirty percent.

Once I'm out of my seat and heading toward the front of the restaurant, Flynn catches up with me and claps a hand over my shoulder.

"Have a good night?" he asks, and I glance at him out of my periphery as he holds open the door for both of us to step out.

"Yeah…Sure…" I pause, getting the vibe that there's more he wants to say.

Which there is. Right off the bat, red flags wave all over the place.

Once the door shuts and it's just me and Flynn standing outside Marco's, he takes three steps closer, and his eyes are narrowed in skepticism. "What are you doing, man?"

"What do you mean?"

"Bringing Sophie tonight. What's that about?"

"I don't know…" I run a hand through my hair and scoff. "She's nice. Why are you acting like it's such a big deal? Do you have a problem with her or something?"

Flynn rolls his eyes. "No, I don't have a fucking problem with her. But bringing a girl to a family event is a big step."

"Get real. Ty brings chicks to family events all the fucking time."

"But that's Ty. That's not you."

A shocked laugh vibrates my throat. "And what? He's somehow excluded from lectures? What the fuck? Why are you in my business? My dick's business, really. Soph and I are just fun."

Right?

Yeah. Fuck yeah. Just a lot of fun.

"Look, Jude, I'm not trying to be a dick. I'm just trying to understand where your head's at. I'm trying to look out for you," Flynn clarifies. "And considering you never bring girls to anything, *ever*, whether you want to admit it or not, this was a big step for you."

I have no idea what to say to that. Or what he wants me to say to that. And when his eagle-like eyes become a little too much, I look down and fixate on the concrete beneath my boots.

I have no fucking clue what he's trying to get at here. I mean, I didn't really think through all of the whys when I asked Sophie to meet me at Lex's school. I just knew I wanted her to be there…for whatever reason.

"Are you ready to get serious with someone?" Flynn asks, and I jerk my eyes back to his.

"*What?* I don't get serious. With anyone. You know this."

"Yeah, but does *she* know this?"

"Of course she does. I'm not a prick. Any woman I'm with knows the score."

Flynn shakes his head, and his far-too-wise eyes observe me. "Sorry to break this to you, man, but even if she did know at one point, I'm not so sure she does now."

"What the fuck is that supposed to mean?"

"It means, if you have no intention of getting serious with her, you just gave her a real fucked-up mixed signal by introducing her to your entire family."

My head feels like a top, fucking spinning around in circles.

"Just…be careful, man. Think about what your actions are showing, you know? That's all I'm going to say, and now, you can consider me officially out of your business." Flynn claps his hand on my back before lifting the motorcycle helmet tucked in the crook of his arm over his head. "See ya tomorrow morning at the gym?"

I just nod. "Of course."

But as I watch my brother retreat to his Harley, I can only stand there, frozen to my spot in front of Marco's.

Did I just screw shit up by bringing her here tonight?

Well, Vegas did get pretty intimate. And you had her to come to your place the other night, even though you've never invited a woman to your place. Add in the meet-the-family stunt you just pulled, and it's a big fat cluster of what-the-fuck, dude.

I scrub a hand down my face. Shiiiit. Flynn is right. This isn't me. This isn't what I do.

Why the fuck am I doing all this shit?

Because you're actually starting to feel something for her…

Yeah. *Now,* I'm feeling terrified.

The drive from Marco's to Sophie's apartment isn't far, but I'm so lost in my own damn head that I don't register the fact that I didn't even turn on the radio until I'm pulling onto her street in Nolita.

It's a little after ten, and the streets are what I'd call calm for a New York evening. So calm that I could easily find a spot to parallel park in, but I know it wouldn't be a good idea to actually go up to her apartment tonight.

The only thing I can do is drop her off and try to get my head straight.

"Tonight was fun," she says, and I hate the uncertainty that lies in her voice. No doubt, my weird mood since we left the restaurant, in combination with the reality that we've been driving for the past ten minutes in absolute silence, hasn't gone unnoticed.

Which is sad because, deep down, I'm glad she came.

And you also want to go upstairs and lose yourself in her, too.

I ignore that reckless thought, and when I come to a stop in front of her building, I don't bother cutting the engine. I just shift into park.

"Thanks for coming, babe. I'm glad you enjoyed it."

"Of course I enjoyed it. Your family is great, Jude," Sophie says, her voice soft and kind and stirring my heart in ways I shouldn't be comfortable with. "And Lexi is one special little girl."

And you're special too.

When my smile touches my eyes, I try like hell to not be so affected by her. Sex and fun and playing around is one thing, but *feeling* something for her? It's not what a guy like me is supposed to do.

I unbuckle my seat belt and hop out of my car, rounding the hood to open her door.

She uses the hand I offer to ease herself out, but when she notices that the car is still on and I'm illegally parked in front of her building, her eyes turn hesitant.

"You're not coming up?"

"Not tonight, babe." I shake my head. "I have to run by Craze to check on a few things."

I don't have shit to do at the club. But I definitely need to quiet my fucking head and get myself right again. Back to the Jude who doesn't let himself feel anything more than fun.

Her brow furrows. "Oh. Okay."

She looks disappointed, and I hate it. Loathe it, actually. The urge to lean down and kiss her is strong, but instead, I settle for a soft, gentle, *very chaste* kiss to her mouth.

Don't leave her hanging like this, dude. It's cruel. You know you still want to see her.

"But you can expect a text from me soon," I tell her and force a smirk to my lips. "With some instructions."

Sophie searches my face for the longest moment, but eventually, a curious smile slides across her mouth. "Instructions?"

"Uh-huh." I nod. "Get ready, babe. Because we're about to experience something *wild* together."

"More wild than an orgasm on a roller coaster?"

I chuckle at the reminder of our Vegas sexcapades. "Ten times wilder."

"Holy smokes." Her eyebrows damn near rise to her forehead, and I just wink at her.

"Oh yeah, sweet Sophie, it's going to be a good time."

"Can't wait." She stands up on her tippy-toes and presses her full mouth to mine. And the temptation to deepen that kiss, to prolong, to savor it, begins to build to an almost uncontrollable level.

Thankfully, Sophie is the one who pulls away, and with a little wave and a soft "*Good night,*" she walks toward the entrance door of her building.

I watch her the whole way, making sure she gets in safely, and once the main door clicks shut, I hop in my car and grab my cell phone.

The first text I send to Sophie is an address that very few people even know exists in this city. It's an underground kind of place that I'm certain will provide the kind of wild, erotic experience that will get Sophie and me back on the right track.

Away from feelings. Away from more.

And solely focused on *just fun*.

And my next and final message is a simple one.

Me: Wednesday. 7pm. Wear the hottest dress you own.

THIRTY-EIGHT

Wednesday, April 4th

Sophie

The cool evening air causes goose bumps to form on my arms and my legs, and even harden my nipples beneath the dress I chose to wear tonight. It's a silky black number that ends just below my knee but has a slit on one side that nearly reaches my right hip. The material is so thin, provides absolutely zero warmth, and is completely open at the back.

Basically, the absolute last dress you want to be wearing when it's anything but over seventy degrees outside. And it *might* be early spring in New York, but it's far from seventy degrees.

I check the address on my phone once more, the one Jude sent to me, and even though the cab driver managed to drop me off on the street where I thought said place was located, I don't see anything but an alleyway that's lit up by one pathetic streetlamp.

This can't be right.

I glance over my shoulder, prepared to seek out my cab driver for some help, but all I witness is retreating red lights, making it apparent that he's hauling ass to his next destination.

On a sigh, I glance down at my phone again, and **6:55 p.m.** stares back at me.

I'm five minutes early, which is a rarity for me, but since I skipped my therapy appointment last minute so I could meet Jude on time, I was dressed and ready about an hour earlier than I normally would.

Besides our daily text conversations, this will be the first time I've seen him since I had dinner with his family. Six days probably shouldn't seem like a long time, but after being inside each other's pockets twenty-four seven in Vegas and the first few days after that, it kind of feels like an eternity.

I've grown so used to seeing him all the time, it feels like there's now a hole inside my chest that only he can fill.

I'm sure Dr. Winters is probably wondering what would keep me from our standing Wednesday appointments, but my track record is starting to show that whenever Jude wants me to meet him somewhere, I drop everything and do it.

Which is kind of preposterous.

Yeah, well, that's what you do when you're falling in love with someone.

I roll my eyes at myself and ignore my pesky subconscious. Instead, I distract my mind by copying the address into Google Maps to figure out where I went wrong.

But when I hit enter and the map updates, I find that I'm right where I'm supposed to be.

Seriously?

I glance around the alleyway and find nothing but a few dumpsters and discarded trash on the sidewalk. And when I look directly in front of me, I just see a big steel door with no windows and a fire escape that resides directly above it.

A shiver of discomfort rolls up my spine and I start to call Jude for an explanation, but just before my finger hits the phone-shaped button under his name, I spot his tall, muscular form turning the corner and heading down the street in my direction.

"Shit, babe," he comments as he comes to a stop in front of me. "You're early." He glances at his watch and grins. "Well, actually, you're right on time, but for you, that's early."

"Uh…mind explaining why you have me standing in the middle of a deserted alley?"

"I will," he says with his notorious playboy smirk, and he reaches out to grip my hips to pull me closer. "But first, I want to say hello."

Lips to mine, he takes my mouth in a deep, tantalizing kiss, and he doesn't release me until I'm breathless and being cold is no longer an issue.

"I missed you, Soph." My heart jolts against my ribs, and he brushes his lips against my mouth, *once, twice, three* times. Then, he leans his head back to lock his now playful gaze with mine. "You look stunning, babe. That dress could give a man a heart attack."

"Thank you." I blush and giggle in the way that only Jude seems to be able to make me do. "And…I missed you too."

The words feel all-too-right on my tongue. Because I did miss him. *A lot.*

"Ready to get wild?" he asks and waggles his brows.

"I *am*, but…I'm still not understanding how this alley leads to anything but getting robbed."

Jude chuckles. "Babe, it's not always what's on the outside, but what's on the *inside*."

He takes my hand and steps up to the windowless door. Two hard knocks and another four rhythmic, smaller ones sound from his knuckles as they rap against the steel.

Ten seconds later, the hinges screech as the door slides open just enough to reveal a man in a black shirt with a shaved head standing behind it.

"Password," he demands, and Jude doesn't waver.

"Eleanor Roosevelt's G-string."

I blink. I'm sorry… *What did he just say?*

To my utter surprise, the door opens farther, and the bald guy gestures for us to walk inside.

Once we step into a darkened entryway, the man shuts the big steel door with a slam that startles me enough that I jump. Jude squeezes my hand for reassurance.

"The rules are simple," the bald guy states firmly and crosses his arms below his beefy chest. "Anything that happens has to be consensual. And if it's consensual, then anything goes."

Consensual? As in sex?

My eyes jolt to Jude's face, but he only offers a wink and another encouraging squeeze of my hand.

"Have fun."

Those are the last two words out of bald dude's mouth right before he opens another door and Jude is whisking me inside and down a long hallway with strip lighting guiding our path.

We walk through another two doors, and then we come face-to-face with the mother lode, and my brain just about wants to explode out of my skull when I take in my surroundings.

Oh. My. God.

I'm rapidly reminded of the underground spot we went to after the Raines Law Room, only this place is *way* different. More refined and opulent, but *intense*. And far more obvious in what is supposed to happen beneath the shadows of the dim lights and between the gold-embossed and velvet-curtained walls.

I say this because the first people I lay eyes on are not at all being discreet about the sex they're having in a private but visible booth that sits to the side of a bar where two women are tongue-kissing each other in front of their glasses of wine.

My ears note the soft, sultry music that adds to the ambiance, but my eyes are still busy trying to make sense of what I'm seeing. My gaze is more of a shocked gape than anything else, and it's being yanked and tugged around the room like a yo-yo on a string.

People kissing. Touching. *Having sex.* Some are dressed. Some are half dressed. And some are completely naked. But all appear to be single-minded in their goal of pleasure.

"Baby, welcome to the *real* Secret Club," Jude breathes hotly into my ear. "Hardly anyone knows about its existence, and the ones that do, come here to experience their deepest, hottest fantasies."

"Is this a…a…*sex club?*" I whisper and have to gulp down the shock once my ears actually hear the last two words leave my body.

"One of the most prestigious underground sex clubs out there."

"W-what exactly are we going to do here?" I ask, even though that might sound like the dumbest question on the planet. Obviously, we're supposed to have sex. *Duh.*

But the real question I'm trying to ask is…*are we going to have sex in front of other people?*

"Think about it, babe." He brushes his hand down my arm and rests it on my hip. "*Fucking in a restaurant? Fingering you on a roller coaster? You giving me oral on an elevator?* You and I, we have some serious exhibitionist tendencies. And we're here to explore them further."

I don't have a response to that, but all I can think is, *but no one knew we were doing those things. It was our secret.*

Jude presses his hand to my lower back and guides me down a corridor, stopping right in front of a wall that is made from clear glass and looks directly into a room that is set up like a normal, sophisticated bedroom. On one wall, a giant king-sized bed is covered in pillows and a thick white comforter that looks cozy to sleep beneath.

There're framed photos hanging on the wall. A nightstand with a lamp that even has a phone charging cord hanging off it. A desk in the far corner with a leather-bound notebook, a gold pen, and a potted green plant sitting on top. And a long, tall bookshelf filled with all sorts of hardback books.

It's actually a really nice, normal bedroom. But again, it's in the middle of a secret sex club with a translucent wall so *anyone* can look inside.

"This is our bedroom for the night," he whispers into my ear. "To do what we want, to fulfill our deepest fantasies. And to let anyone who wants to see it, watch from right here."

There's a part of me that's incredibly aroused by the idea of someone watching Jude kiss me, touch me, *fuck me.* But there's also a part of me that is so undeniably nervous and uncertain of whether or not this is something I can do.

I want to be spontaneous and do wild, crazy things with this man, I really do, but everyone has a limit. *Is this one mine?*

"Are you ready?" he asks, and I look up and examine his face.

I don't know what I want or need to find there, but something about his steady, controlled gaze and the excitement I can see beneath the surface is starting to make me feel like it might be okay to give this a shot. He's never once put me in a dangerous situation. If anything, he's gone out of his way to make sure I'm safe. Sometimes, even in a bit of a territorial way I find to be pretty damn sexy.

But still, the stark reality is that this isn't something I would ever picture myself doing.

Yet, you're here. And you're already turned on.

I think about all the other times with Jude that I've pushed past what I've thought were boundaries, only to find out they were roadblocks I'd set for myself. Unnecessary mental obstacles that were preventing me from doing things I wanted and liked and enjoyed.

And if you're this aroused already, then that's saying something…

"Let's do it," I whisper, letting the response fall from my lips before I can swallow it back down and start a mental loop of doubt and second-guessing.

Jude takes my hand into his and guides me away from the glass, down a back hallway, and into a side door that leads directly into the bedroom I just saw a few moments ago.

But only this time, *I'm on the other side of the glass.* And I'm sitting down on the bed. And I'm doing all of this knowing there's a possibility that people might watch whatever happens within these walls.

Oh boy, I just hope I'm ready for this…

THIRTY-NINE

Jude

Sophie sits on the bed, her legs crossed and her right foot jiggling up and down. Each motion makes the heel of her stiletto tap against the hardwood floor, and I walk over to her to provide some reassurance.

I can tell she's nervous. I even understand why she's nervous.

This is an incredibly erotic thing we're about to do, have sex while other people watch, but it's going to show both her and me that this is what we're all about—fulfilling fantasies and enjoying hot, incredible, no-strings-attached nights together that leave us both satisfied.

Experience wild things together and have a fuckload of pleasurable fun while doing it.

When my knees gently bump against hers, I try to ground her nerves by placing my hands on her shoulders and massaging the tight muscles that lie beneath my fingertips.

She stares up at me with those big, all-encompassing jade eyes of hers, and it suddenly feels as if someone stole all the fucking oxygen out of the room.

God, she's beautiful. The most beautiful woman I've ever known.

She's this dangerous combination of sultry and sweet. Sassy and meek. She makes me want to fuck her senseless but also protect her. Keep her safe. Make sure no one hurts her.

"You okay, babe?" I ask quietly toward her, and she sucks her lips into her mouth before nodding. "Don't worry," I say. "There's no rush. There's no time limit. There's no need for us to do anything but just enjoy each other at our own pace."

"Okay." She nods again, and her shoulders begin to relax beneath my big hands.

For a long moment, I'm not sure how long, Sophie stays rooted to her spot on the bed, her fingers fidgeting into the mattress as I continue to gently massage my hands up and down her shoulders and neck and bare arms.

The more I rub at her soft skin, the more her body starts to inch closer to me, and when I move my hands to the base of her skull and slide my fingers through the silky tresses of her hair, her head falls back and the softest moan escapes from her lips.

Her breathing begins to change then, from tight and rigid to soft and easy, while each inhale of her lungs pushes her breasts up and makes her cleavage more apparent beneath her slinky dress.

She's into this.

She's a fucking vision of wanton desire. A goddess I'm not sure she even understands that she is.

And when I glance over my shoulder to the glass wall behind me, I see that I'm not the only one who has eyes on this mesmerizing woman. I'm not the only who is turned on by simply watching the way her lips are parted or her lashes fan over her cheeks or how her hips shift a little on the bed.

At least ten other people, mostly men from what I can make out beneath the shadowy lighting, stand right there, on the other side of the transparent wall, watching me touch her.

But mostly, watching *Sophie* enjoy being touched.

My chest grows tight, each inhale and exhale getting harder and harder to move air through my lungs, but I push against the discomfort with a hard swallow and force myself to focus back on her.

When Sophie looks up at me again, her lips lax from my touch, her eyes glow with the kind of heat that I know means if I slid my hand up her thigh and beneath her panties, she'd be wet with arousal.

But I hesitate so long to act on the urge to feel that certainty for myself, that eventually, I'm not the one who makes the next move. *Sophie* is.

She stands to her feet and slides her hands into my hair. And I can't stop looking at her.

"Kiss me," she whispers, and I do.

I press my mouth against hers and move our lips in a passionate dance. She moans again and deepens the kiss, her tongue sneaking into my mouth and mingling with mine. She tastes like her fruity mints, and a part of me loves that no one on the other side of that wall will ever know that about her.

They will never know how Sophie tastes. Or how Sophie feels.

And they will never know all the amazing things about her that I know.

Like, the fact that she'll choose dessert over dinner if given the option. Or when she's mad about something, a little crinkle forms between her eyes. Or when something makes her laugh really hard, her contagious giggles will go completely silent, but her face will stay scrunched up in hilarity.

Or that if they challenged her to a game of Texas Hold'em, she could hustle them out of money without even batting an eye.

Or that she earned fifteen badges in Las Vegas. And fourteen of them were earned by an orgasm *I* gave her.

Sophie's hands moving to my belt and tugging it loose pull my attention back to the present, and when she goes to her knees before me, I stare down at her in absolute shock at the brazen move.

My cock grows hard, but my mind and heart wage one hell of a battle against me.

What are you doing, man? This isn't right.

Her lips quirk up into the kind of sexy but mischievously cute smile that threatens to send my mind back to memories of the elevator in Vegas. And when her hands move to my zipper, sliding it down slowly, I have the most intense urge to pick her up and carry her out of the room.

To shield her away from the strangers on the other side of the glass.

To not let anyone see her vulnerable, with her mouth around my cock. Or see how damn beautiful my girl looks when she's about to come.

Fucking stop this, dude. Don't let this go any further.

Sophie's hands grip the edge of my boxers and pants, starting the process of pulling them down, and I don't even have to think about my reaction. I just do. In an outright impulse, I quickly stop her momentum and grab her hands into mine.

Her face creases up in confusion when I don't allow her to go any further. And her green eyes jerk up to my face.

"Jude?"

"I can't." I shake my head. "Not here, babe," I tell her and gently lift her back to her feet. "We're not going to finish this here."

"You want to leave? *Now?*" All sorts of reactions coat her eyes, only half of which I can discern. But I'm not going to waste any time standing here, inside this fucking room with strangers' eyes on her, and try to figure it all out.

"I'm so fucking proud of you, Sophie." I hold my hands on either side of her face, brushing my lips against hers. "Of how you were just giving in to this moment and what you were feeling. But it's time to go."

After I softly kiss her once more, I take her hand into mine and lead her the fuck away from that bedroom. I don't know what's come over me or what I'm even doing, but I know I don't want Sophie here for a minute more with other people's eyes on her.

I want her all to myself.

FORTY

Sophie

I was going to go through with it. At least, I *think* I was going to go through with it.

But in a blink of an eye, everything changed. One moment, I was gripping Jude's pants and boxers, ready to pull them down, ready to make him *and* me feel good. And the next, he was telling me we needed to leave.

A hundred different feelings stirred in my belly. Confusion. Disappointment. *Relief.*

I still don't know what to make of any of it, but with Jude's lips persistent against mine, it's currently the furthest thing I'm thinking about. Hell, I can hardly unlock my door as we stumble into my apartment, his arms around me and his kiss a fierce, determined force guiding and heightening my arousal.

Ever since he decided it was time to leave that club, *leave that bedroom,* we haven't stopped kissing or touching each other. Not during the ride on the subway. Or during the three-block walk to my building.

And not now that we're inside my place either.

I kick off my heels, and Jude lifts me up into his arms, wrapping my thighs around his waist as he strides toward my bedroom.

"Fuck. I need to be inside you," he says. "Now."

For once, I just tell it like it is. Say what I'm feeling out loud. "I need that too."

He groans and presses his mouth to mine again, and our lips and tongues move together in a frenzied, rough tango.

When my back hits my mattress, only then does he disconnect the kiss to slide my dress up my waist and remove my panties. But then, he pauses and says, "Everything off, babe. I need to feel your body against mine."

I don't balk, I just do, and all our clothes become a distant memory on my bedroom floor.

Between one beat of my heart and the next, his body covers mine. Every inch of his skin and my skin are touching, connected, rubbing against each other. And I'm wild with the need to feel him, *all* of him. It's an all-consuming craving that feels impossible to fully satisfy.

He pauses and leans off the mattress, grabbing for a condom in the back pocket of his discarded pants, but my mouth moves before I can even think.

"No. Don't."

He looks at me. "Don't what?"

"I want to feel you inside me. Bare."

"But—"

"I'm on birth control," I add in a rush. "And I'm safe, clean, and—"

"I'm clean too," he cuts me off. "But are you sure, Sophie?"

I nod, but then I quickly say, "Only if you want it, too."

He doesn't respond with words. Instead, he *shows* me his answer through actions.

With his body over mine, he guides himself inside me…*completely bare.* Just like I wanted. *Just like I need.* Inch by inch, I can feel him…*really* feel him, and it's better than anything before.

He slowly stokes our intimate connection as his blue eyes stare deep into mine, and our mouths are so close, we're sharing breaths and moans.

And it's all so soft and sweet and *perfect.* It's eye contact and touching and feeling and just…becoming one. This doesn't feel like just sex anymore. It feels like something entirely different.

It feels like more.

Jude's eyes stay connected with mine, and with each of his thrusts inside me, I feel like another piece of my heart slides out of my chest and into his.

"God, you're everything."

Those words are a mere whisper, a barely heard wisp of sound that my ears almost can't discern, but I swear they come straight from his lips.

I feel the same way, I silently think.

"Sophie."

That time, I *know* it's him. And his sapphire eyes hold the kind of emotion that doesn't stem from a mere good time. The kind of emotion I've been feeling for him for far longer than I can even admit to myself.

And I swear, right there, right then, with softness in his voice and the way I feel like his soul is in his eyes, it's the final blow—*the bull's-eye straight to my heart.*

The mattress shifts, and I pop open my eyes to make out Jude's form sitting on the edge of the bed in the darkness of my room. I have no idea what time it is, but I know that before I fell asleep, I was nestled cozily within the comfort of his arms, right after it felt like the sex we experienced together wasn't just sex. *No, it was far more.*

When he starts to slowly stand up, almost like he's trying to do it without being heard, I can't stop myself from reaching out with my hand and brushing my fingers against his back.

"What are you doing?"

"I gotta go, babe."

"Stay," I whisper toward him. "Don't leave. Stay the night with me."

His muscles tense beneath my fingertips. "I can't stay, Soph."

"Why not?"

"Because I just…can't."

His back is still toward me, and the lack of emotion in his voice makes an uncomfortable ache start in the pit of my stomach. I sit up to turn on the lamp on my nightstand, and the time on my alarm clock reveals it's after two in the morning.

"Jude? What's going on? Did something happen?"

He finally turns around to meet my eyes. "I just can't stay the night, Sophie. That's not what I do."

Not what he does? What the hell?

"What do you mean, that's not what you do?" I ask as inklings of anger start to flood into my veins. Though, there's enough hurt and sadness mixed in to make my lips crease down at the corners too. "We were together for three nights straight in Vegas. How is this any different?"

"Because Vegas was fun, babe. And that's what we are—*fun*," he answers, and I hate how cold his voice sounds. I swear, if I put my hand up to his mouth as those words passed his lips, I'd actually feel my fingertips freeze.

I also hate that he's just written us off like that. After everything we've experienced together. After I met his family. After *tonight*. And he's going to tell me this is still *just fun?*

I saw the way he looked at me. I felt the way he kissed me. Touched me. Slid inside me. It wasn't fucking. It wasn't sex. And it wasn't just fun.

When I just sit there staring up at him, trying to understand how one man can change in what feels like an instant, Jude elaborates.

"Soph, babe, I can't stay because that's not what this is, you know? I thought you understood that. I thought we were on the same page."

"We *were* on the same page," I say, and my voice grows quiet as my fingers fidget mindlessly with my comforter. There's a huge part of me that wants to hold back the truth, but the part that refuses to go along with the façade wins out. "But that page feels like it's turned and turned again, and now, things *have* changed between us, Jude."

"No, Sophie." He stands up with just his boxer briefs covering his body and runs a frustrated hand through his hair. "Things didn't change."

That's such bullshit. I know I have my own issues with putting relationships and commitment on some kind of pedestal that's impossible to reach, but I know what I saw. I know what I felt.

"Are you really going to sit there and try to act like nothing besides just a bunch of sex and fun has happened between us? Please don't do that, Jude. Think about tonight. Think about the way we were together," I practically plead, silently hoping that he'll take a step back and really think about what he's feeling.

But his lips turn into a firm line, and by the way his jaw tenses, I can tell I've hit a nerve. Although, I'm not at all expecting what comes out of his mouth next.

"I don't need to think about anything, Sophie. And it's not my fault if you've made up some shit about us in your head," he answers, and it feels like each one of his words is a sharpened knife stabbed deeper into my chest.

Tears prick my eyes and my hands shake, and I just sit there, gaping at a man I feel like I don't even know anymore.

"I'm sorry, babe," he continues, but it's the furthest thing from an apology. There isn't an ounce of anything but emotionless asshole within those words. "I can't go along with acting like this is more than it is. It's not my style. Jude Winslow will never be attached to anybody."

I want to sob. I want to scream. And I want him to fucking leave. More than that, I *need* him to leave for my own sanity and self-preservation.

"You're right," I say, and my voice is harsh as a whip. "We were just fun, Jude. *Just a bunch of fucking fun*, like you said. Nothing else. Nothing more. And you'll never be attached to me because I deserve a hell of a lot better than someone like you. So, you can leave now. Pretty sure we're done here."

Those stupid tears start to stream down my cheeks in uncontrollable waves, and Jude's eyes flash with a sense of sadness, like he suddenly grew a conscience and feels bad for hurting me or something. And he steps toward me with an outstretched hand in a pathetic attempt to provide comfort for the pain he just created.

"Don't touch me!" I snap and abruptly shift my body so his fingers can't make contact with my skin.

"Sophie," he starts to say, and the way he says my name reminds me too much of the Jude I thought I knew.

"*No*. Get out."

His eyes go wide with shock and other things I don't care about, but he doesn't move from his spot beside my bed.

"Get out!" I scream at the top of my lungs. "Leave! Now!"

And only then does he listen to me.

Right out of my bedroom and out of my apartment and out of my life, Jude leaves.

FORTY-ONE

Jude

I struggle to pull my jeans up my legs and zip them with my hand while simultaneously trying to shove my feet into my boots. I stumble more than a few times and almost fall face first on the hardwood floor right outside of Sophie's apartment door, but I quickly put a hand to the wall and steady myself.

Son of a bitch.

Just as I start the process of buttoning up my shirt, a middle-aged woman in a pair of plaid pajamas with a little white dog tucked in the crook of her arm steps off the elevator. She pauses mid-step as the doors shut behind her, her brow furrowing at my current display of rushed, bumbling hands and disheveled attire.

Normally, I'd offer something, *anything*, to put her at ease, to make her smile, *to give her relief that I'm not a psycho inside her building*, but my mind might as well be on another planet with the way it can't seem to concentrate on anything but snapshots of Sophie's tearstained cheeks and shaking hands.

And all I can hear is the pain that was in her voice when she told me to leave.

God, what did I just do?

You broke her heart. That's what you did.

I yank my hands away from the buttons of my shirt when my fingers can't seem to manage the simple task and scrub a frustrated hand down my face.

"Fuck," I mutter harshly, and it's only then that I note the lady in the pajamas scurries away, moving down the hallway and to her apartment as quickly as her slippers can take her.

Way to go, Jude. You're really hitting it out of the park tonight.

Another visual of Sophie sits prominently behind my eyes, and I grimace as I recall the words I said to her. The way she looked when I told her we were just fun. Nothing else. Nothing more.

You mean, the way you lied to her.

"Goddammit."

I turn to face her door, my hand lifted in the air, prepared to rap against the wood, but I pause halfway and shove that hand back into my pocket.

There is absolutely nothing I can say to her that will fix this.

That realization feels impossible to grasp, and the idea of walking away from her feels even harder, but I don't have any other choice. I *can't* give her what she wants. *What she deserves.*

I'm not the guy you settle down with. Never have been and I vowed that I never will be.

It's the only way I know.

Love and heartbreak and all that bullshit would destroy me from the inside out. I've seen it do those things to too many people I love. I've seen the destruction. The aftermath. And I don't want any part of it. Not for me, and not for Sophie either.

Too bad you've already done that not just to her, but to you, too.

I shake my head at myself, pushing the uncomfortable thoughts as far away as I possibly can, and I turn on my heel.

This is for the best.

Ten steps later, I'm standing in front of the elevator. With one push of the button, the doors open and I'm inside.

And by the time I'm stepping into the lobby and heading toward the entrance, I start to believe that what I'm doing is the right thing, even though every step I take feels like I'm going in the wrong direction.

Obviously, I just need some time to process it all, but once I do, *I know* this is how it has to be because Jude Winslow doesn't get attached to anyone.

And he sure as hell doesn't let himself fall in love.

FORTY-TWO

Thursday, April 5th

Sophie

When I couldn't sleep, couldn't stop the damn tears from streaming down my cheeks, I forced myself to get out of bed. The sky was still dark, but I knew my favorite bakery up the street from my apartment would be open.

So, I threw on some clothes, don't even know what clothes, and walked the two blocks.

But when I got there and ordered my usual—a glazed donut and a coffee—I couldn't even lift the donut to my mouth to take a bite. Couldn't even take a drink. The idea of food or anything else made me want to puke.

I also think the fact that Rose, the little old lady who owns the shop, kept looking at me with sympathy and concern on her face wasn't helping my current distraught state.

Surely my red-rimmed eyes and blotchy cheeks weren't giving her any reassurance.

To be honest, I hate that I'm so affected by what Jude said to me. By how he acted. By the way he seemed to turn into a completely different person when faced with the idea of more happening between us.

I feel as if I've taken ten steps back in the progress I thought I'd made.

I know I come with some serious baggage, but I also know that what I saw and felt couldn't have been a figment of my imagination. He feels something for me.

Or felt something for you, at least.

More tears stream down my cheeks, and I swipe my hands over my face as a shaky breath bounces around in my throat.

Just. Stop. Crying. For. Fuck's. Sake.

On a deep inhale, I force oxygen into my lungs and continue my path to the only place that makes sense right now.

The sun begins to make her way over the horizon just as I pass the doorman standing outside Belle's building and step into the lobby. I know it's early and I know she and John are probably in bed, but I can't seem to find it in me to care.

I need my twin.

On the elevator and up the ten flights to her floor, I stare down at my shoes the whole way. They're the oldest pair of gym shoes I own, and by the looks of the stains and ratty shoestrings, I should've thrown them in the garbage a long-ass time ago.

But who cares about shoes when you feel like someone tore your heart out of your chest, amiright?

The mental joke has the opposite effect. Instead of being a careful avoidance of my reality, it only serves as a stark reminder.

Cue more fucking tears.

Frankly, if Justin Timberlake didn't actually write "Cry Me a River" about Britney Spears, then he could easily just tell the world I was his muse.

Am I pathetic for feeling like this? Maybe it all really was a figment of my imagination?

After another swipe of my hand across my face, I pull the key to Belle's apartment out of my purse. It's the one she gave me for emergencies, and considering I feel like I might be one crying jag away from someone having to put me in a straitjacket and ship me off to Shutter Island, I'd say right now qualifies for this 9-1-1, unexpected arrival.

When I step inside, John's and her apartment is completely quiet, and I meander around in her kitchen for a little while, hoping that maybe she'll wake up and come find her twin sister having a mental breakdown by her fridge.

But when the silence becomes too much for my racing mind and time feels like it doesn't budge a second, I pull a Cristina Yang and walk straight into my sister's bedroom, slip off my ratty shoes, and climb into bed with her and John like they're my Derek Shepherd and Meredith Grey.

Thankfully, from what I can tell, they're not naked. But at this point in my emotional rock bottom, I don't even think I'd care about that.

Belle stirs in her sleep and turns on her side, her eyes blinking open and groggily staring into mine. "Sophie?"

"Hi."

"Am I dreaming?"

I shake my head.

"So, you are, in fact, in bed with me and my husband."

I nod.

John is awake now, sitting up on his elbows a little to look over Belle's shoulder and directly at me. "Ah, hell. This really is happening."

"No offense, sis. I love you very much, and I'm always happy to see you, but…" Belle pauses and clears the sleep from her voice. "It's a little strange waking up to both you and my husband in bed. Mind explaining what's going down here?"

"I need you," I whisper, and it cracks open the flimsy dam, allowing my tears to come back full force.

"Oh no, honey," Belle whispers and quickly pulls me into a tight hug.

"I think now is a good time for me to go make some coffee," John announces quietly, and I feel the mattress shift as he gets out of bed. Without any questioning, he just walks out of their bedroom, and I hear the door click shut, his signal that he's given us privacy.

Why does my brother-in-law have to be such a good guy? I sure as shit know he wouldn't leave Belle in the middle of the night because he's a fucking commitment-phobic asshole.

Another round of sobs, and I officially hate myself.

"Okay, you have to give me something here because I'm starting to get really worried," Belle says quietly, concern very much evident in the inclination of her voice. "What's going on, Soph?"

"Everything."

Belle sighs. "Can you be slightly more specific, maybe? Everything is a lot of ground to cover."

I wish I didn't have to burden my sister with all my bullshit, but the strength it would take to keep all this bottled up inside me any longer is too much. *I can't do it.* I can't keep lying to my sister—or anyone else, for that matter. The only thing that feels right is to tell the truth.

So, through each shuddering, unsteady breath, I do.

"I've been having secret sex rendezvous with a guy I haven't told you about. Even went to Vegas with him for a few days. And now, everything has blown up into flames."

"*What?*" Belle leans her head back to meet my eyes, and the look of shock that is on her face makes me grimace. It also makes me cry harder.

"I'm sorry!" I sob. "I should have told you. I know I should've told you, but everything just got so out of control. And at first, I didn't know what you'd think about me sleeping with the dancer from your bachelorette party, but then, he didn't end up even being a dancer, and before I knew it, I was meeting up with him for hot sex in public places and he was stealing my panties and I was a Girl Scout in Vegas, earning orgasm badges!" I ramble on a wail and shove my face into her pillows.

"What the…?" she says and releases me from her arms to sit up and rest her back against the headboard of her bed. "Who was stealing your underwear? And when were you hanging out with Girl Scouts?"

"No!" I bellow and lift my head to meet her eyes. "There're no Girl Scouts!"

"Holy hell, I feel like my head is going to explode," she mutters and reaches out to shove some of my hair out of my face. "Honey, I'm going to need you to take a breath, calm yourself, and start from the beginning. But much slower this time and with a little more detail because I'm really hoping this story of yours doesn't involve what I'm now thinking it does."

Oh God. I'm really failing at the delivery of all of this.

With deep inhales through my nose and long exhales through my mouth, I try to slow my quick, hiccupping breaths down.

"That's it," Belle encourages with a gentle hand to my shoulder. "That's perfect. Just keep doing that."

Once my breathing slows and the tears stop streaming from my lids, Belle offers a soft smile in my direction. "Better?"

"A little."

"Enough to tell me what's really going on, but this time, in a way I can actually understand?"

"Yeah." I nod.

"Because I have to say, I'm still a little confused and slightly horrified about how Girl Scouts and orgasms go together, you know?"

I should probably laugh at that because it's fucking ridiculous, but humor is not an emotion I can feel right now. But thankfully, telling my sister everything is something I *can* manage. And while it's difficult as hell and I shed more tears than I'd like, I crack my Jude box wide open.

I tell Belle how things started between us. How things progressed. I tell her about all our secret meetups and about Vegas and how I met his family.

I even tell her about the secret sex club where no sex happened because Jude wanted to leave. How it felt like things had changed between us and how horribly wrong everything went last night.

And I tell her how devastated I felt—*still feel*—when he left.

Once I'm finished, Belle just wraps me up in her arms and gives me a tight, loving hug.

"I'm so sorry, Soph," she whispers into my ear. "I wish you would've told me about Jude before now."

"I know. I should have."

"Man, I can't believe my bachelorette party was a catalyst for this," she mutters. "But I can definitely understand the draw. Pretty sure any woman would understand. The man is like an irresistible Greek god with a smile that could light panties on fire. Although, I'm currently struggling with the urge to go track his ass down and straight up kill him for hurting you like this."

Her mere mention of panties threatens to send me spiraling again, but I dig deep to push the unwanted emotion back down into my belly.

Belle runs her fingers through my hair, rooting me in comfort I really needed to feel, and we both just stay in her bed, staring up at the ceiling of her bedroom.

"I don't want to ask you this, but I have to, Soph. Do you really think there's no hope?"

I shake my head and swallow around the thick ball of emotion lodged in my throat. "It's done."

"God, I'm so sorry." Belle frowns, and all I can do is shrug. But then she surprises me with her next line of questions. "Can I put in a request? No more secrets between us, okay?"

My therapy sessions with Dr. Winters pop into my brain, and I cringe.

Unfortunately, Belle doesn't miss it. "What? What is it, Soph? Is there something else?"

I shake my head. Sigh. I even almost lie and tell her I've told her everything, but I realize that all of my lies and secrets played a role in leading me to this desolate state. "I'm not ready to say yet, but just know it's not something you need to freak out about, all right?"

She searches my face, like she's trying to figure it out anyway, but ultimately, she gives up and agrees, "Okay."

A few minutes later, Belle gets out of bed, but I just lie there, mostly numb from all the crying jags, but also, my head still spinning around like a top over thoughts of Jude.

Why does it have to hurt so bad?

Because you're in love with him.

I shove my face into my sister's pillows again and fight back the tears with a groan. I know I shouldn't have fallen in love with Jude Winslow, but it's pretty fucking obvious that's what I went and did.

"Okay, yeah." Belle's voice fills my ears. "I think it's safe to say today is *not* a workday and I need to call Katelynn and let her know her ass better drive into the city because we need a Sage Sister day."

"You don't have to do that," I mutter into the pillow, but my sister is undeterred.

"You're not getting out of this one, Soph. We're having a 'fuck boys' day!"

"Yeah, fuck those boys!" John yells from the kitchen, apparently hearing more of our conversation than he was letting on.

I lift my head from the pillows just in time to see Belle shout back at him with cupped hands around her mouth. "Mind your business! You have a dick, too!"

Before I know it, she's keeping her word and grabbing her cell to call Katelynn. And by the time she hangs up the phone, Belle lets me know that our elder sister is going to meet us at Amelia's Diner for breakfast.

I feel relief to be surrounded by the support of my sisters. But also, I feel dread over the idea of having to be out in public, when on the inside, I feel like half of my heart has been relocated into someone else's body.

But as I watch the way my sister helps me get ready—brushing my hair, letting me borrow some of her clothes, doing everything in her power to lift my mood—I realize that I need to stop hiding shit and let her and Katelynn *all the way* into my life. I have to be more open to their support that I so obviously need.

It's time you finally tell them everything—*even your standing Wednesday appointments with Dr. Winters.*

FORTY-THREE

Saturday, April 7th

Flynn

I pull my Harley to a stop just outside of Club Craze and cut the engine. The beats of house music pound from the inside of the building, and I'm already regretting agreeing to come.

I hate nightclubs.

Give me my bike. Give me the open road. Give me a roomful of people who aren't drunk off booze and dry fucking one another, and I'll show up with bells on.

But this awful scene? Busy nightclubs in New York City? They're the last place a guy like me wants to be.

I hop off my seat, remove my helmet from my head, and secure it to my bike, before turning on my heel to face the madhouse. My black boots crunch into the gravel between the street and sidewalk outside of the club as I head toward the entrance.

Of course, standing behind the clichéd velvet ropes that are guarded by a pair of bouncers, there's a line a mile long of people waiting to get the coveted invite inside.

I'm starting to feel way too fucking old for shit like this.

"Hey there. You're the guy who just rode in on that hot Harley, aren't you?" a female voice asks from behind me, and I turn around to find a skinny blonde with plastic tits standing there giving me the kind of come-hither eyes that say she's down for a lot of things she probably shouldn't be down for.

She's attractive, yes, but not my type.

"Good God, I'd like to do more than take a ride on his bike," the brunette standing beside her whispers loud enough for me to hear.

First of all, honey, I never take anyone on the back of my bike. And secondly… Well, confidence is one thing, but being this obvious and superficial is an absolute turnoff for a bastard like me.

But I don't tell them that. Instead, always sticking with the priority of being a gentleman, no matter the situation, I simply offer a smile and move back to my task of trying to get inside this fucking club.

Once I'm standing closer to the velvet ropes, I grab the attention of one of the bouncers with a head nod. "Hey, man, I know you're busy with all this—" I pause and glance over my shoulder "—bullshit."

"Yeah." He laughs. "What can I do for ya?"

"My brother told me to come by here and grab a drink with him," I explain briefly. "Jude Winslow. You might know him?"

The bouncer nods, his face reacting in a similar way that anyone who knows my baby brother seems to do. "Ah, hell yeah! Jude's a good time."

Yeah. That's what they always say too. It's one of the things I've always loved about Jude. He's just so fucking lovable that it takes a serious effort not to like him.

I grin. "That he is."

"Come on in," he adds and moves the velvet rope for me. "Pretty sure Jude is in the VIP area."

"Thanks."

Once I make it into the club, the house music grows louder and more persistent inside my skull as I near the main area where the dance floor and DJ are located.

I almost pull out my cell and text my brothers to figure out how in the hell I'm supposed to find them in this chaos of gyrating bodies and drunken fools, but I get lucky when I spot Remy at the bar.

"You made it," he says and claps a hand onto my shoulder when I step up beside him.

I did, indeed, make it, made obvious by the fact that I'm standing right here. I don't bother acknowledging the evidence of my presence and, instead, move on to information I don't know. "Where's Ty?"

"Hell if I know. Said he had something come up last minute."

I glance around for the man of the hour, the one who was annoyingly insistent on getting me to come here tonight. But when I don't spot him right away, I meet Rem's eyes again. "And Jude?"

My elder brother lets out a deep sigh. "Fucking hell. He's a mess."

"What do you mean?" I jerk my head back, and Rem simply tosses his thumb over his shoulder to lead my gaze in the direction of our baby brother, who is currently on the dance floor with a bunch of women surrounding him.

A bottle of champagne is in one hand as he shakes it up and squirts the liquid around on the crowd before him.

"Ah, fuck," I mutter.

"You said it, brother. That's spiraling if I've ever seen it."

"What happened?" I ask just as memories of my conversation with Jude outside of Marco's start to float around inside my head.

Don't tell me I had a part in this meltdown…

"Not sure," he answers with a shrug. "Been trying to figure that out for the last hour, but the train wreck is just chugging along, as you can see."

Honestly, I've been feeling guilty about that conversation ever since it happened. I make a point never to put my nose in my brothers' business. That's Remy's and Winnie's job, not mine. But there was just something about his recklessness with Sophie that didn't sit well with me.

She seemed like a really nice girl, and the more I saw the way she looked at Jude, the more I started to get worried that Jude wasn't keen on what was really happening.

I look back at the dance floor just in time to see a woman with long red hair sidle up to my brother. She's in the shortest dress I've ever seen, and she's doing everything in her power to get Jude's attention.

When he looks at her, he smirks, even lifts his bottle of champagne into the air and pours her a long drink. But then something changes. He shoves his bottle of liquid courage into the chest of a random, dancing man a few feet away and proceeds to put as much distance between himself and the flirtatious woman as he can.

What is he doing?

I furrow my brow and look at Remy.

"I know, man. He's all over the place. One minute, he looks as if he's trying to flirt with every skirt in the room, and the next, it's as if he remembers he wore his chastity belt tonight."

Jude has always been a panty-charming kind of guy who downright revels in female attention. And that redhead is a woman I'd expect to see him go home with once last call was announced from the bar.

But he's avoiding her—*completely*—and it tells my strong intuition everything I need to know.

Shit. This is exactly what I was hoping it wasn't…

"I think even a blind man could put these puzzle pieces together."

Rem's eyes move off the freak show our brother is putting on in the center of the dance floor and back to me. "Wait…you think you know what's going on with him?"

"C'mon, Rem," I say through a harsh laugh. "You can't be that dense, bro. There's only one reason for a man to look like *that,* and it's got tits."

"*Oh no.* It's that woman he brought to Lexi's competition, isn't it? Sophie, right?"

I raise my eyebrows and lean into a hard stare that Remy can read well enough. If the reason for this breakdown isn't her, I'll donate my left nut to scientific research.

"Well, shit, Flynn," Rem mutters and looks out at Jude again. "I think it's safe to say this won't resolve without an intervention."

"Copy that."

Just like we've done what feels like a hundred times before—though, most of them occurred when we were all in our early twenties and Jude and Ty were acting like drunken idiots—Rem and I stride away from the bar to remove our brother from the crowd.

Rem on one side, me on the other, we slide our arms beneath his shoulders and drag the mess off the dance floor and up to a quieter, calmer area with fewer distractions.

Jude bitches and complains the whole way, but we ignore him *and* the curious looks we get from clubgoers. And we don't stop until his ass is firmly on one of the couches in what I'm assuming is the VIP section he said he set aside for us tonight.

He glares. "What the fuck are you guys doing?"

"That's funny. We were hoping to ask you the same thing," Rem comments with a smirk. "You're a goddamn lunatic tonight, and it's high time you tell us why."

"There's nothing to tell. I'm just having a good time." Jude rolls his eyes and goes to stand up, but both Rem and I shove him back down.

"Seriously?" he questions, and we nod in synchrony.

"Spill it, man," Rem says. "What's up?"

When Jude doesn't say anything, I call on the last-ditch effort and mention the name of the invisible elephant in the room.

"Where's your friend Sophie?"

I don't miss the way his eyes flash with the kind of pain I've seen before. It's an acute agony of regret and misery—and the exact pain I saw over thirteen years ago when we had to tell Remy that his bride-to-be wouldn't be showing up at the altar.

But Jude doesn't respond. Instead, he just sits there. Mute.

"Dude," Rem chimes in. "I hate to be the one to tell you, but you can't hide from the fact that you look like a psycho. Like a man who is all screwed up inside his head and has bought a one-way ticket to Spiral Town, USA."

Jude searches Remy's steady gaze and then moves to me.

"Rem's right, man," I agree. "You're a mess."

"Oh, is that right?" Jude snaps. "But I thought you'd be happy about this, Flynn?"

"What's that supposed to mean?"

"*You* are the one who pulled me aside and gave me a real good talking-to, remember?" he announces, and every word is wrapped in sarcasm. "Told me I needed to be careful what my actions were telling Sophie. So, yeah, I guess you could say all the *carefulness* is what led me here."

Rem's gaze locks on to me. "What'd you say to him?"

Shit. I sigh. "I just tried to make him realize that bringing Sophie to our family thing was a big fucking step for him. And..." I shrug. "I mean, Rem, if you were paying any attention that night, you would've seen the look in her eyes, and you would know exactly why I said something. Even though, I have to admit, it wasn't my business."

"Definitely wasn't your fucking business," Jude retorts.

"I know, man. I'm sorry." I raise both hands in the air and shake my head. "I shouldn't have said shit."

"Or maybe you should've," Rem states. "And maybe Jude needs to buck the fuck up and tell us what really happened."

"And why would I do that?"

"So we can help you, numbnuts," Rem answers without batting an eye. "Because whether you want to admit it to yourself or not, you invited us here for a reason. And I'm certain it wasn't to watch you play clown show on the dance floor. I mean, *come on.* Think about what's going on here. How many times in your life has *Flynn* given you a *talk* that was unnecessary? Words are like gold to this son of a bitch, dude. You know that."

"Fuuuuuck." Jude leans his head back on the velvet sofa and scrubs his hand down his face, and I roll my eyes to the ceiling. These guys think I'm quiet because they gossip and chatter like a group of high school cheerleaders.

The moment is long, but Rem and I just sit there, waiting patiently for Jude to work through whatever he's currently battling inside that thick, stubborn head of his.

Thankfully, I only have to tolerate the sounds of two eardrum-destroying pop songs before Jude appears to have the *"Aha! I need to just tell my brothers what's up so I can stop looking insane"* moment.

"Okay, fine." He raises his hands and then slaps them onto his knees. "I messed things up with Sophie real goddamn bad."

Rem quirks a brow. "And what do you mean by bad?"

"Fucking *bad,*" he says, and that familiar pain is back in his eyes again. "I hurt her, and ever since then, ever since she kicked me out of her apartment with tears streaming down her cheeks, I feel like someone's rearranged my fucking insides."

I move to sit down beside him, wrapping my arm behind the back of the couch, while Jude leans forward and rests his elbows on his knees, dropping his head into his hands on a groan.

I pat his back with a supportive hand, and in typical Rem fashion, he takes the reins of the conversation.

"What hurt her?"

"Me," Jude answers without reluctance and lifts his head back up to look at us. "*I hurt her. Because commitment isn't my thing, you know.*"

"You sure about that, bro?"

"Of course, I'm sure it's not my thing." Jude scoffs. "Never has been. Never will be."

"And why is that, exactly?"

"For lots of fucking reasons, Rem," he retorts. "Because I saw the bullshit Dad put Mom through. Because I saw what happened to *you*. No fucking thank you. I'm just fine with the way things have always been. I don't need anyone or anything else."

"Well, to be honest, bro, you're looking exactly like I did thirteen years ago."

Jude's head jerks back. "What are you trying to say?"

"That you're sitting here like a heartbroken son of a bitch."

"No, I'm not."

"Yeah, you are," Rem disagrees on a snort. "And trust me, I know, because I've been there."

Jude doesn't say anything to that. He just sits there, looking like a man who's currently in the middle of a difficult revelation.

And Rem stays patient, giving him a few minutes, while I continue to play my usual role. The strong but silent brother who is there for support but only says things when he *really* means them.

"Falling in love with someone, being in a committed relationship with someone you love, isn't a fucking death sentence, Jude. And just because Charlotte and I didn't work out doesn't mean that you shouldn't give a relationship with someone like Sophie a chance," Rem says eventually. "Who, by the way, seems really fucking awesome." His tone is quiet, but his delivered words pack a sucker punch of an effect on Jude—his mouth creases down at the corners, and his eyes briefly go shut.

"She is." The anguish in his voice is palpable.

"Then, if I were you," Rem continues, "and I had someone like Sophie who wanted to be with me so much that it actually caused her *and* me physical pain for things to end? Then, I wouldn't be sitting here."

"What would you do?"

"I'd be trying to make it work with her."

Jude scoffs. "No, you wouldn't."

"Yes, I would," Rem answers so easily that I almost believe him. "Stuff that went down in my past doesn't mean shit about your happiness, Jude. If Sophie means that much to you that it's made you look like a fucking lunatic over the idea of not being with her, then I don't think you should waste that opportunity."

Jude grows quiet for a long moment, but eventually, the hints of a smile touch his face as he so obviously tries to derail the conversation. "Thanks for this," he says and looks at both Rem and me. "For being here. I appreciate it."

"Anytime, man." I clap a hand to his back, and then I show no mercy by pushing him right back to the important shit. "You know what you're going to do?"

Jude shrugs and runs a hand through his hair. "I don't fucking know. I feel like I've got a lot to think about. Hell, there's probably a lot of fucked-up shit I need to work through."

"Well, I could've easily told you that," Rem teases, and Jude rolls his eyes and *almost* laughs.

But then a heavy sigh takes priority. "Man, I really messed things up with her."

"Shit happens," I tell him, something I *do* believe. "We all screw up at times. Doesn't mean we don't deserve a second chance if we show we're willing to apologize for it and put in the work to make it better."

But my truth doesn't stem from things like love. It's more of a blanket statement about life in general.

"Do you think I'm in love with her?" Jude asks so quietly I almost don't hear him, but Rem is quick to volley that question right back.

"Do you feel like you are?"

"I don't know," he mutters and stares down at his clasped hands. "I've never been in love before. How would I know what it feels like?"

"When it's good, it feels like you're fucking flying."

Jude quirks a brow at Remy. "And when it's bad?"

"Like someone rearranged your insides," he repeats Jude's earlier words, and by the outright shocked look on my youngest brother's face, it's safe to say they hit the nail on the head.

"Fuck," he mutters, and Rem looks over at me, his eyes silently communicating what I'm already thinking—*Jude's in love.*

The poor bastard.

"I definitely need a drink now," Jude grumbles. "You guys want anything?"

I shake my head, but Rem says, "I'll take a bourbon."

And once a cocktail waitress Jude waved down brings them their drinks, the mood lightens enough for Rem to ask, "So, how did you meet Sophie, by the way?"

"Oddly enough, it all started with a bet with this dancer Mav—" Mid-sentence, Jude just stops talking, and his face scrunches up in a combination of terror and shock.

"Jude, buddy? You good?" I ask, and he shakes his head.

"I…I have to go."

"*What?*"

"I have to go," he says and hops up from the couch. He starts to walk away from us but turns back around to say, "Tell them to put your drink on my tab."

"Where the fuck are you going?!" Rem shouts toward his retreating back.

"Somewhere important! I'll call you tomorrow!"

And then he's gone, disappearing into the crowd without any further explanation. Leaving Rem and me with gaped jaws and puzzled eyes.

"Well, shit, I guess he's done for the night."

I glance at Remy, and a shocked laugh hops out of my throat. "Yeah, but I guess it's better than seeing him walk around this club like an angry lunatic."

"I hear that." Remy chuckles. "You think he's heading in Sophie's direction?"

"No fucking clue."

"Do you want to stay here any longer?"

I smirk. "Hell no."

"Same." Rem grins and lifts his glass in the air. "What do you say, after I finish this bourbon, we head out of here and grab something to eat?"

"I'm down."

But as we sit there, I can't stop myself from asking him something that's been bugging me since I heard him trying to talk our brother off the ledge. "So, tell me, did you believe all that stuff you were saying to Jude? About how if you were in his shoes, you'd be trying to make it work with Sophie?"

"Fuck no," Remy mutters. "No offense to Sophie, because she seems like an awesome girl, but love has never done me any favors. And I don't plan on being a fan of it anytime soon."

I grin. And also, I can't find it in me to disagree.

FORTY-FOUR

Jude

"Jude?" Tommy, one of my favorite bouncers at Club Craze, calls out toward me as I dash through the door, past the velvet ropes, and onto the pavement like a madman. "You all right, bro?"

"I need a cab."

"On it." He nods and, thankfully, doesn't question me any further.

I have no real plan, just a semblance of a plan, and I'm sure my brothers are currently sitting in the club wondering what in the hell just happened.

But I didn't have time to explain the crazy shit rolling around inside my head.

I pace the sidewalk while I wait for Tommy to get me a cab. The whole time, my back feels rigid with tension and my eyes can't focus on anything.

I can't believe I didn't fucking see it. Remember *it.*

But then again, who would really think that some wack job fortune-teller would even be able to predict my future? Certainly not me.

"Yo, Jude!" Tommy calls my name, and I look up from my boots to see him standing there, holding the back door of a cab open.

Thank fuck.

I'm offering Tommy a quick thanks and hopping into the damn thing in record time. And once I tell the driver an address in Manhattan, he puts his foot on the gas and gets us rolling.

Like always, though, traffic in New York on a Saturday night is a nightmare. Especially since spring is starting to make its debut, and people actually want to be outside doing shit.

Which means, we hit every red light. Get delayed by two fire trucks and another three ambulances that temporarily bring traffic to a halt. And I feel like I age a thousand years by the time the cabbie is pulling onto the street and coming to a stop in front of the address I gave him.

Neon lights of a strip club shine from the top of the building and reflect off the windshield of his taxi.

"All riiiight," he says with a waggle of his brows in the rearview mirror. "Looks like you're about to have a good night."

I ignore his commentary and toss him two twenties beneath the plexiglass divider.

"Thanks," I say, and I get out before he has time to say any weird shit about strippers or tits in my face or god knows what else.

And the instant he pulls away, I spot the Taco Bell my brothers and I dined at the infamous night of Rem's bachelor party, *right after* a stripper tore his boxers with her stilettos.

But when I move my eyes across the street, expecting to see the **Fortune Teller** sign shining like a beacon, that's not what I see at all.

A well-known sign with a little cartoon redhead in pigtails taunts me.

Wendy's.

A Wendy's? What the fuck?

I look around the street, my eyes pinging back and forth on everything I can make out, thinking it's possible that my memory has me a little confused. But when I don't see anything besides a convenience store and a parking garage, I know that what I'm seeing is real.

The fortune-teller is gone. And she's been replaced by a goddamn fast-food restaurant.

Son of a bitch.

Both hands in my hair, I yank at the strands and try to figure out what in the hell I should do now.

All the while, Cleo, the apparently retired or out-of-business fortune-teller's words repeat over and over again inside my head. *"There will come a bet. One that will change the course of your life. One that will mold the shape of you as a man. Be careful, though, child. It won't be a period of easy choices. But if you handle it right, it could lead to a great deal of happiness for you."*

I shouldn't be able to remember all of that after thirteen years, but it's like it got stored in the deep recesses of my head until my brain deemed it the perfect moment to torture me with it.

Obviously, *now* is that absolute perfect moment. *After* I've fucked everything up.

And right on cue, the proverbial cherry on top of this shitty sundae, the sky chooses that exact moment to open up and let the rain come down. Literally. Giant drops of rain pelt me from above and drench my clothes until my white shirt is practically see-through.

Well, this is wonderful. Really wonderful.

And I stand there for the longest moment, just letting my misery and the rain soak me to my core.

Soon, though, my mind starts to clear, and there's only one person in my life that I know could help me figure all this shit out. *If* I can figure it out.

It's not even a full second before I'm in motion.

First, I try to hail a cab, but then, when the first five taxis I see are already occupied, I don't wait any longer.

Feet to the pavement, I run. Away from that fucking Wendy's and straight to the one person who can hopefully help me fix everything.

After three knocks to the door, I stand outside on the front porch, and the sky still hasn't let up. It keeps assaulting me with big beads of rain, but I'm now numb to the cold and to the way my clothes stick to my body and my boots slosh with each step.

When no one answers, I pound my fist against the wood again.

Footsteps sound from the inside, and the front porch light flips on.

"Who the fuck is it?"

I grin when I make out Wes's figure through the windows that run along the side of the door.

He swings it open and just stands there, looking at me like he's not sure what to make of the situation.

"Hey, man." I try to play it cool, you know, like I'm not a man in the middle of a nervous breakdown. "Is Winnie around?"

"Well, she is, but she's *sleeping*," he answers and tilts his head to the side when he starts to recognize my current state. "You okay?"

"Sort of." I shake my head. "Actually, nah, not really."

"Who is it?" my sister's faint voice calls from behind Wes, and the breath I didn't realize I was holding escapes from my chest.

"It's one of your crazy brothers."

"Jude?" Winnie asks, the instant her confused and sleepy gaze meets my face. She steps closer to the door, and her eyes go wide when she looks me up and down, taking in every inch of my drenched attire. "Holy hell, did you run?"

"Cabs were taking too long."

"What are you doing here?" she questions and tightens her robe around her body. "Do you have any idea what time it is?"

Truthfully, no. I don't have a clue. And I don't really care. All this shit in my head. All these racing thoughts and regrets and visions of Sophie's torn-up face when I left her apartment are eating me alive. I have to tell someone, and I need that someone to help me fucking fix it.

And I know if anyone can help me, it's Winnie.

"Jude?"

"The fortune-teller is gone, and her shop is a fucking Wendy's now." It's the first thing that pops out of my mouth, and Winnie's face morphs into concern.

"Why don't you come inside, Jude?" Wes acknowledges the fact that I'm still just standing outside in the rain. "You can dry off, I'll grab you a beer, and you and Winnie can have a chat."

He holds open the door and Winnie steps to the side, but the second I'm in their entryway, she's wrapping her arm around mine, completely ignoring that I'm probably getting her wet, and leading me into the kitchen.

Wes hands me a fluffy cream bath towel and a beer, and I sit down at the table, across from my sister. My brother-in-law, though, doesn't hang around. Instead, it appears, he goes back upstairs for the night.

"All right, Jude," Winnie says, and her eyes peer into mine. "What on earth would make you run, like, I don't even know how many miles in the rain at one in the morning?"

Normally, I would play it all off and joke around the truth. But I can't tonight.

"Sophie."

"Oh boy." She inhales a deep breath and blows it out through pursed lips. "I had a feeling you were going to say that. Although, I'm surprised you spilled the beans without more pushing on my end."

"I'm in love with her, Winnie." I just blurt it out, and my sister's brows nearly hit her forehead.

"And I definitely didn't expect you to say that. Holy shit, Jude!" She reaches out to shove a hand into my arm. "*You're in love?*"

"Don't get too excited, sis. I fucked it all up."

Her shoulders sag.

"But I'm hoping, fucking praying, that you can help me find a way to fix it."

She reaches out her hand and gently covers mine. "We'll figure it out. I promise. But you're going to have to give me all the details. You can't leave *anything* out. And before you get that look, it's not because I'm being nosy. It's because I need to have the full picture of what we're working with here."

A sharp laugh pops from my throat. "A fucking disaster. That's what we're working with."

"It can't be that bad."

"Oh, but, sis, it is." I eye her knowingly, and then I lay it all out there for Winnie—minus all the very intimate details that I know she doesn't want to know and I sure as shit don't want to tell her—I give her the rundown of everything.

How I met Sophie. How I ruined her date with that one dude but ended up taking her on a date to make up for it. How she became this irresistible force in my life, and I just wanted more of her time. More of her.

How we went to Vegas.

How things were after I took her to Lexi's Mathletes competition.

And I tell her how things ended. How badly I messed up. How badly I hurt Sophie.

Winnie just listens, taking it all in, and only occasionally asks me a question to clarify something or simply just nods as she follows along.

Once I'm done, I have to lift the full bottle of beer that Wes left on the table for me and chug half the thing down.

My sister just sits there quietly, like her mind is still trying to wrap itself around everything I just revealed. But then, the teeniest hint of a smile touches the corners of her lips.

"Are you…smiling right now?" I ask, and she shakes her head, but that smile of hers only grows. "Winnie? What the fuck? Are you enjoying my misery?"

She shakes her head again, and a laugh bubbles up from her throat. "I'm sorry! None of this is funny to me, I swear!"

"Then why the happy fucking face?"

"Because I just thought about the conversation we had at the lake house last summer, and how you were saying you were never going to fall in love, and I told you that you were going to eat those words one day."

"Are you really going to play the 'I told you so' game? *Right now?* While I'm sitting here at your kitchen table, feeling like I'm bleeding out?"

"In my defense, I haven't said *I told you so,* even though I probably should tell you *I told you so* since we both know that I was right, and your mouth is pretty full at the moment with the giant bite of bullshit you spewed at the lake house."

"You just said it!" I point at her. "*Twice!*"

"No, I didn't. I said the words *I told you so,* but I didn't say the words directly to you."

"You keep saying it!"

She laughs. And for the first time all night, I find myself laughing too.

Damn, my baby sister is a trip.

But then, once the laughter subsides, the acute, undeniable pain is the most prominent sensation I can feel.

Fuck. I put my head in my hands.

"So, was I hearing things when you were at my door, or did you say that the fortune-teller was gone?"

I sigh and look up at her. "Her shop is now a fucking Wendy's."

"And how, exactly, do you know this?"

"Because I went there first."

Her head jerks back. "But I thought you didn't believe in shit like that?"

"I didn't. Until I made a fucking bet that led me to a woman named Sophie Sage, and I'm now sitting here like a miserable bastard at your kitchen table at one in the morning."

"So, the infamous fortune-teller from Rem's bachelor party was right?"

"About me?" I shake my head on a harsh laugh. "Apparently, she hit the future-predicting nail right on the head."

"What did she say about Rem, Flynn, and Ty?"

"I already told you this last summer. It was thirteen years ago. I don't fucking remember."

"Well, you need to think about it, Jude. Because this feels pretty damn important."

I groan. "Winnie, just because it came true for me doesn't mean it will for the rest of our brothers."

She eyes me knowingly. "You mean it came true for you *and* Remy."

Well, *shit*.

"Seriously, what did she say about everybody?" Winnie asks again, and when I just sit there, trying to recall what happened that night, she gets impatient. "Jude? What did she say?!"

"I'm trying to remember!" I answer back. "You'll have to excuse me for the foggy head, considering I ran to your place in the rain because…you know…I feel like I've made the biggest mistake of my fucking life. But no big deal."

She nods, but she doesn't give it up. "I get that, Jude. And I promise, we're going to fix all that. But right now, I need to know what else that fortune-teller said."

"You're so stubborn, you know that?"

"I do," she retorts and reaches out to tap the side of my head. "So, think with that brain of yours and figure it out."

"Damn, sis," I complain and pull away from her annoying finger. "Just give me a minute here…" I pause and rack my brain for what Cleo the fortune-teller told the rest of my brothers. It's all hazy at best, like trying to figure out the time on an hourglass that's aged a hundred years in the dirt.

But eventually, a few things *do* pop up in my mind.

"I think I remember Ty's," I announce, and Winnie stares at me, her eyes damn near trying to pry it out of my head by sheer force. "It was something about him taking a bite of forbidden fruit and a big secret that he'd have to keep. A secret that would cause turmoil or some shit."

"That doesn't sound too good."

I shrug. "Well, she did tell Remy his wedding wouldn't happen a week before his wedding was supposed to happen, so I don't think Miss Cleo gave a flying fuck about giving people bad news."

Winnie snorts. "And what about Flynn?"

I shake my head. "I can't remember his."

"*What?*" she questions, her voice rife with disappointment. "But you remembered Ty's!"

"Barely."

When Winnie just sits there, looking at me like a woman who won't move past this whole stupid thing until she knows, I decide to give it one last shot.

"I'll text Ty," I say and pull my phone out of my still-damp pants. "Make the fucking professor use that big brain of his for something that doesn't revolve around getting into someone's panties."

Me: Remember that fortune-teller we went to at Rem's bachelor party?

His response comes in a minute later.

Ty: Of course I fucking do. That woman was insane.

Maybe not as insane as we originally thought, I think to myself, but I also keep that to myself.

Me: What was Flynn's fortune?

Ty: Why the fuck do you want to know that?

Me: Just wondering. I know mine was like a bet or something. Yours was a secret. She didn't finish Rem's because he fucking hightailed it out there after the first part kicked him straight in the dick. But I can't remember Flynn's. Do you?

Ty: It was something about a pact. A wild night with a stranger and a pact.

I turn the screen of the phone to show Winnie.

"So, a bet, a pact, a secret, and poor Remy just got told his wedding wouldn't happen?"

"He was out the door before she could say anything else."

"He should've waited."

I laugh. "Win, I'm sorry that this is a big inconvenience for you, but I can tell you, Rem didn't look good when she said the wedding wouldn't happen. Pretty sure he left because it was fucking with his head. Not because he wanted to inconvenience his baby sister over thirteen years later."

A guilty smile consumes her lips. "Gah. Sorry. I just can't help it! I want to know!"

All I can do is shrug. "Well, I did my best, sis. And now, you know, I'm kind of hoping we can get back to the whole reason I came here in the first place."

She cocks her head to the side, almost like she fucking forgot why I'm even here, and then she sits up straight and blurts out, "Right! Right! Sophie!"

Just hearing her name, even from my sister's mouth, brings everything right back to the pain. Back to the regret. Back to the reality that I might've lost the best thing that's ever happened to me.

"Fuck, Win, what am I going to do?"

She reaches out both of her hands and clasps them over mine. "We're going to fix this. Together. That's what we're going to do."

"But is it even fixable?" I question. "I mean, Win, I hurt her so bad. I was a total bastard."

"That you were, but it's because of all that Winslow baggage you've been carrying around."

I want to tell her that's bullshit, but even I know that's a lie. All the crap I've seen my mom and Rem and even Winnie go through over the years when it comes to love and relationships has done nothing but make me put up some kind of wall or some shit. Out of self-protection more than anything else, I think.

"Just tell me this, Jude. How far are you willing to go for her?"

The Jude of the past, *before Sophie*, would've had a real prick answer to that question.

But the Jude of now? Well, his answer is easy.

"Anything and everything. Nothing is off-limits."

Winnie's eyes and mouth go wide. "For real?"

I nod.

Then her mouth quirks up into a grin, and she leans over to wrap her arms around my shoulders tightly. "I love you, Jude. And I promise you, everything is going to work out."

God, I hope so. Because not even a week has passed, and life without Sophie is proving to be the most-painful, un-fun, miserable time of my existence.

FORTY-FIVE

Wednesday, April 11th

Sophie

My phone chimes loudly from my purse, and I snag it out quickly to put it on silent. But I don't miss the name that glares back at me from the screen—**Jude**. He's texted me at least twenty times since Sunday *and* called me another ten times on top of that, but I've made a point not to read any of his messages or, of course, answer his calls.

And I don't really know why. Because the pain is still too raw? Or because I'm scared that the lure of simply being with him because I'm in love with him is still so strong that it could make me give in to something that will only end with more pain?

My heart tells me it's probably a lot of both.

But the temptation to see what he has to say is so real that I even find my finger hovering above the screen, just one tap away from giving in to the urge.

"Sophie?" Dr. Winters's voice yanks me back to the present, and I quickly shove my phone back into my purse, mortified of my appointment faux pas.

Especially because *this* appointment is different from all the rest. More important probably, too.

"So sorry," I apologize and look beside me to where Belle and Katelynn sit. "My phone is on silent now. Promise."

"Let me guess…Jude? *Again?*" Belle asks, and I just offer a small nod.

Belle knows most of the sordid details of my Jude situation, but my eldest sister is mostly clueless. She knows I was seeing someone and it ended badly, but that's about it.

When Katelynn met Belle and me for brunch last Thursday, the day I was at the peak of my mental breakdown after I kicked Jude out of my apartment, I'd felt so numb from telling Belle everything that I couldn't do anything that day but keep myself distracted and avoid rehashing everything both in my head and out loud again.

And for the past week, I've continued to give avoidance my best college try. Although, the persistent attempts by Jude through texts and calls haven't been helping.

I just don't understand why he's trying to reach out to me. Because he feels bad? Because he wants to try to go back to when we were just two people having wild and crazy fun?

Anyone's guess is as good as mine. And truthfully, knowing Jude's past, I probably don't want to know the answer. A player tiger can never change his stripes and all that jazz.

Both Dr. Winters and Katelynn look at me curiously, but my therapist is the first one to ask me outright.

"What's going on with you and Jude?"

"Nothing," I say, and I hate that those words are my reality. "I ended things with him. Well, it was kind of a mutual decision, I guess. A chaotic, drama-filled mutual decision."

"What happened?" Katelynn asks, and I stare down at my hands on a deep inhale of breath as I try to push the tightness out of my chest.

"I guess you could say our relationship had started out as a fun, no-strings-attached kind of thing, but over time, I grew feelings for him. I even felt like he was feeling things for me, too. But when I confronted him about it, he said no."

Both Katelynn and Belle reach out to tenderly pat my shoulders.

"I'm sorry to hear that," Dr. Winters says, and her voice is soft with the kind of sympathy that could have the power to bring back those stupid tears.

Tears I don't think Jude Winslow deserves from me.

"Is it wrong if I ask her what her feelings for him were?" Katelynn directs her question to Dr. Winters. "Is that too pushy?"

"What do you think, Sophie?" Dr. Winters asks, glancing between my eldest sister and me. "Is Katelynn's question too pushy for you? Or are you willing to answer it?"

There's a large part of me that doesn't want to answer, but that would defeat the whole purpose of asking my sisters to come to this appointment with me.

"It's okay, Kate," I finally say and offer a small, albeit pathetic, smile in her direction. "My feelings, well, I…was in love with him. *Am* in love with. Currently trying not to be in love with him."

"That…sucks," Katelynn responds, and I let out a humorless laugh.

"That it does."

"So, tell me, Sophie," Dr. Winters begins, switching gears a little. "What made you decide to bring your sisters to today's appointment?"

"Well…" I pause and try to find the right words to a difficult question. "I'm not entirely sure why I wanted them here, but I think it's because I just need them to know more about me. More about what's going on with me."

"Good. I think that's great, Sophie," Dr. Winters says, nodding, and then she directs her focus toward Belle and Katelynn.

"How did it make you two feel when you found out that Sophie has been going to therapy?"

"I mostly just felt like I dropped the ball somewhere along the line." Katelynn is the first to answer. "I'm busy with my toddlers and my job and my husband, and I feel like I haven't been there for Sophie as much as she needed me to be."

I grimace at the mere idea that Katelynn feels like she let me down. But before I can chime in, Dr. Winters is redirecting the question to my twin.

"And what about you, Belle?"

Belle looks at me and then back at Dr. Winters. "To be honest, I was a little shocked because I don't know why she wouldn't tell me that. It's as if Sophie felt like she needed to hide it from me, and that makes me feel sad. I don't want her to feel like she needs to hide anything from me."

"Why do you think she would hide something like going to therapy from you?"

"I don't know." Belle shrugs. "Maybe because she thought I would judge her?"

Shit. That makes me feel even worse than Katelynn's answer.

"Sophie? Do you have anything you want to say to your sisters after hearing their responses?"

"I do." I sigh and resign myself to stay on this open and honest track, no matter how difficult and bumpy it feels. "Katelynn, you haven't let me down. Anytime I've really needed you, you've dropped everything for me. Take Thursday, for example. You took time off work, found a babysitter for the boys, and came into the city to be with me. And even though I didn't expand much on what was going on, you were there, helping me take my mind off things I wasn't ready to face. Just being exactly what I needed from my big sister."

"Really?" Katelynn questions, and tears start to form a small sheen over her eyes.

"Really. I love you. And I'm incredibly grateful for you."

"Ditto, Soph." One small tear slips down her cheek, and that spurs emotion to form behind my own eyes.

"And what about Belle?" Dr. Winters asks me. "Is there anything you want to say to her now that you've heard her initial reaction to your being in therapy?"

"Belly, I love you, dearly, and even though there're times you can have dramatic reactions to things, if there's one thing I'm certain of, it's that you will never judge me. You will always accept me for who I am."

"I will, I swear."

I nod. "I know."

"I love you too, by the way."

I smile at her, and before I know it, all three of us Sage sisters are blubbering into tissues that Dr. Winters places in our hands. She gives us a minute to get it together but, eventually, keeps the session moving in a productive direction.

"Sophie, have you told your sisters why you started therapy and why you decided to stay in therapy?"

I shake my head.

"Are you ready to tell them?"

"I don't know." I shrug. But then, I nod. "I guess that's probably why I brought them here, huh?"

Dr. Winters smiles knowingly. "I think it is."

I look at both Katelynn and Belle, and once I find the strength and the right words, I tell them why I started therapy. That after Mimi died, I took it pretty hard and needed someone neutral and outside of the family to talk to, and how I think that was mostly because I didn't want to burden them with my grief when I knew they were grieving too.

I tell them about how my sessions with Dr. Winters morphed from Mimi to the fact that I had other baggage I needed to claim. I tell them about my issues with obsessing over the future. Over marriage. Over relationships. And that it had gotten to the point where I wasn't even giving any man a shot if I didn't think he checked off all the things I wanted and needed in a husband.

"I guess the reason I wasn't telling you guys anything about this is because I felt like some kind of abnormal freak, you know?" I continue. "I didn't feel like I had any reason to have this baggage even though I had it. I mean, our parents are happily married. Our childhoods were normal. And you guys were in healthy relationships and didn't appear to have any of the problems that I do."

"Oh, but I definitely had them," Belle answers, and I turn to look at her with surprised eyes. "And I probably should've been talking to Dr. Winters too at one point." She grins. "Luckily, John is so damn patient that he knew how to work through things with me."

"What do you mean?" I ask.

"I was super insecure about myself. With every guy I dated. Always feeling like I wasn't good enough. And it was *not* good for relationships, let me tell you," Belle explains. "It wasn't until I met John that I was able to find some clarity and build the confidence that I should have inside myself."

"Do you think it was you or John that helped you with those things?" Dr. Winters asks, and Belle lifts her hand up in a so-so gesture.

"A little of both. Mostly, I think it had to come from deep within myself. But I think I was also lucky I had a good man beside me who wasn't adding to my toxic tendencies."

Dr. Winters nods. "That's good, Belle. That's really good."

"I can also vouch that I had my issues," Katelynn announces, surprising me for the second time in this session. "I had major issues with trust, and that made me a real shit communicator in relationships." She laughs a little. "Honestly, before Todd, I did some crazy shit with my exes. Checking their phones because I was paranoid they were cheating on me or lying to me. It wasn't good."

Holy hell.

"You both dealt with those things before you got married?" I question, and Belle smiles softly at me.

"Yeah. And the insecurity is still something I have to work past at times. Even in my marriage with John."

"Me too," Kate adds. "Todd and I have good communication and our relationship has a strong foundation of trust, but that doesn't mean I don't have to fight my own demons at times to remember those things."

"So, wait, I'm not the only crazy one?" I tease, and both my sisters laugh.

"Nope," Katelynn says with a shake of her head, and Belle agrees.

"Hell no, sis."

"Well, I'm very proud of all three of you," Dr. Winters states with a soft smile. "And I think you should be proud of yourselves too. It's never easy opening up about things that make us feel vulnerable." She makes eye contact with me. "Are you happy with your decision to bring your sisters here today?"

"Yes, I'm glad they're here," I say and mean every word.

"Tell me where that emotion stems from, Sophie."

"It comes from a lot of things, but mostly, I think it stems from feeling relief that everything is out in the open and knowing that I shouldn't feel the need to hide stuff like this from them. I don't have to go it alone, you know? I can use their support, too."

"Good," Belle says and Katelynn nods.

"I'm happy to hear that, Soph. Because I want to be there for you when you need me."

"We're getting close to the end of our session, but Sophie, do you mind if I check in with you directly about what has happened with Jude?"

My first inclination is to shy away from the question, but I stay strong.

"Sure."

"Do you want Belle and Katelynn to leave?"

I shake my head and reach out to hold both of my sisters' hands. "No, they should stay."

For another fifteen minutes, we sit in Dr. Winters's office. All the while, Belle and Katelynn stay silent and just listen patiently while I tell Dr. Winters my current state of mind. Rehash some of the painful details of what really went down with Jude and me, and talk about why I haven't been looking at his texts or answering his calls.

And by the time I leave her office, I feel the sadness starting to seep into my bones again, but I also feel resolved in my decisions.

Honestly, I even feel proud of myself for setting my own boundaries with Jude. Once I started feeling too much emotion for him and knew I couldn't go on just acting like it was only hot sex and fun, I ended things. Harshly, in a way, but it's what I had to do for me.

Oddly enough, I don't even regret the time I spent with him. There's a part of me that really wants to, but in this case, ironically, I'm taking a page out of Jude's book and choosing not to regret. Just move on.

Now, I guess, all I have left to do is give this broken heart of mine time to heal. And the only way I can achieve that is to stick with my decision and keep the door that leads to Jude completely shut.

But damn does that hurt.

FORTY-SIX

Saturday, April 14th

Jude

I pace on the sidewalk, and every time I look at the entrance door to the building, I have to force oxygen in and out of my lungs.

Just stay calm, man.

And when the pacing is only causing me to freak out more, I stop and pull my phone out of my pocket and look at the last few text exchanges between my sister and me.

Winnie: It's go time, bro. She's going to be at her apartment soon.

Me: Are you sure, Win? It's Saturday night. She usually has wedding events on the weekends.

Winnie: I'm positive. Get your ass in gear and head to her apartment, stat.

That was the last message she sent me, but it's been nearly two hours and I'm too impatient to just stand here clueless and waiting.

Me: We all set, Win? What's her ETA? Give me an update, for fuck's sake.

But a full minute goes by and no response.

And then another full minute goes by. Still, no text back.

When the count moves to four minutes and only radio silence, I begin to demon-dial Winnie. Over and over *and over* again, I call her, get voice mail, hang up, and call again.

"Oh my God!" she snaps into my ear once she finally answers. "Relax. I swear to you that everything is all set."

"You know," I retort back and run a hand through my hair. "You could've just texted me back and told me that."

"I'll have *you* know, Mr. Attitude, that I was on the phone with a certain someone by the name of Julie."

Sophie's assistant.

"For real? What'd she say? How is Sophie? Did she say anything about me?"

I am officially a man in love, and apparently that means I act like a fool. But honestly, after spending the last week trying to get in touch with Sophie—*more texts and calls than I'm certain I've ever sent anyone in my life*—I don't care about anything besides seeing her.

"Shit," Winnie mutters. "Hold on just a sec, Jude."

Hold on? Fucking hold on?!

"Oh my God," I breathe out in frustration and resume the pacing again.

When I was a teenager, I can remember my mom wearing the life out of two DVDs. Repeatedly, she watched those damn movies. They were her go-to when nothing else was on.

One was a movie called *Twister*. It was a love story wrapped up in a dramatic tornado, storm-chasers plot. The visual effects made it seem like they filmed it with a potato, and the acting, in my opinion, wasn't all that great either.

The other movie was the famous *When Harry Met Sally*.

And truthfully, I always thought the one monologue Harry delivers when he's trying to make Sally realize that he loves her was gag-worthy. I'd cringe if I heard those clichéd lines coming from our living room television, and trust me, I heard them a lot with Wendy Winslow's frequent viewership.

I thought Harry was a fucking sap. Pathetic, even. But right now, standing outside Sophie's apartment, I realize that I *am* Harry. I'm Harry, and I'm desperate to make the woman I love, the woman I know I screwed things up with, understand that I need her.

And the urgency to do all that is pressing around my neck like a vise.

"Okay, I'm back." Winnie's voice is in my ear again.

"What the hell, Win?" I question and stop pacing so I can give my full focus to the conversation.

"I'm sorry, okay!" she apologizes, but it's more sass than apology. "Julie was calling me on the other line again."

"Oh, well, you should've fucking said that. What'd she say? Did she tell you if Sophie has said anything about me?"

"Jude," Winnie responds on a snort. "We've been through this. I am not calling Julie to get the girl gossip. She thinks I'm a flipping bride trying to find an event planner, even though I'm just carefully trying to figure out what Sophie is up to so my brother can give her the big romantic gesture that will make her realize he may be an idiot, but he's an idiot who loves her."

"Yeah, I keep forgetting about that."

Frankly, ever since Winnie said she'd help me, she wasn't lying. And once it was apparent that I'd fucked things up so bad with Sophie that she wasn't even answering my calls or texts, Winnie's been on the case, even dragged two of her best friends, Cassie and Georgia, in on the charade. They've basically been undercover CIA agents, trying to figure out Sophie's where-abouts and shit.

It all sounds pretty stalkerish, but what can I say? I'm new at this whole being-in-love thing.

"But don't worry, I got enough info about Sophie to know we're still a definite go."

"Really?"

"Yes. You're at her apartment, right?"

"Standing outside her building like a stalker as we speak."

"Perfect."

"You realize that you probably shouldn't be encouraging this sad behavior, right?"

"Jude, it's not sad when you're putting it all on the line for the woman you love."

"Yeah, yeah, you keep telling me that. I just hope you don't have it all wrong."

"I don't," she says, and her voice doesn't falter. "Now, since Julie let me know that Sophie just texted that she's done running errands but is going to call me in about thirty minutes when she's back at her apartment to talk about my fake wedding plans, I also know that you're exactly where you need to be, and the rooftop is ready."

"What? *How?* Are you here?"

"No, Jude, but I'm just that good," she answers through a confident laugh. "And I also had a little help from some of my friends."

I glance around the mostly empty sidewalk, but besides an old man with a cane and a small group of teenagers near the bodega on the corner, I see zero familiar faces.

But then, when I turn on my heel to look toward Sophie's building, one big, familiar-as-hell dude is highlighted beneath the glow of the entry lights as he comes striding out with an even bigger smile on his face.

"Uh…Win? By any chance, did you happen to have Thatch help you?" I ask her, a part of me hoping that what I'm seeing isn't real.

"He had to pitch in last minute," she answers. "Between an issue at Wes's restaurant and an off-season knee injury for one of my players, I couldn't be the one to do the setup on two hours' notice."

Thatcher Kelly and his wife Cassie are two of Wes and Winnie's best friends. But Thatch is also one wild motherfucker. Frankly, the two of us are kind of kindred spirits when it comes to seeking out fun and good times.

But I'm not so sure he's the man I want at the helm of this.

Instantly, visuals of last summer when we caught a canoe on fire while shooting off fireworks for the Fourth of July flash in my head.

God, no.

"You didn't happen to plan a big fireworks show or anything, right?"

She cackles. "After the two of you almost lit the lake house on fire? Um, no. There're no fireworks."

"Jude, the man of the hour!" Thatch exclaims and walks toward me.

"Wait…is that Thatch? Is he still there?" Winnie questions in my ear.

"Hey, man," I greet, and Winnie is now yelling.

"Oh my God, tell him he needs to leave! Now!"

"By the way, my sister says you need to leave."

He chuckles. "Tell Winnie to cool her jets and that ole Thatcher was just making sure everything was fluffing perfect." He winks. "Which it is. Made sure it's extra special just for you, bud."

Now, I'm really starting to wonder if I should be terrified that Thatcher Kelly was a part of this planning process. This is a big moment, what feels like the most important in my life, and I can't have anything go wrong.

"You want me to hang around?" Thatch asks. "There're plenty of places I can hide on that rooftop and make sure everything goes smoothly."

"Tell him to leave!" Winnie shouts into the receiver. "You're not his own personal rom-com movie!"

"Nah, man, I'm good, but I appreciate the help." *Also, please tell me "extra special" doesn't mean you added a last-minute fireworks show or explosion or, you know, anything else that might put Sophie in too much physical danger to allow her to focus on me telling her I'm in love with her.*

"Anytime, son," he responds, completely oblivious to my current concern. "Anyway, I better head out of here before Cassie calls me again. I told her I'd be home in twenty minutes, but that was thirty minutes ago. So, yeah, if I don't get home soon, she'll kick me in the dick."

I grimace.

"Love is grand, isn't it?" he chuckles and pulls me into a tight hug. "I'm just kidding, my man. This, what you're doing, it takes giant gonads. But I can tell you, it's worth it. When you find the woman who makes you want to show all your fluffing cards and put your balls on the line, you do everything in your power to make her yours."

I step back and meet his eyes. But the usual sarcasm and humor aren't what I find. Just steady, serious, and full-on honesty.

"Anyway, son," he continues and claps a hand onto my back. "Good luck. Although, I don't think you'll need it. I've got a good feeling about this."

Once Thatch leaves and I end the call with Winnie, the weight that sits on my shoulders feels like a thousand pounds as I use the entry key my sister somehow managed to commandeer by what I hope weren't illegal means, and I head inside.

Once I'm on Sophie's floor, standing beside her door, my phone chimes with a text.

Winnie: I'm proud of you. I love you. Everything is going to be okay. And most importantly, YOU GOT THIS.

God, I hope she's right. Because I feel like I'm standing on an actual ledge right now, and I'm not even on the rooftop yet.

In less than twenty minutes, you're going to find out…

Twenty minutes turns into forty minutes, and I start to wonder if Julie doesn't know what the fuck she was talking about, but then, the elevator doors open and there she is.

Sophie.

She looks more beautiful than my mind even allowed me to recall over the past week and half. Most likely, out of self-preservation. No doubt, I'm in enough pain as it is, but my mind hasn't lost clarity on anything about this woman.

I know her. To the depths of my heart, I know her.

I know her laugh. And her smile. I know her adorable quirks. I know who she is on the outside as much as I know who she is on the inside.

And I know all those things because I love her. Plain and simple.

With her arms full of bags, she juggles carrying them while also typing something on her phone, and her eyes don't look up from the screen until she's steps away from where I stand beside her apartment door.

Her eyes flash with instant, intimate familiarity, and my presence is such a shock that the bags in her arms start to fall.

Quickly, I step forward and snag them before they topple over and to the ground.

But she doesn't say anything. She is a statue, her feet rooted to their spot on the floor.

"I know you're surprised to see me," I hedge carefully.

"H-how? W-why?" she fumbles over her words. "W-what are you doing here?"

"I know you haven't answered any of my calls or texts, and that you most likely don't want to talk to me, but this, *you,* are too important for me not to try as hard as I can to get you to hear what I need to say."

She shakes her head, like she still can't understand what is happening.

"I just need five minutes of your time, Sophie," I say, and I know that my voice borders on pleading, but I don't care. I'll do whatever it takes to get her to hear me out.

"Jude, I'm pretty sure that everything that needed to be said was already said."

Fuck.

"Just hear me out for five minutes, and then if you never want to see me again, I'll leave you alone." *But please don't make me leave you alone. I love you too much.*

"I'm supposed to call a client that's been riding my assistant's ass for the past week to get in touch with me," she answers, but also, she searches my eyes for a beat before adding, "So, you're going to have to make this quick."

She unlocks her apartment door and pointedly holds it open for me to step inside. Which I do, but after I set the bags down on her kitchen counter, I turn to her.

"I know this might be a big ask, but can you follow me somewhere?"

"Jude."

"Please?" I beg.

"Where am I supposed to follow you to?"

"I have a feeling you're really going to hate this answer…" I pause and cringe a little. "But I can't tell you that until we get there."

She sighs. "I don't think—"

I cut her off by walking over and pulling her hands into mine. They come easily, like they want to be there, and she doesn't pull away, which I take as a good sign.

"Just five minutes, Soph. And I promise it's not anything crazy."

She sighs again. Stares down at our interlocked hands, and just as she lets go of mine and my heart feels as if it drops out of my stomach, she says, "Fine. Lead the way."

An inkling of hope. I'll fucking take it.

Out of her apartment and into the elevator, she follows me, and I'm sure

I glance over my shoulder a hundred times to make sure she doesn't attempt to run.

But she doesn't. She also doesn't look at me at all, her eyes fixated on the ground and her arms crossed below her breasts, but she stays.

The elevator doors open directly onto the rooftop, and Sophie's brow furrows as she steps out to find a hundred LED tealight candles—not a fire risk, thank fuck—covering every surface of the ground around us. Along with what have to be at least fifty large vases filled with flowers that guide an open pathway toward a perfect spot on the deck that showcases the city.

"Oh my God." A hand goes to her mouth. "Did you do all this?"

"With some help, yes."

Sure, I didn't actually do the setup, but I was part of the planning process. Especially when it came to the flowers. I made sure exact replicas of bouquets I'd watched her quietly admire at the Venetian were made.

Her green eyes move to mine, and I swear it looks as if a few tears sit behind her lids.

I reach out with my hand, hoping she'll at least let me lead her a little farther, and my heart starts pounding wildly inside my chest when she actually does, placing her small hand in mine again.

If I could just hold this woman's hand for the rest of my life, I'd be happy.

I stop right at the end of the path of flowers and grasp both of her hands in mine. She looks up at me with eyes that clearly don't know what to expect, and I know now is the time for me to man the fuck up.

And on a deep breath, I do.

"Do you remember on the plane to Vegas when you asked me if I had any regrets, and I said I had none?"

She nods.

"Well, I do, Sophie." I begin to tell her everything I desperately need her to hear. "I have one giant regret, and it was the night you had to kick me out of your apartment because of the horrible things I said. The way I acted like I didn't have feelings for you—and especially because I made you cry." I admit the painful events out loud. "Seeing you cry and knowing I was the one responsible? That crushed me. *Still* crushes me. I never should've left that night. I should've stayed. I should've faced what I was feeling for you, and I should've told you the truth."

One small tear slips down her cheeks, and there's a part of me that wants to stop, fearful that I'm somehow hurting her all over again, but there's another part of me that needs her to hear the rest. Needs her to understand the truth.

I gently squeeze her hands and continue.

"You scared the hell out of me, babe. But it's because you're everything I want and need, and I've never felt like I needed anyone. But fuck, *I need you*. You make me a better man. You make me want all of the things I've always told myself I didn't want. And you've stolen my heart," I say while my eyes plead for her to really listen to these next words. "I'm in love with you, Sophie. *I love you*. With everything inside of me. And I know it took me far too fucking long to realize that, but see, I've never been in love before. So, I guess I'm hoping you'll understand that it's a bit of a learning curve for a man like me."

Her lips part, and her eyes frantically search mine. "You love me?"

"More than anything." I nod. "I just want you. Only you. Twenty-four-fucking-seven with Sophie Sage. That's all I want and need."

All of a sudden, the sensation of something I purchased two days ago sits heavy in my back pocket. This something wasn't in the plans for tonight, but when I saw it, I knew it had to be hers. And I had to be the one to give it to her.

Honestly, I don't know why I brought it with me, but I think something deep inside my heart told me this moment wouldn't be complete without it.

And before I know it, I'm getting down on one knee in front of her, pulling that something, which is a Tiffany blue box, out of my pocket.

"Babe, I need you to understand that I'm not the same Jude you first met at Club Craze," I tell her, and her eyes grow wide with disbelief. "I'm the Jude after Sophie. The one who loves you with everything inside himself. The one who sees and wants and needs forever with you. You might be the first woman I've ever loved, but I know with absolute certainty, you're the *only* woman I'll ever love."

I pop open the ring box to reveal a round diamond solitaire on a rose gold band. It's beautiful and elegant and belongs on her finger.

"Sophie Sage, will you marry me?"

She takes the longest blink I've ever seen, and her eyes bounce between my face and the ring in my hand more times than I can track.

But eventually, she answers. And I'll be damned if it doesn't stab a knife right into my nuts.

"*No.*"

FORTY-SEVEN

Sophie

"No?" Jude repeats, and it's then I realize that everything that's running through my mind hasn't come past my lips.

Besides that one word—*no*.

Oh my God, Sophie!

His face is shocked, and his blue eyes look so sad that it feels as if my heart is trying to pound its way out of my chest so *it* can be the one to tell Jude how I really feel.

"So, no?" he repeats again, shakes his head, and starts to move to get off his knee. "You don't want—"

"Wait! That didn't come out right!" I blurt and dive toward him so aggressively that I knock him backward onto the roof deck and my body lands on top of his.

"Holy hell, Soph," Jude mutters, but I don't give him time to say anything else.

"I love you, Jude!" I shout far too loudly, considering my face is just inches from his. "I'm in love with you!"

"You are?"

"I am." I nod, and big, fat, elated tears start to stream down my cheeks.

This man just put everything on the line for me because he loves me. I'm certain I've never felt this kind of happiness inside my heart in my entire life.

His face pinches in confusion. "Then why the hell did you just say no to my proposal?"

"Not because I don't want to marry you, because I do, Jude. I really, *really* do," I answer with blunt honesty and a small, *I know I'm a little crazy* smile. "But just like you're the guy who needed to propose to show his commitment, I'm the girl who needs to take it slow because of my messed-up view of marriage being this insane thing I need to achieve."

"So…you want to marry me, but right now, you're saying *no?*"

"Yes."

An amused smile begins to lift his lips. "Yes, you're saying no."

"Correct." *God, my heart feels like it's going to pump right out of my chest.*

"So, let me get this straight. You love me and you want to be with me, and you even want forever with me, but you're saying no to marrying me right now?"

I nod again, and my nose brushes against his. "Yes to all of those things."

"But you love me?"

"I do, Jude. More than anything. I just want to be with you. No one else. Just you."

"That's all I want too, babe."

"Because you love me?" I ask, even though I'm certain of his answer. I just want to hear him say it again.

"You're the *only* woman I've ever loved, Sophie. And you're the only one I ever will."

"Funnily enough, Jude, you're my first love, too. Even with how badly I've always wanted it, I never actually let it happen until you came along."

He wraps his arms around my back and holds me close. "Damn, it feels good hearing you say that."

"Do you think that maybe now we seal this all with a kiss?"

He smirks. "Yes, among many other things that need to happen tonight because I've been missing you so bad."

"I've missed you too." I brush my lips against his. "I kept telling myself I would get through this, I would move on from you, but every day without you has felt harder than the one before it."

"Well, my sweet Sophie, since you weren't answering any of my calls or texts, I resorted to getting Winnie to help me stalk you because I missed you so much it was causing me physical pain."

"Sounds like we were both a bit of a mess, huh?"

He nods and presses a soft kiss to my lips. "But it's okay, because now, we have each other."

"That's right." I stare deep into his eyes. "Now we have each other."

He kisses me then, and our lips are persistent against each other. A mess of passion and relief and love. *Oh-so-much* love.

As our kisses grow more heated and uncontrolled, Jude rises to his feet, holding me tightly in his arms, and starts to walk toward the elevator. "I need you to know three things right now."

"And what are those?"

"You don't have a client to call. That was my sister playing investigator to find out where you were for me."

I laugh. "Seriously?"

"What can I say?" He shrugs one shoulder. "I'm a man willing to do anything to be with the woman he loves."

"And the other two things?"

"There's not going to be much sleeping tonight."

"Got it." I giggle. "And what else?"

"One day soon, I'm going to get you to say *yes*."

"Is that right?"

"So right that I'd bet everything on it."

And I wouldn't take that bet because I also know he's right.

Jude and I, we're not just wild sex and fun. *No way.*

We're all the things. And we're forever.

EPILOGUE

Jude

At a little after eight in the evening, I head out of Sophie's and my apartment in Nolita and lock the door behind me. The place is a stone's throw from her old place, but it's bigger, has an even better view, and there's always a doorman to make me feel okay when I'm pulling late hours working at a club and Sophie is by herself.

That's right. We are officially *living together*.

Every morning, I get to wake up to Sophie's gorgeous face, and every night, I get to hold her in my arms. Not to mention, we're *always* together, and I never have to miss a moment when she has a bare pussy. Honestly, I don't know why more men aren't considering this important "bare pussy" detail when deciding whether or not to put long-term commitment on their vision boards. And yes, I learned about vision boards from Sophie.

It's the best fucking time of my life, and I'm a man who is *almost* living the dream. But there's one thing that still needs to occur to make that "almost" a reality—*marrying her*.

Laughable, right? I know.

Trust me, our unmarried status has nothing to do with my lack of trying.

Three proposals I've attempted so far. The one on her rooftop. One that involved taking her to my uncle Brad and aunt Paula's lake house and proposing while we were out on the water. And the last one involved showing her how much I love her by surprising her with a fluffy blond ball of Labrador puppy and the engagement ring around his little collar.

You'd think she would've said yes to one of those, right? *Wrong.* Three proposals have only led me to three no's *and* a puppy that Sophie named Frankie.

It's incredibly ironic that I spent so much of my young life running from marriage and am now chasing after it like a dog with the mailman, but now that I've given myself over to loving Sophie, I need the commitment.

I need to lock her down, seal the deal, and make it official that she's not going anywhere for the rest of our lives.

But soon, that's all going to change.

Once I'm outside the door of our building, I start the four-block walk toward the restaurant where I reserved a table for two. An Italian place my niece Lexi loves and has the perfect intimate ambiance for tonight.

Paesano is a well-known spot for locals in Little Italy, and its quaint charm and romantic vibes of candlelight and wood beams and classical Italian music are exactly what I need to set the mood that ends in Sophie finally saying *yes.*

I pull my cell out of my pocket and shoot her a message as I come to a stop in front of the restaurant.

Me: Where ya at, babe?

Her answer comes in a minute later.

Sophie: Running about ten minutes behind. Had some issues getting everything broken down after the event. But I'm on my way! And please please please, tell me there's no wait because I'm starving!

Little does she know, there's no line because I'm a man with a plan. A proposal plan, that is. But in the name of taking her by surprise—*which is a hard thing when I've already done this three times*—I send her back a little white lie.

Me: Hostess said there's only a ten-to-fifteen-minute wait. So, by the time you get here, our table should be ready.

I don't make a point to lie to my girl, the woman I *will* marry someday real fucking soon, but sometimes, there're exceptions, and it goes without saying, tonight is one.

Sophie: Wooo-hooo! Thank everything! See you soon, baby!

I grin and go to slide my phone back into the pocket of my jeans, but when it vibrates in my hand, I lift up the screen to find a few messages inside my group chat with my brothers.

Ty: Starting a pool. $50 bucks to play. Who is betting that Sophie says yes? Who is betting that Sophie says no? Personally, I'm on Team No.

Flynn: LOL. I got $50 on yes.

Remy: Put me down for no. Soph is hard-core. No way she's saying yes tonight.

I roll my eyes.

Me: She's going to say YES, you fucks.

Ty: Uh oh…is someone feeling a little nervous?

Me: I have no reason to be nervous because Soph is going to say yes.

Remy: I have to hand it to her, she keeps shit entertaining.

*Ty: For real. I love that she's made it clear she wants to marry Jude, but *she's got him proposing all over the fucking city because he doesn't know when she'll say yes.*

Me: I've only proposed three times, dude.

Flynn: About to be four.

Ty: HAHAHAHA

Me: One day, you smug bastards are going to be knocked on your ass by a woman, and I'm going to laugh MY ass off.

Ty: Is this woman knocking me on my ass because she wants to fuck me? Because then, I can definitely get down with that cause.

I just shake my head. He knows *exactly* what I'm talking about. They all do. But currently, they're still deep in their ways of noncommitment and avoidance.

I can't really blame them, though. Not too long ago, I *was* them, oblivious to what I was missing and the fact that I wasn't really living by carrying the heavy weight of avoidance.

Thank fuck for Sophie.

I glance at my watch and see I've been bullshitting with these assholes for far too long, and I send them one final message.

Me: Whoever put their money on no, be prepared to pay the fuck up.

And then I shove my phone back into my pocket and head inside to the restaurant, where the hostess leads me straightaway to the table I reserved, tucked away in the far corner of the room and already set up for the big night.

Surprisingly, Sophie isn't far behind me, and in another ten minutes, I spot her gorgeous face walking through the main doors.

I lift my hand to grab her attention, and the second her gaze meets mine, she smiles.

Fuck. I love this woman.

The instant she's within reach of my arms, I stand up and pull her into a hug. "Missed you so much."

"You just saw me this morning," she says through a cute laugh.

"Exactly." I groan and breathe in the sweet, flowery scent of her hair. "Twelve hours is too long."

"It's like you're obsessed with me or something," Sophie teases, and I press a kiss to her lips before pulling out her chair and helping her sit down.

"Oh, baby, you have no idea."

But soon, you're about to find out.

⌒

Sophie

Right after our friendly server drops our meals at our table, I excuse myself to go to the restroom. But the instant I'm safely locked inside the one-stall bathroom, I grab my phone from my purse and call Julie.

It takes her three rings before she answers.

"Everything all set?"

"Uh…almost. How much time do I have left?"

"What do you mean, almost?" I question. "We already have our meals, Julie!"

"Well, Frankie was whining in his crate, and I couldn't ignore him!" she retorts back, and I sigh. But also, I understand. My little buddy, the one Jude gave to me the last time he proposed, is irresistibly cute. I wouldn't have been able to ignore him either.

"But don't worry," she continues. "He's officially been fed, watered, and taken out, and I'm just finishing up in your bedroom."

"Okay. Good. That's good." I breathe out a sigh of relief. "What's your ETA on leaving?"

"If you stop asking me damn questions? Ten minutes, tops."

"Okay, I get it." I grin. "I'm officially leaving you alone."

"Good," she says, and it sounds like she's breathing so heavy I'm wondering if she's actually running around our apartment. "I'll text when I'm out."

"Perfect."

"Okay, seeyabye!"

The line clicks off, and I meet my reflection in the bathroom mirror. *It's almost go time, Soph.*

Once I do a quick check of my hair and makeup, I head back out to the table and sit down across from Jude. But when I look at him, expecting him to simply be enjoying his meal, that's not what I find.

He's looking at me in a way I've seen before. Sparkling, blue eyes and a soft smile, I've seen this look exactly three times before now.

Oh no. No-no-no!

"Sophie." He reaches across the table and takes my hand in his. "I love you, baby."

Ah, shit. He's going to do it.

"I love you too," I say and quickly try to change the subject. "How's your… uh…" I glance down at his plate, where the fettuccine Alfredo he ordered sits untouched. "Pasta? Good?"

"Who cares about the food, babe?" His smile reaches his eyes, turning them warm like blue-colored honey. "I want to tell you something."

"Uh…how about you hold that thought while we eat?" I blurt out. "You know, otherwise, the food will get cold."

He just shakes his head and scoots his chair closer to mine, and I know that if I don't think of something quick, everything that I've planned is about to be ruined.

"Baby, I—"

"I'm not feeling well!" I shout at the top of my lungs, so loud that even a couple on the other side of the restaurant hears me.

"Huh?"

"I'm…uh…not feeling well?" I respond, but when I realize it sounds more like *I'm* asking him, I shake my head and rephrase. "I feel sick, Jude. I think we need to go home."

"You're sick?"

"Yep. Not good. We should go." I nod manically as I stand up from my chair with such force the damn thing topples over and onto the ground.

"Shit. Babe, do you need a doctor?"

Oh God. This web of lies is starting to get way bigger than you want…

"No, no." I brush it off. "It's fine. Just…I should probably take a hot shower and lie in bed. That's it. Sick enough to need to leave, but not so sick that we should be worried. Like, half sick. Can't-be-out-in-public sick."

Jude just looks at me in bewilderment, surely because the shit coming out of my mouth doesn't make sense, but I somehow manage to get him to follow my lead.

Once he tosses some money onto the table, he wraps his arm around my shoulders, tucking me close to his side, and guides us out of the restaurant.

And as we head toward our apartment, only a few blocks away, all I can think is, *Holy moly. I really hope Julie is gone by the time we get there.*

Jude

I have no idea what's wrong with my girl, but I sure as shit am doing everything in my power to get her back home so I can try to figure it out.

Looks like the proposal plan isn't happening tonight.

Hell, it *almost* happened. I was about two minutes away from getting down on one knee for the fourth time, but all of a sudden, Sophie said she wasn't feeling well and started knocking shit over and acting a bit crazy with her need to leave the restaurant.

Damn, I hope she's okay.

I keep her close to my side as we walk back to our place, and the whole way, I keep glancing down at her face, ensuring that she's okay.

So far, so good. She doesn't have to stop to puke or anything, and it's not long before we're inside our building and stepping onto the elevator.

Her phone pings with a text notification when we're in the cart, and when she looks at the screen, the tension I noted in her shoulders earlier appears to dissipate.

"Everything okay?"

She nods.

"You still feel sick?"

"A little?" She just shrugs. "But I'm sure I'll be fine."

Just a little? After that mad dash out of Paesano's?

I furrow my brow, examining her closer, but she turns her face away just enough that I can't get a good read on her eyes.

What the fuck is happening?

The cart dings our arrival, and Sophie exclaims, "We're here!" like she's never been in an elevator before. And then she's off the cart and scurrying toward our door, unlocking it, but at the same time not actually opening it, and turns to face me.

"I love you, Jude," she says, and it's all so odd that I feel my head cock to the side.

"Uh…I love you too?" I respond, but my confusion makes it sounds like more of a question than an answer. "Are you sure you're okay, babe?"

"I'm perfect." She smiles, stands up on her tippy-toes to press a kiss to my lips, and then she pushes the door open.

I shake my head and step inside, my eyes focused more on the ground than anything else, but when I notice a random rose petal on our entryway floor, I look up to find *more* rose petals, along with candles and flowers strategically placed all around our apartment.

And I'm not talking a small amount of flowers and candles; I'm talking a lot. So much so that if Thatch would've set this up, I'd already be calling the fire department.

It's downright breathtaking, but it only makes me more fucking confused.

What the hell is this?

Unless I've suffered a stroke or all of a sudden gained superhuman powers that I'm not aware of, there's no way I got my fifth proposal attempt together this fucking quickly...*right?*

"Jude." Sophie grabs my attention and takes my hands into hers as she gets down on her knees before me. "I love you so much. I want forever with you. I want to be—"

"Whoa, whoa, whoa!" I cut her off. "What are you doing? Are you proposing to me?"

"Well...I'm *trying* to."

"Wait..." I pause and look around the room as my mind puts all the pieces of the puzzle together. "You were faking being sick at the restaurant, weren't you?"

"Maybe?" She grimaces, and that's when I know that *she fucking knew* I was about to propose to her back there.

"You knew!" I exclaim and pull her to her feet before she has a chance to ask me to marry her. Lord knows I wouldn't be able to say no to her. *No fucking way.* "You knew I was going to propose, and you faked being sick so that *you* could propose?!"

"I'm sorry, but do you realize how long it took Julie to set this up?" she shouts back at me with that sexy sass I love so much. "Hours of work, Jude! I couldn't ruin it!" She turns on her heel and heads over to our fireplace, grabbing an iPad—*her* iPad—that was discreetly hiding behind a potted plant.

"Okay. Okay," she says and puts a hand to her hip. "Now, we both just need to chill out and relax for a hot second. And then, I'm going to hit record on my iPad because I promised Julie I would record the whole thing, and we're going to start from the beginning. But this time, you're actually going to let me propose, okay?"

She's in event planner mode, rambling and gesturing with her hands, and it's the cutest fucking thing in the world. So much so that it makes laughs spill from my lips.

Immediately, Sophie stops mid-step and looks at me.

"Are you laughing right now?"

"Fuck yes, I'm laughing right now."

She crinkles her nose. "Why?"

"Because you're crazy and I love you."

Her brow furrows, but I don't give her any time to toss any more sassy responses my way. I stride right for her, take the iPad from her hands, and hit record. Once the video is on, I look right into the camera.

"Julie, honey, you really outdid yourself," I say. "Although, I hate to be the bearer of bad news here, but Sophie isn't going to be proposing to me tonight."

I peer up to look at Sophie and find her standing there in absolute shock.

But I don't let it stop me.

"She's not proposing because I'm proposing to her. *Right now.*"

And right then, I set down the iPad, pull the Tiffany's box I've been carrying around for six long fucking months out of my back pocket, and get down on one knee.

"Sophie, my love, my heart, my wild, adorable girl, I love you. You know this. Hell, anyone who sees the way I look at you knows this."

Her hand goes to her mouth, and one tear falls down her cheek.

"Baby, I need you to be my wife. *Please*, I'm begging you, *marry me*. Spend the rest of your life with me. Let me love you forever."

"*Yes.*"

Her answer is so immediate that I almost don't believe my ears, but then she says it again.

"Yes."

Hope blooms inside my chest, and it is so huge, so persistent, it feels like my lungs and heart have to shift to make room. "You'll marry me?"

"Of course I'll marry you, Jude," she says through fresh tears. "I love you so much."

Fuck yes!

Once I *finally* secure the ring on her finger, I stand to my feet and pull her into my arms, swinging us around on a hearty, exuberant chuckle.

"Thank fuck!" I exclaim so loud that Frankie barks from his crate in our bedroom. But Sophie just stares at me with her heart in her eyes and giggles leaving her lips. "Now, baby, are you ready to go to Vegas and get hitched?"

"No way." She snorts. "I want a real wedding, Jude. With all our friends and family there to witness the day I say *I do* to the man of my dreams."

"So, that's a no on Vegas?"

"Definitely a no on Vegas." Her mouth morphs into a mischievous grin. "But would you like to make a wager with me?"

"I'm listening."

"I'll bet you anything you want, anything your heart desires, that you and I are going to get married and be blissfully happy for the rest of our lives."

I shake my head. "That's a horrible fucking bet, babe."

"Why?"

"Because I'd never bet against us. You and I are the one thing I'm certain about."

"Ditto," she whispers as she brushes her lips gently against mine. "Our love is a forever kind of love, Jude. It's strong and stable. It's sweet and kind. It's wild and fierce. It's passion personified. And it's the most fun this girl has ever had."

Her words make me grin. "Well, soon-to-be Mrs. Winslow, get ready for a lifetime of fun."

THE END

Love Jude, Sophie, and the rest of the Winslow crew and want to read
MORE
Winslow Brothers?

Well, we have *great* news!

You can cure your Winslow Brothers' cravings right now and
find out what really happened during Remy's bachelor party in
this FREE novella!

GOTTA HAVE FATE!
https://dl.bookfunnel.com/1dvqktv6el

It's completely **FREE** and not-to-be missed!

AND

You can preorder the next book in the
Winslow Brothers Collection today!

The sexy, mysterious Flynn Winslow is next.

The Pact is coming soon!
mybook.to/ThePact_Ebook

Completely new to the Winslow Brothers and Winnie and Wes and the
Billionaire gang?

Grab ***Tapping the Billionaire*** to read more about our favorite
billionaires, and of course, find out how Wes and Winnie's love story
began. Trust us, you won't regret it.
mybook.to/TtBWorldwide

BEEN THERE, DONE THAT TO ALL OF THE ABOVE?
Never fear, we have a list of nearly FORTY other titles to keep you busy
for as long as your little reading heart desires! Check them out at our
website: *www.authormaxmonroe.com*

**COMPLETELY NEW TO MAX MONROE AND DON'T
KNOW WHERE TO START?**

Check out our Suggested Reading Order on our website!
www.authormaxmonroe.com/max-monroe-suggested-reading-order

WHAT'S NEXT FROM MAX MONROE?
Stay up-to-date with our characters and our upcoming releases by
signing up for our newsletter on our website:
www.authormaxmonroe.com/newsletter!

You may live to regret much, but we promise it won't be
subscribing to our newsletter.
Seriously, we make it fun! Character conversations about royal babies,
parenting woes, embarrassing moments, and shitty horoscopes are just
the beginning! If you're already signed up, consider sending us a message
to tell us how much you love us. We really like that. ;)

Follow us online:

Facebook: www.facebook.com/authormaxmonroe
Reader Group: https://www.facebook.
comgroups/15616401054166388/
Twitter: www.twitter.com/authormaxmonroe
Instagram: www.instagram.com/authormaxmonroe
TikTok: vm.tiktok.com/ZMe1jv5kQ
Goodreads: https://goo.gl/8VUIz2

ACKNOWLEDGMENTS

First of all, THANK YOU for reading. That goes for anyone who has bought a copy, read an ARC, helped us beta, edited, or found time in their busy schedule just to make sure we stayed on track. Thank you for supporting us, for talking about our books, and for just being so unbelievably loving and supportive of our characters. You've made this our MOST favorite adventure thus far.

THANK YOU to each other. Max is thanking Monroe. Monroe is thanking Max. We know, *we know*! We do this every book. Every. Single. Book. But guess what? We're going to keep doing it because that's how we roll. If you don't believe us, we challenge you to go read all of them and see for yourself. HAHA!

THANK YOU, Lisa, for continuing to kick our 2021-insane-schedule's ass. We couldn't do this without you, and that is a fact, Jack! On a sidenote, we're certain now that we all deserve a trip somewhere tropical after this.

THANK YOU, Stacey, for making the insides of our book look so damn pretty and rolling with the crazy schedule punches we throw your way. You are the absolute best!

THANK YOU, Peter (aka Banana), for rocking our covers and making Jude Winslow look like the sexy, charming, perfect good-time guy that he is.

THANK YOU to every blogger who has read, reviewed, posted, shared, and supported us. Your enthusiasm, support, and hard work do not go unnoticed. We love youuuuuuuuuuuuu!

THANK YOU to the people who love us—our family. You are our biggest supporters and motivators. We couldn't do this without you. Although, it should be noted, sometimes you guys are hella distracting. But the ones who are the most distracting are under the age of eleven, so we're not going to hold that against you. HAHA.

THANK YOU to our Camp members! You guys are the best! THE BEST, we tell you! You've made Camp the coolest place to be and one of our favorite places to go to procrastinate. We can't wait for all the fun we've got planned for this year!

As always, all our love.
XOXO,
Max & Monroe

www.ingramcontent.com/pod-product-compliance
Lightning Source LLC
Chambersburg PA
CBHW070556300726
48975CB00006B/1607